MILDRED
PIERCE

JAMES M.CAIN

MILDRED
PIERCE

VINTAGE CRIME

Vintage Books
A DIVISION OF RANDOM HOUSE, INC.
NEW YORK

Vintage Books Edition, may 1989

Copyright 1941 by James M. Cain
Copyright renewed 1969 by James M. Cain
All rights reserved under International and Pan-American Copyright Conventions. Published in the United States by Random House, Inc., New York, and simultaneously in Canada by Random House of Canada Limited, Toronto. Originally published by Alfred A. Knopf, Inc., in 1941.

Library of Congress Cataloging in Publication Data
Cain, James Mallahan, 1892–1977.
Mildred Pierce.
I. Title.
PZ3.C11993Mi   1978   [PS3505.A3113]   813'.5'2
77-92632
ISBN 0-679-72321-8 (pbk.)

Designed by Ann Gold

Manufactured in the United States of America

30 29 28 27 26 25 24 23

MILDRED
PIERCE

CHAPTER

1

In the spring of 1931, on a lawn in Glendale, California, a man was bracing trees. It was a tedious job, for he had first to prune dead twigs, then wrap canvas buffers around weak branches, then wind rope slings over the buffers and tie them to the trunks, to hold the weight of the avocados that would ripen in the fall. Yet, although it was a hot afternoon, he took his time about it, and was conscientiously thorough, and whistled. He was a smallish man, in his middle thirties, but in spite of the stains on his trousers, he wore them with an air. His name was Herbert Pierce. When he had finished with the trees, he raked the twigs and dead branches into a pile, carried them back to the garage, and dropped them in a kindling box. Then he got out a mower and mowed the lawn. It was a lawn like thousands of others in southern California: a patch of grass in which grew avocado, lemon, and mimosa trees, with circles of spaded earth around them. The house, too, was like others of its kind: a Spanish bungalow, with white walls and red-tile roof. Now, Spanish houses are a little outmoded, but at the time they were considered high-toned, and this one was as good as the next, and perhaps a little bit better.

The mowing over, he got out a coil of hose, screwed it to a spigot, and proceeded to water. He was painstaking about this too, shooting the water all over the trees, down on the spaded circles of earth, over the tiled walk, and finally on the grass. When the whole place was damp and smelled like rain, he turned off the water, pulled the hose through his hand to drain it, coiled it, and put it in the garage. Then he went around front and examined his trees, to make sure the water hadn't drawn the slings too tight. Then he went into the house.

The living room he stepped into corresponded to the lawn he left. It was indeed the standard living room sent out by department stores as suitable for a Spanish bungalow, and consisted of a crimson velvet coat of arms, displayed against the wall; crimson velvet drapes, hung on iron spears; a crimson rug, with figured border; a settee in front of the fireplace, flanked by two chairs, all of these having straight backs and beaded seats; a long oak table holding a lamp with stained-glass shade; two floor lamps of iron, to match the overhead spears, and having crimson silk shades; one table, in a corner, in the Grand Rapids style, and one radio, on this table, in the Bakelite style. On the tinted walls, in addition to the coat of arms, were three paintings: one of a butte at sunset, with cow skeletons in the foreground; one of a cowboy, herding cattle through snow, and one of a covered-wagon train, plodding through an alkali flat. On the long table was one book, called Cyclopedia of Useful Knowledge, stamped in gilt and placed on an interesting diagonal. One might object that this living room achieved the remarkable feat of being cold and at the same time stuffy, and that it would be quite oppressive to live in. But the man was vaguely proud of it, especially the pictures, which he had convinced himself were "pretty good." As for living in it, it had never once occurred to him.

Today, he gave it neither a glance nor a thought. He hurried through, whistling, and went back to a bedroom, which was filled with a seven-piece suite in bright green, and showed feminine touches. He dropped off his work clothes, hung them in a closet, and stepped naked into the bathroom, where he turned on water for a bath. Here again was reflected the civilization in which he lived, but with a sharp difference. For whereas it was, and still is, a civilization somewhat naïve as to lawns, living rooms, pictures, and other things of an aesthetic nature, it is genius itself, and has forgotten more than all other civilizations ever knew, in the realm of practicality. The bathroom that he now whistled in was a utile jewel: it was in green tile and white tile; it was as clean as an operating room; everything was in its proper place and everything worked. Twenty seconds after the man tweaked the spigots, he stepped into a bath of exactly the temperature he wanted, washed himself clean, tweaked the drain, stepped out, dried himself on a clean towel, and stepped into the bedroom again, without once missing a bar of the tune he was whistling, or thinking there was anything remarkable about it.

After combing his hair, he dressed. Slacks hadn't made their appearance then, but gray flannels had: he put on a fresh pair, with polo shirt and blue lounge coat. Then he strolled back to the kitchen, a counterpart of the bathroom, where his wife was icing a cake. She was a small woman, considerably younger than himself; but as there was a smear of chocolate on her face, and she wore a loose green smock, it was hard to tell what she looked like, except for a pair of rather voluptuous legs that showed between smock and shoes. She was studying a design, in a book of such designs, that showed a bird holding a scroll in its beak, and now attempted a reproduction of it, with a pencil, on a piece of tablet paper. He watched for a few moments, glanced at the cake, said it looked swell. This was perhaps an understatement, for it was a gigantic affair, eighteen inches across the middle and four layers high, covered with a sheen like satin. But after his comment he yawned, said: "Well—don't see there's much else I can do around here. Guess I'll take a walk down the street."

"You going to be home for supper?"

"I'll try to make it, but if I'm not home by six don't wait for me. I may be tied up."

"I want to know."

"I told you, if I'm not home by six—"

"That doesn't do me any good at all. I'm making this cake for Mrs. Whitley, and she's going to pay me three dollars for it. Now if you're going to be home I'll spend part of that money on lamb chops for your supper. If you're not, I'll buy something the children will like better."

"Then count me out."

"That's all I want to know."

There was a grim note in the scene that was obviously out of key with his humor. He stood around uncertainly, then made a bid for appreciation. "I fixed up those trees. Tied them up good, so the limbs won't bend down when the avocados get big, the way they did last year. Cut the grass. Looks pretty nice out there."

"You going to water the grass?"

"I *did* water it."

He said this with quiet complacency, for he had set a little trap for her, and she had fallen into it. But the silence that followed had a slightly ominous feel to it, as though he himself might have fallen into a trap that he wasn't aware of. Uneasily he added: "Gave it a good wetting down."

"Pretty early for watering the grass, isn't it?"

"Oh, one time's as good as another."

"Most people, when they water the grass, wait till later in the day, when the sun's not so hot, and it'll do some good, and not be a waste of good water that somebody else has to pay for."

"Who for instance?"

"I don't see anybody working around here but me."

"You see any work I *can* do that I *don't* do?"

"So you get done early."

"Come on, Mildred, what are you getting at?"

"She's waiting for you, so go on."

"Who's waiting for me?"

"I think you know."

"If you're talking about Maggie Biederhof, I haven't seen her for a week, and she never did mean a thing to me except somebody to play rummy with when I had nothing else to do."

"That's practically all the time, if you ask me."

"I wasn't asking you."

"What do you do with her? Play rummy with her a while, and then unbutton that red dress she's always wearing without any brassieres under it, and flop her on the bed? And then have yourself a nice sleep, and then get up and see if there's some cold chicken in her icebox, and then play rummy some more, and then flop her on the bed again? Gee, that must be swell. I can't imagine anything nicer than that."

His tightening face muscles showed his temper was rising, and he opened his mouth to say something. Then he thought better of it. Then presently he said: "Oh, all right," in what was intended to be a lofty, resigned way, and started out of the kitchen.

"Wouldn't you like to bring her something?"

"Bring her—? What do you mean?"

"Well, there was some batter left over, and I made up some little cakes I was saving for the children. But fat as she is, she must like sweets, and—here, I'll wrap them up for her."

"How'd you like to go to hell?"

She laid aside the bird sketch and faced him. She started to talk. She had little to say about love, fidelity, or morals. She talked about money, and his failure to find work; and when she mentioned the lady of his choice, it was not as a siren who had stolen his love, but as the cause of the shiftlessness that had lately come over him. He broke in frequently, making excuses for himself, and repeating that there *was* no work, and insisting bitterly that if Mrs. Beiderhof had come into his life, a guy was entitled to some peace, instead of a constant nagging over things that lay beyond his control. They spoke quickly, as though they were saying things that scalded their mouths, and had to be cooled with spit. Indeed, the whole scene had an ancient,

almost classical ugliness to it, for they uttered the same recrim-
inations that have been uttered since the beginning of marriage, and added little of originality to them, and nothing of
beauty. Presently they stopped, and he started out of the kitchen
again, but she stopped him. "Where are you going?"

"Would I be telling you?"

"Are you going to Maggie Biederhof's?"

"Suppose I am?"

"Then you might as well pack right now, and leave for good,
because if you go out of that door I'm not going to let you
come back. If I have to take this cleaver to you, you're not
coming back in this house."

She lifted the cleaver out of a drawer, held it up, put it back,
while he watched contemptuously. "Keep on, Mildred, keep
right on. If you don't watch out, I may call you one of these
days. I wouldn't ask much to take a powder on you, right now."

"You're not calling me. I'm calling you. You go to her this
afternoon, and that's the last you've seen of this house."

"I go where I goddam please to go."

"Then pack up, Bert."

His face went white, and their eyes met for a long stare.
"O.K., then. I will."

"You better do it now. The sooner the better."

"O.K. . . . O.K."

He stalked out of the kitchen. She filled a paper cornucopia
with icing, snipped the end off with a pair of scissors, and
started to ice the bird on the cake.

By then he was in the bedroom, pitching traveling bags from
the closet to the middle of the floor. He was pretty noisy about
it, perhaps hoping she would hear him and come in there, begging him to change his mind. If so, he was disappointed, and
there was nothing for him to do but pack. His first care was for
an outfit of evening regalia, consisting of shirts, collars, studs,
ties, and shoes, as well as the black suit he called his "tuxedo."
All these he wrapped tenderly in tissue paper, and placed in the

bottom of the biggest bag. He had, in truth, seen better days. In his teens he had been a stunt rider for the movies, and was still vain of his horsemanship. Then an uncle had died and left him a ranch on the outskirts of Glendale. Glendale is now an endless suburb, bearing the same relation to Los Angeles as Queens bears to New York. But at that time it was a village, and a pretty scrubby village at that, with a freight yards at one end, open country at the other, and a car track down the middle.

So he bought a ten-gallon hat, took possession of the ranch, and tried to operate it, but without much success. His oranges didn't grade, and when he tried grapes, the vines had just started when Prohibition came along and he dug them out, in favor of walnuts. But he had just selected his trees when the grape market zoomed on the bootleg demand, and this depressed him so much that for a time his land lay idle, while he tried to get his bearings in a dizzily-spinning world. But one day he was visited by three men who made him a proposition. He didn't know it, but southern California, and particularly Glendale, was on the verge of the real-estate boom of the 1920's, such a boom as has rarely been seen on this earth.

So, almost overnight, with his three hundred acres that were located in the exact spot where people wanted to build, he became a subdivider, a community builder, a man of vision, a big shot. He and the three gentlemen formed a company, called Pierce Homes, Inc., with himself as president. He named a street after himself, and on Pierce Drive, after he married Mildred, built this very home that he now occupied, or would occupy for the next twenty minutes. Although at that time he was making a great deal of money, he declined to build a pretentious place. He told the architect: "Pierce Homes are for folks, and what's good enough for folks is good enough for me." Yet it was a little better, in some ways, than what is usually good enough for folks. It had three bathrooms, one for each bedroom, and certain features of the construction were almost luxurious. It was a mockery now, and the place had been mortgaged and remortgaged, and the money from the mortgages long since spent. But once it had been something, and he liked to thump the walls, and comment on how solidly they were built.

Instead of putting his money in a bank, he had invested it in A. T. & T., and for some years had enjoyed daily vindication of his judgment, for the stock soared majestically, until he had a $350,000 "equity" in it, meaning there was that much difference between the price of the stock and the margin on which he carried it. But then came Black Thursday of 1929, and his plunge to ruin was so rapid he could hardly see Pierce Homes disappear on his way down. In September he had been rich, and Mildred picked out the mink coat she would buy when the weather grew cooler. In November, with the weather not a bit cooler, he had had to sell the spare car to pay current bills. All this he took cheerfully, for many of his friends were in the same plight, and he could joke about it, and even boast about it. What he couldn't face was the stultification of his sagacity. He had become so used to crediting himself with vast acumen that he could not bring himself to admit that his success was all luck, due to the location of his land rather than to his own personal qualities. So he still thought in terms of the vast deeds he would do when things got a little better. As for seeking a job, he couldn't bring himself to do it, and in spite of all he told Mildred, he hadn't made the slightest effort in this direction. So, by steady deterioration, he had reached his present status with Mrs. Biederhof. She was a lady of uncertain years, with a small income from hovels she rented to Mexicans. Thus she was in relative affluence when others were in want, and had time on her hands. She listened to the tales of his grandeur, past and future, fed him, played cards with him, and smiled coyly when he unbuttoned her dress. He lived in a world of dreams, lolling by the river, watching the clouds go by.

He kept looking at the door, as though he expected Mildred to appear, but it remained closed. When little Ray came home from school, and scampered back for her cake, he stepped over and locked it. In a moment she was out there, rattling the knob, but he kept still. He heard Mildred call something to her, and she went out front, where other children were waiting for her. The child's name was really Moire, and she had been named by the principles of astrology, supplemented by numerology, as had the other child, Veda. But the practitioner had neglected to include pronunciation on her neatly typewritten slip, and Bert and Mildred didn't know that it was one of the Gaelic variants of Mary, and pronounced Moyra. They took it for a French name of the more exclusive kind, and pronounced it Mwaray, and quickly shortened it to Ray.

His last bag strapped up, he unlocked the door and walked dramatically to the kitchen. Mildred was still at work on the cake, which by now was a thing of overwhelming beauty, with the bird sitting on a leafy green twig, holding the scroll, "Happy Birthday to Bob," perkily in its beak, while a circle of rosebuds, spaced neatly around the rim, set up a sort of silent twittering. She didn't look up. He moistened his lips, asked: "Is Veda home?"

"Not yet she isn't."

"I laid low when Ray came to the door just now. I didn't see any reason for her to know about it. I don't see any reason for either of them to know about it. I don't want you to tell them I said good-bye or anything. You can just say—"

"I'll take care of it."

"O.K., then. I'll leave it to you."

He hesitated. Then: "Well, good-bye, Mildred."

With jerky steps, she walked over to the wall, stood leaning on it, her face hidden, then beat on it once or twice, helplessly, with her fists. "Go on, Bert. There's nothing to say. Just—go on."

When she turned around he was gone, and then the tears came, and she stood away from the cake, to keep them from falling on it. But when she heard the car back out of the garage, she gave a low, frightened exclamation, and ran to the window. They used it so seldom now, except on Sundays if they had a little money to buy gas, that she had completely forgotten about it. And so, as she saw this man slip out of her life, the only clear thought in her head was that now she had no way to deliver the cake.

She had got the last rosebud in place, and was removing stray flecks of icing with a cotton swab wound on a toothpick, when there was a rap on the screen door, and Mrs. Gessler, who lived next door, came in. She was a thin, dark woman of forty or so, with lines on her face that might have come from care, and might have come from liquor. Her husband was in the trucking business, but they were more prosperous than most truckers were at that time. There was a general impression that Gessler trucks often dropped down to Point Loma, where certain low, fast boats put into the cove.

Seeing the cake, Mrs. Gessler gave an exclamation, and came over to look. It was indeed worth the stare which her beady eyes gave it. All its decorations were now in place, but in spite of their somewhat conventional design, it had an aroma, a texture, a totality that proclaimed high distinction. It carried on its face the guarantee that every crumb would meet the inexorable confectioners' test: It must melt on the tongue.

In an awed way, Mrs. Gessler murmured: "I don't see how you do it, Mildred. It's beautiful, just beautiful."

"If you have to do it, you can do it."

"But it's *beautiful!*"

Only after a long final look did Mrs. Gessler get to what she came for. She had a small plate in her hand, with another plate clamped over it, and now lifted the top one. "I thought maybe you could use it. I fricasseed it for supper, but Ike's had a call to Long Beach, and I'm going with him, and I was afraid it might spoil."

Mildred got a plate, slid the chicken on it, and put it in the icebox. Then she washed Mrs. Gessler's plates, dried them and handed them back. "I can use practically anything, Lucy. Thanks."

"Well, I've got to run along."

"Have a nice time."

"Tell Bert I said hello."

". . . I will."

Mrs. Gessler stopped. "What's the matter?"

"Nothing."

"Come on, baby. Something's wrong. What is it?"

"Bert's gone."

"You mean—for good?"

"Just now. He left."

"Walked out on you, just like that?"

"He got a little help, maybe. It had to come."

"Well what do you know about that? And that floppy-looking frump he left you for. How can he even look at her?"

"She's what he wants."

"But she doesn't even *wash!*"

"Oh, what's the use of talking? If she likes him, all right then, she's got him. Bert's all right. And it wasn't his fault. It was just—everything. And I did pester him. I nagged him, he said, and he ought to know. But I can't take things lying down, I don't care if we've got a Depression or not. If she can, then they ought to get along fine, because that's exactly the way he's built. But I've got my own ideas, and I can't change them even for him."

"What are you going to do?"

"What am I doing now?"

A grim silence fell on both women. Then Mrs. Gessler shook her head. "Well, you've joined the biggest army on earth. You're the great American institution that never gets mentioned on Fourth of July—a grass widow with two small children to support. The dirty bastards."

"Oh Bert's all right."

"He's all right, but he's a dirty bastard and they're all dirty bastards."

"We're not so perfect."

"We wouldn't pull what they pull."

The front door slammed and Mildred held up a warning finger. Mrs. Gessler nodded and asked if there was anything she could do, today. Mildred wanted desperately to say she could give her a lift with the cake, but there had been one or two impatient taps on an automobile horn from across the yard, and she didn't have the nerve. "Not right now."

"I'll be seeing you."

"Thanks again for the chicken."

The child who now entered the kitchen didn't scamper in, as little Ray had a short time before. She stepped in primly, sniffed contemptuously at the scent left by Mrs. Gessler, and put her schoolbooks on the table before she kissed her mother. Though she was only eleven she was something to look at twice. In the jaunty way she wore her clothes, as well as the handsome look around the upper part of her face, she resembled her father more than her mother: it was commonly said that "Veda's a Pierce." But around her mouth the resemblance vanished, for Bert's mouth had a slanting weakness that hers didn't have. Her hair, which was a coppery red, and her eyes, which were light blue like her mother's, were all the more vivid by contrast with the scramble of freckles and sunburn which formed her complexion. But the most arresting thing about her was her walk. Possibly because of her high, arching chest, possibly because of the slim hips and legs below it, she moved with an erect, arrogant haughtiness that seemed comic in one so young.

She took the cake her mother gave her, a chocolate muffin with a white V iced upon it, counted the remaining ones, and calmly gave an account of her piano practice. Through all the horrors of the last year and a half, Mildred had managed fifty cents a week for the lessons, since she had a deep, almost religious conviction that Veda was "talented," and although she didn't exactly know at what, piano seemed indicated, as a sound, useful preliminary to almost anything. Veda was a satisfactory pupil, for she practiced faithfully and showed lively interest. Her piano, picked out when Mildred picked out her coat, never actually arrived, so she practiced at her Grandfather Pierce's, where there was an ancient upright, and on this account always arrived home from school somewhat later than Ray.

She told of her progress with the Chopin *Grand Valse Bril-*

lante, repeating the title of the piece a number of times, somewhat to Mildred's amusement, for she employed the full French pronunciation, and obviously enjoyed the elegant effect. She spoke in the clear, affected voice that one associates with stage children, and indeed everything she said had the effect of having been learned by heart, and recited in the manner prescribed by some stiff book of etiquette. The waltz disposed of, she walked over to have a look at the cake. "Who's it for, Mother?"

"Bob Whitley."

"Oh, the paper boy."

Young Whitley's sideline, which was soliciting subscriptions after school hours, Veda regarded as a gross social error, and Mildred smiled. "He'll be a paper boy without a birthday cake if I don't find some way to get it over there. Eat your cake now, and then run over to Grandfather's and see if he minds taking me up to Mrs. Whitley's in his car."

"Can't we use our car?"

"Your father's out with it, and—he may be late. Run along now. Take Ray with you, and Grandfather'll ride you both back."

Veda stalked unhurriedly out, and Mildred heard her call Ray in from the street. But in a minute or two she was back. She closed the door carefully and spoke with even more than her usual precision. "Mother, where's Father?"

"He—had to go somewhere."

"Why did he take his clothes?"

When Mildred promised Bert to "take care of it," she had pictured a vague scene, which would end up with "Mother'll tell you more about it some day." But she had forgotten Veda's passion for her father's clothes, the proud inspection of his tuxedo, his riding breeches, his shiny boots and shoes, which was a daily ritual that not even a trip to her grandfather's was going to interfere with. And she had also forgotten that it was impossible to fool Veda. She began examining some imaginary imperfection on the cake. "He's gone away."

"Where?"

"I don't know."

"Is he coming back—"

"No."

She felt wretched, wished Veda would come over to her, so she could take her in her arms and tell her about it in some way that didn't seem so shame-faced. But Veda's eyes were cold, and she didn't move. Mildred doted on her, for her looks, her promise of talent, and her snobbery, which hinted at things superior to her own commonplace nature. But Veda doted on her father, for his grand manner and fine ways, and if he disdained gainful work, she was proud of him for it. In the endless bickerings that had marked the last few months, she had invariably been on his side, and often withered her mother with lofty remarks. Now she said: "I see, Mother. I just wanted to know."

Presently Ray came in, a chubby, tow-haired little thing, four years younger than Veda, and the picture of Mildred. She began dancing around, pretending she was going to poke her finger into the cake, but Mildred stopped her, and told her what she had just told Veda. She began to cry, and Mildred gathered her into her arms, and talked to her as she had wanted to talk in the first place. She said Father thought the world of them both, that he hadn't said good-bye because he didn't want to make them feel badly, that it wasn't his fault, but the fault of a lot of things she couldn't tell about now, but would explain later on some time. All this she said to Ray, but she was really talking to Veda, who was still standing there, gravely listening. After a few minutes Veda evidently felt some obligation to be friendly, for she interrupted to say: "If you mean Mrs. Biederhof, Mother, I quite agree. I think she's distinctly middle-class."

Mildred was able to laugh at this, and she seized the chance to gather Veda to her, and kiss her. Then she sent both children off to their grandfather's. She was glad that she herself hadn't said a word about Mrs. Biederhof, and resolved that the name should never pass her lips in their presence.

Mr. Pierce arrived with the car and an invitation to supper, and after a moment's reflection, Mildred accepted. The Pierces had to be told, and if she told them now, after having supper with them, it would show there were no hard feelings, and that she wanted to continue relations as before. But after the cake had been delivered, and she had sat around with them a few minutes, she detected something in the air. Whether Bert had already stopped by, or the children had made some slip, she didn't know, but things weren't as usual. Accordingly, as soon as supper was over and the children had gone out to play, she got grimly at it. Mr. Pierce and Mom, both originally from Connecticut, lived in a smaller, though just as folksy Pierce Home, on a pension he received as a former railroad man. But they were comfortable enough, and usually took their twilight ease in a small patio back of the house. It was here that Mildred broke the news.

A silence fell on them, a glum silence that lasted a long time. Mom was in the swing. She began touching the ground with her foot and it began rocking, and as it rocked it squeaked. Then she began to talk, in a bitter, jerky way, looking neither at Mildred nor at Mr. Pierce. "It's that Biederhof woman. It's her fault, from beginning to end. It's been her fault, ever since Bert started going with her. That woman's a huzzy. I've known it ever since I first laid eyes on her. The idea, carrying on like that with a married man. And her own husband not dead a year yet. And the filthy way she keeps house. And going around like she does with her breasts wobbling every which way, so any man's got to look at her, whether he wants to or not. What did she have to pick on my boy for? Wasn't there enough men, without she had to ..."

Mildred closed her eyes and listened, and Mr. Pierce sucked his pipe, and put in melancholy remarks of his own. It was all about Mrs. Biederhof, and in a way this was a relief. But then a sense of vague apprehension stirred within her. This evening, she knew, was important, for what was said now would be written indelibly on the record. For the children's sake, if no other, it was vital that she give no word of false testimony, or omit words essential to a fair report, or in any way leave a suspicion of untruthfulness. Also, she felt a growing annoyance at the facile way in which everything was being blamed on a woman who really had very little to do with it. She let Mom run down, and after a long silence, said: "It's not Mrs. Biederhof."

"Who is it, then?"

"It's a whole lot of things, and if they hadn't happened, Bert wouldn't any more have looked at her than he would have looked at an Eskimo woman. It's—what happened to Bert's business. And the awful time we had getting along. And the way Bert got fed up. And—"

"You mean to tell me this is *Bert*'s fault?"

Mildred waited a minute, for fear the rasp in Mom's voice would find an answering rasp in her own. Then she said: "I don't say it was *anybody*'s fault, unless it was the Depression's fault, and certainly Bert couldn't help that." She stopped, then doggedly plowed on with what she dreaded, and yet felt had to be said: "But I might as well tell you, Bert wasn't the only one that got fed up. *I* got fed up too. He didn't start this thing today. *I* did."

"You mean—*you put Bert out?*"

The rasp in Mom's voice was so pronounced now, her refusal to admit basic realities so infuriating, that Mildred didn't trust herself to speak at all. It was only after Mr. Pierce had interposed, and a cooling five minutes had passed, that she said: "It had to come."

"It certainly did have to come if you went and put that poor boy out. I never heard of such a thing in my life. Where's he at now?"

"I don't know."

"And it's not even your *house*."

"It'll be the bank's house pretty soon if I don't find a way to raise the interest money."

When Mom replied to that, Mr. Pierce quickly shushed her down, and Mildred smiled sourly to herself that the barest mention of interest money meant a rapid change of subject. Mr. Pierce returned to Mrs. Biederhof, and Mildred thought it diplomatic to chime in: "I'm not defending her for a minute. And

I'm not blaming Bert. All I'm trying to say is that what had to come had to come, and if it came today, and I was the one that brought it on, it was better than having it come later, when there would have been still more hard feelings about it."

Mom said nothing, but the swing continued to squeak. Mr. Pierce said the Depression had certainly hit a lot of people hard. Mildred waited a minute or two, so her departure wouldn't seem quite so pointed, then said she had to be getting the children home. Mr. Pierce saw her to the door, but didn't offer a ride. Falteringly, he said: "You need anything right now, Mildred?"

"Not yet a while, thanks."

"I sure am sorry."

"What had to come had to come."

"Good night, Mildred."

Shooing the children along, Mildred felt a hot resentment against the pair she had just left, not only for their complete failure to get the point, but also for their stingy ignoring of the plight she was in, and the possibility that their grandchildren, for all they knew, might not have anything to eat. As she turned into Pierce Drive the night chill settled down, and she felt cold, and swallowed quickly to get rid of a forlorn feeling in her throat.

After putting the children to bed she went to the living room, pulled a chair to the window, and sat there in the dark looking out at the familiar scene, trying to shake off the melancholy that was creeping over her. Then she went to the bedroom and turned on the light. It was the first time she had slept here since Bert started his attentions to Mrs. Biederhof; for several months, now, she had been sleeping in the children's room, where she had moved one of the twin beds. She tiptoed in there, got her pajamas, came back, took off her dress. Then she sat down in front of the dressing table and started combing her hair. Then she stopped and began looking at herself, grimly, reflectively.

She was a shade under medium height, and her small size, mousy-blond hair, and watery blue eyes made her look considerably younger than she actually was, which was twenty-eight. About her face there was no distinction whatever. She was what is described as "nice-looking," rather than pretty; her own appraisal she sometimes gave in the phrase, "pass in a crowd." But this didn't quite do her justice. Into her eyes, if she were provoked, or made fun of, or puzzled, there came a squint that was anything but alluring, that betrayed a rather appalling literal-mindedness, or matter-of-factness, or whatever it might be called, but that hinted, nevertheless, at something more than complete vacuity inside. It was the squint, Bert confessed afterwards, that first caught his fancy, and convinced him there was "something to her." They met just after her father died, when she was in her third year at high school. After the garage business had been sold and the insurance collected, her mother had toyed with the idea of buying a Pierce Home, using her small capital as a down payment, and taking in roomers to pay the rest. So Bert came around, and Mildred was excited by him, mainly on account of his dashing ways.

But when the day of the grand tour of Pierce Homes arrived, Mrs. Ridgely was unable to go, and Bert took Mildred. They drove in his sports roadster, and the wind was in her hair, and she felt a-tingle and grown-up. As a grand climax they stopped at the Pierce Model Home, which was really the main office of Pierce Homes, Inc., but was built like a home, to stimulate the imaginations of customers. The secretaries had gone by then, but Mildred inspected everything from the great "living room" in front to the cozy "bedrooms" at the rear, lingering longer in these than was perhaps exactly advisable. Bert was very solemn on the way home, as befitted one who had just seduced a minor, but gallantly suggested a re-inspection next day. A month later they were married, she quitting school two days before the ceremony, and Veda arriving slightly sooner than the law allowed. Bert persuaded Mrs. Ridgely to give up the idea of a Pierce Home for boardinghouse purposes, possibly fearing deficits, and she went to live with Mildred's sister, whose husband had a ship chandler's business in San Diego. The small capital, at Bert's suggestion, was invested in A. T. & T.

And Mildred's figure got her attention in any crowd and all crowds. She had a soft, childish neck that perked her head up at a pretty angle; her shoulders drooped, but gracefully; her brassiere ballooned a little, with an extremely seductive burden. Her hips were small, like Veda's, and suggested a girl, rather than a woman who had borne two children. Her legs were really beautiful, and she was quite vain of them. Only one thing about them bothered her, but it bothered her constantly, and it had bothered her ever since she could remember. In the mirror they were flawlessly slim and straight, but as she looked down on them direct, something about their contours made them seem bowed. So she had taught herself to bend one knee when she stood, and to take short steps when she moved, bending the rear knee quickly, so that the deformity, if it actually existed couldn't be noticed. This gave her a mincing, feminine walk, like the ponies in a Broadway chorus; she didn't know it, but her bottom switched in a wholly provocative way.

Or possibly she did know it.

The hair finished, she got up, put her hands on her hips, and surveyed herself in the mirror. For a moment the squint appeared in her eyes, as though she knew this was no ordinary night in her life, and that she must take stock, see what she had to offer against what lay ahead. Leaning close, she bared her teeth, which were large and white, and looked for cavities. She found none. She stood back again, cocked her head to one side, struck an attitude. Almost at once she amended it by bending one knee. Then she sighed, took off the rest of her clothes, slipped into her pajamas. As she turned off the light, from force of long habit she looked over to the Gesslers', to see if they were still up. Then she remembered they were away. Then she remembered what Mrs. Gessler had said: "... the great American institution that never gets mentioned on Fourth of July, a grass widow with two small children to support"—and snick-ered sourly as she got into bed. Then she caught her breath as Bert's smell enveloped her.

In a moment the door opened, and little Ray trotted in, weeping. Mildred held up the covers, folded the little thing in, snuggled her against her stomach, whispered and crooned to her until the weeping stopped. Then, after staring at the ceiling for a time, she fell asleep.

2

For a day or two after Bert left, Mildred lived in a sort of fool's paradise, meaning she got two orders for cakes and three orders for pies. They kept her bustlingly busy, and she kept thinking what she would say to Bert, when he dropped around to see the children: "Oh, we're getting along all right—no need for you to worry. I've got all the work I can do, and more. Just goes to show that when a person's willing to work there still seems to be work to be done." Also, she conned over a slightly different version, for Mr. Pierce and Mom: "Me? I'm doing fine. I've got more orders now than I can fill—but thank you for your kind offers, just the same." Mr. Pierce's fainthearted inquiries still rankled with her, and it pleased her that she could give the pair of them a good waspish sting, and then sit back and watch their faces. She was a little given to rehearsing things in her mind, and having imaginary triumphs over people who had upset her in one way and another.

But soon she began to get frightened. Several days went by, and there were no orders. Then there came a letter from her mother, mainly about the A. T. & T., which she had bought outright and still held, and which had fallen to some absurd figure. She was quite explicit about blaming this all on Bert, and seemed to feel there was something he could do about it, and should do. And such part of the letter as wasn't about the A. T. & T. was about Mr. Engel's ship-chandler-business. At the moment it seemed that the only cash customers were bootleggers, but they all used light boats, and Mr. Engel was stocked with heavy gear, for steamers. So Mildred was directed to drive down to Wilmington and see if any of the chandlers there would take this stuff off his hands, in exchange for the lighter articles used by speedboats. Mildred broke into a hysterical laugh as she read this, for the idea of going around, trying to get rid of a truckload of anchors, struck her as indescribably comic. And in the same mail was a brief communication from the gas company, headed "Third Notice," and informing her that unless her bill was paid in five days service would be discontinued.

Of the three dollars she got from Mrs. Whitley, and the nine she got from the other orders, she still had a few dollars left. So she walked down to the gas company office and paid the bill, carefully saving the receipt. Then she counted her money and stopped by a market, where she bought a chicken, a quarter pound of hot dogs, some vegetables, and a quart of milk. The chicken, first baked, then creamed, then made into three neat croquettes, would provision her over the weekend. The hot dogs were a luxury. She disapproved of them, on principle, but the children loved them, and she always tried to have some around, for bites between meals. The milk was a sacred duty. No matter how gritty things got, Mildred always managed to have money for Veda's piano lessons, and for all the milk the children could drink.

This was a Saturday morning, and when she got home she found Mr. Pierce there. He had come to invite the children over for the weekend—"no use coming back here with them. I'll bring them direct to school Monday morning, and they can come home from there." By this Mildred knew there was dirty work afoot, probably a trip to the beach, where the Pierces had friends, and where Bert would appear, quite by coincidence.

She resented it, and resented still more that Mr. Pierce had delayed his coming until she had spent the money for the chicken. But the prospect of having the children fed free for two whole days was so tempting that she acted quite agreeably about it, said of course they could go, and packed a little bag for them. But unexpectedly, as she ran back in the house after waving them good-bye, she began to cry, and went in the living room to resume a vigil that was rapidly becoming a habit. Everybody in the block seemed to be going somewhere, spinning importantly down the street, with blankets, paddles, and even boats lashed to the tops of their cars, and leaving blank silence behind. After watching six or seven such departures Mildred went to the bedroom and lay down, clenching and unclenching her fists.

Around five o'clock the bell rang. She had an uneasy feeling it might be Bert, with some message about the children. But when she went to the door it was Wally Burgan, one of the three gentlemen who had made the original proposition to Bert which led to Pierce Homes, Inc. He was a stocky, sandy-haired man of about forty, and now worked for the receivers that had been appointed for the corporation. This was another source of irritation between Mildred and Bert, for she thought he should have had the job, and that if he had bestirred himself a little, he *could* have had it. But Wally had got it, and he was out there now, without a hat, greeting her with a casual wave of the cigarette that seemed to accompany everything he did. "Hello, Mildred. Is Bert around?"

"Not right now he isn't."

"You don't know where he went?"

"No, I don't."

Wally stood thinking a minute, then turned to go. "All right, I'll see him Monday. Something came up, little trouble over a title, I thought maybe he could help us out. Ask him if he can drop over, will you?"

Mildred let him get clear down the walk before she stopped him. She hated to wash the dirty linen in front of any more people than she could help, but if straightening out a title would mean a day's work for Bert, or a few dollars in some legal capacity, she had to see that he got the chance. "Ah—come in, Wally."

Wally looked a little surprised, then came back and stepped into the living room. Mildred closed the door. "If it's important, Wally, you'd better look Bert up yourself. He—he's not living here anymore."

"*What?*"

"He went away."

"Where?"

"I don't know exactly. He didn't tell me. But I'm sure old Mr. Pierce would know, and if they've gone away, why—I think Maggie Biederhof might know, at least how to reach him."

Wally looked at Mildred for a time, then said: "Well—when did all this happen?"

"Oh—a few days ago."

"You mean you've busted up?"

"Something like that."

"For good?"

"As far as I know."

"Well, if you don't know I don't know who does know."

"Yes, it's for good."

"You living here all alone."

"No, I have the children. They're away with their grandparents for the weekend, but they're staying with me, not with Bert."

"Well say, this is a hell of a note."

Wally lit another cigarette and resumed looking at her. His eyes dropped to her legs. They were bare, as she was saving stockings, and she pulled her skirt over them self-consciously. He looked several other places, to make it appear that his glance had been accidental, then said: "Well, what do you do with yourself?"

"Oh, I manage to keep busy."

"You don't look busy."

"Saturday. Taking a day off."

"I wouldn't ask much to take it off with you. Say, I never did mind being around you."

"You certainly kept it to yourself."

"Me, I'm conscientious."

They both laughed, and Mildred felt a little tingle, as well as some perplexity that this man, who had never taken the slightest interest in her before, should begin making advances the moment he found out she had no husband anymore. He talked along, his voice sounding a little unnatural, about the swell time they could have, she replying flirtatiously, aware that there was something shady about the whole thing, yet a bit giddy at her unaccustomed liberty. Presently he sighed, said he was tied up for tonight, "But look."

"Yes?"

"What you doing tomorrow night?"

"Why, nothing that I know of."

"Well then—?"

She dropped her eyes, pleated her dress demurely over her knee, glanced at him. "I don't know why not."

He got up and she got up. "Then it's a date. That's what we'll do. We'll step out."

"If I haven't forgotten how."

"Oh, you'll know how. When? Half past six, maybe?"

"That suits me fine."

"Make it seven."

"Seven o'clock I'll be ready."

Around noon next day, while Mildred was breakfasting off the hot dogs, Mrs. Gessler came over to invite her to a party that night. Mildred, pouring her a cup of coffee, said she'd love to come, but as she had a date, she wasn't sure she could make it. "A date? Gee, you're working fast."

"You've got to do something."

"Do I know him?"

"Wally Burgan."

"Wally—well, bring him!"

"I'll see what his plans are."

"I didn't know he was interested in you."

"Neither did I. . . . Lucy, I don't think he was. I don't think he'd ever looked at me. But the second he heard Bert was gone, well it was almost funny the effect it had on him. You could see him get excited. Will you kindly tell me why?"

"I ought to have told you about that. The morals they give you credit for, you'd be surprised. To him, you were a red-hot mamma the second he found out about you."

"About *what?*"

"Grass widow! From now on, you're fast."

"Are you serious?"

"I am. And they are."

Mildred, feeling no faster than she had ever felt, pondered this riddle for some little time, while Mrs. Gessler sipped her coffee and seemed to be pondering something else. Presently she asked: "Is Wally married?"

"Why—not that I know of. No, of course he's not. He was always gagging about how lucky the married ones were on income-tax day. Why?"

"I wouldn't bring him over, if I were you."

"Well, as you like."

"Oh, it's not that—he's welcome, so far as that goes. But—you know. These are business friends of Ike's, with their lady friends, all-right guys, trying to make a living same as anybody else, but a little rough, and a little noisy. Maybe they spend too much time on the sea, playing around in their speedboats. And the girls are the squealing type. None of them are what you ought to be identified with, specially when you've got a single young man on your hands, that's already a little suspicious of your morals, and—"

"Do you think I'm taking Wally seriously?"

"You ought to be, if you're not. Well if not, why not? He's a fine, upstanding, decent young man, that looks a little like a pot-bellied rat, but he's single and he's working, and that's enough."

"I don't think he'd be shocked at your party."

"I haven't finished yet. It's not a question of whether you're making proper use of your time. What *are* your plans, so far as you know them?"

"Well, he's coming here and—"

"When?"

"Seven."

"That's mistake No. 1. Baby, I wouldn't let that cluck buy your dinner. I'd sit him right down and give him one of those Mildred Pierce specials—"

"What? Me work when he's willing to—"

"As an investment, baby, an investment in time, effort, and raw materials. Now shut up and let me talk. Whatever outlay it involves is on me, because I've become inspired and when inspired I never count little things like costs. It's going to be a perfectly terrible night." She waved a hand at the weather, which had turned gray, cold, and overcast, as it usually does at the peak of a California spring. "It won't be no fit night out for man nor beast. And what's more, you've already got dinner half fixed, and you're not going to have things spoil just because he's got some foolish notion he wants to take you out."

"Just the same, that was the idea."

"Not so fast, baby—let us pause and examine that idea. *Why* would he want to take you out? Why do they ever want to take us out? As a compliment to us, say they. To show us a good time, to prove the high regard they have for us. They're a pack of goddam liars. In addition to being dirty bastards, and very dumb clucks, they are also goddam liars. There's practically nothing can be said in favor of them, except they're the only ones we've got. They take us out for one reason, and one reason only: so *they* can get a drink. Secondarily, so *we* can get a drink, and succumb to their fell designs after we get home, but mainly so *they* can have a drink. And, baby, right there is where I come in."

She ducked out the screen door, ran across the yards, and presently was back with a basket, in which were quite a few bottles. She set them out on the kitchen table, then resumed her talk. "This stuff, the gin and the Scotch, is right off the

boat, and better than he's tasted in years. All the gin needs is
a little orange juice, and it'll make a swell cocktail; be sure you
cut it down plenty with ice. Now this other, the wine, is straight
California, but he doesn't know it, and it's O.K. booze, so lean
on it. That's the trick, baby. Handle the wine right and the
high-priced stuff will last and last and last. Fill him up on it—
much as he wants, and more. It's thirty cents a quart, half a
cent for the pretty French label, and the more he drinks of that,
the less he'll want of Scotch. Here's three reds and three whites,
just because I love you, and want you to get straightened out.
With fish, chicken and turkey, give him white, and with red
meat, give him red. What are you having tonight?"

"Who says I'm having anything?"

"Now listen, have we got to go all over that? Baby, baby,
you go out with him, and he buys you a dinner, and you get a
little tight, and you come home, and something happens, and
then what?"

"Don't worry. Nothing'll happen."

"Oh something'll happen. If not tonight, then some other
night. Because if it don't happen, he'll lose interest, and quit
coming around, and you wouldn't like that. And *when* it happens, it's Sin. It's Sin, because you're a grass widow, and fast.
And he's all paid up, because he bought your dinner, and that
makes it square."

"He must have a wonderful character, my Wally."

"He's got the same character they've all got, no better and
no worse. *But*—if you bought *his* dinner, and cooked it for him
the way only you can cook, and you just happened to look cute
in that little apron, and something just happened to happen,
then it's Nature. Old Mother Nature, baby, and we all know
she's no bum. Because that grass widow, she went back to the
kitchen, where all women belong, and that makes it all right.
And Wally, he's not paid up, even a little bit. He even forgot
to ask the price of the chips. He'll find out. And another thing,
this way is quick, and the last I heard of you, you were up
against it, and couldn't afford to waste much time. You play it
right, and inside of a week your financial situation will be greatly

eased, and inside of a month you'll have him begging for the chance to buy that divorce. The other way, making the grand tour of all the speako's he knows, it could go on for five years, and even then you couldn't be sure."

"You think I want to be kept?"

"Yes."

For a while after that, Mildred didn't think of Wally, at any rate to know she was thinking of him. After Mrs. Gessler left, she went to her room and wrote a few letters, particularly one to her mother, explaining the new phase her life had entered, and going into some detail as to why, at the moment, she wouldn't be able to sell the anchors. Then she mended some of the children's clothes. But around four o'clock, when it started to rain, she put the sewing basket away, went to the kitchen, and checked her supplies from the three or four oranges in reserve for the children's breakfast to the vegetables she had bought yesterday in the market. The chicken she gave a good smelling, to make sure it was still fresh. The quart of milk she took out of the icebox with care, so as not to joggle it, and using a tiny ladle intended for salt, removed the thick cream at the top and put it into a glass pitcher. Then she opened a can of huckleberries and made a pie. While that was baking she stuffed the chicken.

Around six she laid a fire, feeling a little guilty that most of the wood consisted of the dead limbs Bert had sawed off the avocado trees the afternoon he left. She didn't build it in the living room. She built it in the "den," which was on the other side of the chimney from the living room and had a small fireplace of its own. It was really one of the three bedrooms, and had its own bathroom, but Bert had fixed it up with a sofa, comfortable chairs, and photographs of the banquets he had spoken at, and it was here that they did their entertaining. The fire ready to light, she went to the bedroom and dressed. She put on a print dress, the best she had. She examined a great many stockings, found two that showed no signs of runs, put them on. Her shoes, by careful sparing, were in fair shape, and she put on simple black ones. Then, after surveying herself in the mirror, admiring her legs, and remembering to bend the right knee, she threw a coat around her and went to the den. Around ten minutes to seven she put the coat away and turned on one button of heat. Then she pulled down the shades and turned on several lamps.

Around ten after seven, Wally rang the bell, apologetic for being late, anxious to get started. For one long moment Mildred was tempted: by the chance to save her food, by the chance to eat without having to cook, most of all by the chance to go somewhere, to sit under soft lights, perhaps even to hear an orchestra, and dance. But her mouth seemed to step out in front of her, and take charge in a somewhat gabby way. "Well, my goodness, I never even dreamed you'd want to go out on a night like this."

"Isn't that what we said?"

"But it's so awful out! Why can't I fix you something, and maybe we could go out some other night?"

"Hey, hey, I'm taking *you* out."

"All right, but at least let's wait a few minutes, in case this rain'll let up a little. I just hate to go out when it's coming down like this."

She led him to the den, lit the fire, took his coat, and disappeared with it. When she came back she was shaking an orange blossom in a pitcher, and balancing a tray on which were two glasses.

"Well say! *Say!*"

"Thought it might help pass the time."

"You bet it will."

He took his glass, waited for her to take hers, said "Mud in your eye," and sipped. Mildred was startled at how good it was. As for Wally, he was downright reverent at how good it was. "What do you know about that? Real gin! I haven't tasted it since—God knows when. All they give you in these speaks is smoke, and a guy's taking his life in his hands, all the time. Say, where did *you* tend bar?"

"Oh, just picked it up."

"Not from Bert."

"I didn't say where."

"Bert's hooch was God-awful. He was one of these home-laboratory guys, and the more stuff he put in it to kill the taste, the worse it tasted. But this—say, Bert must be crazy if he walked out on *you*."

He looked at her admiringly and she refilled his glass. "Thanks, Mildred. I couldn't say no if I tried. Hey, what about yours?"

Mildred, not much of a drinker under any circumstances, had decided that tonight might be an excellent time to exercise a certain womanly restraint. She laughed, shook her head. "Oh—one's all I take."

"Don't you like it?"

"I like it all right, but I'm really not used to it."

"You've got to get educated."

"I can see that right now. But we can attend to that part a little bit at a time. Tonight, the rest of it's yours."

He laughed excitedly, strolled over to the window, stood looking out at the rain. "You know, I'm thinking about something. . . . Maybe you were right about not going out. That looks wetter than a Chinaman's wash. Did you really mean it, what you said about knocking something together that we could eat?"

"Of course I meant it."

"Putting you to one hell of a lot of trouble, though."

"Don't be silly, it's no trouble at all. And I bet you get a better meal here than you would outside. That's another thing you might have noticed, all the time you've been coming here. I don't know how much of a bartender I am, but I'm an awfully good cook."

"Quit kidding me. That was the hired girl."

"That was me. Want to watch?"

"I sure do."

She really was a marvelous cook, and he watched delightedly while she popped the chicken into the oven, scraped four potatoes, shelled a little dish of peas. They went back to the den until it should be time to put the vegetables on to boil, and he had another cocktail. By now she was wearing a little blue apron, and he oafishly admitted that he "sure would like to give those apron strings a pull."

"You better not."

"Why?"

"I might tie it on you, and put you to work."

"O.K. by me."

"Would you like to eat here? By the fire?"

"I'd love it."

She got a bridge table out of the closet and set it up in front of the fireplace. Then she got out silver, glassware, and napkins, and arranged them for two. He followed her around like a puppy, his cocktail glass in his hand. "Hey, this looks like a real dinner."

"I told you. Maybe you weren't listening."

"From now on, I'm nothing but ears."

The dinner was a little more of a success than she bargained for. For soup, she served some chicken jelly she had had left over from the middle of the week, and it struck him as very high-toned. When she had taken away the cups, she came in with the wine, which by a curious coincidence had been in the icebox since Mrs. Gessler left, and poured it, leaving the bottle on the table. Then she came in with the chicken, the potatoes, and peas, all deftly arranged on one platter. He was enthusiastic about everything, but when she came in with the pie, he grew positively lyrical. He told how his mother made such pies, back in Carlisle, Pa. He told about the Indian School, and Mt. Pleasant, the quarterback.

But the food, much as it delighted him, seemed almost incidental. He insisted that she sit beside him, on the sofa, and wear the apron. When she came in with the coffee, she found he had turned out the lights, so they drank it by firelight alone. When they finished it he put his arm around her. Presently, deciding she ought to be sociable, she dropped her head on his shoulder, but when he touched her hair with his finger she got up. "I've got to take these things out."

"I'll put the table away for you."

"Then all right, and when you get done with that, if you want the bath, it's right beyond you, and that's the door over there. As for the cook, as soon as she gets the dishes out of sight, she's going to put on a warmer dress."

What with the rain, and the general clammy feel of the night, the little print dress was becoming more and more uncomfortable, despite its pleasing appearance. She went to the bedroom, slipped out of it, and hung it up in the closet. But when she reached for her dark blue woolen dress, she heard something and turned around. He was standing in the door, a foolish grin on his face. "Thought you might need a little help."

"I don't need help, and I didn't ask you in here."

She spoke sharply, for her resentment at this invasion of her privacy was quick and real. But as she spoke, her elbow touched the closet door, and it swung open, revealing her. He caught his breath and whispered "Jesus." Then he seemed bewildered, and stood looking at her and yet not looking at her.

Badly annoyed, she took the woolen dress off its hanger and slipped it over her head. Before she could close the snaps, however, she felt his arms around her, heard him mumbling penitently in her ear. "I'm sorry, Mildred. I'm sorry as hell. But it didn't break like I figured it would. I swear to God, I came in here for nothing but to pull those apron strings. It was just a gag, that's all. Hell, you know I wouldn't pull any cheap tricks like that on you, don't you?" And as though to prove his contempt for all cheap tricks, he reached over and turned out the light.

Well, was she angry at him or not? In spite of the way in which she had followed all instructions, and the way he had justified all predictions, she still didn't know what she wanted to do about Wally. But as she twisted her head to keep her mouth from meeting his, it flitted through her mind that if she didn't have to open the Scotch, she might be able to get six dollars for it somewhere.

Along about midnight, Wally lit a cigarette. Feeling warm, Mildred kicked the covers off and let the cold damp air prickle her quite lovely nakedness. She raised one leg, looked at it judiciously, decided once and for all it was not bowed, and that she was going to stop worrying about it. Then she wiggled her toes. It was a distinctly frivolous operation, but there was nothing frivolous about Wally as he set an ashtray near him, and pulled the covers over his more or less lovely nakedness. He was silently, almost ostentatiously glum as he lay there and smoked, so much so that Mildred said: "Penny."

"I'm thinking about Bert."

Without hearing any more about it, she knew what this meant: Wally had had his fun, and now he was getting ready to get out from under. She waited a moment or two, as she often did when angered, but in spite of her effort to sound casual, her voice had a vibrant sound to it. "And what about Bert?"

"Oh—you know."

"If Bert left me, and he's out of my life, why do you have to do all this thinking about him, when nobody else is?"

"We're good friends. Goddam good friends."

"But not so goddam good that you wouldn't block him off from a job he was entitled to have, and then go around playing all the politics you knew how, to get it for yourself."

"Mildred, cussing's no good, coming from you."

"And double-crossing's no good, coming from anybody."

"I don't like that."

"I don't care whether you like it or not."

"They needed a lawyer."

"After you talked to them they did. Oh yes, at least a dozen people came to Bert, and warned him what you were doing and begged him to go down and put his claim in, and he wouldn't do it, because he didn't think it was proper. And then he found out what was proper. And what a pal you were."

"Mildred, I give you my word—"

"And what's that worth?"

She jumped out of bed and began marching around the dark room, bitterly reviewing the history of Pierce Homes, Inc., the incidents of the crash, and the procedure of the receivers. He started a slow, solemn denial. "Why don't you tell the truth? You've had all you wanted of me, haven't you? A drink, a dinner, and other things I'd prefer not to mention. And now you want to duck, and you start talking about Bert. Funny you didn't think about Bert when you came in here, wanting to pull those apron strings. You remember them, don't you?"

"I didn't hear you saying no."

"No, I was a sap."

She drew breath to say he was just like the rest of them, and then add Mrs. Gessler's phrase, "the dirty bastards," but somehow the words didn't come. There was some core of honesty within her that couldn't quite accept Mrs. Gessler's interpretations of life, however they might amuse her at the moment. She didn't really believe they were dirty bastards, and she had set a trap for Wally. If he was wriggling out of it the best way he could, there was no sense in blaming him for things that were rapidly becoming too much for her, but that he certainly had nothing to do with. She sat down beside him. "I'm sorry, Wally."

"Hell, that's all right."

"I've been a little upset lately."

"Who wouldn't be?"

Next morning, Mildred was glumly washing the dinner dishes when Mrs. Gessler dropped over, to give an account of the party. She rather pointedly didn't refer to Wally until she was leaving, and then, as though she had just thought of it, asked how he was. Mildred said he was all right, and listened while Mrs. Gessler added a few more details about the party, and then said abruptly: "Lucy."

"Yes?"

"I'm on the town."

"Well—you don't mean he actually left the money on the bureau, do you?"

"All but."

Mrs. Gessler sat on the corner of the table, looking at Mildred. There didn't seem to be much to say. It had all seemed so pat, so simple, and amusing yesterday, but neither of them had allowed for prophecies that merely half came true, or for dirty bastards that were goddam liars, but not quite such clucks as they should have been. A wave of helpless rage set over Mildred. She picked up the empty wine bottle, heaved it into the pantry, laughed wildly as it smashed into a hundred pieces.

From then on, Mildred knew she had to get a job. There came another little flurry of orders for cakes and pies, and she filled them, but all the time she was thinking, in a sick, frightened kind of way, or trying to think, of something she could do, some work she could get, so she could have an income, and not be put out of the house on the 1st of July, when the interest would be due on the mortgages Bert had put on the house. She studied the help-wanted advertisements, but there were hardly any. Each day there would be notices for cooks, maids, and chauffeurs, but she skipped quickly by them. The big advertisements, headed "Opportunity," "Salesmen Wanted," and "Men, Women, Attention,"—these she passed over entirely. They savored too much of Bert's methods in getting rid of Pierce Homes. But occasionally something looked promising. One advertisement called for: "Woman, young, pleasing appearance and manners, for special work." She answered, and was excited a day or two later when she got a note, signed by a man, asking her to call an address in the Los Feliz section of Hollywood.

She put on the print dress, made her face up nicely, and went over there.

The man received her in sweat shirt and flannels, and said he was a writer. As to what he wrote, he was quite vague, though he said his researches were extensive, and called him to many different parts of the world, where, of course, she would be expected to travel with him. He was equally vague about her duties: it appeared she would help him "collect material," "file documents," and "verify citations"; also take charge of his house, get some order into it, and check his bills, on which he feared he was being cheated. When he sat down near her, and announced he felt sure she was the person he was looking for, she became suspicious. She hadn't said a word that indicated any qualifications for the job, if indeed a job existed, and she came to the conclusion that what he wanted wasn't a research assistant, but a sweetie. She left, feeling sullen over her wasted afternoon and wasted bus fare. It was her first experience with the sexological advertiser, though she was to find out he was fairly common. Usually he was some phony calling himself a writer, an agent, or a talent scout, who had found out that for a dollar and a half's worth of newspaper space he could have a daylong procession of girls at his door, all desperate for work, all willing to do almost anything to get it.

She answered more ads, got repeated requests to call, and did call, until her shoes began to show the strain, and she had to take them constantly to the shoemaker's, for heel-straightening and polishing. She began to feel a bitter resentment against Bert, for taking the car when she needed it so badly. Nothing came of the ad-answering. She would be too late, or not qualified, or disqualified, on account of the children, or unsuitable in one way and another. She made the rounds of the department stores, and became dismally familiar with the crowd of silent people in the hallway outside the personnel offices, and the tense, desperate jockeying for position when the doors opened at ten o'clock. At only one store was she permitted to fill out a card. This was at Corasi Bros., a big place in downtown Los Angeles that specialized in household furnishings. She was first through the door here, and quickly sat down at one of the little glass-topped tables reserved for interviews. But the head of the department, addressed by everybody as Mrs. Boole, kept passing her by, and she grew furious at this injustice. Mrs. Boole was rather good-looking, and seemed to know most of the applicants by name. Mildred was so resentful that they should be dealt with ahead of her that she suddenly gathered up her gloves and started to flounce out, without being interviewed at all. But Mrs. Boole held up a finger, smiled, and came over. "Don't go. I'm sorry to keep you waiting, but most of these people are old friends, and it seems a pity not to let them know at once, so they can call at the other stores, and perhaps have a little luck. That's why I always talk to new applicants last, when I really have a little time."

Mildred sat down again, ashamed of her petulant dash for the door. When Mrs. Boole finally came over, she began to talk, and instead of answering questions in a tight-lipped defensive way, as she had at other places, opened up a little. She alluded briefly to the break-up of her marriage, stressed her familiarity with all things having to do with kitchens, and said she was sure she could be useful in that department, as saleswoman, demonstrator, or both. Mrs. Boole measured her narrowly at that, then led her into an account of what she had been doing about getting a job. Mildred held nothing back, and after Mrs. Boole cackled gaily at the story of Harry Engel and his anchors, she felt warm tears swimming into her eyes, for she felt if she didn't have a job, at least she had a friend. It was then that Mrs. Boole had her fill out the card. "There's nothing open right now, but I'll remember what you said about the kitchenware, and if anything comes up, at least I'll know where to get hold of you."

Mildred left in such a pleasant glow that she forgot to be disappointed, and she was halfway down the hall before she realized that her name was being called. Mrs. Boole was standing in the hallway, the card still in her hand, and came toward her nervously. She took Mildred's hand, held it a moment or two while she looked down at the street, many stories below. Then: "Mrs. Pierce, there's something I've got to tell you."

"Yes?"

"There aren't any jobs."

"Well, I knew things were slack, but—"

"Listen to me, Mrs. Pierce. I wouldn't say this to many of them, but you seem different from most of the applicants that come in here. I don't want you to go home thinking there's any hope. There isn't. In this store, we've taken on just two people in the last three months—one to take the place of a gentleman who was killed in an automobile accident, the other to take the place of a lady who had to retire on account of ill health. We see everybody that comes in, partly because we think we ought to, partly because we don't want to close up the department altogether. There just aren't any jobs, here or in the other stores either. I know I'm making you feel bad, but I don't want you to be—kidded."

Mildred patted her arm, and laughed. "Well my goodness, it's not your fault. And I know exactly what you mean. You don't want me to be wearing out shoes, for nothing."

"That's it. The shoes."

"But if you *do* have something—"

"Oh, if I have anything, don't worry. I'll be only too glad to let you know—by paid telegram. And, if you're down this way again, will you drop in on me? We could have lunch."

"I'll be only too glad to."

Mrs. Boole kissed her, and Mildred left, feeling footsore, hungry, and strangely happy. When she got home there was a notice hanging on the door, asking her to call for a paid telegram.

"Mrs. Pierce, it was like something in a movie. You had hardly stepped into the elevator, honestly. In fact I had you paged downstairs, hoping you hadn't left the store."

They sat down, in Mrs. Boole's private office this time, Mrs. Boole behind her big desk, Mildred in the chair beside it. Mrs. Boole went on: "I was watching you step into the down car, I was admiring your figure if you have to know why I was watching you, when this call came from the restaurant."

"You mean the store restaurant?"

"Yes, the tea room on the roof. Of course, the store doesn't have anything to do with that. It's sublet, but the manager likes to take people from our lists, just the same. He feels it makes a better tie-up, and then of course we do quite a lot of sifting ourselves, before we place a name on file, and it puts him in touch with a better class of girls."

"And what is the job?"

Mildred's mind was leaping wildly from cashier to hostess to dietician: she didn't quite know what a dietician was, but she felt she could fill the bill. Mrs. Boole answered at once: "Oh, nothing very exciting. One of his waitresses got married, and he wants somebody to take her place. Just a job—but those girls do very well for a four-hour day; they're only busy at lunch, of course—and it would give you plenty of time with your own children, and home—and at least it's a job."

The idea of putting on a uniform, carrying a tray, and making her living from tips made Mildred positively ill. Her lips wanted to flutter, and she ran her tongue around inside them to keep them under control. "Why, thanks ever so much, Mrs. Boole. I realize, of course, that it's quite a nice opening—but I doubt if I'm really fitted for it."

Mrs. Boole suddenly got red, and began to talk as though she didn't quite know what she was saying. "Well, I'm sorry, Mrs. Pierce, if I got you down here about something that— perhaps you don't feel you could accept. But I somehow got the idea that you wanted work—"

"I do, Mrs. Boole, but—"

"But it's perfectly all right, my dear—"

Mrs. Boole was standing now, and Mildred was edging toward the door, her face feeling hot. Then she was in the elevator again, and when she got out on the street she hated herself, and felt that Mrs. Boole must hate her, and despise her, and regard her as a fool.

Shortly after this, she registered with an employment agency. To decide which agency, she consulted the phone book, and decided on Alice Brooks Turner, mainly on account of the crisp succinctness of her advertisement:

JAMES M. CAIN

ACCOUNTANTS
CASHIERS
SALESMEN
OFFICE MANAGERS
Alice Brooks Turner
Skilled Personnel Only

Miss Turner, who had a small suite in one of the downtown office buildings, turned out to be a trim little person, not much older than Mildred, and a little on the hard-boiled side. She smoked her cigarette in a long holder, with which she waved Mildred to a small desk, and without looking up, told her to fill out a card. Mildred, remembering to write neatly, furnished what seemed to her an absurd amount of information about herself, from her age, weight, height, and nationality, to her religion, education, and exact marital status. Most of these questions struck her as irrelevant, and some of them as impertinent. However, she answered them. When she came to the question: What type of work desired?—she hesitated. What type of work did she desire? Any work that would pay her something, but obviously she couldn't say that. She wrote: Receptionist. As in the case of Dietician, she wasn't quite sure what it meant, but it had caught her ear these last few weeks, and at least it had an authoritative sound to it.

Then she came to the great yawning spaces in which she was to fill in the names and addresses of her former employers. Regretfully she wrote: Not previously employed. Then she signed the card, walked over, and handed it in. Miss Turner waved her to a chair, studied the card, shook her head, and pitched it on the desk. "You haven't got a chance."

"Why not?"

"Do you know what a receptionist is?"

"I'm not sure, but—"

"A receptionist is a lazy dame that can't do anything on earth, and wants to sit out front where everybody can watch her do it. She's the one in the black silk dress, cut low in the neck and high in the legs, just inside the gate, in front of that little

— 44

one-position switchboard, that she gets a right number out of now and then, mostly then. You know, the one that tells you to have a seat, Mr. Doakes will see you in just a few minutes. Then she goes on showing her legs and polishing her nails. If she sleeps with Doakes she gets twenty bucks a week, if not she gets twelve. In other words, nothing personal about it and I don't want to hurt your feelings, but by the looks of this card I'd say that was you."

"It's quite all right. I sleep fine."

If this bravado had any effect on Miss Turner, there was no sign of it. She nodded, and said: "I'm sure you sleep fine. Don't we all? But I'm not running a house of call, and it just happens that at the moment receptionists are out. That was then. In those good old days. When even a hockshop had to have this receptionist thing out there in front to show it had class. But then they found out she wasn't strictly necessary. They began sleeping with their wives, and I guess it worked out all right. Anyway, the birth rate went up. So I guess you're out of luck."

"Receptionist isn't the only thing I can do."

"Yes, it is."

"You don't give me much chance to tell you."

"If there was something else you could do, you'd have put it down in great big letters, right on this card. When you say receptionist, that's all I want to know. There's no more after that, and no use your wasting my time, and me wasting yours. I'll file your card, but I told you once and I'm telling you again, you haven't got a chance."

The interview, obviously, was ended, but Mildred forced herself to make a little speech, a sales talk. As she talked she warmed up to it, explaining that she was married before she was seventeen, and that while other women were learning professions, she had been making a home, raising two children, "not generally regarded as a disgraceful career." Now that her marriage had broken up, she wanted to know if it was fair that she be penalized for what she had done, and denied the right to earn her living like anybody else. Furthermore, she said, she hadn't been asleep all that time, even if she had been married.

She taught herself to be a good housekeeper and a fine cook, was in fact earning such little income as she had by peddling her cookery around the neighborhood. If she could do that, she could do other things. She kept repeating: "What I do, I do well."

Miss Turner pulled out a lot of drawers, set them in a row on her desk. They were filled with cards of different colors. Looking intently at Mildred, she said: "I told you you're not qualified. O.K., you can take a look here and see what I mean. These three drawers are employers, people that call me when they want somebody. And they call me, too. They call me because I'm on the level with them and save them the trouble of talking to nitwits like you. You see those pink ones? That means 'No Jews.' See the blues? 'No Gentiles'—not many of them, but a few. That's got nothing to do with you, but it gives you an idea. People are sold over this desk just like cattle in the Chicago yards, and for exactly the same reason: they've got the points the buyer wants. All right, now take a look at something that does concern you. See those greens? That means 'No Married Women.' "

"Why, may I ask?"

"Because right in the middle of rush hour you wonderful little homemakers have a habit of getting a call that Willie's got the croup, and out you run, and maybe you come back next day, and maybe you come back next week."

"Somebody has to look after Willie."

"These people, these employers on the greens, they're not much interested in Willie. And another habit you wonderful homemakers have got is running up a lot of bills you thought friend husband would pay, and then when he wouldn't you had to get a job. And then the first paycheck you draw, there's eighteen attachments on it—and life's too short."

"Do you call that fair?"

"I call them green. I go by the cards."

"I don't owe a cent."

"Not one?"

Mildred thought guiltily of the interest that would be due

July 1, and Miss Turner, seeing the flicker in her eye, said: "I thought so.... Now take a look at these other drawers. They're all applicants. These are stenographers—a dime a dozen, but at least they can do *something*. These are qualified secretaries— a dime a dozen too, but they rate a different file. These are stenographers with scientific experience, nurses, laboratory assistants, chemists all able to take charge of a clinic, or run an office for three or four doctors, or do hospital work. Why would I recommend you ahead of any of them? Some of those girls are Ph.D.'s and Sc.D.'s from U.C.L.A. and other places. Here's a whole file of stenographers that are expert bookkeepers. Any one of them could take charge of all the office work for a small firm, and still have time for a little sleeping. Here are sales people, men and women, every one of them with an A-1 reference—they can really move goods. They're all laid off, there's no goods moving, but I don't see how I could put you ahead of them. And here's the preferred list. Look at it, a whole drawerful, men and women, every one of them a real executive, or auditor, or manager of some business, and when I recommend one, I know somebody is getting something for his money. They're all home, sitting by their phones, hoping I'll call. I won't call. I've got nothing to tell them. What I'm trying to get through your head is: You haven't got a chance. Those people, it hurts me, it makes me lie awake nights, that I've got nothing for them. They deserve something, and there's not a thing I can do. But there's not a chance I'd slip you ahead of any one of them. You're not qualified. There's not a thing on earth you can do, and I hate people that can't do anything."

"How do I qualify?"

Mildred's lips were fluttering again, the way they had in Miss Boole's office. Miss Turner looked quickly away, then said: "Can I make a suggestion?"

"You certainly can."

"I wouldn't call you a raving beauty, but you've got an A-1 shape and you say you cook fine and sleep fine. Why don't you forget about a job, hook yourself a man, and get married again?"

"I tried that."

"Didn't work?"

"I don't seem to be able to kid you much. It was the first thing I thought of, and just for a little while I seemed to be doing all right. But then, I guess two little children disqualified me, even there. That wasn't what he said, but—"

"Hey, hey, you're breaking my heart."

"I didn't know you had a heart."

"Neither did I."

The cold logic of Miss Turner's harangue reached Mildred's bowels, where the tramping, waiting, and hoping of the last few weeks hadn't. She went home, collapsed, and wept for an hour. But next day she doggedly registered at three more agencies. She took to doing desperate things, like turning suddenly into business places, as she was passing them on the street, and asking for an opening. One day she entered an office building and, beginning at the top floor, called on every firm, in only two places getting past the gate. All the time the thought of July 1 haunted her, and she got weaker, paler, and tackier-looking. The print dress was pressed so many times that she searched the seams anxiously every time she put the iron on it. She lived on oatmeal and bread, reserving for the children such eggs, chicken, and milk as she could buy.

One morning, to her surprise, there came a card from Miss Turner, asking her to call. She dressed in about four minutes, caught the nine o'clock bus, and was in the familiar little office by nine thirty. Miss Turner waved her to a seat. "Something's come up, so I dropped you that card."

"What is it?"

"Housekeeper."

". . . Oh."

"It's not what you think, so don't employ that tone of voice. I mean, there's no sleeping in it, so far as I know. And it means nothing to me. I don't handle domestic help, so I won't collect a dime. But I was over in Beverly the other night, and got talking with a lady that's going to marry a director, and he doesn't know it yet, but his house is due for a big shake-up. So she wants a housekeeper. So, on account of all that fine domestic efficiency you were telling me about, I told her about you, and I think it's yours if you want it. Children O.K. You'll have your own quarters and I think you can nick her for one fifty if you get tough, but you'd better ask for two hundred and come down. That's over and above all your uniforms, food, laundry, heat, light, and quarters, and quite a lot more than most of my talented stable are making."

"I hardly know what to say."

"Make up your mind. I've got to let her know."

"Why did you think of me, for this?"

"Didn't I tell you? You broke my goddamn heart."

"Yes but—it's the second time lately I've had an offer of this kind. Not long ago a lady offered me a job as—as a waitress."

"And you turned it *down?*"

"I had to."

"Why?"

"I can't go home and face my children if they know I've been working all day at taking tips, and wearing a uniform, and mopping up crumbs."

"But you can face them with nothing for them to eat?"

"I'd rather not talk about that."

"Listen, this is just one woman's opinion, and it may be all wrong. I've got my own little business, and it's all shot, and I'm just about holding my own if I eat in the tea rooms instead of the Biltmore. But if that goes, and I have to choose between my belly and my pride, I'm telling right now, I'm picking my belly every time. I mean, if I had to wear a uniform, I'd do it."

"I'll go over there, as a courtesy to you."

For the first time, Miss Turner departed from her hard-boiled manner, and showed some sign of annoyance. "What have I got to do with it? Either you want this place or you don't. If you don't just say so and all I've got to do is call her up and tell her, and that lets me out. But if you do want it, for God's sake get over there and act like you mean it."

"I'll go, as a courtesy to you."

Miss Turner got out a card and savagely wrote a note on it, her eyes snapping as she handed it over to Mildred. "All right, you wanted to know why that lady offered you a job as waitress, and why I recommended you for this. It's because you've let half your life slip by without learning anything but sleeping, cooking, and setting the table, and that's all you're good for. So get over there. It's what you've got to do, so you may as well start doing it."

Shaken, Mildred got on the Sunset bus, but the address was unfamiliar to her, and she had to ask the conductor where to get off. At Coldwater Cañon Drive, where he set her down, there was no sign of the street, and she started wandering around an unfamiliar neighborhood, trying to get her bearings. The houses were big and forbidding, with driveways in front of them and clipped grass all around, and she couldn't find the courage to approach one. Of pedestrians there were none, and she plodded around for the better part of an hour, peering at each street sign, losing all sense of direction in the winding streets. She got into a hysteria of rage at Bert, for taking the car, since if she had that, she would not only be saved walking, but could slip into a filling station and inquire in a self-respecting way, having the attendant produce maps. But here there were no filling stations, nobody she could ask, nothing but miles of deserted pavements, shaded by frowning trees. Finally a laundry truck pulled up, and she got the driver to straighten her out. She found the house, a big mansion with a low hedge around it, went up to the door and rang. A white-coated houseman appeared. When she asked for Mrs. Forrester he bowed and stepped aside for her to enter. Then he noticed she had no car, and froze. "Housekeeper?"

"Yes, I was sent by—"

"Back way."

His eyes glistening with suddenly secreted venom, he closed the door, and she savagely trudged around to the back. Here he admitted her, and told her to wait. She was in a sort of service foyer, and in the kitchen, which was only a few steps away, she could see a cook and a waitress eyeing her. He returned, led her through dark, cool halls to a library, and left her. She sat down, glad to rest her aching feet. In a few minutes Mrs. Forrester came in. She was a tall woman in flowing negligee, who wafted graciousness all around her, putting the world at its ease. Mildred got up, handed over Miss Turner's note, and sat down while Mrs. Forrester read it. Evidently it was flattering, for it evoked one or two nods and clucks. Then Mrs. Forrester smilingly looked up. "It's customary, Mildred, for the servant to sit on the *Mistress's* invitation, not on her own *initiative.*"

Mildred was so startled at hearing herself addressed by her first name that it was a second or two before the sense of this made its way to her mind. Then she shot up as though her legs were made of springs, her face hot, her mouth dry. "Oh. I beg your pardon."

"It's perfectly all right, but on little things, especially with an inexperienced woman, I find it well to begin at the beginning. Do sit down. We've many things to talk about, and it'll make me quite uncomfortable to have you standing there."

"This is all right."

"Mildred, I *invited* you to sit *down.*"

Her throat throbbing, tears of rage swimming into her eyes, Mildred sat down, while Mrs. Forrester spoke grandly of her plans for reorganizing the house. Apparently it was her intended husband's house, though what she was doing in it, in negligee, a full month before the wedding, she didn't bother to explain. Mildred, it appeared, would have her own quarters, above the garage. She herself had two children by a former marriage, and of course no fraternization between children could be permitted, though there need be no trouble about that, as Mildred would have her own entrance on the lane, and "all such questions can be worked out." Mildred listened, or tried to, but suddenly a vision leaped in front of her eyes. She saw Veda, haughty, snobbish Veda, being told that she had to come in the back way, and that she couldn't fraternize with Forrester offspring. Then Mildred knew that if she took this place she would lose Veda. Veda would go to her father, her grandfather, the police, or a park bench, but not even whips could make her stay with Mildred, in the Forrester garage. A surge of pride in the cold child swept over her, and she stood up. "I don't think I'm quite the person you want here, Mrs. Forrester."

"The *Mistress* terminates the *interview*, Mildred."

"Mrs. Pierce, if you don't mind. And I'm terminating it."

It was Mrs. Forrester's turn to shoot up as though her legs were made of springs, but if she contemplated further instruction in the relation of the servant to the Mistress, she thought better of it. She found herself looking into Mildred's squint, and it flickered somewhat ominously. Pressing a button, she announced coldly: "I'll have Harris show you out."

"I'll find my way, thank you."

Picking up her handbag, Mildred left the library, but instead of turning toward the kitchen, she marched straight for the front door, closing it calmly behind her. She floated to the bus stop on air, rode into Hollywood without seeing what she was passing. But when she found she had got off too soon, and had to walk two blocks for the Glendale connection, she wilted and moved on trembling legs. At Hollywood Boulevard, the bench was full, and she had to stand. Then everything began spinning around, and the sunshine seemed unnaturally bright. She knew she had to sit down, or topple over, right there on the sidewalk. Two or three doors away was a restaurant, and she lurched into it. It was crowded with people eating lunch, but she found a small table against the wall, and sat down.

After picking up the menu, and dropping it quickly so the girl wouldn't notice her trembling hands, she asked for a ham sandwich, with lettuce, a glass of milk, and a glass of water, but she was an interminable time getting served. The girl puttered about, complained of the service that was demanded of her, and the little that she got for it, and Mildred had a vague suspicion that she was being accused of stealing a tip. She was too near collapse for argument, however, and beyond repeating that she wanted the water right away, said nothing. Presently her order arrived, and she sat apathetically munching it down. The water cleared her head, and the food revived her, but there was still a quivering in her bowels that didn't seem to have anything to do with the walking, fretting, and quarreling she had done all morning. She felt gloomy indeed, and when she heard a re-sounding *slap*, a few inches from her ear, she barely turned her head. The girl who had served her was facing another girl, and even as Mildred looked, proceeded to deal out a second loud slap. "I caught you, you dirty little crook! I caught you red-handed, right in the act!"

"Girls! *Girls!*"

"I caught her! She's been doing it right along, stealing tips off my tables! She stole ten cents off eighteen, before that lady sat down, and now she stole fifteen out of a forty-cent tip right here—*and I seen her do it!*"

In a moment the place was like a beehive, with other girls shouting their accusations, the hostess trying to restore order, and the manager flying out of the kitchen. He was a rotund little Greek, with flashing black eyes, and he summarily fired both girls and apologized profusely to the customers. When the two of them suddenly paraded out, in their street clothes, a few minutes later, Mildred was so lost in her reflections that she didn't even give her girl a nod. It was not until the hostess appeared in an apron, and began serving orders, that she woke up to the fact that she was face to face with one of the major decisions of her life. They needed help, that was plain, and needed it now. She stared at the water glass, twisted her mouth into a final, irrevocable decision. She would not do this kind of work, if she starved first. She put a dime on the table. She got up. She went to the cashier's desk, and paid her check. Then, as though walking to the electric chair, she turned around, headed for the kitchen.

The next two hours, to Mildred, were a waking nightmare. She didn't get the job quite as easily as she had supposed she would. The proprietor, whose name was apparently Makadoulis, but whom everybody addressed as Mr. Chris, was willing enough, especially as the hostess kept shrilling in his ear: "You've got to put somebody on! It's a mess out there! It's a mess!" But when the girls saw Mildred, and divined what she was there for, they gathered around, and passionately vetoed her application, unless Anna was taken back. Anna, she gathered, was the girl who had waited on her, and the aggressor in the fight, but as all of them apparently had been victims of the thefts, they seemed to regard her as their representative in a sense, and didn't propose to have her made a goat. They argued their case in quite noisy fashion, letting the counters pile up with orders while they screamed, and making appropriate gestures. One of these gestures wiped a plate into space, with a club sandwich on it. Mildred caught it as it fell. The sandwich was wholly wrecked, but she put it together again, with deft fingers, and restored it to its place on the counter. The Chef, a gigantic man addressed as Archie, watched her exhibition of juggling with impassive stolidity, but when the reconstructed sandwich was back on the counter he gave her a curt nod. Then he began banging on the steam table with the palm of his hand. This restored quiet as nothing else had been able to do. Mr. Chris turned to the girls. "Hokay, hokay."

The question of Anna being thus settled, the hostess hustled Mildred back to the lockers, where she unlocked a door and held out a menu. "Take off your dress and while I'm finding a uniform to fit, study this menu, so you can be some use. What size do you wear?"

"Ten."

"You worked in a restaurant before?"

"No."

"Study it, specially prices."

Mildred took off her dress, hung it in the locker, and stared at the menu. There were fifty-five- and sixty-five-cent lunches on it, as well as appetizers, steaks, chops, desserts, and fountain drinks, most of these bearing fancy names that were unintelligible to her. In spite of her best concentration most of it was a jumble. In a minute or two the hostess was back with her uniform, a pale blue affair, with white collar, cuffs, and pockets. She slipped into it. "And here's your apron. You furnish your uniform; it comes off your first check, three ninety-five; you get it at cost, and you keep it laundered. And if you don't suit us, we charge you twenty-five cents' rent on the uniform; that comes out of your check too, but you don't have the whole uniform to pay for unless we really take you on. The pay is twenty-five cents an hour, and you keep your own tips."

"And what's your name, Miss?"

"Ida. What's yours?"

"Mildred."

They started for the dining room, but going through the kitchen Ida kept talking into her ear. "I'm giving you a light station, see? Three, four, five, and six, all them little booths against the wall. That's so you don't get no fours. Singles and twos are easier. All them that's just come in, you take them, and them that's already started on their lunches, I'll take care of them myself. That's so you don't get mixed up on them other girls' books."

They reached the dining room, and Ida pointed out the station. Three of the tables were occupied by people who had given their orders before the fight started, the fourth by a pair of women who had just come in. All were getting annoyed at the delay in service. But still Mildred wasn't permitted to start. Ida led her to the cashier, a fish-faced blonde who began savagely telling Ida of the complaints she had received, and of the five people who had already walked out. Ida cut her off, had her issue Mildred a new book. "You've got to account for every check, see? In here you mark your number, you're No. 9. Here you mark the number of the table, here the number of customers on the check. Down here, put down everything they order, and the first thing you got to learn: don't make no mistake on a check. It's all booked against you, and if you make a mistake, it's deducted, *and you got to pay for it.*"

With this ominous warning in her ears, Mildred at last approached the two women who were waiting to have their orders taken, handed them their menus, and inquired what they were going to have. They replied they weren't sure they were going to have anything, and wanted to know what kind of place this was anyway, to let people sit around without even asking them if they minded waiting. Mildred, almost in hysteria by now with what she had been through that day, felt a hot impulse to take them down a few notches, as she had taken Mrs. Forrester. However, she managed a smile, said there had been a little trouble, and that if they could just be patient a minute or two, she would see they were served at once. Then, taking a quick lunge at the only thing she remembered about the menu, she added: "The roast chicken is awfully good today."

Slightly mollified, they chose chicken on the sixty-five-cent lunch, but one of them said loudly: "See there's no gravy on mine in any way, shape, or form. I hate brown gravy."

"Yes, Miss. I'll remember."

Mildred started for the kitchen, barely missing a girl who

appeared at the *out* door. Swerving in time, she dived through the *in* door and called to Archie: "Two roast chicken. One without gravy."

But the ubiquitous Ida was at her elbow, calling frantically to Archie: "Hold one gravy, hold it!" Then she yanked Mildred aside, and half screamed at her. "You got to call it right! You can't work nowhere without you're in good with the Chef, and you got to call it right for him. Get this: If there's any trimmings they don't want, you don't call it *without* 'em, you call it *hold 'em!*"

"Yes, Miss."

"You got to be in good with the Chef!"

Dimly Mildred began to understand why that great paw, banging on the steam table, had restored order when Mr. Chris had been mobbed like a Junebug in a flock of angry hens. She had observed that the waitresses dipped their own soup, so she now got bowls and filled them with the cream of tomato that her customers had ordered. But there was no surcease from Ida. "Pick up your starters! Pick up your starters!" At Mildred's blank look, Ida grabbed two plates of salad from the sandwich counter, whipped two pats of butter into two small plates, and motioned Mildred to get the four plates in there, quick. "Have they got water?"

"Not yet."

"For crying out loud."

Ida made a dive for the lift spigot, drew two glasses of water, slid them expertly so they fetched up beside the four plates. Then she pitched two napkins up against the water glasses. "Get in there with them—if they haven't walked out on you."

Mildred blinked helplessly at this formidable array. "Well—can I have a tray?"

In despair, Ida picked up plates, glasses, and napkins, so they were spread across her fingers like playing cards, and balanced halfway up her arm. "Get the soup, and come on." She was gone before Mildred could recover from the speed of her legerdemain. The soup Mildred picked up gingerly, kicking the *out* door open as she saw the others doing. Taking care not to spill any of it, she eventually reached the table. Ida was smoothing the two women down, and from their glances Mildred knew it had been fully explained to them that she was a new girl, and that allowances had to be made for her. At once they began amusing themselves by calling her January and Slewfoot. Lest she show resentment, she started for the kitchen, but it seemed impossible to get away from Ida. "Pick up something! Don't never make a trip, in or out, without something in your hand. You'll trot all day and you'll never get done! Get them dirty dishes over there, on No. 3. Pick up something!"

The afternoon dragged on. Mildred felt stupid, heavy, slow, and clumsy. Try as she would to "pick up something," dirty dishes piled on her tables, and unserved orders in the kitchen, until she thought she would go insane from the confusion. Her trouble, she discovered, was that she hadn't the skill to carry more than two dishes at a time. Trays were prohibited here, Ida informed her, because the aisles were so narrow they would lead to crashes, and this meant that everything had to be carried by hand. But the trick of balancing half a dozen dishes at a time was beyond her. She tried it once, but her hand crumpled under the weight, and a hot fudge sundae almost went on the floor. The climax came around three o'clock. The place was empty by then and the fish-faced cashier came back to inform her she had lost a check. The subsequent figuring showed that the check was for fifty-five cents, which meant that her whole hourly wage was lost. She wanted to throw everything in the place at the cashier's head, but didn't. She said she was sorry, gathered up the last of her dirty dishes, and went back with them.

In the kitchen, Mr. Chris and Ida were in a huddle, evidently talking about her. From their expressions as they started toward her, she sensed that the verdict was unfavorable, and she waited miserably for them to get it over with, so she could get away from Ida, and the Filipino dish washers, and the smell, and the noise, and drearily wonder what she was going to do next. But as they passed Archie, he looked up and made a gesture such as an umpire makes in calling a man safe at the plate. They looked surprised, but that seemed to settle it. Mr. Chris said "hokay, hokay," and went into the dining room. Ida came over to Mildred. "Well, personally, Mildred, I don't think you're suited to the work at all, and Mr. Chris, he wasn't a bit impressed either, but the Chef thinks you'll do, so against our better judgment we're going to give you a trial."

Mildred remembered the reconstructed club sandwich and the little nod she had received from Archie, realized that it was indeed important to be in good with the Chef. But by now her dislike of Ida was intense, and she made no effort to keep the acid out of her voice as she said: "Well please thank Archie for me and tell him I hope I won't disappoint him." She spoke loud enough for Archie to hear, and was rewarded with a loud, ursine cackle.

Ida went on: "Your hours are from eleven in the morning, ten thirty if you want breakfast, to three in the afternoon, and if you want lunch then, you can have it. We don't do a big dinner business here, so we only keep three girls on at night, but they take turns. You're on call twice a week from five to nine, same wages as in the daytime. Sundays we're closed. You'll need white shoes. Ask for nurses' regulation at any of the stores, two ninety-five. Well what's the matter, Mildred, don't you want the job?"

"I'm a little tired, that's all."

"I don't wonder, the way you trot."

When she got home, the children had just arrived from school. She gave them milk and cookies and shooed them out to play. Then she changed her dress and put slippers on her aching feet. She was about to lie down, when she heard a yoo-hoo, and Mrs. Gessler joined her, in a somewhat dark humor. Ike, it appeared, hadn't come home last night. He had phoned around nine, telling her of a hurry call that would prevent his arrival until next morning. It was all in his line of work, he had appeared at ten as he said he would, and yet. ... The extent to which Mrs. Gessler trusted Ike, or anybody, was evidently very slight.

Mildred presently asked: "Lucy, can you lend me three dollars?"

"More if you want it."

"No, thanks. I've taken a job, and need some things."

"Right away?"

"In the morning."

Mrs. Gessler went out, and Mildred went back to the kitchen to make her some tea. When she came back she sat down gratefully to the smoking cup, and flipped Mildred a bill. "I didn't have three, but here's five."

"Thanks. I'll pay it back."

"What kind of a job?"

"Oh—just a job."

"I'm sorry.... But if it's that kind of a job, I hope you picked a five-dollar house. You're too young for the two-dollar trade, and personally I wouldn't like sailors."

"I'm a waitress. In a hash-house."

"It rhymes up the same way."

"Just about."

"That's funny, though. It was none of my business, but all the time you were answering those ads, and trying to get hired on as a saleswoman, or whatever it was—I kept wondering to myself why you didn't try something like this."

"Why, Lucy?"

"Suppose you did get a job as a saleswoman? What would you get for it? No matter how they figure it up, when you're selling goods you get paid on commission, because it stands to reason if you weren't making commission they wouldn't pay you. But who's buying any goods? You'd have just stood around some store, all day long, waiting for the chance to make a living, and not making it. People *eat*, though, even now. You'll have something coming in. And then, I don't know. It may sound funny, but at selling, I'd say you just weren't the type. At *this*, though—"

All that Mrs. Boole had said, all that Miss Turner had said, all that her bowels had told her, after that trip to Beverly Hills, came sweeping over Mildred, and suddenly she dived for the bathroom. The milk, the sandwich, the tea, all came up, while moaning sobs racked her. Then Mrs. Gessler was beside her, holding her head, wiping her mouth, giving her water, leading her gently to bed. Here she collapsed in a paroxysm of hysteria, sobbing, shaking, writhing. Mrs. Gessler took her clothes off, massaged her back, patted her, told her to let it come, not to try to hold back. She relaxed, and cried until tears gushed down her face, and let Mrs. Gessler wipe them away as they came. After a long time she was quiet, but it was a glum, hopeless quiet. Then: "I can't do it, Lucy! I—just—can't—do—it."

"Baby! Do what?"

"Wear a uniform. And take their tips. And face those awful people. They called me names. And one of them grabbed my leg. Ooh—I can feel it yet. He put his hand clear up to—"

"What do they pay you?"

"Twenty-five cents an hour."

"And tips extra?"

"Yes."

"Baby, you're nuts. Those tips will bring in a couple of dollars a day, and you'll be making—why, at least twenty dollars a week, more money than you've seen since Pierce Homes blew up. You've got to do it, for your own sake. Nobody pays any attention to that uniform stuff any more. I bet you look cute in one. And besides, people have to do what they can do—"

"Lucy, stop! I'll go mad! I'll—"

At Mrs. Gessler's look, Mildred pulled herself together, at least tried to make intelligible her violent outburst. "That's what they've been telling me, the employment people, everybody, that all I'm good for is putting on a uniform and waiting on other people, and—"

"And maybe they're right, just at the present moment. Because maybe what they're trying to tell you is exactly what I'm trying to tell you. You're in a spot. It's all right to be proud, and I love you for it. But you're starving to death, baby. Don't you suppose my heart's been heavy for you? Don't you know

I'd have sent roast beef in here, or ham, or whatever I had, every night, except that I knew you'd hate me for it? You've just got to take this job—"

"I know it. I can't, and yet I've got to."

"Then if you've got to, you've got to, so quit bawling."

"Promise me one thing, Lucy."

"Anything."

"Don't tell anybody."

"I wouldn't even tell Ike."

"I don't care about Ike, or any of these people, what they think. It's on account of the children, and I don't want anybody at all to know it, for fear somebody'll say something to them. They mustn't know it—and specially not Veda."

"That Veda, if you ask me, has some funny ideas."

"I respect her ideas."

"I don't."

"You don't understand her. She has something in her that I thought I had, and now I find I haven't. Pride, or whatever it is. Nothing on earth could make Veda do what I'm going to do."

"That pride, I wouldn't give a snap of my finger for it. You're quite right about her. Veda wouldn't do it herself, but she's perfectly willing to let you do it and eat the cake."

"I want her to have it. Cake—not just bread."

During the six weeks Mildred had been looking for work, she had seen quite a little of Wally. He had dropped around one night, after the children had gone to bed, and was quite apologetic about what he had said, and penitently asserted he had made a sap of himself. She said there were no hard feelings, and brought him into the den, though she didn't bother to light a fire or serve a drink. But when he sat down beside her and put his arm around her, she got up and made one of her little speeches. She said she would be glad to see him any time, she wanted him as a friend. However, it must be distinctly understood that what was past was past, not to be brought up again under any circumstances. If he wanted to see her on that basis, she would try to make him welcome, and she really wanted him to come. He said gee that was swell of her, and if she really meant it, it was okey-doke by him.

Thereafter he dropped by rather often, arriving usually around nine, for she didn't want the children to know quite how much she was seeing him. Once, when they were spending a weekend at the Pierces', he came on Saturday evening and "took her out." She expressed a preference for a quiet place, for she was afraid the print dress wouldn't pass muster anywhere else, so they took a drive and ate in a roadside inn near Ventura. But one night, when her affairs were beginning to get desperate, he happened to sit beside her on the sofa again, and she didn't move. When he put his arm around her, in a casual, friendly kind of way, she didn't resist, and when he pulled her head on his shoulder she let it stay there. They sat a long time without speaking. So, with the door tightly locked, the shades pulled down, and the keyhole stuffed up, they resumed their romance, there in the den. Romance, perhaps, wasn't quite the word, for of that emotion she felt not the slightest flicker. Whatever it was, it afforded two hours of relief, of forgetfulness.

This evening, she found herself hoping that Wally might come, so she wouldn't have to think about the uniform she would have to buy in the morning, or the sentence she would begin serving. But when the bell rang she was a little surprised, for it was only a few minutes after seven. She went to the door, and instead of Wally standing there, it was Bert. "Oh. Why— hello, stranger."

"Mildred, how are you?"

"Can't complain. How's yourself?"

"O.K. Just thought I'd drop around for a little visit, and maybe pick up a couple of things I left in the desk, while I'm about it."

"Well come in."

But suddenly there were such whoops from the back of the house that any further discussion of his business had to be postponed indefinitely. Both children came running, and were swept into his arms, and solemnly measured, to determine how much they had grown since he saw them. His verdict was "at least two inches, maybe three." As Mildred suspected he had seen them both the previous weekend, this seemed a rapid rate of growth indeed, but if this was supposed to be a secret, she didn't care to unmask it, and so acquiesced in three inches, and it became official. She brought them all back to the den, and Bert took a seat on the sofa, and both children snuggled up beside him. Mildred told him the main news about them: how they had good report cards from school, how Veda was doing splendidly with her piano practice, how Ray had a new tooth. It was forthwith exhibited, and as it was a molar, required a deal of cheek-stretching before it came clearly into view. But Bert admired it profusely, and found a penny to contribute, in commemoration thereof.

Both children showed him their new possessions: dolls, brought by Mrs. Gessler from San Pedro a few days before; the gold crowns they were to wear at the pageant that would mark the closing of school in two weeks; some balls, translucent dice, and perfume bottles they had obtained in trades with other children. Then Bert asked Mildred about various acquaintances, and she answered in friendly fashion. But as this took the spotlight off the children, they quickly became bored. After a spell of ball-bouncing, which Mildred stopped, and a spell of recitations from the school pageant, which wound up in a quarrel over textual accuracy, Ray began a stubborn campaign to show Daddy the new sand bucket her grandfather had given her. As the bucket was in the garage, and Mildred didn't feel like going out there, Ray began to pout. Then Veda, with an air of saving a difficult situation, said: "Aren't you terribly thirsty, Father? Mother, would you like me to open the Scotch?"

Mildred was as furious as she ever permitted herself to get at Veda. It was the same old Scotch, and she had been saving it against that dreadful day when she might have to sell it, to buy bread. That Veda even knew it existed, much less how to open it, she had no idea. And if it were opened, that meant that Bert would sit there, and sit there, and sit until every drop of it was gone, and there went her Scotch, and there went her evening.

At Veda's remark, Ray forgot about the sand bucket, and began to shriek: "Yes, Daddy, we're going to have a drink, we're going to get drunk!" When Bert said, "I might be able to stand a drink, if coaxed," Mildred knew the Scotch was doomed. She went to the bedroom, got it out of the closet, went to the kitchen, and opened it. She turned out ice cubes, set glasses on a tray, found the lone seltzer siphon that had been there since winter. When she was nearly done, Veda appeared. "Can I help you, Mother?"

"Who asked you to go snooping around my closet to find out whether there was any liquor there or not?"

"I didn't know there was any secret about it."

"And hereafter, I'll do the inviting."

"But, Mother, it's Father."

"Don't stand there and look me in the eye and pretend you don't know what I'm talking about. You know you had no business saying what you did, and you knew it at the time, I could tell by the cheeky look on your face."

"Very well, Mother. It shall be as you say."

"And stop that silly way of talking."

"But I remind you, just the same, that there was none of this kind of stinginess when Father was doing the inviting. Things have indeed changed here, and not for the better, alas. One might think peasants had taken over the house."

"Do you know what a peasant is?"

"A peasant is a—very ill-bred person."

"Sometimes, Veda, I wonder if you have good sense."

Veda stalked out, and Mildred grimly arranged the tray, wondering why Veda could put her so easily on the defensive, and hurt her so.

Having a drink was a gay ritual in the household, one that had started when Bert made his bathtub gin, and that proceeded on its prescribed course tonight. First he poured two stiff drinks

for the children, cluck-clucking loudly at what rummies they
were getting to be, and observing that he didn't know what the
younger generation was coming to anyway. Then he poured two
light drinks for himself and Mildred, containing perhaps two
drops of liquor apiece. Then he put in ice and fizz water, set
the drinks on the tray and offered them around. But by a fascinating switcheroo, which Mildred never quite understood, he
always contrived to give the children the light drinks, himself
and Mildred the others. So adroit was this sleight-of-hand, that
the children, in spite of their sharpest watching and concen-
trating, never got the drinks that were supposedly prepared for
them. In the day when all the drinks were exactly the same
color, there was always a delightful doubt about it: Bert said
the children *had* got their drinks, and as there was at least a
whiff of juniper in all the glasses, they usually decided to agree.
Tonight, although the switcheroo went off as smoothly as ever,
the color of the Scotch betrayed him. But on his plea of fatigue,
and the need of a stimulant, they agreed to accept the light
drinks, so he set one of the stiff ones for Mildred, and took the
other himself.

It was a ritual, but after the preliminaries were out of the
way, it was enjoyed by each child differently. To Veda, it was
an opportunity to stick out her little finger, to quaff elegantly,
to play Constance Bennett. She regarded it as an occasion for
high-toned conversation, and plied her father with lofty questions about "conditions." He replied seriously, and at some
length, for he regarded such inquiries as signs of high mentality
on Veda's part. He said that while things had been mighty bad
for some time, he now saw definite signs of improvement, and
believed "we're due to turn the corner pretty soon."

But to Ray, it was a chance to "get drunk," as she called it,
and this she did with the utmost enthusiasm. As soon as she
got half of her fizz water down, she jumped up and began
spinning around in the middle of the floor, laughing at the top
of her lungs. Mildred caught her glass when this started, and
held it for her, and she spun around until she was dizzy and
fell down, in a paroxysm of delight. Something always caught

in Mildred's throat when this wild dance began. She felt, in some vague way, that she ought to stop it, but the child was so delightful that she never could make herself do it. So now she watched, with the tears starting out of her eyes, for the moment forgetting the Scotch. But Veda, no longer the center of the stage, said: "Personally, I think it's a disgusting exhibition."

Ray now went in to the next phase of the ritual. This was a singsong recitation her father had taught her, and went as follows:

> *I went to the animals' fair,*
> *The birds and the beasts were there,*
>> *The old baboon*
>> *By the light of the moon*
> *Was combing his auburn hair;*
> *The monkey he got drunk,*
> *And fell on the elephant's trunk,*
>> *The elephant sneezed*
>> *And fell on his knees—*
> *And what became of the monkety-monk?*

However, as Ray recited it, there were certain changes. "Beasts," was a little beyond her, so the line became "the birds and the bees." "Auburn" was a little difficult too, so the old baboon acquired a coat of "old brown hair." The "monkety-monk" was such a tempting mouthful that he became the "monkety-monkety-monkety-monkety-*monk*," a truly fabulous beast. While she was reciting, her father contrived to slip off his belt and stuff the buckle down the back of his neck, so that suddenly, when he pulled the free end over his head and began trumpeting on all fours, he was a sufficiently plausible elephant for any animals' fair. Ray began circling around, coming nearer and nearer with her recitation. When she was almost on him, and had tweaked his trunk two or three times, he gave a series of mighty sneezes, so that they completely prostrated him. When he opened his eyes Ray was nowhere to be seen. He now went into a perfect dither of anxiety over what had happened to her, put his head in the fireplace and called loudly up the chimney: "Monkety, monkety, monk."

"Have you looked in the closet?"

"Mildred, I bet that's just where she is."

He opened the closet, put his head in, and called: "Hey." Mildred suggested the hallway, and he looked out there. Indeed, he looked everywhere, becoming more alarmed every minute. Presently, in a dreadful tone, he said: "Mildred, you don't suppose that monk was completely *atomized,* do you?"

"I've heard of things like that happening."

"That would be terrible."

Veda picked up her glass, stuck out her little finger, took a fastidious sip. "Well, Father, I don't really see why you should get so upset about it. It seems to me anybody could see she's right behind the sofa."

"For that, you can go to bed."

Mildred's eyes blazed as she spoke, and Veda got up very quickly. But Bert paid no attention. He draped the belt over his head again, got down on his hands and knees, said "woof-woof," and charged around the sofa with the cutout open. He grabbed the ecstatically squealing Ray in his arms, said it was time they both went to bed, and how would they like Daddy to tuck them in? As he raised the child high in the air, Mildred had to turn her head, for it seemed to her that she loved Bert more than she could love any man, so that her heart was a great stifling pain.

But when he came back from the tucking in, put the belt on his trousers again, and poured himself another drink, she was thinking sullenly about the car. It didn't occur to her that he was the half-dozenth person she had been furious at that day, and that all of them, in one way or another, were but the faces worn by her own desperate situation. She was a little too literal-minded for such analysis: to her it was a simple matter of justice. She was working, he wasn't. He wasn't entitled to something that would make things so much easier for her, and that he could get along well enough without. He asked her again how she had been, and she said just fine, but all the time her choler was gaining pressure, and she knew that before long it would have to come out.

The bell rang, and she answered. But when Wally gave her a friendly pat on the bottom she quickly whispered: "Bert's here." His face froze for a moment, but then he picked up his cue with surprising convincingness. In a voice that would be heard all over the house, he bellowed: "Why, Mildred! Say I haven't seen you in a coon's age! Gee you're looking great! Say, is Bert in?"

"He's right in here."

"I'll only be a minute, but I got to see him."

If Wally elected to believe Bert still lived here, Bert evidently preferred to follow suit. He shook hands with a fine show of hospitality, offered a drink as though the liquor were his own, and asked how was every little thing quite as though nothing had happened. Wally said he had been trying to see him for a couple of months now, over something that had come up, and so help him God, this was the first chance he had had. Bert said don't tell him he simply didn't know what made the time fly. Wally said it was those three houses in Block 14, and what he wanted to know was, had any verbal promise been made at the time of the sale that the corporation would put a retaining wall in the rear? Bert said absolutely not, and launched into details as to how the lots were sold. Wally said it had all sounded pretty funny to him, but he wanted to make sure.

Mildred half listened, no longer in any humor for Wally, her mind on the car, and thinking only how she would begin. But then a perfectly hellish idea entered her mind, and she no sooner thought of it than she acted on it. "My but it's hot in here! Aren't you boys uncomfortable in those coats? Don't you want to take them off?"

"I think she said something, hey, Bert?"

"I'll say she did."

"Don't get up. I'll take them."

They took off their coats, and she draped them over her arm, and stepped into the closet to put them on hangers. When she had them nicely hung up, she slipped her fingers into Bert's change pocket, and there, as she knew it would be, was the key to the car. She took it out, slipped it into her shoe. When she came out of the closet she picked up her drink, which she had barely touched. "I think *I'll* get tight."

" 'Atta girl!"

"Lemme freshen it for you."

Bert put fresh ice in her glass, and a little more liquor, and a squirt of seltzer, and she took two or three quick swallows. She tinkled her ice, told the story of Harry Engel and the anchors, which amused the two gentlemen greatly. When she finished, she felt the key tickling her instep, and let out the first ripple of real laughter that had come out of her in months. She had a charming laugh, a little like Ray's, and it startled the two men, too, so for a time they laughed with her, as though there had never been a Depression, a break-up of marriage, or a sour feeling over who got the job with the receiver.

But Wally, evidently a little nervous, and more than a little uncertain about his status, decided presently that he had to leave. Bert took him ceremoniously to the door, but he discovered that he had forgotten his coat, and this gave him a chance to dash back for a quick word with Mildred. "Hey, is he back? I mean, is he living here?"

"Just saying hello."

"Then I'll be seeing you."

"I certainly hope so."

When Bert came back he resumed his seat, took a meditative sip out of his glass, and said: "Looked like he hadn't heard anything. About us, I mean. I figured there was no need to tell him."

"You did exactly right."

"What he don't know won't hurt him."

"Certainly not."

The bottle was getting low now, but he poured himself another drink, and got around to what he had come for. "Before

I go, Mildred, remind me to get a couple things out of the desk. Nothing important, but might as well take them along."

"Can I find them for you?"

"My insurance policy."

His voice was a little ugly, as though he expected an argument. The policy was for $1,000, paid-up value $256, and he had never taken out more because he didn't believe in insurance as an investment, preferring A. T. & T. There had been wrangles about it, Mildred insisting that if anything happened to him "it's the one thing between the children and the poorhouse." Yet she knew it was the next item for sacrifice, and obviously he was bracing himself for opposition. But she blandly got it for him, and he said "Thanks, Mildred." Then, apparently relieved at the easy way he got it, he said: "Well, goddam it, how you been, anyway?"

"Just fine."

"Let's have another drink."

They had the last two in the bottle, and then he said he had to go. Mildred got him his coat, and took him to the door, and submitted to a teary kiss, and he went. Quickly she turned out the lights, went to the bedroom, and waited. Sure enough, in a few minutes the bell rang. She opened, and he was standing there, looking a little foolish. "Sorry to bother you, Mildred, but my car key must have fallen out of my pocket. You mind my looking?"

"Why, not at all."

He went back to the den, snapped on the light, and looked all over the floor where he had been playing with Ray. She watched him with pleased, slightly boozy interest. Presently she said: "Well come to think of it, perhaps *I* took that key."

"*You* took it?"

"Yes."

"Well gimme it. I got to go home. I . . ."

She stood smiling as the dreadful truth dawned on him, and his face sagged numbly. Then she stepped quickly aside as he pawed at her. "I'm not going to give it to you, and there's no use in your trying to take it from me, because I've got it in a place where I don't think you'll find it. From now on, that car's mine. I'm working, and I need it, and you're not, and you don't need it. And if you think I'm going to pound around on my feet, and ride busses, and lose all that time, and be a sap, while you lay up with another woman and don't even use the car, you're mistaken, that's all."

"You say you're working?"

"Yes, I am."

"Then O.K. Why didn't you say so sooner?"

"Would you like me to ride you back?"

" 'Preciate that very much."

"You staying with Maggie?"

"Prefer not to say where I'm staying. I'm staying where I'm staying. But if you drop me by Maggie's, it's all right. Got to see her for a minute, so you can drop me there—if it's convenient for you."

"Anywhere's convenient for me."

They went out together, and got in the car. Fishing the key out of her shoe they started off, and rode silently to Mrs. Biederhof's, where she said she was awfully glad he dropped around, and wanted him to feel welcome any time, not only for the children's sake but for her sake. He solemnly thanked her, said he had enjoyed the evening, and opened the door to get out. Then he grabbed for the key. However, she had foreseen exactly that contingency, and palmed the key as soon as she turned on the ignition. She laughed, quite gaily malicious. "Didn't work, did it?"

"Guess it didn't."

"Good night, Bert. And I have a couple of old brassieres at the house, tell her. They're clean and fresh and she can have them any time she drops around."

"Listen, goddam it, you got the car. Now kindly shut up."

"Anything you say."

She pulled away and drove home. When she got there the light was still on, and everything was as she had left it. Glancing at the gas, she saw there were two gallons in the tank, and kept on straight ahead. At Colorado Avenue she turned. It was the first through boulevard she had been on, and the traffic signals were off, with yellow blinkers showing. She gave the car the gun, excitedly watching the needle swing past 30, 40, and 50. At 60, on a slight upgrade, she detected the gravelly sound of ping, made a mental note to have the carbon removed. Then she eased off a little on the gas, breathed a long, tremulous sigh. The car was pumping something into her veins, something of pride, of arrogance, of regained self-respect, that no talk, no liquor, no love, could possibly give. Once more she felt like herself, and began thinking about the job with cool detachment, instead of shame. Its problems, from balancing the dishes to picking up starters, flitted through her mind one after another, and she almost laughed that a few hours ago they had seemed formidable.

When she put the car in the garage, she inspected the tires with a flashlight, to see how they looked. She was pleased to find that there was considerable rubber left, so that new ones wouldn't be needed at once. Then she ran humming into the house, turned out the light, and undressed, in the dark. Then she went to the children's room, put her arms around Veda, and kissed her. As Veda stirred sleepily, she said: "Something very nice happened tonight, and you were the cause of it all, and I take everything back that I said. Now go to sleep and don't think about it any more."

"I'm so glad, Mother."

"Good night."

"Good night."

5

Within a few days, Mildred's financial troubles had eased a little, for she quickly became the best waitress in the place, not only at giving service, but at bagging tips. The trick of balancing dishes she learned by practicing after the children had gone to bed. She used tin plates, weighting them with stones from the garden, and got so that she could spread three on the fingers of her left hand, lay two more on her arm, remember not to stick her tongue out, and go sailing around the kitchen table without dropping any.

Tips, she knew instinctively, were a matter of regular customers who left dimes instead of nickels. She cultivated men, as all the girls did, as they were better tippers than women. She thought up little schemes to find out their names, remembered all their little likes, dislikes, and crotchets, and saw that Archie gave them exactly what they wanted. She had a talent for quiet flirtation, but found that this didn't pay. Serving a man food, apparently, was in itself an ancient intimacy; going beyond it made him uncomfortable, and sounded a trivial note in what was essentially a solemn relationship. Simple friendliness, coupled with exact attention to his wants, seemed to please him most, and on that basis she had frequent invitations to take a ride, have dinner, or see a show. At first she didn't quite know what to do about them, but soon invented a refusal that wasn't a rebuff. She would say she wanted him to "keep on liking her," that he "might feel differently if he saw her when she wasn't in uniform." This had the effect of arousing a good lively fear that perhaps she wasn't so hot in her street clothes, and at the same time of leaving enough pity for the poor working girl to keep him coming back, so she could serve his lunch. Having her leg felt, it turned out, was practically a daily hazard, and this she found best not to notice. Even a leg feeler, if properly handled, could be nursed into a regular who left good tips, no doubt to prove he really had a heart of gold.

She held aloof from the restaurant itself, and the people connected with it. This wasn't entirely due to her ideas of social superiority. In her own mind, she was highly critical of the kitchen, and was afraid to get drawn into talk, for fear she would say what she thought, and lose her job. So she confined her observations to Mrs. Gessler, and every night gave a savage account of the way things were done. Her special grievance was the pies. They were bought from the Handy Baking Company, and Mrs. Gessler often laughed loudly at Mildred's description of their uninviting appearance, their sticky, tasteless filling, and their hard, indigestible crusts. But in the restaurant she held her peace, until one day she heard Ida bawling out Mr. Chris. "I'm that ashamed to put it on the table! I'm that ashamed to ask a customer to eat it! It's just awful, the pie you put out here, and expect people to pay for it." Mr. Chris, who took all bawlings-out with a martyred shrug, merely said: "Maybe a pie is lousy, but what you expect, times like these now? If he no eat, see me, I hokay a new check." Mildred opened her mouth to take Ida's side, and hotly proclaim that a new check wouldn't make the pie taste any better. But at that moment it flashed through her mind that perhaps the real remedy was to get the pie contract herself. With the chance to make these precious dollars, her whole attitude changed. She knew she had to capture Ida, and not only Ida, but everybody else in the place.

That afternoon she was rather more helpful to the other girls than strict ethics demanded, and later, at lunch, sat down with them and got sociable. Meanwhile, she reflected what she was going to do about Ida. She was working that evening, and after the place closed, noticed Ida hurrying out with a glance at the clock, as though she might be catching a bus. Holding the door open, she asked: "Which way do you go, Ida? Maybe I could give you a lift."

"*You* got a car?"

"Anyway, it goes."

"Me, I live on Vermont. Up near Franklin."

"Why it's right on my way. I live in Glendale."

The iciness was gone by the time they climbed in the car. As they parted, Mildred asked Ida if she'd like her to stop by and pick her up, on the way over in the morning. From then on Ida had a ride, and Mildred had a better station, and more importantly, she had Ida's ear, with no possible interruptions, for a considerable time every day. They became bosom friends, and somehow the talk always got around to pies. Ida was bitter indeed at the product Mr. Chris offered his customers, and Mildred listened sympathetically. And then one night she innocently inquired: "What does he pay for those pies?"

"If he pays two bits, he's being swindled."

"Yes, but *how* much."

"I don't know.... Why?"

"*I* make pies. And if he pays anything at all, I'd meet the price and make him some that people would really want to eat. I'd make him some that would be a feature."

"Could you do it, honest?"

"I sell them all the time."

"Then I'll find out what he pays."

From then on, pies became a feverish conspiracy between Mildred and Ida, and one Sunday Mildred drove over to Ida's with a fine, wet, beautifully made huckleberry pie. Ida was married, to a former plasterer not working at the moment, and Mildred suspected that a pie might help with the Sunday night supper. Next day, during the luncheon rush, while Mr. Chris had stepped over to the bank to get more change, Ida stopped Mildred in the aisle, and said in a hoarse stage whisper: "He pays a straight thirty-five cents for them and takes three dozen a week."

"Thanks."

That night, Ida was full of the information she had filched from the file, and on Mildred's calculation that she could furnish pies at thirty-five cents, she became masterful. "You leave it to me, Mildred. Just leave it to me. You won't have to say one word. I've been knowing it all along I had to have a showdown about them pies, and now it's coming. Just leave it all to me."

The showdown, next morning, was a little noisier than Mildred had expected. Mr. Chris said he had dealt with the Handy Baking Company for years, and wasn't going to change, and Ida said he'd been losing customers for years too, and didn't have sense enough to know it. And besides, Ida went on, here's a girl that makes grand pies, and what was the matter, didn't he *want* customers? Mr. Chris said not to bother him, he was busy. Ida said look at the variety she's got, cherry, huckleberry, strawberry—

"No chilly, no hooklabilly, no strawbilly!" Mr. Chris fairly shouted his emphasis. "All a pieces fall down in a juice, waste half a pie, no good! Appliss, poomkin, limmon—no other kind, won't have'm."

At this Ida went into the dining room, beckoning Mildred after her. When they were alone she whispered excitedly: "You heard what he said? Apple, pumpkin, lemon—no other kind. That means he wants to switch, but he's too bullheaded to say so. Now listen, Mildred. Tomorrow you bring three pies, one apple, one pumpkin, one lemon. Just three, no more. And I'll see that they're served. They're samples, but you've got to remember one thing: It's got to be *his* idea."

Ida put her head through the door and beckoned, and Anna came out. Anna, the girl with the sock, had been reinstated some time before. Ida pulled her into the huddle. "Listen, Anna, you heard what I said to him in there?"

"Ida, them pies are a disgrace, and—"

"O.K., then you do just like I say, and we'll get Mildred's pies in here, 'stead of them cow pies we got now. Anna, they're just wonderful. But you know how he is, so tomorrow, when I put out the samples Mildred's going to bring, you put the bee on him and say that's what he's been up to all along. Then he thought it up, and we break through his bullheadedness."

"Just leave it to Little Orphan Annie."

"And put it on thick."

"I'll take that Greek like Grant took Richmond. Don't worry, Mildred. We'll sell your pies for you."

Mildred had a warm, wet-eyed feeling toward them both, and decided that Anna rated a free pie now and then, too. That afternoon she made the samples, and next morning Ida took charge of them herself, hurrying back to the kitchen with them like a spy carrying bombs. Changing into her uniform, Mildred was as nervous as an actress on opening night, and when she went into the kitchen there was expectancy in the air. Mr. Chris was at his desk, in the corner, and presently got up and went over to the *out* door. Here he posted, with a thumbtack, a piece of cardboard on which was written, in his Mediterranean hand-writing the special order for the day:

Sell
Ham & S Potato

All gathered around and looked at it. Ida went over to the desk, picked up the blue pencil, came back to the door and added:

& Pie

One by one, the girls filed in the dining room.

Lunch had barely started when Mildred managed to sell two pieces of pie. Mr. Rand, one of her regular customers, came in early with another man, and when she handed him the menu to pick out his dessert, she asked innocently: "Would you care for a piece of pie, Mr. Rand? The lemon is very good today."

Mr. Rand looked at his companion. "That just shows how much principle she's got. The pie stinks, she knows it stinks, and yet she says the lemon is very good today. Lay off the pie—unless you're really tired of this life, and prefer to be dead."

"We have a new line of pie today, Mr. Rand."

"Well—is it any *good?*"

"You try a piece. I think you'll like it."

The other man chose chocolate ice cream, and Mildred hurried to the kitchen to get the orders. As she came back with both desserts and the coffee, her heart gave a leap as she heard a customer say: "That pie looks good." When she set it in front of Mr. Rand the other man didn't even let her put the ice cream down. "Say, I want some of that! Can I switch?"

"Why certainly!"

"Principle? She's got principle plus. Say, that meringue looks two inches thick."

By noon, the lemon pie was a few smears of filling in an empty plate, and by one o'clock, all three pies were gone. By three, Ida had opened up on Mr. Chris, with everybody standing around, to watch the result. She said just look how them pies went. She said the lemon was gone before she could even turn around, and one customer wanted a second cut, and she didn't have it to give him. She said it was just terrible what the people said, when Mildred's pies ran out and she had to serve the bakery pies. To all of this, Mr. Chris made no reply whatever, merely hunching over his desk, and acting as though he was deaf. Ida plowed on, louder and louder. She said there was one lady, in a party of four, that wanted to know where they got such wonderful pies, and when she pointed out Mildred, she was that amazed. Mr. Chris twisted uneasily, and said not to bother him, he was busy, and—

"So that's what you was up to!"

He jumped up, and found Anna's finger not six inches from his nose, leveled at him as though it were a six-shooter. Giving him no time to recover, she went on: "So that's why you been asking all them questions about Mildred! That's why you been foxing around! And who told you she made pies, I'd like to know? Well can you beat that. Every time you take your eye off him he's up to something!"

To this not unflattering harangue Mr. Chris at first returned a blank stare. Then he burst into loud laughter, and pointed a derisive finger at Ida, as though it was a great joke on her. Ida professed to be highly indignant, that he should "let her go on like that" when he knew about Mildred's pies all the time, and had already made up his mind to take them. The more she talked the louder he laughed, and then, after he had wiped his streaming eyes, the bargain was struck. There was a little difficulty about price, he trying to beat Mildred down to thirty cents, but she held out for thirty-five, and presently he agreed. That night Mildred stood treat to Ida and Anna in a speako Wally had taken her to, and helped Anna pick up a man at a nearby table. Still with her first half-dozen pies to make, she drove home very late, full of a gulpy love for the whole human race.

On the strength of her new contract, she had a phone put in, and began to drum up more trade with the neighborhood customers, on the theory that a few extra pies were no more trouble, but that the extra money would be so much velvet. For pies one at a time, she had charged, and still charged, eighty-five cents each. Shortly, as a result of the neighborhood trade, there dropped into her lap another restaurant contract. Mr. Harbaugh, husband of one of her customers, spoke of her pies one night at the Drop Inn, a cafeteria on Brand Boulevard, not far from Pierce Drive, and they called her up and agreed to take two dozen a week. So within a month of the time she went to work as a waitress, she was working harder than she knew she could work, and still hold out until Sunday, when she could sleep. Taking care of the children was out of the question, so she engaged a girl named Letty, who cooked the children's lunch and dinner, and helped with the washing, stirring, and drudgery that went with the pies. She bought two extra uniforms, so she could launder all three at once, over the weekend. This chore, however, she did in the bathroom, behind locked doors. She made no secret of the pies; she couldn't very well. But she had no intention that either the children or Letty should know about the job.

And yet, tired as she was most of the time, there was a new look in her eye, even a change in her vocabulary. Talking with Mrs. Gessler, she spoke of "my pies," "my customers," "my marketing"; the first personal pronouns predominated. Unquestionably she was becoming a little important, in her own eyes, at least, a little conceited, a little smug. Well, why not? Two months before, she barely had pennies to buy bread. Now she was making eight dollars a week from her Tip-Top pay, about fifteen dollars on tips, more than ten dollars clear profit on pies. She was a going concern. She bought a little sports suit, got a permanent.

Only one thing bothered her. It was now late in June, and on July 1 seventy-five dollars was due on the mortgages. Her affluence was recent, and she had saved less than fifty dollars toward what she needed, but she was determined not to worry. One night, driving with Wally, she said abruptly: "Wally, I want fifty dollars out of you."

"You mean—now?"

"Yes, now. But it's to be a loan, and I'll pay you back. I'm making money now, and I can let you have it in a month, easy. But the interest is due on those mortgages Bert took out, and I'm not going to be foreclosed out of my home for a measly fifty bucks. I want you to get it to me tomorrow."

"O.K. I think I got it."

"Tomorrow."

"Hell, I'll write you a check tonight."

One day not long after that, she came home to find Letty in one of her uniforms. She hadn't bought uniforms for Letty yet. She had her put an apron on, over the wash dresses she came to work in, and said the uniform question would be postponed until it was certain she was satisfactory. Now, seeing Letty in

restaurant regalia, she felt her face prickle, but left the kitchen
for fear of what she might say. But Letty caught the look and
followed. "I told her you wouldn't like it, Mrs. Pierce. I told
her right off, but she hollered and carried on so I put it on,
just to keep her quiet."

"*Who* hollered and carried on?"

"Miss Veda, ma'am."

"*Miss* Veda."

"She makes me call her that."

"And she told you to put that uniform on?"

"Yes'm."

"Very well. It's quite all right, if that's how it happened, but
you can take it off now. And hereafter, remember I'm giving
orders around here, not Miss Veda."

"Yes'm."

Mildred made her pies, and nothing more was said about it
that afternoon, or at dinner, Veda taking no notice of Letty's
change of costume. But after dinner, when Letty had gone home,
Mildred summoned both children to the den, and talking mainly
to Veda, announced they were going into the question of the
uniform. "Certainly, Mother. It's quite becoming to her, don't
you think?"

"Never mind whether it's becoming or not. The first thing I
want to know is this: Those uniforms were on the top shelf of
my closet, under a pile of sheets. Now how did you happen to
find them there?"

"Mother, I needed a handkerchief, and went to see if any of
mine had been put with your things by mistake."

"In the closet?"

"I had looked everywhere else, and—"

"All your handkerchiefs were in your own top drawer, and
they still are, and you weren't looking for any handkerchief at
all. Once more you were snooping into my things to see what
you could find, weren't you?"

"Mother, how can you insinuate such—"

"*Weren't* you?"

"I was not, and I resent the question."

Veda looked Mildred in the eye with haughty, offended dignity. Mildred waited a moment, and then went on: "And how did you happen to give one of those uniforms to Letty?"

"I merely assumed, Mother, that you had forgotten to tell her to wear them. Evidently they had been bought for her. If she was going to take my things to the pool, I naturally wanted her decently dressed."

"To the pool? What things?"

"My swimming things, Mother."

Little Ray laughed loudly, and Mildred stared bewildered. School being over, she had left a book of bus tickets, so the children could go down and swim in the plunge at Griffith Park. But that Letty was included in the excursion she had no idea. It quickly developed, however, that Veda's notion of a swim in the pool was for herself and Ray to go parading to the bus stop, with Letty following two paces behind, all dressed up in uniform, apron, and cap, and carrying the swimming bags. She even produced the cap, which Mildred identified as the collar of one of her own dresses. It had been neatly sewed, so as to make a plausible white corona, embroidered around the edges.

"I never heard of such goings-on in my life."

"Well, Mother, it seems to me wholly proper."

"Does Letty go in swimming?"

"Certainly not."

"What does she do?"

"She sits by the pool and waits, as she should."

"For *Miss* Veda, I suppose?"

"She knows her place, I hope."

"Well hereafter, there'll be no more Miss Veda. And if she goes with you to the pool, she goes in her own clothes, and she has a swim. If she hasn't a suit, I'll get her one."

"Mother, it shall be as you say."

Little Ray, who had been listening to all this with vast delight, now rolled on the floor, screaming with laughter, and kicking her heels in the air. "She can't swim! She can't swim, and she'll get drownded! And Red will have to pull her out! He's the life guard, *and he's stuck on her!*"

At this, Mildred began to understand Letty's strange conduct, and had to laugh in spite of herself. Veda thereupon elected to regard the inquest as closed. "Really, Mother, it seems to me you made a great fuss over nothing. If you bought the uniforms for her, and certainly I can't imagine who else you could have bought them for—then why shouldn't she wear them?"

But Veda had slightly overdone it. In a flash, from the special innocence with which she couldn't imagine who *else* the uniforms could have been bought for, Mildred divined that she knew the truth, and that meant the whole thing had to be dealt with fundamentally. For Veda's purpose, in giving Letty the uniform, might be nothing more sinister than a desire to make a peafowl's progress to the pool, but it might be considerably more devious. So Mildred didn't act at once. She sat looking at Veda, the squint hardening in her eye; then she scooped up Ray in her arms, and announced it was time to go to bed. Undressing her, she played with her as she always did, blowing into the buttonholes of the little sleeping suit, rolling her into bed with a loud whoosh and a final blow down the back of her neck. But all the time she was thinking of Veda, who never took part in these frivolities. Out of the corner of her eye, she could see her, cramped in front of the dressing table for a period of primping, whose main object seemed to be the spreading of as many combs, brushes, and bottles in front of her as the table would hold. She was none too agreeable about it when Mildred finished with Ray, and ordered her to the den for more talk. She got up angrily and threw down a brush. "Yee gods—what now?"

When they got to the den, Mildred closed the door, sat down in the armchair, and stood Veda in front of her. "Why did you give Letty that uniform?"

"For heaven's sake, Mother, haven't I told you once? How often do I have to tell you? I won't have you questioning me this way. Good night—I'm going to bed."

Mildred caught her arm, pulled her back. "You knew, when you gave it to Letty, that that was my uniform, didn't you?"

"*Your* uniform?"

Veda's simulation of surprise was so cool, so calculated, so insolent, that Mildred waited longer than she usually did, when angered. Then she went on: "I've taken a job as a waitress in a restaurant in Hollywood."

"As a—*what?*"

"As a waitress, as you very well know."

"Yee gods! Yee—"

Mildred clipped her on the cheek, but she gave a short laugh, and brazenly finished: —"gods and little fishes!"

At this, Mildred clipped her a terrific wallop on the other cheek, that toppled her to the floor. As she lay there, Mildred began to talk. "So you and your sister can eat, and have a place to sleep, and a few clothes on your backs. I've taken the only kind of a job I could get, and if you think I'm going to listen to a lot of silly nonsense from you about it, you're mistaken. And if you think your nonsense is going to make me give up the job, you're mistaken about that, too. How you found out what I was doing I don't know—"

"From the uniform, stupid. You think I'm dumb?"

Mildred clipped her again, and went on: "You may not realize it, but everything you have costs money, from the maid that you ordered to go traipsing with you to the pool, to your food, and everything else that you have. And as I don't see anybody else doing anything about it—"

Veda had got up now, her eyes hard, and cut in: "Aren't the pies bad enough? Did you have to degrade us by—"

Mildred caught her by both arms, threw her over one knee, whipped the kimono up with one motion, the pants down with another, and brought her bare hand down on Veda's bottom with all the force her fury could give her. Veda screamed and bit her leg. Mildred pulled loose, then beat the rapidly reddening bottom until she was exhausted, and Veda screamed as though demons were inside of her. Then Mildred let Veda slide to the floor, and sat there panting and fighting the nausea that was swelling in her stomach.

Presently Veda got up, staggered to the sofa, and flung herself down in tragic despair. Then she gave a soft laugh, and whispered, in sorrow rather than in anger: "A waitress."

Mildred now began to cry. She rarely struck Veda, telling Mrs. Gessler that "the child didn't need it," and that she "didn't believe in beating children for every little thing." But this wasn't the real reason. The few times she had tried beating, she had got exactly nowhere. She couldn't break Veda, no matter how much she beat her. Veda got victory out of these struggles, she a trembling, ignoble defeat. It always came back to the same thing. She was afraid of Veda, of her snobbery, her contempt, her unbreakable spirit. And she was afraid of something that seemed always lurking under Veda's bland, phony toniness: a cold, cruel, coarse desire to torture her mother, to humiliate her, above everything else, to hurt her. Mildred apparently yearned for warm affection from this child, such as Bert apparently commanded. But all she ever got was a stagy, affected counterfeit. This half loaf she had to accept, trying not to see it for what it really was.

She wept, then sat with a dismal feeling creeping over her, for she was as far from settling the main point as she had ever been. Veda had to be made to accept this job she had taken, else her days would be dull misery, and in the end she would have to give it up. But how? Presently, not conscious of having hatched any idea, she began to talk. "You never give me credit for any finer feelings, do you?"

"Oh, Mother, please—let's not talk about it anymore. It's all right. You're working in a—in Hollywood, and I'll try not to think about it."

"As a matter of fact, I felt exactly about it as you do, and I certainly would never have taken this job if it hadn't been that I—" Mildred swallowed, made a wild lunge at something, anything, and went on: "—that I had decided to open a place of my own, and I had to learn the business. I had to know all about it and—"

At least Veda did sit up at this, and show some faint sign of interest. "What kind of a place, Mother? You mean a—"

"Restaurant, of course."

Veda blinked and for a dreadful moment Mildred felt that this didn't quite meet Veda's social requirements either. Desperately she went on: "There's money in a restaurant, if it's run right, and—"

"You mean we'll be *rich?*"

"Many people have got rich that way."

That did it. Even though a restaurant might not be quite the toniest thing that Veda could imagine, riches spoke to the profoundest part of her nature. She ran over, put her arms around her mother, kissed her, nuzzled her neck, insisted on being punished for the horrible way she had acted. When Mildred had given her a faltering pat on the bottom, she climbed into the chair, and babbled happily to Mildred about the limousine they would have, and the grand piano, on which she could practice her music.

Mildred gladly promised all these things, but later, when Veda was in bed and she herself was undressing, she wondered how long she could keep up the pretense, and whether she could get another job before her bluff was called. And then a hot, electric idea flashed through her mind. Why not have her own restaurant? She looked in the mirror, and saw a calculating, confident woman's face squinting back at her. *Well, why not?* Her breath began to come just a little bit fast as she canvassed her qualifications. She could cook, she had such a gift for it as few ever have. She was learning the business; in fact, so far as pies went, she was in business already. She was young, healthy, stronger than she looked. She had two children, all she wanted, all she could be expected to bring into the world, so there need be no more of that. She was implacably determined to get ahead, somehow. She put on her pajamas, turned out the light, but kept walking around the room, in the dark. In spite of herself, the limousine, the chauffeur, and the grand piano began to gleam before her eyes, but as real this time, not imaginary. She started for bed, then hurried to the children's room. "Veda?"

"Yes, Mother. I'm awake."

She went over, knelt down, put her arms around the child, hugged her passionately. "You were right, darling, and I was wrong. No matter what I say, no matter what anybody says, never give up that pride, that way you have of looking at things. I wish I had it, and—never give it up!"

"I can't help it, Mother. It's how I feel."

"Something else happened tonight."

"Tell me."

"Nothing to tell. Only now I feel it, now I *know* it, that from now on things are going to get better for us. So we'll have what we want. Maybe we won't be rich, but—we'll have something. And it'll all be on account of you. Every good thing that happens is on account of you, if Mother only had sense enough to know it."

"Oh Mother, I love you. Truly I do."

"Say it again. . . . Say it—just once—more."

6

Again Mildred's attitude toward the restaurant changed, from critical disapproval to eager curiosity. Mr. Chris, while his cuisine might not excite her, had been in business many years, and it dawned on her now that his system was the ancient system that any restaurant must use, if it is to run at all. She began to study it hard, noting the bookkeeping, the marketing, the method of using up leftovers, particularly the tricks used by Archie, who did many things that annoyed her, but never used two motions where one would suffice, never wondered if a dish was done, but always knew, and at that moment picked it up. Some of his principles she adopted at once in making her pies, for she was addicted to a deal of peeping into the oven, and giving them one more minute, just to make sure. Now she put them in by the clock and took them out by the clock, and saved herself much fretting, and made better pies.

All the time her confidence was growing, her ideas clarifying as to the kind of place she meant to have. But one thing vexed her constantly. Where was she going to get the money? In the afternoons, if she had an hour, she drove to the restaurant supply houses on Main Street, in Los Angeles, and priced, cal-culated, and added up. As well as she could tell, she would need a thousand dollars' worth of equipment before she could start, even in a small way. A range, icebox, steam table, and sink were going to cost at least half that, and furniture, dishes, silver, and linen would account for the rest. To save this money, at her present income, was going to take a long time, and there was always the risk that she would lose her job, or that some shift in the pie situation would wipe her out completely, and leave her exactly where she was in the spring. She had to get started, but on whose money she didn't know. She thought about Wally, and even about Mrs. Gessler, but she doubted if they were good for such a sum, and some instinct told her not to ask them.

For a short time she flirted with the idea of getting it from Mr. Otis, a retired butcher turned federal meat inspector, who was a regular customer, and always left her a quarter. She worked on his romantic nature to the point where he suggested meeting her outside, and then realized she should have her notes and memoranda in some kind of order if she was to im-press him enough to make a deal. So one night, when Wally had reached the stage of yawns and a cigarette, she turned on the light and sat down at the desk. "Wally, want to help me with something?"

"Not particularly."

"I have to have it soon. Tomorrow, maybe."

"What is it?"

"I don't know what you'd call it. An estimate of costs, some-thing like that. For a man that may back me in business. But I want it all written down, with the right words for what I mean, so it looks businesslike."

Wally, snapping his cigarette ashes into the fireplace, turned around and blinked. "What kind of business?"

"Just a restaurant."

"Hey, wait a minute, *wait* a minute."

He squashed his cigarette and came over to her. Then he pulled up a chair and sat down. "Start all over again. And at the beginning. Not in the middle."

Haltingly, feeling suddenly self-conscious about it, she told him her plan: a small restaurant, where she would do the cooking herself, and sell nothing but chicken. "They have steak places. And fish places. And I thought—well, down where I work practically every other order is for chicken, so it looks to me as though I ought to have plenty of customers. And then I wouldn't have to fool with all those à la carte prices, or bookkeeping, or menus, or leftovers, or anything like that. Everybody gets a chicken-and-waffle dinner, or chicken and vegetables, if they want, but all at the same price. And then I'll have pies to take out, and keep on getting all the wholesale pie business that I can, and—well, it looks like one would help the other. I mean, the pies would help the restaurant and the restaurant would help the pies."

"And who is this guy?"

"Just an old fogy that eats lunch with me every day. But I think he's got money. And if I could show him it was a good investment he might let me have what I need."

Wally took several turns around the room, looking at her as he went. She was so accustomed to think of him as a fat blob that she occasionally forgot what a cold little eye he really had. Presently he asked: "You really think you can put that across?"

"Well—don't you?"

"I'm asking *you.*"

"It seems as though it ought to pay. I've worked it all out in my mind and I'm pretty *sure* I've thought of everything. I can certainly cook. And I've studied the business down there, every little thing I could think of. I mean, the system. And how to save money. That's the main thing, Wally, about this idea of mine. What costs in a restaurant is waste, and the extras, like printing, for the menus, and the people you have to have, for every little feature you put in. But this way, there wouldn't *be* any waste. All the leftovers would go into gravy and soup, and there wouldn't be any printing, or extras of any kind. *I* certainly think I can put it across."

"Then if you can, I might be able to put you in on a deal.

One that would start you off with a bang. A deal that would leave you sitting so pretty you wouldn't even *need* a backer."

"Wally! If you don't look out, I'll cry."

"You do the crying later and listen to what I'm going to say to you. You know that model home we had? That dream house that Bert built, so we could take the prospects in there and show them what their place was going to look like if they spent twice as much dough as any of them had?"

"Yes, of course." She had special, rather romantic reasons for remembering the model home.

"O.K. They got to get rid of it."

"Who?"

"The receivers. For Pierce Homes, Inc. The outfit that pays me to be their attorney, and messenger boy, and thief, and anything else they can think of. They've got to get rid of it, and if you'll take it over and put this chicken place in it, it's yours. And believe me, Mildred, if that's not a natural for a restaurant, I never saw one. Why, that place even smells like chicken. Right there under the trees, with the old colonial architecture that Bert spent all that dough on—is that a place to gnaw wishbone! Dump a little gravel on one side—free parking for everybody that comes in. That big reception room—perfect for the restaurant part. The model Pierce bedroom—there's your pantry. The streamlined Pierce office—there's your kitchen. Every stick in the place complies with the fire law and the health law, even to the toilets, and there's two of them, not just one. If you really mean this, I can get it for you for four thousand bucks, house, lot, and every improvement that's on it."

"Wally, now I *am* going to cry."

"Was I asking if you had four thousand bucks? I know what you've got and what you haven't got, and I'm telling you, if you want it, it's yours."

He leaned down close, looked melodramatically around, as though to make sure nobody could hear. Then, in a low voice: "They've got to establish losses."

"Who?"

"The receivers! On their federal income tax, the return due next March, for the year 1931, they've got to show losses. If they don't, they're sunk. That's why it's yours, for four thousand bucks."

"Wally, I'd still have to have money!"

"Who says you would? That's the beauty of it. Once you take title to a piece of property around this town, that's all they want to know—you can get all the credit you want, more than you can use. You think those supply houses aren't feeling this Depression too? They can't give the stuff away, and all they ask is: Do you own property or not? They'll deliver anything you want, and connect it up for you, too. You need a little cash, two, three hundred dollars, maybe, I can take care of that. All you've got to do is take over that property and get going, quick."

For the first time in her life, Mildred felt the quick, hot excitement of a conspiratorial deal. She comprehended the credit aspect of it, once Wally explained it, and she didn't need to be told how perfect the place was for her purposes. In her mind's eye she could already see the neon sign, a neat blue one, without red or green in it:

MILDRED PIERCE
Chicken   Waffles   Pies
Free Parking

But it all seemed too good to be true, and when she asked eager questions about it, Wally explained: "There's no catch to it. They're in one hell of a hole. On those other properties, even if they did get rid of one, the federal rulings leave them worse off than they were before. I mean, when *we* didn't build the houses, even if we had to recapture when the buyer defaulted, there's no way we can show losses. But on this, there's the twenty-five hundred the corporation paid Bert for the lot, that not even a government auditor can question. And there's the eleven thousand five hundred that Bert spent on the house, and the corporation's money, not his. Fourteen grand all together, and if we let you have it for four, there's a loss of ten thousand dollars that just about takes care of every little thing for 1931, and then some."

"But why *me?*"

"Why not? Who else wants it? Nobody can live in that dump, you know. All Bert was building was a real-estate office, but for some reason nobody seems to want a real-estate office right now. It's got to be somebody that can use it for something else, and that means you."

"I know, but before I get too excited about it, you'd better make sure. Because if they're just giving it away, it looks as though there'd be somebody, on the inside—"

"Oh—I see what you mean. As a matter of fact, a couple of them did have that bright idea. I put my foot down. They were original incorporators, and I've dealt with the government enough to know that if some fast stuff like that was pulled, we'd all land in jail. On a thing like this, it's got to be bona fide, and that's where *you* come in. If the government agent don't like it, he can go up and see your place, and eat the chicken, and satisfy himself you're using it for the purposes you said you were going to use it for. And then he can take a look at our files and see that we took the best offer we could get. It'll be on the up-and-up. You're no insider. You're no original incorporator. You're—"

He broke off, sat down, and began cursing, first softly, then with rising vehemence. Sensing something wrong, she asked: "What is it, Wally?"

"Bert."

"What's he got to do with it?"

"Original incorporator."

"Well?"

"He's an original incorporator, and you're married to him, and there goes your restaurant, and the prettiest deal I've had a chance to put across since Pierce Homes folded."

It was ten minutes before Mildred could get through her head the ramifications of community property, and the fact that Bert, by merely being married to her, would be co-owner of the restaurant, and therefore subject to a ruling. Then she argued about it, indignantly and passionately, but she could see by Wally's face that the point was serious. He left presently, saying he would talk to his colleagues and look up the law, and she went to bed frantic lest this, her first big chance, would be lost on a legal technicality. She had a recurrence of her bitter fury against Bert, and the way he seemed to thwart her at every turn. Next night Wally was back, looking more cheerful. "Well, it's O.K., but you'll have to get a divorce."

"Is that the only way?"

"Well? Bert left you, didn't he?"

"I wish there was some other way."

"Why?"

"Because I don't know how Bert's going to act about it. You never can count on Bert. If it was just his heart, that would be all right. But he's got some twist in his head, and you never know what he's going to do. He might make trouble."

"How?"

"He'd think of some way."

"There's no way. If he'll let you get a divorce on the ground of cruelty, do it nice and quiet, all well and good. If he gets tough, you spring that Biederhof woman on him, and he's got to give way, because on infidelity he can't block it. You don't ask him. You tell him."

"It takes a year, doesn't it?"

"You getting cold feet?"

"No, but if it's no use, why do it?"

"It takes a year before your decree becomes final. But as soon as it's entered, that ends the community property, and that's all you've got to worry about."

"Well—I'll see him."

"Cut out that 'well' stuff. Look, Mildred, you might as well get this thing cleaned up. Because even if it wasn't for this federal thing, you'd hardly dare go into business, still married to Bert. You don't know where he gets his money. For all you can tell, you'd no sooner hang out a sign than you'd have more judgments and attachments and garnishees slapped on you than you could count. You'd be broke before you started. But, soon as you shake Bert, you're all right."

"I said I'd see him."

"If it's money that's worrying you, forget it. In court, I'll represent you myself, and the rest of it's nothing. But get going. The deal's hot, and you haven't got one day to lose."

Next Sunday, when the children were invited to dinner by the Pierces, Mildred knew Bert was coming over. She had sent word to him that she wanted to see him, and this obviously was an arrangement that would insure his finding her alone. She started her pies early, in the hope she would be done before he got there, but she was up to her elbows in dough when he walked in the kitchen door. He asked how she had been, and she said just fine, and she asked how he had been, and he said he couldn't complain. Then he sat down quite sociably and watched her work. It was some time before she could bring herself to broach the subject, and when she did broach it, she did so after considerable beating around the bush. She told about the model home, and the legal points involved, and quoted Wally in places that became difficult. Then, gulping a little, she said: "So, it looks as though we've got to get a divorce, Bert."

He received this statement with a very grave face, and waited a long time before he spoke. Then he said: "That's something I'll have to think about."

"Have you any *particular* objections?"

"... I've got plenty of objections. For one thing, I belong to a church that's got some pretty strict rules on this matter."

"Oh."

She couldn't keep the acid out of her voice as she spoke. That he should bring up his perfunctory connection with the Episcopal church struck her as pretty farfetched, particularly as her understanding was that what his church objected to wasn't divorce itself, but remarriage of divorced persons. But before she could make the point, he went on: "And I'd have to know more about this deal of Wally Burgan's. A whole lot more."

"What have you got to do with that?"

"You're my wife, aren't you?"

She turned away quickly, thrust her hands into the dough, tried to remember that arguing with Bert was like arguing with a child. Presently she heard him saying: "I probably know ten times as much about federal taxes as Wally Burgan does, and all I can say is it sounds to me like a lot of hooey. It comes down to a straight question of collusion: Is there any, or isn't there? In all cases involving collusion, the burden of proof is on the government, and in this case there can't be any proof, because I can testify, any time they call me, that there wasn't any."

"Bert, don't you see that it isn't a question of proving anything to a court, one way or another? It's whether they *let* me have the property or they don't. And if I don't get a divorce, they won't."

"No reason for them to act that way at all."

"And what am I going to tell Wally?"

"Just refer him to me."

Bert patted his thighs, stood up, and seemed to regard the discussion as closed. She worked furiously at the dough, tried to keep quiet, then wheeled on him. "Bert. I want a divorce."

"Mildred, I heard all you said."

"What's more, I'm going to get one."

"Not unless I say the word."

"How about Maggie Biederhof?"

"And how about Wally Burgan?"

In his palmiest days as a picture extra, Bert never did such a take'm as he did at that moment, with the dough doing service as a pie. It caught him square in the face, hung there a moment, then parted to reveal tragic, injured dignity. But by the time it had cascaded in big blobs to the floor, dignity had given way to hot anger, and he began to talk. He said he had friends, he knew what was going on. He said she ought to know by now she couldn't pull the wool over his eyes. Then he had to go to the sink to wash his face, and while he clawed the dough away, she talked. She taunted him with not making a living for his family, with standing in her way every time she tried to make the living. He tried to get back to the subject of Wally, and she shrilled him down. He said O.K., but just let her try to bring Maggie Biederhof into it, and see what happened to her. He'd fix it so she'd never get a divorce, not in this state she wouldn't. As she screamed once more that she would have a divorce, she didn't care what he did, he said they'd see about that, and left.

Mrs. Gessler listened, sipped her tea, shook her head. "It's the funniest thing, baby. Here you lived with Bert—how long was it?—ten or twelve years, and still you don't understand him, do you?"

"He's got that contrary streak in him."

"No he hasn't. Once you understand Bert, he's not contrary at all. Bert's like Veda. Unless he can do things in a grand way, he's not living, that's all."

"What's grand about the way he acted?"

"Look at it, for once, the way he looks at it. He doesn't care about the church, or the law, or Wally. He just put all that in to sound big. What's griping him is that he can't do anything for the kids. If he has to stand up in court and admit he can't pay one cent for them, he'd rather die."

"Is he doing anything for them now?"

"Oh, but now is just a trifling detail, a temporary condition that he doesn't count. When he puts over a deal—"

"That'll be never."

"Will you just let me talk for a while? It's his fear of being a flat tire, I'm telling you, at one of those big dramatic moments of any man's life, that's making him dog it. But he can't hold out very long. For one thing, there's the Biederhof. She won't like it when she finds out you asked for a divorce and he wouldn't give it to you. She's going to wonder if he really loves her—though how anybody could love her is beyond me. And all the time, he's got it staring him in the face that the harder he makes it for you the harder he's making it for the kids. And

Bert, he loves those kids, too. Baby, Bert's on the end of the plank, and there's nowhere for him to jump but off."

"Yes, but *when?*"

"When he gets the pie."

"What pie?"

"The pie you're going to send him. It's going to be a very special pie. It doesn't appeal to his stomach, except incidentally. It appeals to his higher nature, and in Bert, that means his vanity. It's a pie you've been fooling around with, and you want his opinion on its commercial possibilities."

"I don't really mind making Bert a pie."

"Then get at it."

So Mildred made him a pie, a deep-dish creation, filled with crabapples cunningly candied with sugar so as to bring out the tart of the apples as well as the crystal sweetness of the sugar. It was about as commercial as a hand-whittled clothespin, but she wrote a little note, asking his opinion, and a little P.S., saying she had put his initials on it to see if she could still do monograms. She sent it by Letty, and sure enough, around the middle of the week, there came another invitation to the children, for Sunday dinner. That time she took care to have her pies out of the way early, and to make a cold lunch. It was Letty's Sunday on, and Mildred had her serve the lunch in the den, preceding it with a cocktail. These attentions Bert accepted gravely, and discussed the pie at length, saying he thought it would be a knockout. There was a great field, he said, in ready pastries, since people no longer kept the servants they used to, and were often stumped for a company dessert. All this was what Mildred had been thinking for some time, but that didn't occur to her particularly, and she was genuinely happy to hear such hopeful opinion. Then Bert said it all over again, and then a pause fell between them. Then he said: "Well Mildred, I told you I'd think that little matter over, and I have."

"Well?"

"Of course any way you look at it, it's unpleasant."

"It certainly is for me."

"It's just one of those things that two people hate to think about. But we really got nothing to do with it."

"I don't know what you mean, Bert."

"I mean, whether it's unpleasant for us, that's not it. It's what's best for those kids that counts, and that's what we got to think about. And talk about."

"Did I ever have any other reason? It's for them that I want to take advantage of this opportunity. If I can make a go of it, I can give them what I want them to have, and what you ought to want them to have, too."

"I want to do my share."

"Nobody's asking you to do anything. I know that when you're able, you'll be only too glad to do anything you can. But now—did I say one word about it? Did I?"

"Mildred, there's one thing I can do, and if you're set on this, I want to do it. I can see that you have a place to sleep, and that the kids have, and that nobody can take it away from you. I want to give you the house."

Mildred, caught wholly by surprise, wanted to laugh and wanted to cry. The house had long ceased to be a possession, so far as she was concerned. It was a place that she lived in, and that crushed her beneath interest, taxes, and upkeep. That Bert, with a straight face, should offer it to her at this time struck her as merely grotesque. And yet she remembered what Mrs. Gessler had said, and knew she was in the presence of a man and his pride. She got up suddenly, went over, and put her arms around him. "You don't have to do that."

"Mildred, I want to."

"If you want to, there's only one thing I can do, and that is, take it. But you don't have to. I want you to know that."

"All right, but you've got to take it."

"I'm sorry I said what I did about Mrs. Biederhof."

"I've been hating myself for what I said about Wally. Christ, I know there'd never be anything between you and that fat slob. But—"

"We keep saying things."

"That's it. That we don't mean."

"That we couldn't mean, Bert. Don't you think I hate this just as much as you do? But it's got to be. For their sake."

"Yeah, for their sake."

They talked low and close for a long time, and then got to laughing over the way he looked when she hit him with the dough. Then they got to laughing over the charges she would have to bring, and the cruelties he had been guilty of. "I guess you'll have to hit me, Bert. They all say the defendant hit her, and caused her great mental and physical anguish."

"You talk like Veda. She's always wanting to be hit."

"I'm glad there's a little of me in her."

He doubled his fist, brushed her chin with it. Then they both burst into shaking, uncontrollable sobs.

"The gams, the gams! Your face ain't news!"

It was a moment before Mildred quite knew what was meant, but then she gave her skirt a little hitch, and wasn't exactly displeased when a photographer whistled.

Mrs. Gessler, having no gams to speak of, stood behind her, and the bulbs went off. Next thing she knew, she was in court, raising her hand, swearing to tell the truth, the whole truth, and nothing but the truth, so help her God, and giving her name, address, and occupation, which she described as "housewife." Then she was answering questions put to her by a Wally she had never seen before, a solemn, sympathetic, red-haired man who gently urged her to tell an elderly judge the story of Bert's unendurable cruelties: his silences, during which he wouldn't speak to her for days on end; his absences from home, his striking her, "in an argument over money." Then she was sitting beside Wally, and Mrs. Gessler was up there, corroborating everything she said, with just the right shade of repressed indignation. When Mrs. Gessler got to the blow, and Wally asked her sternly if she had actually seen it, she closed her eyes and whispered, "I did."

Then Mildred and Mrs. Gessler were out in the corridor where Wally presently joined them. "O.K. Decree's entered."

"My—so soon?"

"That's how it goes when you got a properly prepared case. No trouble about a divorce if it's handled right. The law says cruelty, and that's what you got to prove, but that's all you got to prove. That sock in the jaw was worth two hours of argument."

He drove them home, and Mildred made drinks, and Bert came in, to sign papers. She was glad, somehow, that since the real-estate deal started, Wally had been curiously silent about romance. It permitted her to sit beside Bert without any sense of deceit, and really feel friendly toward him. The first chance she got, she whispered in his ear: "I told them the property settlement had been reached out of court. The reporters, I mean. Was that all right?"

"Perfectly."

That this elegant announcement should come out in the papers, she knew, meant a great deal to him. She patted his hand, and he patted back. Wally left, and then Bert, after a wistful look at his glass, decided he had to go too. But something caught in Mildred's throat as he went down the walk, his hat at what was intended to be a jaunty angle, his shoulders thrown bravely back. Mrs. Gessler looked at her sharply. "Now what is it?"

"I don't know. I feel as though I'd picked his bones. First his kids, and then his car, and now the house, and—everything he's got."

"Will you kindly tell me what good the house would do *him?* On the first call for interest he'd lose it, wouldn't he?"

"But he *looked* so pitiful."

"Baby, they all do. That's what gets us."

7

It was a hot morning in October, her last at the restaurant. The previous two weeks had been a mad scramble in which it had seemed she would never find time for all she had to do. There had been visits to Los Angeles Street, to order the equipment her precious credit entitled her to; calls on restaurant proprietors, to get her pie orders to the point where they would really help on expenses; endless scurrying to the model home, where painters were transforming it; hard, secret figuring about money; work and worry that sent her to bed at night almost too exhausted to sleep. But now that was over. The equipment was in, particularly a gigantic range that made her heart thump when she looked at it; the painters were done, almost; three new pie contracts were safely past the sample stage. The load of debt she would have to carry, the interest, taxes, and installments involved, frightened her, and at the same time excited her. If she could ever struggle through the first year or two, she told herself, then she would "have something." So she sat with the girls at breakfast, listening to Ida instruct Shirley, who was to take her place, with a queer, light feeling, as though she were made of gas, and would float away.

Ida talked with her customary earnestness. "Now when you got to make a customer wait, you can't just leave him sit there, like you done with that old party yesterday. You got to take an interest in him, make him feel you're watching out for him. Like you could ask him if he wouldn't like a bowl of soup or something, while he's waiting."

"At leas' ask him don't he want to feel your leg."

Ida took no notice of Anna's interruption, but went grimly on. When a customer came in and sat down at Anna's station, Mildred motioned Anna back to her coffee. "Sit down, I'll take care of him."

She paid little attention to the customer, except to wonder whether his bald spot was brown by nature, or from sunburn. It was a tiny bald spot, with black hair all around it, but it was a bald spot just the same. While he fingered the menu, she decided for sunburn. Then she noticed he was heavily sunburned all over, but even this didn't account for a slightly Latin look about him. He was quite tall, and rather lanky, and a bit boyish looking in his battered flannels. But his eyes were brown, and the little clipped moustache was decidedly Continental. All these things, though, she noted without interest until he put down the menu and glanced at her. "What in the hell am I looking at that for? Why does anybody ever look at a menu for breakfast? You know exactly what you're going to have, and yet you keep looking at it."

"To find out the prices, of course."

She had no intention of making a gag, but his eyes were friendly, and it slipped out on her. He snapped his fingers as though this were the answer to something that had worried him all his life, and said: *"That's* it." Then they both laughed, and he got down to business. "O.K.—you ready?"

"Shoot."

"Orange juice, oatmeal, bacon and eggs, fried on one side and not too much, dry toast, and large coffee. You got it?"

She recited it back to him, with his own intonations, and

they laughed again. "And if you could step on it slightly, show just a little speed—why, I might get to Arrowhead in time for a little swimming before the sun goes down."

"Gee, I wish *I* could go to Arrowhead."

"Come on."

"You better look out, I might say yes."

When she came back with his orange juice, he grinned and said: "Well? I mean it."

"I told you to look out. Maybe I did too."

"You know what would be a highly original thing for you to do?"

"What's that?"

"Say yes, right away—like that."

A wild, excited feeling swept over her. It suddenly occurred to her that for the moment she was free as a bird. Her pies were all made and delivered, the children were with the Pierces at the beach, the painters would be done by noon, there was nothing to detain her at all. It was as though for just a little while she was unlisted in God's big index, and as she turned away from him she could feel the wind in her hair. She went to the kitchen, and beckoned to Ida. "Ida, I think the real trouble with that girl is me. I think I make her nervous. And she's got to start some time. Why don't I just quietly get out?"

Ida looked over toward Mr. Chris, who was doing his morning accounts. "Well *he'd* just love to save a buck."

"Of course he would."

"All right, Mildred, you run along, and I wish you all kinds of luck with your little restaurant, and I'll be out the very first chance I get, and—oh, your check!"

"I'll pick it up next week."

"That's right, when you come with the pies."

Mildred got the bacon and eggs, went out with them. His eyes met hers before she was through the kitchen door, and she couldn't repress a little smile as she approached. As she set down the plate she asked: "Well, what are you grinning about?"

"And what are *you* grinning about?"

"Oh—might as well be original once in a while."

"Damn it, I *like* you."

The rest of it was quick, breathless, and eager. He wanted to get started, she insisted she had to take her car home. He wanted to tail her there, she said she had an errand to do after she got there. The errand was to see that the model home was locked after the painters got out, but she didn't go into that. They made the rendezvous at the Colorado Pharmacy, at twelve fifteen. Then Anna approached, to take over and collect her tip. Mildred hurried to her locker, changed, said her hasty good-byes, and scooted.

She didn't, however, go home at once. She raced over to the Broadway Hollywood and bought swimming things, thanking her luck that she had money enough with her to pay for them. Then she raced to her car and started home. It was fourteen minutes to twelve, by the dash clock, when she whirled up the drive. She put the car away, closed the garage, and ran into the house with her bundles, glancing from habit toward the Gesslers', but the shades were all down, they apparently having gone away for the weekend. Inside, she pulled her own shades down, locked all doors, checked icebox, range, water heater, and spigots. Then she whipped off her dress, changed into the little sports suit and floppy hat. She ripped open the new beach bag, stuffed her purchases into it. From her dressing table she took a comb, dropped that in. From the bathroom she got a clean towel and cake of soap, dropped them in. Then she closed the bag, got out a light coat, and dived out the door. Then, trying it to make sure it was locked, she started down the drive, but at a pace in comic contrast with the haste of a moment before. For the benefit of all who might be looking, she proceeded at demure leisure, merely a lady out for a Saturday swim, the beach bag dangling innocently from her hand, the coat thrown carelessly over one arm.

But when she got out of the block her pace quickened. She was almost running when she reached the model home. It was properly locked, and a glance through the windows told her the painters had gone. She tiptoed around it, her eyes shooting into every precious part. Then, satisfied that everything was in order, she started for the drugstore. She had gone only a block or two when she heard a horn, so close it made her jump. He was within a few feet of her, at the wheel of a big blue Cord. "I honked you before, but I couldn't make you stop."

"Anyway, we're both on time."

"Get in. Say, you look great."

Going through Pasadena they decided it was time to tell names, and when he heard hers, he asked if she was related to Pierce Homes. When she said she was "married to them for a while," he professed to be delighted, saying they were the worst homes ever built, as all the roofs leaked. She said that was nothing to how the treasury leaked, and they both laughed gaily. His name, Beragon, he had to spell for her before she got it straight, and as he put the accent on the last syllable she asked: "Is it French?"

"Spanish, or supposed to be. My great-*great*-grandfather was one of the original settlers—you know, the gay caballeros that gypped the Indians out of their land, the king out of his taxes, and then sold out to the Americans when Polk started annexing. But if you ask me, the old coot was really a wop. I can't prove it, but I think the name was originally Bergoni. However, if he Spanished it up, it's all right with me. Wop or spig, I wouldn't trust either one as far as a snail can hop, so it doesn't make much difference, one way or the other."

"And what's your first name?"

"Montgomery, believe it or not. But Monty's not so bad."

"Then, if I ever get to know you well enough to call you by your first name, I'll call you that."

"Is that a promise, Mrs. Pierce?"

"It is, Mr. Beragon."

She was pleased at all these particulars about himself, for they told her he was giving her his real name, and not a phony invented for a somewhat irregular occasion. She settled back, lost a slightly uneasy feeling she had had, of being just a pick-up.

■ ■

From Glendale to Lake Arrowhead, for any law-abiding citizen, is a trip of two hours and a half. But Mr. Beragon didn't pay much attention to the law. The blue car climbed into the seventies and stayed there, and when they pulled up at the gate of the settlement it was only a little after two. They didn't enter it, however. They took the little road to the right, and in a moment were stealing through great mountain pines that ladened the air with their smell. Presently they nosed down a rough dirt track, twisted through bushes that whacked the windshield, and pulled up with a jerk behind a little shingled shack. Mr. Beragon set his brake, started to get out, and then said, as though he had just thought of it: "Or would you prefer a bathhouse, around on the other side? I keep this shack here, but—"

"I think this is fine."

He took her bag, and they went clumping around a boardwalk to the front. He unlocked the door, and they stepped into the hottest, stuffiest room that Mildred had ever been in.

"Wooh!"

He strode around, throwing up windows, going out back and opening doors, letting air circulate in a place that evidently hadn't been opened for a month. While he was doing this she looked around. It was the living room of a rough mountain shack, with a rough board floor through whose chinks she could see the red earth beneath. Two or three Mexican rugs were scattered around, and the furniture was oak, with leather seats. However, there was a stone fireplace, and a horsy, masculine look to everything, so she half liked it. He reappeared presently, and said: "Well, are you hungry? We can get lunch at the tavern, or would you rather swim first?"

"Hungry? You just *had* breakfast!"

"Then we'll swim."

He picked up her bag and led the way to a small back room whose only furnishings were a cotton rug, a chair, and an iron bed, made up neatly with blankets. "If you can manage here, I'll use the front room, and—see you in a few minutes."

"I won't be long."

Both of them spoke with elaborate casualness, but she was no sooner alone than she pitched the bag on the bed and zipped it open even more quickly than she had zipped it shut. She was terrified he would reappear before she had finished dressing. Yet the possible consequences, as such, weren't what frightened her. The heat, and now the piny breeze that was blowing in, filled her with a heavy, languorous, South Seas feeling that wanted to dawdle, to play, to get caught half dressed, without any shame whatever. But as he left her, she had caught a whiff of her hair, and it reeked of Archie's bacon grease. It often did, she knew, specially when she was a day or so late at the beauty shop, but as to whether Wally noticed this, or liked it, or didn't like it, she cared no more than she cared whether he dropped by or didn't drop by. But that this man should notice it was a possibility that made her squirm. She had an obsession to get overboard, to get washed, before he came near her.

She slipped feverishly out of her clothes, put them on a chair, slipped on the suit. This was before the day of sarongs, and it was a simple maroon affair that made her look small, soft, and absurdly childish. She put on the rubber slippers, picked up the soap. Near her was a door that seemed to lead to some sort of small corridor. She opened it and peeped. Out back was a lattice, and beyond that the walk that circled the house. She pattered out and around, then ran straight down to the little jetty, with its small float. Clutching the soap in her hand, she dived off. The water was so cold she flinched, but she swam down until she was within a few inches of the stones she could see on bottom. Now safely out of sight, she ground the soap into her hair, swimming down with her free hand, holding her breath until her heart began to pound.

When she came up he was standing there, on the float, so she let the soap flutter to the bottom. "You were certainly in one hell of a hurry."

"I was hot."

"You forgot your cap."

"I—? I must be a sight."

"You look like a drowned rat."

"If you could only see what *you* look like!"

At this pert remark he dived in, and there ensued an immemorial chase, with the immemorial squeals, kicks, and splashes. She retreated out of his reach, he followed with slow, lazy strokes; sometimes they stopped and floated, then resumed, as he thought of some new stratagem to catch her. After a while she tired, and began circling to get back to the float. Then he was in front of her, having swum under water to cut her off. Then she was caught, and the next thing she knew was being carried bodily into the shack. As she felt its warmth again, the dopey South Seas feeling returned. She felt limp and helpless, and barely had strength to kick the beach bag off the bed.

It was dark when they got up, and they drove over to the tavern for dinner. When they got back it was cold, and they decided to build a fire, of pine knots. But then they decided they hadn't had enough to eat, and got in the car, and drove down to San Bernardino, for a steak, which she offered to broil. When they got back it was late, but they gathered pine knots by the car lights, and carried them in, and started them going. When they were glowing red she laid the steak on them, to burn it, and then held it with the tongs while it cooked. Then he got plates, and they cut hungrily into it, chewing it down like a pair of wolves. Then he helped her wash up. Then he asked solemnly if she was ready to go home, and she solemnly replied that she was. Then he carried her into the bedroom, and they shivered at the unexpected cold, and in five minutes were exclaiming at how good the blankets felt.

After a while they got to talking, and she learned that he was thirty-three years old, that he had attended the University of California at Los Angeles, that he lived in Pasadena, that his family lived there too, or at any rate his mother and sister, who seemed to be all the family he had. When she asked him what he did, he said: "Oh I don't know. Fruit I guess. Oranges, grapefruit, something like that."

"You mean you work for the Exchange?"

"I should say not. That damned California Fruit Growers' Exchange is taking the bread right out of my mouth. I hate *Sunkist,* and *Sunmaid,* and every other kind of a label with that wholesome-looking girl on it."

"You mean you're an independent?"

"Damn it, what difference does it make what I am? Yes, I guess I'm an independent. I have a company. Fruit export. I don't *have* it. I own part of it. Land too, part of an estate I came into. Every quarter they send me a check, and it's been getting smaller since this Sunkist thing cut it, too. I don't *do* anything, if that's what you mean."

"You mean you just—loaf?"

"You can call it that, I suppose."

"Aren't you ever going to do something?"

"Why should I?"

He seemed quite nettled, and she stopped talking about it, but she found it disturbing. She had a complex on the subject of loafing, and hated it, but she detected there was something about this man's loafing that was different from Bert's loafing. Bert at least had plans, grandiose dreams that he *thought* would come true. But this loafing wasn't a weakness, it was a way of life, and it had the same effect on her that Veda's nonsense had: her mind rejected it, and yet her heart, somehow, was impressed by it; it made her feel small, mean, and vulgar. The offhand dismissal of the subject put her on the defensive too. Most of the men she knew were quite gabby about their work, and took the mandate of accomplishment seriously. Their talk might be tiresome, but it was what she accepted and believed in. This bland assumption that the whole subject was a bore, not worth discussing, was beyond her ken. However, her uneasiness vanished with a little ear-twiddling. At daybreak she felt cold, and pushed her bottom against him. When he took her in his arms she wriggled into his belly quite possessively, and dropped off to sleep with a sigh of deep content.

Next day they ate and swam and snoozed, and when Mildred opened her eyes after one of these naps, she could hardly be-

JAMES M. CAIN

lieve it was late afternoon and time to go home. But still they
dawdled, he arguing they should stay another day, and make a
weekend of it. The Monday pies, however, were on her mind,
and she knew she had to get at them. It was six o'clock when
they drove over to the tavern for an early dinner, and seven
before they got started. But the big blue Cord went down even
faster than it had come up, and it was barely nine as they
approached Glendale. He asked where she lived, and she told
him, but then she got to thinking. "Want to see something,
Monty?"

"What is it?"

"I'll show you."

He kept following Colorado Boulevard, and then at her direction he turned, and presently stopped. "You wait here. I
won't be a minute."

She got out her key and ran to the door, her feet crunching
on the gravel that had been dumped for the free parking. Inside, she groped her way to the switchbox, and threw on the
neon sign. Then she ran out to observe its effect. He was already under it, peering, blinking. It was, indeed, a handsome
work of art, made exactly as she had pictured it, except that it
had a blazing red arrow through its middle. Monty looked first
at the sign, then at Mildred. "Well what the hell? Is this yours?"

"Don't you see whose name is on it?"

"Wait a minute. The last I heard, you were slinging hash in
that—"

"But not anymore. Yesterday was my last day. I quit early
to run off with you. From now on, I'm a businesswoman."

"Why didn't you tell me?"

"I didn't get any chance, that I noticed."

At this tribute to his prowess as a lover, he grinned, and she
pulled him inside, to see the rest of it. She switched on the
lights and took him through, lifting the painters' cloths to show
him the new maple tables, pointing out the smart linoleum floor
covering, explaining it was required by the Department of
Health. She took him to the kitchen, opened up the great range.
He kept asking questions, and she poured out the whole story,

excitedly flattered that a professional loafer could be interested. Yet it was an amended version. There was little in it of Wally, or Bert, or any of the circumstances that had actually figured in it, a great deal about her ambitions, her determination "to be something before I die." Presently he asked when she was going to open. "Thursday. The cook's night out. I mean everybody's cook."

"Next Thursday?"

"At six o'clock."

"Am I invited?"

"Of course you are."

She switched off the lights, and for a moment they were standing there in the dark, with the smell of paint all about them. Then she caught him in her arms. "Kiss me, Monty. I guess I've fallen for·you."

"Why didn't you tell me about all this?"

"I don't know. I was going to, but I was afraid you might just think it was funny."

"I'll be here Thursday. With bells."

"Please. It won't be the same without you."

He took her home, handed her to the door, made sure she had her key. As she was waving good-bye to the disappearing Cord she heard her name called. Automatically she looked toward the Gesslers', but their house was still dark. Then she saw a woman coming across lawns, and saw it was Mrs. Floyd, who lived two doors away.

"Mrs. Pierce?"

There was a sharp note in the voice, and Mildred had a quick prescience that something was wrong. Then, in a tone of virtuous indignation that the whole street could hear, Mrs. Floyd cut loose. "Where in the world have you been? They've been a-trying to reach you ever since last night, and—*where have you been?*"

Mildred choked back an impulse to tell her it was none of her business where she had been, managed to inquire civilly: "What did they want with me, Mrs. Floyd?"

"It's your daughter."

"My—"

"Your daughter Ray. She's got the flu, and they've taken her to a hospital, and—"

"Which hospital?"

"I don't know which hospital, but—"

Mildred dashed into the house and back to the den, snapping on lights as she went. As she picked up the phone a horrible feeling came over her that God had had her number, after all.

8

As Mom made her dozenth remark about Mildred's disappearance over the weekend, Mildred's temper flared. It had been, indeed, a trying hour. She had rung a dozen numbers without finding out anything, while Mrs. Floyd sat there and kept up a running harangue about mothers who run off with some man and leave other people to take care of their children. As a last resort she had rung Mrs. Biederhof, and while that lady told her which hospital Ray had been taken to, and one or two other things, her syrupy good wishes hadn't exactly put Mildred in a good humor. Now, after a dash to Los Angeles and a quick look at Ray, she was sitting with Bert, Veda, Mom, and Mr. Pierce at one end of the hospital corridor, waiting for the doctor, listening to Bert rehearse exactly what had happened: Ray had been dull Friday night, and then yesterday at the beach, when she seemed to be running a temperature, they had called Dr. Gale, and he had advised taking her to a hospital. Mom interrupted Bert and corrected: The doctor hadn't done no such a thing. He had ordered her home and they had taken her home. But when they got there with her the house was all locked up and they rang him again. It was *then* that he ordered her to a hospital, because there was no other place to take her. Mildred wanted to ask what was the matter with the Pierces' house, but made herself swallow it back.

Bert took up the story again: There was nothing serious the matter, just a case of grippe, not flu, as Mildred had been told. "That strip of adhesive on her lip don't mean a thing. They opened a little pimple she had, that's all." Mom took the floor again, making more insinuations, until Mildred said: "I don't know that it's any of your business where I was, or anybody else's."

Mom turned white, and sat bolt upright, but Mr. Pierce spoke quickly, and she sank back, her lips compressed. Then Mildred, after trying to keep quiet, went on: "I was at Lake Arrowhead, if you have to know. When some friends invited me up to their cottage by the lake, I didn't see why I was the one person on earth that had to stay home. Of course I should have. That I readily admit. But I didn't know at the time that I had a set of in-laws that couldn't even find a place for a sick child that had been left in their care. I'll certainly know better next time."

"I think Mother's perfectly right."

Up to now, Veda had been coldly neutral, but when she heard about the swank cottage by the lake, she knew exactly where she stood. Bert looked unhappy, and said nothing. Mr. Pierce had a solemn rebuke: "Mildred, everybody did the best they knew, and I don't see any need for personal remarks."

"Who started these personal remarks?"

Nobody had an answer for this, and for a time there was silence. Mildred had little appetite for the wrangle, for deep down in her heart she had a premonition that Ray was really sick. After an interminable time Dr. Gale arrived. He was a tall, stooped man who had been the family doctor ever since Veda was born. He took Mildred into the sickroom, looked at Ray, listened to the night nurse's whisper. Then he spoke reassuringly: "We get a lot of these cases, especially at this time of year. They shoot up a temperature, start running at the nose, refuse everything you give them to eat, and you'd think they were blowing up something really bad. Then next day they're out running around. Though I don't mind telling you I'm glad we've got her here instead of home. Even in a case of grippe you can't be too careful."

"I'm glad you opened that pimple. I meant to, day before yesterday—and then I forgot it."

"Well I'm glad you didn't open it. Those things, the rule is to let them strictly alone, especially on the upper lip. I didn't open it. I put that little strip over it to keep her fingers off it, that's all."

Mildred took Veda home, improvising a tale about the people who had stopped by Saturday and invited her up to the lake. She named no names, but made them quite rich and high-toned. She undressed, with the light out, before she remembered her pies. It was three o'clock before she got to bed, and she was exhausted.

All next day she had an unreasoning, hysterical sense of being deprived of something her whole nature craved: the right to sit with her child, to be near it when it needed her. And yet the best she could manage was a few minutes in the morning, an hour after supper. She had got to the hospital early, and wasn't at all reassured by the nurse's cheery talk. And her heart had contracted when she saw Ray, all her bubbling animation gone, her face flushed, her breathing labored. But she couldn't stay. She had to go, to deliver pies, to pay off painters, to check on announcements, to contract for chickens, to make more pies. It was dinnertime before she got another respite, and then she couldn't eat. She fidgeted while Letty served Veda, then loaded Veda in the car, and took her in for another vigil. Home again, she put Veda to bed, but when she went to bed herself, she couldn't sleep.

She called the hospital at eight the next morning, and after getting a favorable report, stayed on the phone, crowding her business into the next two hours. Around ten, she loaded her pies into the car, made the rounds of delivery, and arrived at the hospital about eleven. She was surprised to find Dr. Gale already there, whispering in the corridor with a big hairy man in an undershirt, with tattoo marks on his arm. He called Mildred aside. "Now I don't want you to get alarmed. But her temperature's gone up. It's a hundred and four now, and I don't like it. I don't like it, and I don't like that thing on her lip."

"You mean it could be infected?"

"I don't know, and there's no way to tell. I've taken a smear from the pimple, another from the mucus that's coming from her nose, and a couple of CC's of blood. They're on their way to the laboratory now. They'll ring me as soon as they possibly can. But Mildred, here's the point. If we've got trouble there, she can't wait for any lab report. She's got to have a transfusion, right away. Now I've got this man here, he's a professional donor, but it's his means of livelihood, and he won't go in the room till he gets his twenty-five dollars. It's entirely up to you, but—"

Without a thought of what twenty-five dollars would do to her little reserve, Mildred was writing the check before he finished talking. The man demanded an indorsement. Dr. Gale signed, and Mildred, her hands sweating with fear, went into the sickroom. She had that same terrible feeling in her bowels that she had had that day on the boulevard. The child's eyes were dull, her face hot, her whimpering a constant accompaniment to her rapid breathing. There was a new strip on her lip, a bigger one, covering a pack of gauze stained with the livid red of mercurochrome. A nurse looked up, but didn't stop spooning ice into the fluttering little mouth. "This happened after I talked to you, Mrs. Pierce. She had a nice night, temperature constant, and we thought she'd be all right in a few hours. Then just like that it went up."

Ray began to fret, and the nurse began talking to her, saying it was her mother, and didn't she know her mother? Mildred spoke to her. "It's Mamma, darling."

"Mamma!"

Ray's voice was a wail, and Mildred wanted to gather her into her arms, but she merely took one of the little hands and patted it. Then Dr. Gale came in, and other doctors, in white smocks, and nurses, and the donor, his sleeves rolled high this time, showing a veritable gallery of tattoo marks. He sat down, and Mildred stood like a woman of stone while a nurse swabbed his arm. Then she went out in the corridor and started walking up and down, quietly, slowly. Somehow, by a supreme effort of will, she made time pass. Then two nurses came out of the room, then one of the doctors, then the donor, and some order-lies. She went in. The same nurse, the one who had spoken to her before, was at the head of the bed, busy with thermometer and watch. Dr. Gale was bent over, peering intently at Ray. "Her temperature's down, Doctor."

"Good."

"A hundred and one."

"That's just great. How's the pulse?"

"Down too. To ninety-six."

"That's wonderful. Mildred, I've probably put you to a lot of expense over nothing. Just the same—"

They walked out to the corridor, came to an angle, went on. He resumed talking in a casual way: "I hated to do it, Mildred, just hated to slap that outlay on you—though I'll see that every charge is as reasonable as they can make it. But if I had it to do over again, I'd tell you just what I told you before. You see, here's what we're up against. Any infection above the mouth drains into the lateral sinus, and that means the brain. Now with that little pip on her lip there was no way to tell. Every symptom she had spelled grippe, but just the same, all of those symptoms *could* have been caused by strep, and if we had waited until we were sure, it would have been too late. The way she's reacting to that transfusion shows it was all a false alarm—but I'm telling you, if it had been that other, and we hadn't moved fast, I'd never have forgiven myself, and neither would you."

"It's all right."

"These things happen, they can't be helped."

Somewhere on the floor a buzzer sounded, then sounded again, sharply, insistently. It seemed to Mildred that Dr. Gale turned rather quickly, that their saunter was no longer a saun-ter. As they approached the room an orderly hurried past them, carrying hot-water bottles. He entered the room. When they went in, the nurse was jamming them under the covers, which were thick with the extra blankets she had already piled on. "She's having a chill, doctor."

"Orderly, get Dr. Collins."

"Yes sir."

From the ice that was forming around her heart, Mildred knew it was no false alarm this time. She sat down, watched Ray's face turn white, then blue; when the little teeth began to chatter she looked away. An orderly came in with more bottles, which the nurse pushed under the covers without looking up. He was followed by Dr. Collins, a short, heavy man who bent over Ray and studied her as though she were an insect. "It's the pimple, Dr. Gale."

"I can't believe it. She reacted to that transfusion—"

"I know it."

Dr. Collins turned to an orderly and snapped orders in a curt, clipped voice: for oxygen, adrenaline, ice. The orderly went. Both doctors studied Ray in silence, the chattering of her teeth the only sound in the room. After a long time the nurse looked up. "Her pulse is faster, Dr. Collins."

"What is it?"

"A hundred and four."

"Take off the hot-water bottles."

As the nurse pulled out the hot-water bottles and dropped them to the floor the room began to fill. Other nurses appeared, wheeling an oxygen apparatus and a white table full of vials and syringes. They stood around, as though waiting. Ray's teeth stopped chattering and her face lost the blue look. Then red spots appeared on her cheeks, and the nurse felt her forehead. "Her temperature's rising, Dr. Collins."

"Take off the blankets."

Two nurses stripped off the blankets and a third stepped forward with icebags, which she packed around Ray's head. For a long time they were all motionless, and there was no sound except Ray's labored breathing, and the first nurse's report on the pulse: "A hundred and twelve.... A hundred and twenty-four.... A hundred and thirty-two...."

Presently Ray was panting like a little dog, and her whimpering had a pitiful note in it that made Mildred want to cry out against the injustice that one so small, so helpless, should have to bear such agony. But she sat perfectly still, not distracting by so much as a movement the attention of those on whom Ray's chance depended. The child's struggle went on and on, and then suddenly Mildred tightened. The breathing stopped for a second, then resumed in three or four short, harrowing gasps, then stopped altogether. Dr. Collins motioned quickly, and two nurses stepped forward. They had scarcely begun their rapid lifting and lowering of Ray's arms before Dr. Gale had the mask of the oxygen apparatus over her face, and Mildred caught the thunderstorm smell of the gas. Dr. Collins filed the neck of a vial, snapped it off. Quickly filling a syringe, he lifted the covers and jabbed it into Ray's rump. The first nurse had Ray's wrist, and Mildred saw her catch Dr. Collins's eye and glumly shake her head. The artificial respiration went steadily on. After a minute or two, Dr. Collins refilled his syringe, again jabbed it into Ray's rump. Another minute went by, and Mildred saw glances exchanged between nurses. As Dr. Collins refilled his syringe, she stood up. She knew the truth, and she also knew that one more jab into the lifeless little bottom would be more than she could stand. She lifted the mask of the oxygen apparatus, bent down, kissed Ray on the mouth, and pulled the sheet over her face.

She was sitting in the alcove again, but here it was Dr. Gale who broke down, not she. The cruel suddenness of it had left her numb, as though she had no capacity to feel, but as he approached, his stoop was a tottering slump. He dropped down beside her, took off his glasses, massaged his face to keep it from jerking. "I knew it. I knew it when I saw that orderly, running with the bottles. From then on there was no hope. But—we do everything we can. We can't give up."

Mildred stared straight ahead of her, and he went on: "I loved her like she was mine. And there's only one thing I can say. I did everything I could. If anything could have saved her, that transfusion would—and she had it. And you too, Mildred. We both did everything that could have been done."

They sat for a few minutes, both swallowing, both locking their teeth behind twitching lips. Then, in a different tone, he asked: "You got any choice on an undertaker, Mildred?"

"I don't know any undertaker."

"I generally recommend Mr. Murock, out there in Glendale, just a few blocks from you. He's reasonable, and won't run up charges on you, and he'll attend to everything the way most people want it done."

"If you recommend him, then it's all right."

"I'll call him."

"Is there a phone around?"

"I'll find you one."

He took her to a little office on the same floor, and she sat down and dialed Mrs. Biederhof. She asked for Bert, but he was out, and she said: "Mrs. Biederhof, this is Mildred Pierce. Will you tell Bert that Ray died a few minutes ago? At the hospital. I wanted him to know, right away."

There was a long, bellowing silence, and then: "Mrs. Pierce, I'll tell him. I'll tell him just as soon as I can find him, but I want to tell you that I'm sorry from the bottom of my heart. Now is there anything I can do?"

"No, thank you."

"Can I take Veda for a little while?"

"No, thanks ever so much."

"I'll tell him."

"Thank you, Mrs. Biederhof."

She drove home mechanically, but after a few blocks she began to dread the stop signals, for sitting there, waiting for the light to change, she would have time to think, and then her throat would clutch and the street begin to blur. When she got home, Bert came out to meet her, and took her into the den, where

Letty was trying to quiet Veda. Letty went back to the kitchen, and Veda broke into loud sobs. Over and over, she kept saying: "I owed her a nickel! Oh, Mother, I cheated her out of it, and I meant to pay it back, but—*I owed her a nickel!*"

Soothingly, Mildred explained that if she really meant to pay it back, this was the main thing, and presently Veda was quiet. Then she began to fidget. Mildred kissed her and said: "Would you like to go over to your grandfather's, darling? You could practice your piano lessons, or play, or whatever you want to do."

"Oh Mother, do you think it would be right?"

"Ray wouldn't mind."

Veda trotted out of the house, and Bert looked a little shocked. "She's a child, Bert. They don't feel things the way we feel them. It's better that she not be here while—arrangements are being made."

Bert nodded, wandered about the room. A match in the fireplace caught his attention, and he stooped to pick it up. So doing, he bumped his head. If he had been hit with an axe he couldn't have collapsed more completely. Instinctively, Mildred knew why: poking into the fireplace had brought it all back, the game he used to play with Ray, all the gay nonsense between the elephant and the monk. Mildred led him to the sofa, took him in her arms. Then together, in the darkened room, they mourned their child. When he could speak, he babbled of Ray's sweet, perfect character. He said if ever a kid deserved to be in heaven she did, and that's where she was, all right. *Goddam* it, that's where she was. Mildred knew this was a solace from a pain too great for him to bear: that he was taking refuge in the belief she wasn't really dead. Too realistic, too literal-minded, to be stirred much by the idea of heaven, she nevertheless craved relief from this aching void inside of her, and little heat lightnings began to shoot through it. They had an implication that terrified her, and she fought them off.

The phone rang. Bert answered, and sternly said there had been a death in the family, and that Mrs. Pierce couldn't possibly talk business today. Mildred barely heard him. The restaurant seemed remote, unreal, part of a world that no longer concerned her.

Around three thirty, Mr. Murock arrived. He was a roly-poly little man, and after seven seconds of purring condolences, he got down to brass tacks. Everything in connection with the body had been taken care of. In addition, notices had been placed in the afternoon papers, though the morning notices would have to wait until Mildred decided when she wanted the funeral, so perhaps that should be the first thing to consider. Mildred tried to get her mind on this, but couldn't. She was grateful to Bert when he patted her hand and said he would attend to all that. "Fact of the matter, Pop wants to stand the expense, anyhow. He and Mom, they both wanted to come over when I came, but I told them to wait a little while."

"I'm glad you came alone."

"But Pop, he wants to stand the expense."

"Then you attend to it."

So Bert talked to Mr. Murock, apparently knowing instinctively what she wanted. He set the time of the funeral at noon the next day. "No use stringing it out," a point to which Mr. Murock instantly agreed. The grave could be dug in the Pierce family plot in Forest Lawn Cemetery, which had been acquired on the death of the uncle who left Bert the ranch. Services were to be conducted at the house, by the Rev. Dr. Aldous, whom Mr. Murock said he knew very well, and would call at once. Dr. Aldous was Bert's rector, and for a miserable moment Mildred felt ashamed that she could claim no rector as her own. As a child she had gone to the Methodist Sunday school, but then her mother had begun to shop around, and finally wound up with the astrologers who had named Veda and Ray. Astrologers, she reflected unhappily, didn't quite seem to fill the bill at this particular time.

On the choice of a casket, Bert haggled bravely, bringing all his business judgment to bear, and presently settled on a white enamelled one, with silver handles and satin lining, which would be furnished complete for $200, with two limousines and the usual bearers. Mr. Murock got up. The body, he said, would be delivered at five, and they took him to the door, on which two assistants had already fastened a white crepe. Mr. Murock paused a moment to inspect the wire frames they were erecting in the living room, for flowers. Then he started. "Oh—I almost forgot. The burial clothes."

Mildred and Bert went back to the children's room. They decided on the white dress Ray had worn at the school pageant, and with the little pants, socks and shoes, they packed it in one of the children's little valises. It was the gilt crown and fairy wand that broke Bert up again, and Mildred once more had to pat him back to normal. "She's in heaven, she's *got* to be."

"Of course she is, Bert."

"I know goddam well she's not anywhere else."

A minute or two after Mr. Murock left, Mrs. Gessler came over and joined them in the den. She slipped in without greeting, sat down beside Mildred, and began patting her hand with the infinite tact that seemed to be the main characteristic of her outwardly bawdy nature. It was a minute or two before she spoke. Then: "You want a drink, Bert?"

"Not right now, Lucy."

"It's right there, and I'm right here."

"Thanks, I'd rather not."

Then to Mildred: "Baby, Mamma's listening."

"There's a couple of things, Lucy."

Mildred took her to the bedroom, wrote a number on a piece of paper. "Will you call my mother for me, and tell her? Say I'm all right, and the funeral is tomorrow at twelve, and—be nice to her."

"I'll do it on my phone. Anything else?"

"I have no black dress."

"I'll get one for you. Size twelve?"

"Ten."

"Veil?"

"Do you think I should?"

"I wouldn't."

"Then no veil. And no hat. I have one that's all right. And

no shoes. I have them too. But—gloves. Size six. And I think I ought to have a mourning handkerchief."

"I'll have everything. And—"

"What is it, Lucy?"

"They'll be dropping in now. People, I mean. And—I'll probably pull something. I just thought I'd tell you, so you'll know I had a reason."

So a little while later, Mrs. Gessler was back, and certainly pulled something. By then, quite a few people were there: Mrs. Floyd, Mrs. Harbaugh, Mrs. Whitley, Wally, and to Mildred's surprise, Mr. Otis, the federal meat inspector, who had seen the notice in one of the afternoon papers. Letty's contribution was tea and sandwiches, which she had just begun to pass when Mrs. Gessler came in, hatted, gloved, and carrying a gigantic set of lilies. With a wave of the hand she dismissed the florist's driver, and finding the card, read: "Mr. and Mrs. Otto Hildegarde—oh, aren't they beautiful, just *beautiful!*" Then, to everybody in the room: "You know, the couple Mildred visited over the weekend, up at the lake. Lovely people. I'm just crazy about them."

Then Mildred knew that there had indeed been talk, serious talk. But she also knew, from the look that went around, that now it was squelched, once and for all. She felt a throb of gratitude to Mrs. Gessler, for dealing with something she would have been helpless to deal with herself. Bert took the lilies outside, where he spread them on the lawn. Then, coupling up the hose, he attached the revolving nozzle, so they were gently refreshed by the edge of the whirling spray. Other flowers came, and he set them out too, until there was a canopy of blossoms on the grass, all glistening with tiny drops. There was a basket of gladioluses from the Drop Inn, which touched Mildred, but the one that made her swallow hardest was a mat of white gardenias, to which was attached a bluebird card, reading:

Ida	Anna	Chris Makadoulis
Ernestine	Maybelle	Archie
Ethel	Laura	Sam
Florence	Shirley	x (Fuji)

As she was fingering this a hush fell over the room, and she turned to see Mr. Murock's assistants carrying Ray in the door. Under Bert's direction, they set up trusses near the window, arranged the casket, and stepped back to permit the guests to pass by. Mildred couldn't look. But then Mrs. Gessler caught her arm, and she was looking in spite of herself. In the setting sun, a rainbow was shimmering over the spray, framing Ray's head. This broke Bert up again, and most of the guests tiptoed silently out. But it left Mildred unstirred. There was something unreal about Ray's appearance. The hot flush of the last few minutes was gone, also the animation of life, also the deadly pimple. All that remained was a waxy pallor that suggested nothing but heaven, which Bert was now babbling about for the fourth or fifth time.

Letty served the rest of the sandwiches for supper, and Bert and Mildred ate tremulously, silently, hardly tasting what was put in front of them. Then Mr. Pierce and Mom arrived, with Veda, and after viewing Ray, came back to the den. Then Dr. Aldous arrived, a tall, gray, kindly man who sat near Mildred, and didn't put her on the defensive at all for not being a member of his church. Then Mom and Dr. Aldous were in an argument, or rather Mom was, with Dr. Aldous having little to say, and Mr. Pierce correcting Mom on a number of points of ritual. The trouble was that Mom, who had been originally a Methodist, only joining the Episcopal Church after marrying Mr. Pierce, was somewhat confused as to the service that was to be used tomorrow. As Mr. Pierce told her, she had the burial service, the communion service, the psalms, and perhaps even the wedding service, so thoroughly mixed up that it was rather difficult to disentangle them. Mom said she didn't care, she wanted the Twenty-third Psalm, it was only right they should have it when the child was dead, and also there was no use telling her there would be no praying for the child's soul. What were they doing there, anyway? Mr. Pierce sharply reminded her that the burial service had nothing to do with a soul. The whole point was that the soul had already gone, and the burial was nothing but the commitment of a body. As Bert listened unhappily, Mr. Pierce kept calling on Dr. Aldous, as a sort of referee. That gentleman, listening with bowed head, presently said: "As the child wasn't baptized, certain changes will have to be made in the service anyway. Small omissions, but I'm required to make them. Now, in that case, there's no reason why the Twenty-third Psalm, and the little passage in the Communion Service that Mrs. Pierce evidently has in mind, and whatever else we want, can't be included. At the end of the service, special prayers can be, and often are, offered, and I'll be very glad to include these passages—that is, if the mother feels the need of them too."

He looked at Mildred, who nodded. At first, she had resented Mom's taking charge in this high-handed way, and felt mean remarks rising within her. Just in time, she had remembered that the Pierces were paying for everything, and kept her reflections to herself. Now she went to the children's room and packed Veda's things, so the Pierces could have her back in the morning, properly dressed. When she came out with the little suitcase, the Pierces decided it was time to go. Dr. Aldous, however, stayed a few minutes longer. Taking Mildred's hand, he said: "I've often thought the burial service could be a little more intimate, a little more satisfying to the emotions, than it is. It's quite true, as Mr. Pierce said, that it is the commitment of a body, not the consecration of a soul. Just the same, most people find it hard to make the distinction, and—to them, what they see isn't a body. It's a person, no longer alive, but still the same person, loved and terribly mourned. . . . Well, I hope I can arrange a little service that will be satisfactory to the old lady, and the mother, and father, and—everybody."

After Dr. Aldous left, Bert and Mildred were able to talk a little more naturally. She still had to make the inexorable pies, and as he kept her company in the kitchen, and even helped her where he could, he gave details of what had happened at the beach, and she reciprocated with a final version of what happened at the lake, making it correspond with Mrs. Gessler's version, though not feeling any particular desire to deceive. She merely wanted to be friendly. Bert nodded when she got to the part about Mrs. Floyd. "One hell of an end to a nice vacation."

"I didn't care what she thought. But about Ray, I could feel it, even before I got to the hospital. I knew it, even then."

When the pies were made, they sat with Ray for a time, then went back to the den. She said: "You don't have to worry about me, Bert. If Mrs. Biederhof is waiting up for you, why don't you run along?"

"She's not waiting up."

"You sure?"

"Yeah, I'm sure."

". . . She was awfully nice."

"Mildred, can I tell you something? About what really happened Saturday?"

"Certainly."

"Mom, she was just scared, that was all. Mom was never any good in a spot like that. And me, maybe I take after her, because I was scared too. That's why, when Doc Gale began talking hospital I fell for it so quick. But Maggie, she wasn't scared. We had to stop there, on our way to the hospital, because I was still in my beach shorts, and I had to put on some pants. And Maggie, she raised hell about taking Ray to the hospital. She wanted to bring her right in, then and there. That's what I wanted too. It seemed a hell of a note, a poor little kid, and nobody even had a place for her. But—I didn't know how you'd feel about it."

"If that's what happened, it does her credit."

"She's a goddam good friend."

"If that's what she did, I want you to thank her for me, and tell her I would have been only too glad. It was better that she *was* brought to the hospital, but if she had been put in Mrs. Biederhof's care, I wouldn't have had any objection at all. And I know she'd have been properly taken care of, *well* taken care of."

"She's as broken up as if it was her own child."

"I want you to tell her."

"And will she be glad to hear it."

Bert got wood, and made a fire, and lit it. The next Mildred knew, it was daylight, and one arm was asleep, and her head was on Bert's shoulder. He was staring into the embers of the fire. "Bert! I must have been asleep."

"You slept three or four hours."

"Did you sleep?"

"I'm all right."

They went in with Ray for a few minutes, and then Bert went out to look at the flowers. The spray was still whirling, and he reported they were "as fresh as when they were cut."

She got a dustcloth and began moving about the house, cleaning, dusting, putting things in order. Presently she got breakfast, and they ate it in the kitchen. Then he took his departure, to dress.

Around ten, Mrs. Gessler came over, with the black dress, and took the pies, for delivery. Then the Pierces arrived, with Bert, in a dark suit, and Veda, in white. Then Letty arrived, in a Sunday dress of garnet silk. Before her clean apron could be issued, Mildred saw the Engels drive up with her mother, and sent her out to let them in. When Mildred heard them in the den, she sent Veda to say she would be there in a minute. Then she tried on the dress, noted with relief that it was a fair fit. Quickly she got into the rest of her costume. Carrying the black gloves, she went to the den.

Her mother, a small, worried-looking woman, got up and kissed her, as did her sister Blanche. Blanche was several years older than Mildred, and had a housewifey look, with some touch about her of the ineffectuality that seemed to be the main characteristic of the mother. Neither of them had the least trace of the resolute squint that was the most noticeable thing about Mildred's face, nor did they share her voluptuous figure. Harry Engel, the unfortunate possessor of the anchor inventory, got up and shook hands, awkwardly and self-consciously. He was a big, raw-boned man, with a heavy coat of sunburn and a hint of the sea in his large blue eyes. Then Mildred saw William, a boy of twelve, in what was evidently his first long-pants suit. She shook hands with him, then remembered she should kiss him, which she did to his acute embarrassment. He sat down, and resumed his unwinking stare at Veda. To Veda, the Engels were the scum of the earth, and William was even scummier than his parents, if that was possible. Under his stare she became haughtily indifferent, crossing one bored leg over the other, and fingering the tiny cross which hung from a gold chain around her neck. Mildred sat down, and Mr. Pierce resumed his account of the catastrophe, giving a fair version this time, with full faith and credence to Mildred's visit to the Hildegardes, at Lake Arrowhead. Mildred closed her eyes and hoped he would make it long and complete, so she wouldn't have to talk herself. Bert tiptoed over and took the receiver off the hook, so there would be no jangling phone bell.

But when Letty, now aproned, came in to ask if anybody wanted coffee, the Engels stiffened, and Mildred knew something had gone wrong. As soon as the girl had gone, it developed that when she had let them in, they had all shaken hands, taking her for "a friend." Mildred tried to shrug it off, but Blanche was quite bitter about it, obviously feeling that Letty had compromised her social position in front of the Pierces. Mildred began getting annoyed, but it was Veda who put an end to the discussion. With an airy wave of her hand, she said: "Well personally, I don't see why *you* should object to shaking hands with *Letty*. She's really a *very* nice *girl.*"

While all of Veda's delicately shaded accents were soaking in, the sound of the hose stopped. When Mildred went to look, Mr. Murock was carrying flowers in the front door, to place them on the wire racks, and his assistants were carrying in chairs.

I am the resurrection and the life, saith the Lord; he that believeth in me, though he were dead, yet shall he live; and whosoever liveth and believeth in me, shall never die.

■ ■

It wasn't the words, it was the voice, that crumpled Mildred as though something had struck her. Sitting here in the bedroom with Bert and Veda, the door open so they could hear, she had expected something different, something warm, something soothing, particularly after Dr. Aldous's remarks of last night. And then this flat, faraway whine, with a dreadful note of cold finality in it, began intoning the service. Not naturally religious, she bowed her head as if from some ancient instinct, began shuddering from the oppression that closed over her. Then Veda said something. Somewhere she had dug up a prayer book, and it was a moment before Mildred realized she was reading responses: *"For they shall see God. . . . Henceforth, world without end. . . . And let our cry come unto thee. . . ."* To the critical ear, Veda's enunciation might have seemed a bit too loud, a shade too clear, as though intended for the company in the living room, rather than God. But to Mildred, it was the purest of childish trebles, and once more the heat lightnings began to flicker within her, and once more she fought them down. After a long time, when she thought she would scream if she didn't get some relief from her woe, the faraway voice stopped, and Mr. Murock appeared at the door. She wondered if she could walk to the curb. But Bert took her arm and Veda her hand, and she went slowly through the living room. Quite a few people were there, half-remembered faces from her youth, grotesquely marked by time.

Jesus saith to his disciples, Ye now therefore have sorrow.
It was the same cold, faraway voice, and looking across the open grave, with the casket over it, Mildred saw it indeed came from Dr. Aldous, though he looked old and frail in his white robes. In a moment, however, he dropped his voice, adopted a softer more sympathetic tone, and as she caught the familiar words, "The Lord is my shepherd; I shall not want," Mildred knew that the moment had come for the special prayers made necessary by Mom's stipulations, and for intimate solace. They murmured on, and her lips began to twitch as she realized they

were mainly for her benefit, to ease her pain. They only made her feel worse. Then, after an interminable time, she heard: *"O God, whose mercies cannot be numbered; Accept our prayers on behalf of the soul of Moire, thy servant departed, and grant her an entrance into the land of light and joy, in the fellowship of the saints, through Jesus Christ our Lord, Amen."*

And as the child sank down, on Mr. Murock's patent pulleys, Mildred realized, with bitter shame, that now for the first time, in death, it heard itself correctly addressed, that it had lived its brief life without even knowing its name.

The worst came that evening, when she was left alone, with nobody to console, nobody to be brave in front of, nobody to face but herself. The Pierces left in the afternoon, taking Bert with them, and the Engels shortly after, taking her mother, so as to reach San Diego before dark. Then, after an early supper, she had Letty take Veda to a moving picture show. Then she found herself in a house from which all flowers, all chairs, all wire racks had been removed, which was exactly as it had been before. Desolation swept over her. She tramped around, then changed into her smock and began making pies. Around eleven she drove to the theatre, took Letty home, and held tight to Veda's hand on the way back to the house. Veda had a glass of milk, and talked gaily about the picture. It was called *The Yellow Ticket,* and Mildred winced at the circumstantial account of how Miss Elissa Landi had pulled out the gun and shot Mr. Lionel Barrymore in the stomach. When Veda went to bed, Mildred helped her undress, and couldn't bring herself to leave. Then: "Would you like to sleep with me tonight, darling?"

"But Mother, of *course!*"

Mildred was pretending to herself that she was doing Veda a kindness, but Veda wasn't one to let such a spot go to somebody else. She immediately began to *give* comfort, in large, clearly articulated, perfectly grammatical gobs. "Why you poor, dear Mother! You *lamb.* Think of all she's been through today, and the beautiful way she's looked after everybody, without giving one thought to herself! Why of *course* I'll sleep with you, Mother! You poor darling!"

To Mildred it was fragrant, soothing oil in a gaping wound. They went to her bedroom, and she undressed, and got into bed, and took Veda into her arms. For a few minutes she breathed tremulous, teary sighs. But when Veda nestled her head down, and blew into her pajamas, the way she used to blow into Ray's, the heat lightnings flickered once, then drove into her sorrow with a blinding flash. There came torrential shaking sobs, as at last she gave way to this thing she had been fighting off: a guilty, leaping joy that it had been the other child who was taken from her, and not Veda.

9

Only an act of high consecration could atone for this, and some time during the night Mildred knew what it would be, and so knowing, found peace. She may have found a little more than peace. There was something unnatural, a little unhealthy, about the way she inhaled Veda's smell as she dedicated the rest of her life to this child who had been spared, as she resolved that the restaurant must open today, as advertised, and that it must not fail. She was up at daybreak carrying out this resolution, setting out pie plates, flour, utensils, cans of supplies, all sorts of things, for removal to the model home. There was a great deal of stuff and she packed it carefully into the car, but it required several trips. On the last one, she found her staff waiting for her: a waitress named Arline and a Filipino, to do double service as dish washer and vegetable peeler, named Pancho. Both had been engaged the previous week, on the recommendation of Ida. Arline, a small, half pretty girl of twenty-five, hadn't looked very promising, but Ida had recommended her highly. Pancho, it seemed, was addicted to flashy clothes, and had thus incurred the enmity of Archie, but once he was in his kitchen regimentals he was absolutely all right.

Mildred noted Pancho's cream-colored suit, but wasted no time on it. She handed out uniforms and put them both to work. They were to give the place a thorough cleaning, and as soon as the front room was done, they were to hang the percale drapes that lay in a pile on the floor. She showed how the fixtures worked, and on Pancho's assurance that he was a virtuoso with the screwdriver, she drove back to the house, picked up her pies, and made the rounds of delivery.

When she got back she caught her breath at what she saw. Pancho had indeed made a fine job of the drapes: the fixtures were all up and he was hanging the last of them. Arline had put the tables around, so that what had been a dreary pile of wood, metal, and cloth in one corner was now a restaurant, warm, clean, and inviting. Mildred still had many things to do, but when the laundry service delivered her napkins and doilies, she couldn't resist setting a table to see how it looked. To her, it was beautiful. The red-and-white check of the linen combined pleasantly with the maple, and with Arline's brick-red uniform, just as she had hoped it would. For a few minutes she lingered, drinking in the picture with her eyes. Then, after pointing out what was to be done in the kitchen, she got in the car again, to resume her errands.

At the bank, she drew $30, filling out the stub quickly, and trying not to think of the 7 she had to write, under "Balance Forward." She asked for $10 in change, against the requirements of the evening, dropped the rolls of coin into her handbag, and went on. At the ranch where her chickens were on order, she found twenty-six waiting for her, instead of the stipulated twenty. Mr. Gurney, the rancher, was quite voluble about it, saying them birds was in such prime condition he hated to see anybody else get them. Just the same, she was annoyed. He did raise fine chickens, honestly corn-fed, not milk-fed, and fine chickens she had to have. And yet she couldn't have him over-selling her like this. After fingering them for a time, she rejected two because they weren't properly picked and took the rest, paying $8, the price being three for a dollar. Loading them into the car, she went to the U-Bet market, for vegetables, eggs, bacon, butter, and groceries. She spent $11, almost having to dig into her reserve of coin.

Back at the restaurant, she inspected the kitchen, found it fairly satisfactory. Arline had mopped the floor, and Pancho had washed the new dishes without breaking any. Letty arrived, and Mildred had her make lunch for Arline and Pancho, then settled down to what she really liked, which was cooking. She got out the chickens, went over them carefully for pinfeathers, found Mr. Gurney's picking a great deal better than most market picking. Then she took a small cleaver and sectioned them up. She was going to serve half a fried chicken, with vegetables or waffle, for 85¢, but she hated the half chicken that was served in most places. It came on the table in one loathsome piece, and she wondered how people could possibly eat it. She was going to do it differently. First, she cut off the necks, then cut the chicken in half. Then she took off the wings and the legs. The legs she separated into second joints and drumsticks, and then she trimmed the breasts so there was only a sliver of breastbone backing them, without any wishbone or rib. Then, remembering Archie's system for such things, she packed breasts, drumsticks, second joints, and wings into four different dishes, and placed them in the icebox so she could pick up a portion with one motion. The necks and bones she pitched into a pot, for soup. The giblets she cut up and put in a pan, for gravy. She started her other soup, the cream of tomato, and put Pancho to preparing vegetables.

Around four, Wally came in, to inspect the alterations, and report. His main activity, since she had seen him, had been to send out the announcements, and for this he had drafted his secretary. She had utilized all the old Pierce Home lists, so that every person who had bought a home, or had even thought of buying a home, had been covered. Mildred listened, pleased that all this had been so well attended to, but he kept hanging around, and she wished he would go, so she could work. Then she noticed him looking at the showcase. This was the most expensive piece of furniture she had, and the only one that had been made to order. The base and back were of maple, but the sides, top, and shelves were of glass. It was to display the pies she hoped to sell to the "take-out" trade, and presently, looking rather self-conscious, Wally asked: "Well, how did you like that little surprise I fixed up for you?"

"—? What surprise?"

"Didn't you see it?"

"I haven't seen anything."

"Hey—you go back to the kitchen, then, and wait, and believe me pretty soon you're going to see something."

Mystified, she went to the kitchen, and still more mystified, saw Wally appear there in a moment or two, find her pies, and carry two into the restaurant, then two more, then two more. Then she could see him arranging the pies in the showcase. Then she could see him fumbling with something against the wall. Then suddenly the showcase lighted up, and she gave a little cry, and went running out. Wally beamed. "Well, how do you like it?"

"Why Wally, it's *beautiful!*"

"Something I did for you while—well, the last few days. I slipped in here at night and worked on it." He proudly pointed out the tiny reflectors that screwed into the maple, almost invisibly, to shoot the light downward, on the pies; the bulbs, no bigger than her finger; the wiring, cunningly tacked to the back in such manner as to leave the panels free to slide. "You know how much that little job cost?"

"I haven't any idea."

"Well, let's see now, the reflectors, they were seven cents apiece, six of them, that's forty-two cents. The lights, a nickel apiece—say, they're Christmas tree bulbs, can you beat that? Thirty cents for them, that's seventy-two cents. The wire, ten cents. The sockets, screws, and plug, maybe a dollar. Say altogether, a couple of bucks. How's that?"

"I just can't believe it."

"Took me maybe an hour. But it ought to sell pies."

"And get a free dinner."

"Oh, never mind that."

"A free dinner, and second helpings."

But the clock was ticking inexorably on, and she hurried back to work as soon as he left, though in a pleasant glow now, feeling that everybody was trying to help her. The vegetables, started before Wally came, were now ready, and they took them up. She put them in their pots and turned the hot water into the steam table. She made waffle batter, laid beside it the dipper that held exactly one waffle. She made pie crust, for biscuits. Her ice cream arrived: chocolate, strawberry, and vanilla. She had Pancho set all three freezers on a bench, where they could be easily reached, and showed Arline how to dip it up, reminding her she would be responsible for desserts as well as starters. She made salad, started the coffee.

At five thirty she went to the ladies' room to change for the evening. She had given considerable thought to what she would wear. She had decided on white, but not the sleazy white of the nurse uniforms then becoming so common. She went to Bullocks, and bought sharkskin dresses, of a shade just off white, white with a tint of cream in it, and had little Dutch caps made to go with them. Always vain of her legs, she had the dresses shortened a little. Now, she hurriedly got into one, put on her Tip-Top shoes, stuck on the little cap. As she hurried out carrying the apron she would wear in the kitchen, and slip off when she came out to greet the customers, she looked like the cook in a musical comedy.

However, she didn't go into a number. She assembled Pancho, Letty, and Arline for final instructions, paying most attention to Arline. "I'm not expecting many people, because it's my first night and I haven't had a chance yet to build up my trade. But if you should be rushed, *remember:* Get their orders. I've got to know whether they're having vegetables or waffle before I can start, so don't keep me waiting."

"Call them both?"

"Call the waffle only."

"Call biscuits?"

"I'll keep biscuits out all the time, and you pick them up yourself. Pick up your own bread and your own biscuits, but put them in separate baskets and don't forget that biscuits call for a napkin, to keep them hot. Three biscuits to a person, more if they want them, but don't be stingy with them and don't take time to count. Pick them up quick, and pick up enough."

Arline surveyed the place with a practiced eye, counting tables. There were eight tables for two, around the wall, and two tables for four, in the middle. Mildred saw the look, and went on: "You'll be able to take care of them, *if* you get their orders. There's plenty of room here, you're using a tray, and that'll help. Any time you need her, I'll send Letty out to bus up your tables for you, and—"

"Can't she do that right from the start? So we get used to working together, and don't commence bumping and stepping all over each other's feet?"

"Then all right."

Letty nodded, with a self-conscious grin. She was already in the brick-red uniform, which was quite becoming to her, and obviously wanted to be part of the show. Mildred went back to the kitchen, lit the oven, and started the waffle irons to heat. She was using a gas waffle, instead of the usual electric waffle, "because that's the old-fashioned kind of round waffle that people really like." She went to the switch box, put on the lights. The last switch worked the outside sign, and when it was on, she went out to look. There it was, as beautiful as ever, casting a bluish light over the trees. She drew a deep breath and came inside. At last she was open, at last she had her own business.

There ensued a long wait. She sat nervously at one of the tables for two, while Arline, Letty, and Pancho stood in a corner whispering. Then they started to giggle, and a horrible pain shot through Mildred. It was the first time it had occurred to her that she could open a restaurant, and then have nobody show up. She lurched suddenly to her feet and went to the kitchen.

She kept touching the waffle irons, to see if they were hot. Outside a car door slammed. She looked up. A car was there, and four people were entering the restaurant.

She had a moment of complacency as she reached for the chicken: now she would reap her reward for all her observing, thinking, and planning. She had had the free parking located in the rear, so she could see exactly how many customers she had, even before they came in; she had simplified her menu, so she could start the chicken without waiting for the waitress to report; she had placed her icebox, range, materials, and utensils so she could work with the minimum of effort. Feeling as though she were starting a well-tuned machine, she took out four each of breasts, second joints, drumsticks, and wings, rolled them in the flour box beside the range, gave them a squirt from the olive oil bottle that stood beside the flour. She shoved them in the oven, for the brief baking that preceded frying in butter. Not yet closing the oven door, she shoved a pan of biscuits in, beside them. Arline appeared. "Four at No. 9, soup right and left, two and two, one waf."

She reminded Arline she was not to call soup, but dip it up herself, then went out to greet her first guests. They were strangers to her, a man, woman, and two children, but she made them a pretty little speech, saying they were her first guests, and she hoped they liked her place and would keep on being her guests. Arline came in with the starters, the soup, crackers, butter, napkins, water, and salad. Salad, for some reason, is served first in California. Mildred's eye checked the tray, finding it in order. Two more people came in. She vaguely remembered them as Pierce Homes buyers of six or seven years ago, but her waitress training came at once to her aid. Their names were on her tongue before she fairly saw their faces: "Why how do you do, Mrs. Sawyer, and Mr. Sawyer! I'm so glad you were able to come!"

They seemed pleased, and she seated them at a table in the corner. As soon as Arline came over to get their orders, she went back to the kitchen, to start more chicken.

The first order went out smoothly, with Letty bussing the

dirty dishes to Pancho, who went to work at once. But then Arline appeared, looking worried. "Two at No. 3, but one of them's a kid that won't have soup. Says she wants tomato juice with a piece of lemon and some celery salt—I told her we don't serve it, but she says she's got to have it and what do I do now?"

It was no trouble to guess who that was.

She found Bert and Veda, at one of the tables for two. Bert was in a light suit, conscientiously groomed and brushed, but with a black band on one arm. Veda was in a school dress that hadn't been worn yet, and Mildred's floppy hat. Both of them looked up with a smile, Veda exclaiming how pretty Mildred's dress was, Bert nodded approvingly at the restaurant. "By God, this looks like something. You got yourself a piece of property this time, Mildred. This place is real."

He stamped his foot. "And it's built. I saw to that. I bet there was no trouble with the Department of Health when they inspected *this* floor."

"They passed it without even looking."

"How about those toilets?"

"They passed them too. Of course, we had to cut a door through, so both of them opened into the old secretary's office. We made that into a kind of lounge. It's against the law for a toilet to open into the kitchen, you know. But that, and the painting, and the gravel and the swing doors, were about all we had to do. It cost money, though. Whew!"

"I bet it did."

"Would you like to look around?"

"I'd love it."

She took them both through, and felt proud when Bert admired everything profusely, not quite so proud when Veda said: "Well, Mother, I think you've done very well, considering everything." Then she heard a car door slam, and turned to greet her new customer. It was Wally, and he was quite excited. "Say, you're going to have a mob. You heard me, a mob. That's the thing to remember with direct-mail advertising. It's not what you send. It's where you send it. I got that stuff of yours right

MILDRED PIERCE

to the people that know you, and they're coming. I bumped
into six different people that told me they'd be here—and that's
just six I happened to bump into. I said a mob."

Wally pulled over a chair and sat down with Bert and Veda.
Bert asked him sharply if he had attended to the transfer of
beneficiary on the fire insurance. Wally said he figured he'd
wait till the place burned down. Bert said O.K., he was just
asking.

When Mildred looked up, Ida was standing in the door. She
went over and kissed her, and listened while she volubly explained that her husband had wanted to come, but got a call
on a job, and simply had to look into it. Mildred took her to
the table that now had only one chair, the other having been
borrowed by Wally. Ida looked around, taking things in.
"Mildred, it's just grand. And the space you got. You can get
two more fours in easy, just by shifting those twos a little bit.
And you can use trays, big as you want. You got no idea how
that'll help. It'll save you at least one girl. At least."

It was high time for Mildred to get back to the kitchen, but
she lingered, patting Ida's hand, basking in her approval.

The well-oiled machine was in high now, humming smoothly,
pulling its load. So far, Mildred had found a few seconds for
each new arrival, and particularly for each new departure to
give a little reminder of the homemade pies she had for sale,
and wouldn't they like to take home one? But now she was
working a bit feverishly, frying chickens, turning waffles. When
she heard a car door slam she didn't have a chance to look out
and count customers. Then she heard another door slam. Then
Arline appeared. "Two fours just come in, Mrs. Pierce. I got
room for one but what do I do with the other? I can shove two
twos together, but not till I get Miss Ida moved out—"

"No no! Let her alone."

"But what'll I do?"

"Seat four, ask the others to wait."

In spite of herself, her voice was shrill. She went out, asked

143

the second party of four if they minded waiting. She said she was a little rushed now, but it would only be for a few minutes. One of the men nodded, but she hurried away, ashamed that she hadn't foreseen this, and provided extra chairs. When she got to the kitchen, Arline was jabbering at Pancho, then turned furiously to Mildred: "He's washing plates, and the soup bowls are all out, and if he don't let me have them I can't serve my starters! *Soup bowls, stupid,* soup bowls!"

Arline screamed this at Pancho, but as Mildred shushed her down, Letty came in, heavy-footed and clumsy at unaccustomed work, and dumped more soup bowls on the pile, which went down with a crash, three breaking. Mildred made a futile dive to save them, and heard another car door slam. And suddenly she knew that her machine was stalled, that her kitchen was swamped, that she had completely lost track of her orders, that not even a starter was moving. For one dreadful moment she saw her opening turning into a fiasco, everything she had hoped for slipping away from her in one nightmare of an evening. Then beside her was Ida, whipping off her hat, tucking it with her handbag beside the tin box that held the cash, slipping into an apron. "O.K. Mildred, it's them dishes that's causing it all. Now *she* ain't no good out there, none whatever, so let *her* wipe while *he* washes, and that'll help."

As Mildred nodded at Letty and handed her a towel, Ida's quick eye spotted dessert dishes, and she set them out on a tray. Then, to Arline: "Call your soup."

"I want a right and left for two, three and one, chicken and tomato for four, and they been waiting for—"

Ida didn't wait to hear how long they had been waiting. She dipped soup into the dessert dishes, dealt out spoons with one hand and crackers with the other, and hurried out with the tray, leaving butter, salad, and water to Arline. In a minute she was back. "O.K., Mildred, I got your family to take a walk outside. They was all through eating anyway. Then I put two at my table, and that took care of four. Then soon as I get the check for that first party of four, that'll take care of four more, and—"

The twanging voice, the voice that Mildred had hated, twanged on, and Mildred responded to it with a tingle that started in her heart and spread out through the rest of her. Her nerve came back, her hands recovered their skill, as things began moving again. She was pouring a waffle when Mrs. Gessler appeared at the door, and came tiptoeing over to her. "Anything I can do, baby?"

"I don't think so, Lucy. Thanks just the—"

"Oh yes there is."

Ida seized Mrs. Gessler by the arm as she usually seized the members of her command. "You can take off that hat and get out there and sell pies. Don't bother them while they're eating but stay near the showcase and when they get through see what you can do."

"I'll be doing my best."

"Containers in the drawer under the case, they're out flat and you'll have to fold them, then tie them up and put the carrying handles on. If you have any trouble, just call for me or ask Mildred."

"What's the price, Mildred?"

"Eighty-five cents. Everything's eighty-five cents."

Mrs. Gessler laid her hat beside Ida's and went out. Soon Mildred saw her come back, lay a dollar bill in the tin box, take change, and go out. In a short time she saw many bills in the box, as Ida repeatedly came in, made change, and sent Arline out with it, so she would get her tip. When she had a lull, she slipped off her apron and went out. Nobody was standing now, but every seat was filled, and she felt as she had felt yesterday, at the funeral, when she walked through the living room and saw all those half-remembered faces. These were people she hadn't seen in years, people reached by Wally's clever system of mailing. She spoke to them, asked if everything was all right, received their congratulations, and from a few, words of sympathy about Ray.

It was well after eight when she heard another car door slam. Bert, Wally, and Veda had adjourned their meeting, on Ida's invitation, to the running board of Wally's car, and for some time she had heard them talking out there, while she worked. But now, as a foot crunched on the gravel, the conversation stopped, and then Veda burst in the back door. "Mother! Guess who just came in!"

"Who was it, darling?"

"Monty Beragon!"

Mildred's heart skipped a beat, and she looked at Veda sharply. But Veda's shining eyes didn't suggest knowledge of scandal, so cautiously she asked: "And who is Monty Beragon?"

"Oh, Mother, don't you *know?*"

"I guess not."

"He plays polo for Midwick, and he lives in Pasadena, and he's rich, and good-looking, and all the girls just *wait* for his picture to come out in the paper. He's—*keen!*"

It was the first she had known that Monty was anybody in particular, but she was too busy to be excited much. Veda began dancing up and down, and Bert came in, followed by Wally, who looked as though he had just beheld God. "Sa-a-a-a-ay! If that guy's here, Mildred, you're in! Why there's not a restaurant in L.A. that wouldn't pay him to eat there. Isn't that so, Bert?"

"He's very well known."

"Known? Hell, he's a shot."

Arline came in, from the dining room. "One waf."

Veda went to the *out* door, peeped, and disappeared into the dining room. Wally began speculating as to how Monty knew about the opening. He wasn't on any list, and it seemed unlikely he had seen the Glendale papers. Bert, with some irritation, said that Mildred's reputation as a cook had spread far and wide, and that seemed sufficient reason, at least to him, without doing any fancy sleuthing about it. Wally said by God he had a notion to find out, when all of a sudden he was standing there with open mouth, and Mildred felt herself being turned slowly around. Monty was there, looking down at her gravely, intently. "Why didn't you tell me about the little girl?"

"I don't know. I—couldn't call anybody."

"I didn't hear about it until her sister told me, just now."

"She seems to be quite an admirer of yours."

"She's the most delightful little thing I've met in a long time, but never mind about her. I'd like you to know that if I'd had any idea about it, you'd have heard from me."

As though to corroborate this declaration, a box of flowers appeared suddenly under Mildred's nose, together with a slip the messenger was offering her to sign. She opened the box, found herself staring at two gigantic orchids. But Monty took the card and tore it up. "I doubt if you're in the humor for gags."

She put the flowers in the icebox, and introduced Bert and Wally. She was relieved when Ida came over, demanding that the kitchen be cleared. Monty gave her a little pat and went to the dining room. Bert and Wally went outside, eyeing her a little queerly.

By nine o'clock there were only two customers left, and as they were eating the last of the chickens, Mildred went to the switchboard and cut off the sign. Then she counted her cash. She had hoped for thirty people, and had ordered five extra chickens to be safe. Now, having been high-pressured into taking four more than that, she had barely had enough. Truly, as Wally had promised, there had been a mob, and she found she had taken in $46, or $10 more than her wildest hopes. She folded all the bills together, so she could feel their fat thickness. Then, having little to do until Arline, Pancho, and Letty finished up, she slipped off her apron, pinned on her orchids, and went into the dining room.

Ida was still waiting on the last customers, but Bert, Wally, Monty, Veda and Mrs. Gessler were sitting sociably at one of the tables for four. Bert and Monty were discussing polo ponies, a subject that Bert seemed impressively familiar with. Veda had curled herself into the crook of his arm and was drinking in the heavenly words about the only world that could mean anything to her. Mildred pulled up a chair and sat down beside Mrs. Gessler, who at once began making queer noises. Staring into each face, she repeated "H'm? H'm?" in an insistent way, evoking only puzzled stares. It was Monty who got it. His face lit up and he bellowed "Yes!"

Then everybody bellowed yes, and Mrs. Gessler went out to her car. When she came back she had Scotch and White Rock. Mildred had Arline bring glasses, ice, and an opener, and Mrs. Gessler began her ancient rites. Bert took charge of Veda's drink, but Mildred forbade the usual switcheroo. She knew it would remind him of Ray, and she didn't want that. Veda received her drink, with its two drops of Scotch, without any tricks, and Bert suddenly got to his feet. Raising his glass to Mildred, he said: "To the best little woman that any guy was crazy enough to let get away from him."

"You ought to know, you cluck."

Mrs. Gessler was quite positive about it, and everybody laughed, and raised a glass to Mildred. She didn't know whether to raise her glass or not, but finally did. Then Ida, having disposed of the customers, was standing beside her, taking in the conviviality with a twisted grin that seemed strange and pathetic on her extremely plain face. Mildred jumped up, quickly made her a drink, and said: "Now *I'm* going to propose a toast." Raising her glass, she intoned: "To the best little woman that nobody was *ever* crazy enough to let get away from them." Wally said: " 'Ray!" Everybody said " 'Ray!" Ida was flustered, and first giggled, then looked as though she was going to cry, and paid no attention when Mildred introduced her around. Then she plopped down in a chair and began: "Well, Mildred, I wish you could have heard the comment. You got no idea how they went for that chicken. And how amazed they was at them waffles. Why, they said, they never got such waffles since they was little, and they had no idea anybody knew how to make them anymore. It's a hit, Mildred. It's going to do just grand." Mildred sipped her drink, feeling trembly and self-conscious and unbearably happy.

She could have sat there forever, but she had Veda to think of, and Ida to think of too, for after such help, she had to give her a lift home. So she reminded Bert that Veda had to go to school, stuffed the precious cash into her handbag, and prepared to lock up. She shook hands with them all, looking away quickly when she came to Monty, and finally got them outside. On the lawn, the party gathered around Mrs. Gessler's car, and Mildred suspected the Scotch was being finished somewhat informally, but she didn't wait to make sure. Calling to Bert not to keep Veda up late, she loaded Ida into her car, and went roaring down the boulevard.

When she got home she was surprised to find the blue Cord outside. Inside, the house was dark, but she could see a flicker of light from the den, and there she found Monty and Veda, in the dark except for the fire they had lit for themselves, and evidently getting on famously. To Mildred, Monty explained: "We had a date."

"Oh, you did."

"Yes, we made a date that I was to take her home, so I did. Of course we had to take Pop home first—"

"Or at least, to the B—"

But before Veda could finish her languid qualification, she and Monty burst into howls of laughter, and when she could get her breath she gasped: "Oh Mother! We saw the Biederhof! Through the window! And—*they flopped!*"

Mildred felt she ought to be shocked, but the next thing she knew she had joined in, and then the three of them laughed until their stomachs ached and tears ran down their faces, as though Mrs. Biederhof and her untrammelled bosom were the funniest things in the world. It was a long time before Mildred could bring herself to send Veda to bed. She wanted to keep her there, to warm herself in this sunny, carefree friendliness that had never been there before. When the time finally came, she took Veda in herself, and helped her undress, and put her in bed, and held her tight for a moment, still ecstatic at the miracle that had come to pass. Then Veda whispered: "Oh Mother, isn't he just *wonderful!*"

"He's terribly nice."

"How did you meet him?"

Mildred mumbled something about Monty's having come into the Hollywood restaurant once or twice, then asked: "And how did *you* meet him?"

"Oh Mother, I didn't! I mean, I didn't say anything to him. *He* spoke to *me*. He said I looked so much like you he knew who I was. Did you tell him about me?"

"Yes, of course."

"Then he asked for Ray, and when I told him about her, he turned perfectly pale, and jumped up, and—"

"Yes, I know."

"And Mother, those orchids!"

"You want them?"

"Mother! Mother!"

"All right, you can wear them to school."

From the sofa came a voice, a little thick, a little unsteady: "I've been looking at that damned costume all night, and with great difficulty restrained myself from biting it. Now, get it off."

"Oh, I'm not much in the humor for—"

"Get it off."

So the costume came off, and she submitted to what, on the whole, seemed a reasonably appropriate finale to the evening. Yet she was too excited really to have her mind on Monty. When she went to bed she was tired, happy, and weepy, and Bert, Wally, Mrs. Gessler, Ida, Monty, the sign, the restaurant, and the $46 were all swimming about in a moonlit pool of tears. But the face that shimmered above it, more beautiful than all the rest, was Veda's.

10

One morning, some months after this, she was driving down from Arrowhead with Monty. He was part of her life now, though on the whole not quite so satisfactory a part as it had seemed, in that first week or two, that he might be. For one thing, she had discovered that a large part of his appeal for her was physical, and this she found disturbing. So far, her sex experiences had been limited, and of a routine, tepid sort, even in the early days with Bert. This hot, wanton excitement that Monty aroused in her seemed somehow shameful; also, she was afraid it might really take possession of her, and interfere with her work, which was becoming her life. For in spite of mishaps, blunders, and catastrophes that sometimes reduced her to bitter tears, the little restaurant continued to prosper. Whether she had any real business ability it would be hard to say, but her common sense, plus an industry that never seemed to flag, did well enough. She early saw that the wholesale pie business was the key to everything else, and doggedly kept at the job of building it up, until it was paying all expenses, even above the wages of Hans, the baker that she hired. The restaurant intake had been left as clear profit, or what would become profit as soon as her debts, somewhat appalling still, were paid. That Monty might throw her out of step with this precious career was a possibility that distinctly frightened her.

And for another thing, she felt increasingly the sense of inferiority that he had aroused in her, that first night at the lake. Somehow, by his easy flippancy, he made her accomplishments seem small, of no consequence. The restaurant, which to her was a sort of Holy Grail, attained by fabulous effort and sacrifice, to him was the Pie Wagon, a term quickly taken up by Veda, who blandly shortened it to The Wagon. And even though he sometimes brought his friends there, and introduced them, and asked her to sit down, she noticed they were always men. She never met any of his women friends, and never met his family. Once, unexpectedly, he had pointed the car at Pasadena, and said he wanted her to see his home. She was nervous at the idea of meeting his mother, but when they got there it turned out that both mother and sister were away, with the servants off for the night. At once she hated the big stuffy mansion, hated the feeling she had been smuggled in the back door, almost hated him. There was no sex that night, and he professed to be puzzled, as well as hurt, by her conduct. She had a growing suspicion that to him she was a servant girl, an amusing servant girl, one with pretty legs and a flattering response in bed, but a servant girl just the same.

Yet she never declined his invitations, never put on the brake that her instinct was demanding, never raised the hatchet that she knew one day would have to fall. For there was always this delicious thing that he had brought into her life, this intimacy with Veda that had come when he came, that would go, she was afraid, when he went. Monty seemed devoted to Veda. He took her everywhere, to polo, to horse shows, to his mother's, granting her all the social equality that he withheld from Mildred, so that the child lived in a horsy, streamlined heaven. Mildred lived in a heaven too, a heaven of more modest design, one slightly spoiled by wounded pride, but one that held the music of harps. She laved herself in Veda's sticky affection, and bought, without complaining, the somewhat expensive gear that heaven required: riding, swimming, golf, and tennis outfits; overnight kits, monogrammed. If Mildred knew nobody in Pasadena, she had the consolation that Veda knew everybody, and had her picture on the society pages so often that she became quite blasé about it. And so long as this went on, Mildred knew she would put up with Monty, with his irritating point of view, his amused condescension, his omissions that cut her so badly—and not only put up with him, but cling to him.

This particular morning, however, she was in pleasant humor. She had slept well, after a romantic night; it was early fall again, with the mountain trees turning yellow, and she was pontificating amiably about Mr. Roosevelt. She pontificated a great deal now, particularly about politics. She hadn't been in business very long before she became furiously aware of taxes, and this led quite naturally to politics and Mr. Roosevelt. She was going to vote for him, she said, because he was going to put an end to all this Hoover extravagance and balance the budget. Why the very idea, she said, of all those worthless people demanding help, and this Hoover even considering doing anything for them. There was nothing the matter with them except they were too lazy to work, and you couldn't tell her that anybody couldn't get along, even if there was a Depression, if they only had a little gump. In this, Monty may have detected a smug note, an allusion to what *she* had done with a little gump. At any rate, he listened with half an ear, and then asked abruptly: "Can I tell you something?"

"If it's pro-Hoover I don't want to hear it."

"It's about Veda."

"What's she up to now?"

"Music. . . . Well what the hell, it's not up to me to give you any advice. All I know is how the kid feels."

"She takes lessons."

"She takes lessons from some cheap little ivory thumper over in Glendale, and she has a squawk. She doesn't think she's getting anywhere. Well—it's none of my affair."

"Go on."

"I think she's got something."

"I always said she had talent."

"Saying she has talent and doing the right thing about it are two different things. If you don't mind my saying so, I think you know more about pies than you do about music. I think she ought to be put under somebody that can really take charge of her."

"Who, for instance?"

"Well, there's a fellow in Pasadena that could do wonders with her. You may have heard of him—Charlie Hannen, quite well known, up to a few years ago, in the concert field. Then his lungs cracked up and he came out here. Doesn't do much now. Organist, choirmaster, whatever you call it, at our church, leads a quiet life, but takes a few pupils. I'm sure I can get him interested in her. If he takes her on, she'll be getting somewhere."

"When did *you* learn so much about music?"

"I don't know a thing about it. But my mother does. She's been a patroness of the Philharmonic for years and she knows all about it. She says the kid's really got it."

"Of course I never met your mother."

This slightly waspish remark Monty let pass without answering, and it was some minutes before he went on. "And another thing that makes *me* think she's got it is the way she works at it. All right, all I know is horses, but when I see a guy on top of one, out there in the morning when there's nobody else around, popping away with a mallet to improve his backhand, I think to myself, maybe one day he'll be a polo player."

"Isn't *that* something to be."

"It's the same way with her. So far as I know, she never misses a day on that dry-goods box at her grandfather's, and even when she comes over to Mother's she does her two hours of exercises every morning, before she'll even talk about tennis, or riding, or whatever Mother has in mind for her. She *works,* and you don't even have to be a musician to figure that out."

In spite of her almost religious conviction that Veda had talent, Mildred wasn't much impressed: she knew Veda too well to read the evidence quite as Monty read it. Veda's earnest practicing at Mrs. Beragon's might mean a consuming passion for music, and it might mean a consuming passion for letting the whole household know she was around. And Mr. Hannen might have been a celebrated pianist once, but the fact that he was now organist at one of Pasadena's swank churches cast a certain familiar color over his nomination as teacher. All in all, Mildred was sure she detected one of Veda's fine schemes. And in addition to that, she resented what was evidently becoming a small conspiracy to tell her what she should do about her child, and the implication that what she was already doing, by Pasadena standards, wasn't anything like good enough.

So for some time she said nothing about this subject to Veda. But it kept gnawing on her mind, setting up the fear that perhaps she was denying the child something she really ought to have. And then one night Veda broke into a violent denunciation of Miss Whittaker, the lady to whom Mildred had been paying 50¢ a week to give Veda lessons; but something about the tirade didn't have the usual phony sound to it. Troubled, Mildred asked suddenly if Mr. Hannen, of Pasadena, would be better. This produced such excited dancing around that she knew she was in for it. So she called up, made an engagement, and on the appointed afternoon rushed through her work so she could dash home and take Veda over there.

For the occasion, she laid out some of Veda's new finery: a brown silk dress, brown hat, alligator-skin shoes, and silk stockings. But when Veda got home from school, and saw the pile on the bed, she threw up her hands in horror. "Mother! I can't be dressed *up!* Ooh! It would be so *provincial!*" Mildred knew the voice of society when she heard it, so she sighed, put the things away, and watched while Veda tossed out her own idea of suitable garb: maroon sweater, plaid skirt, polo coat, leather beret, woollen socks, and flat-heeled shoes. But she looked away when Veda started to dress. A year and a half had indeed made some changes in Veda's appearance. She was still no more than medium height, but her haughty carriage made her seem taller. The hips were as slim as ever, but had taken on some touch of voluptuousness. The legs were Mildred's, to the last graceful contour. But the most noticeable change was what Monty brutally called the Dairy: two round, swelling protuberances that had appeared almost overnight on the high, arching chest. They would have been large, even for a woman: for a child of thirteen they were positively startling. Mildred had a mystical feeling about them: they made her think tremulously of Love, Motherhood, and similar milky concepts. When Monty had denounced them as indecent, and told Veda for Christ's sake to get a hammock to sling them in, Mildred had been shocked, and pink-faced, and furious. But Veda had laughed gaily, and got brassieres in a completely matter-of-fact way. It would have been hard to imagine her pink-faced about anything. What with the chest, the Dairy, and the slightly swaying hips, she moved like some proud, pedigreed pigeon.

Mr. Hannen lived just off the Pasadena traffic circle, in a house that looked usual enough from the outside, but which, inside, turned out to be one gigantic studio, with all the first floor and most of the second given over to it. It startled Mildred, not only by its size, but by its incredible bareness. There was nothing in it but a big piano, long shelves of music, a wooden wall seat across one end, and a bronze bust, in one corner, labelled BAUER. Mr. Hannen himself was a squat man of about forty, with bandy legs, thick chest, and big hands, though a slight stoop, as well as streaky white hair, hinted at the illness that Monty had mentioned. He was quite friendly, and chatted with Mildred until she was off guard, and grew gabby. When she mentioned the restaurant, Veda tossed her head impatiently, but Mr. Hannen said "Ah!" in a flattering way, remembered he had heard of it, copied down the address, and promised to come in. Then, rather casually, he got around to Veda, had a look at the music she had brought, and said they might as well get the horrible part over. Veda looked a little set back on her heels, but he waved her to the piano and told her to play something—anything, so it was short. Veda marched grandly over, sat down on the bench, twisted her hands in a professional way, and meditated. Mr. Hannen sat down on the wall seat, near Mildred, and meditated. Then Veda launched into a piece known to Mildred as Rachmaninoff Prelude.

It was the first time, in recent months, that Mildred had heard Veda play, and she was delighted with the effect. The musical part she wasn't quite sure about, except that it made a fine noisy clatter. But there could be no mistaking the authoritative way in which Veda kept lifting her right hand high in the air, or the style with which she crossed her left hand over it. The piece kept mounting to a rousing noisy climax, and then inexplicably it faltered. Veda struck a petulant chord. "I always want to play it *that* way."

"I'll tell Mr. Rachmaninoff when I see him."

Mr. Hannen was slightly ironical about it, but his brows knit, and he began eyeing Veda sharply. Veda, a little chastened, finished. He made no comment, but got up, found a piece of music, and put it in front of her. "Let's try the sight-reading."

Veda rattled through this piece like a human pianola, while Mr. Hannen alternately screwed up his face as though he were in great pain, and stared hard at her. When silence mercifully stole into the room, he walked over to the shelves again, got out a violin case, set it beside Mildred, opened it, and began to resin the bow. "Let's try the accompanying. What's your name again?"

"Miss Pierce."

"Ah—?"

"Veda."

"Have you ever accompanied, Veda?"

"Just a little."

"Just a little, what?"

"—I beg your pardon?"

"I might warn you, Veda, that with young pupils I mix quite a general instruction, in with the musical. Now if you don't want a clip on the ear, you'll call me *sir.*"

"Yes sir."

Mildred wanted to kick up her heels and laugh at a Veda who was suddenly meek and humble. However, she affected not to be listening, and fingered the silk of Mr. Hannen's violin cover as though it was the most interesting piece of sewing she had ever seen. He picked up the violin now, and turned to Veda. "This isn't my instrument, but there must be *something* for you to accompany, so it'll have to do. Sound your A."

Veda tapped a note, he tuned the violin, and set a piece of music on the piano. "All right—a little briskly. Don't drag it."

Veda looked blankly at the music. "Why—you've given me the violin part."

"—?"

"Sir."

"Ah, so I have."

He looked on the shelves for a moment, then shook his head. "Well, the piano part's around somewhere, but I don't seem to see it at the moment. All right, keep the violin part in front of you and give me a little accompaniment of your own. Let's see—you have four measures before I come in. Count the last one aloud."

"Sir, I wouldn't even know how to—"

"Begin."

After a desperate look at the music, Veda played a long, faltering figure that ended somewhere up in the tinkle notes. Then, thumping a heavy bass, she counted: "One, two, three, four *and—*"

Even Mildred could detect that the violin was certainly not Mr. Hannen's instrument. But Veda kept up her bass, and when he stopped, she repeated the long figure, thumped her bass, counted, and he came in again. This went on for a short time, but little by little, Mildred thought, it was getting smoother. Once, when Mr. Hannen stopped, Veda omitted the long figure. In its place, she repeated the last part of the air he had been playing, so that when he came in again it joined up quite neatly. When they finished, Mr. Hannen put the violin away and resumed staring at Veda. Then: "Where did you study harmony?"

"I never studied harmony, sir."

"H'm."

He walked around a few moments, said "Well" in a reflective way, and began to talk. "The technique is simply God-awful. You have a tone like a xylophone that fell in love with a hand organ, but that may respond to—whatever we do about it. And the conceit is almost beyond belief. That certainly will respond. It's responded a little already, hasn't it?"

"Yes sir."

"But—play that bit in the Rachmaninoff again, the way you said you always wanted to play it."

Rather weakly, Veda obeyed. He was beside her on the bench now, and dropped his big paw on the keys as he played after her. A tingle went through Mildred at the way it seemed to reach down into the vital of the piano, and find sounds that were rich, dark, and exciting. She noted that it no longer seemed hairy and thick, but became a thing of infinite grace. He studied the keys a moment, then said: "And suppose you did play it that way. You'd be in a little trouble, don't you think?" He played another chord or two. "Where would you go from *there?*"

Veda played a few more chords, and he carefully played them after her. Then he nodded. "Yes, it could have been written that way. I really think Mr. Rachmaninoff's way is better—I find a slight touch of banality in yours, don't you?"

"What's banality, sir?"

"I mean it sounds corny. Cheap. It's got that old Poet and Peasant smell to it. Play it an octave higher and put a couple of trills in it, it would be *Listen to the Mocking Bird* almost before you knew it."

Veda played it an octave higher, twiddled a trill, did a bar of *Listen to the Mocking Bird,* and got very red. "Yes sir, I guess you're right."

"But—it makes musical *sense.*"

This seemed so incredible to him that he sat in silence for some little time before he went on: "I got plenty of pupils with talent in their fingers, very few with anything in their heads. Your fingers, Veda, I'm not so sure about. There's something about the way you do it that isn't exactly—but never mind about that. We'll see what can be done. But your head—that's different. Your sight-reading is remarkable, the sure sign of a musician. And that trick I played on you, making you improvise an accompaniment to the little gavotte—of course, you didn't really do it well, but the amazing thing was that you could do it at all. I don't know what made me think you could, unless it was that idiotic monkey-shine you pulled in the Rachmaninoff. So—"

He turned now to Mildred. "I want her over here twice a week. I'm giving her one lesson in piano—my rate is ten dollars an hour, the lesson is a half hour, so it'll cost you five dollars. I'm giving her another lesson in the theory of music, and that lesson will be free. I can't be sure what will come of it, and it isn't fair to make you pay for my experiments. But, she'll learn *something*, and at the very least get some of the conceit knocked out of her."

So saying, he took a good healthy wallop at Veda's ribs. Then he added: "I suppose nothing will come of it, if we're really honest about it. Many are called, in this business, but few are chosen, and hardly any find out how good you have to be before you're any good at all. But—we'll see.... God, Veda, but your playing stinks. I ought to charge a hundred dollars an hour, just to listen to you."

Veda started to cry, as Mildred stared in astonishment. Not three times in her life had she seen this cold child cry, and yet there she was, with two streams squirting out of her eyes and cascading down on the maroon sweater, where they made glistening silver drops. Mr. Hannen airily waved his hand. "Let her bawl. It's nothing to what she'll be doing before I get through with her."

So Veda bawled, and she was still bawling when they got in the car and started home. Mildred kept patting her hand, and gave up all thought of a little light twitting on the subject of "Sir." Then, in explosive jerks, Veda started to talk. "Oh Mother—I was so afraid—he wouldn't take me. And then—he *wanted* me. He said I had something—in my head. Mother—in my *head!*"

Then Mildred knew that an awakening had taken place in

Veda, that it wasn't in the least phony, and that what had awakened was precisely what she herself had mutely believed in all these years. It was as though the Star of Bethlehem had suddenly appeared in front of her.

So Monty was vindicated, but when Mildred snuggled up to him one night in the den, and wanted to talk about it, the result left a great deal to be desired. He lit a cigarette and rehearsed his reasons for thinking Veda "had it"; they were excellent reasons, all in praise of Veda, but somehow they didn't hit the spot. When she tried to break through his habit of treating everything with offhand impersonality, saying wasn't it wonderful, and how did *he* ever think up something like that, he seemed uncomfortable at her kittenishness, and rather curtly brushed her off. To hell with it, he said. He had done nothing that anybody couldn't have done that knew the child, so why give him any credit? Then, as though bored with the whole subject, he began stripping off her stockings.

But there was a great hunger in Mildred's heart: she had to *share* this miracle with somebody, and when she had stood it as long as she could she sent for Bert. He came the next afternoon, to the restaurant, when the place was deserted and she had him to herself. She had Arline serve lunch and told him about it. He had already heard a little, from Mom, who had got a brief version from Veda, but now he got it all, in complete detail. Mildred told about the studio, the Rachmaninoff prelude, the sight-reading, the accompaniment to the violin selection. He listened gravely, except for the laugh he let out over the "Sir" episode. When Mildred had finished he thought a long time. Then, solemnly, he announced: "She's some kid. She's some kid."

Mildred sighed happily. This was the kind of talk she wanted, at last. He went on, then, flatteringly reminding her that she had always said Veda was "artistic," gallantly conceding that he himself had had his doubts. Not that he didn't appreciate Veda, he added hastily, hell no. It was only that he didn't know of any music on Mildred's side or his, and he always understood this kind of thing ran in families. Well, it just went to show how any of us can be wrong, and goddam it, he was glad it had turned out this way. *Goddam* it he was. Then, having polished off the past, he looked at the future. The fingers, he assured Mildred, were nothing to worry about. Because suppose she didn't become a great pianist? From all he had heard, that market was shot anyhow. But if it was like this guy said, and she had talent in her head, and began to *write* music, that was where the real dough was, and it didn't make a bit of difference whether you could play the piano or not. Because, he said dramatically, look at Irving Berlin. He had it straight that the guy couldn't play a note, but with a million bucks in the bank and more coming in every day, *he* should worry whether he could tickle the keys or not. Oh no, Mildred needn't worry about Veda now. The way it looked to *him*, the kid was all set, and before very long she'd be pulling off something big.

Having Veda turn into Irving Berlin, with or without a million bucks in the bank, wasn't exactly what Mildred had in mind for her. In her imagination she could see Veda already, wearing a pale green dress to set off her coppery hair, seated at a big piano before a thousand people, grandly crossing her right hand over her left, haughtily bowing to thunderous applause—but no matter. The spirit was what counted. Bert spun her dreams for her, while she closed her eyes and breathed deeply, and Arline poured him more coffee, from a percolator, the way he liked it. It was the middle of the afternoon before Mildred returned to earth, and said suddenly: "Bert, can I ask a favor?"

"Anything, Mildred."

"It's not why I asked you here. I just wanted to tell you about it. I knew you'd want to hear."

"I know why you asked me. Now what is it?"

"I want that piano, at Mom's."

"Nothing to it. They'll be only too glad—"

"No, wait a minute. I don't want it as a gift, nothing like that at all. I just want to borrow it until I can get Veda a piano that—"

"It's all right. They'll—"

"No, but wait a minute. I'm going to get her a piano. But the kind of piano that she ought to have, I mean a real grand, costs eleven hundred dollars. And they'll give me terms, but I just don't dare take on any more debt. What I'm going to do, I'm going to open a special account, down at the bank, and keep putting in, and I know by next Christmas, I mean a year from now, I can manage it. But just now—"

"I only wish I could contribute a little."

"Nobody's asking you to."

Quickly she put her hand over his and patted it. "You've done plenty. Maybe you've forgotten how you gave me the house outright, and everything that went before, but I haven't. You've done your share. Now it's my turn. I don't mind about that, but I do want them to know, Mom and Mr. Pierce I mean, that I'm not trying to *get* anything from them. I just want to borrow the piano, so Veda can practice at home, and—"

"Mildred."

"Yes?"

"Will you just kindly shut up?"

"All right."

"Everything's under control. Just leave it to me."

So presently, the piano was carted down, and on January 2, Mildred went to the bank and deposited $21, after multiplying carefully, and making sure that $21 a week, at the end of a year, would almost exactly equal $1,100.

Mildred was in such a panic over the bank holiday, as well as other alarms that attended to Mr. Roosevelt's inauguration, that she paid scant attention to anything except her immediate concerns. But when her apprehension slacked off, she began to notice that Monty seemed moody and abstracted, with little of the flippancy that was normally part of him. Then, in a speak-easy one night, the sharp way he glanced at the check told her he didn't have much money with him. Then another night, when he revoked an order for a drink he obviously wanted, she knew he was hard up. But it was Veda who let the cat out of the bag. Walking home from the restaurant one night, she suddenly asked Mildred: "Heard the news?"

"What news, darling?"

"The House of Beragon is ge-finished. It is ffft, fa-down-go-boom, oop-a-doop-whango. Alas it is no more. Pop goes the weasel."

"I've been suspecting something like that."

Mildred said this quickly, to cover the fact that she actually had been told nothing at all, and, for the rest of the walk home was depressed by the realization that Monty had suffered some sort of fantastic reverses without saying a word to her. But soon curiosity got the better of her. She lit a fire in the den, had Veda sit down, and asked for more details. "Well, Mother, I really don't know a great deal about it, except that it's all over Pasadena, and you hardly hear anything else. They had some stock, the Duenna, that's his mother, and the Infanta, that's his sister. Stock in a bank, somewhere in the East. And it was assessable, whatever that means. So when the bank didn't open it was most unfortunate. What *is* assessable?"

"I heard some talk about it, when the banks were closed. I think it means that if there's not enough money to pay the depositors, then the stockholders have to make it good."

"*That's it.* That explains about their assets being impounded, and why they've gone to Philadelphia, the Duenna and the Infanta, so papers can't be served on them. And of course when Beragon Brothers, dear old Beragon Brothers, founded in 1893—when they went bust, that didn't help any, either."

"When did that happen?"

"Three or four months ago. Their growers, the farmers that raised the fruit, all signed up with the Exchange, and *that* was what cooked Monty's goose. He didn't have any bank stock. His money was in the fruit company, but when that folded his mother kicked in. Then when the bank went under she had nothing to kick. Anyway there's a big sign on the lawn, 'For

Sale, Owner Must Sacrifice,' and Monty's showing the prospective buyers around."

"You mean their *house?*"

"I mean their palatial residence on Orange Grove Avenue, with the iron dogs out front and the peacock out behind—but a buyer had better show up pretty soon, or Monty'll be eating the peacock. It certainly looks as though the old buzzard will have to go to work."

Mildred didn't know whether she was more shocked at the tale she heard or Veda's complete callousness about it. But one thing was clear: Monty wanted no sympathy from her, so for a time she ate with him, drank with him, and slept with him under the pretense that she knew nothing whatever. But presently the thing became so public, what with pieces in the paper about the sale of his polo ponies, the disappearance of the Cord in favor of a battered little Chevrolet, and one thing and another, that he did begin to talk about it. But he always acted as though this were some casual thing that would be settled shortly, a nuisance while it lasted, but of no real importance. Never once did he let Mildred come close to him in connection with it, pat him on the head, tell him it didn't really matter, do any of the things that in her scheme of life a woman was expected to do under these circumstances. She felt sorry for him, terribly upset about him. And yet she also felt snubbed and rebuffed. And she could never shake off the feeling that if he accepted her as his social equal he would act differently about it.

And then one night she came home to find him with Veda, waiting for her. They were in the den, having a furious argument about polo, which continued after she sat down. It seemed that a new team had been organized, called The Ramblers: that its first game would be at San Diego, and that Monty had been invited to make the trip. Veda, an expert on such matters, was urging him to go. "There'd better be *one* eight-goal man with that outfit, or they can stop calling it The Ramblers and call it Mussolini Reviewing the Cavalry, because that's what it's going to be, all right. Just a one-way parade of horses, and they won't wake up until the score is about forty to nothing."

"I've got too much to do."

"Such as what?"

"This and that."

"Nothing whatever, if I'm any good at guessing. Monty, you've got to go with them. If you don't, they're sunk. It'll be embarrassing. And they'll simply ruin your horses. After all, *they've* got some rights."

Polo was a complete mystery to Mildred. How Monty could sell his ponies and still be riding them she couldn't understand, and chiefly she couldn't understand *why* he was riding them, or anybody was. And yet it tore her heart that he should want to go, and not be able to, and it kept bothering her long after Veda had gone to bed. When he got up to go she pulled him down beside her, and asked: "Do you need money?"

"Oh Lord no!"

His voice, look, and gesture were those of a man pained beyond expression at an insinuation utterly grotesque. But Mildred, nearly two years in the restaurant business, was not fooled. She said: "I think you do."

"Mildred—you leave me without any idea—what to say to you. I've—run into a little bad luck—that's true. My mother has—we all have. But—it's nothing that involves—small amounts. I can still—hold up my end of it—if that's what you're talking about."

"I want you to play in that game."

"I'm not interested."

"Wait a minute."

She found her handbag, took out a crisp $20 bill. Going over to him she slipped it in the breast pocket of his coat. He took it out, with an annoyed grimace, and pitched it back at her. It fell on the floor. She picked it up and dropped it in his lap. With the same annoyed grimace, very much annoyed this time, he picked it up, started to pitch it back at her again, then hesitated, and sat there snapping it between his fingers, so it made little pistol shots. Then, without looking at her: "Well—I'll pay it back."

"That's all right."

"I don't know when—two or three things have to be straightened out first—but it won't be very long. So—if it's understood to be strictly a loan—"

"Any way you want."

That week, with the warm June weather, her business took a sharp drop. For the first time, she had to skip an installment on Veda's piano.

The next week, when he changed his mind about going to a speakeasy that he liked, she slipped $10 into his pocket, and they went. Before she knew it, she was slipping him $10's and $20's regularly, either when she remembered about it, or he stammeringly asked her if he could tap her for another small loan. Her business continued light, and when the summer had gone, she had managed to make only three deposits on the piano, despite hard scrimping. She was appalled at the amount of money he cost, and fought off a rising irritation about it. She told herself it wasn't his fault, that he was merely going through what thousands of others had already gone through, were still going through. She told herself it was her duty to be helping somebody, and that it might as well be somebody that meant something to her. She also reminded herself she had practically forced the arrangement on him. It was no use. The piano had become an obsession with her by now, and the possibility that it was slipping away from her caused a baffled, frustrated sensation that almost smothered her.

And she was all too human, and the cuts she had received from him demanded their revenge. She began to order him around: timid requests that he haul Veda to Mr. Hannen's, so she wouldn't have to take the bus, now became commands; she curtly told him when he was to show up, when he was to be back, whether he was to have his dinner at the restaurant or at the house, and when she would join him afterwards. In a hundred small ways she betrayed that she despised him for taking her money, and on his side, he did little to make things better. Monty, alas, was like Bert. A catastrophic change had taken place in his life, and he was wholly unable to adjust himself to it. In some way, indeed, he was worse off than Bert, for Bert lived with his dreams, and at least they kept him mellow. But Monty was an amateur cynic, and cynics are too cynical to dream. He had been born to a way of life that included taste, manners, and a jaunty aloofness from money, as though it were beneath a gentleman's notice. But what he didn't realize was that all these things rested squarely on money: it was the possession of money that enabled him to be aloof from it. For the rest, his days were dedicated to play, play on which the newspapers cast a certain agreeable importance, but play nevertheless. Now, with the money gone, he was unable to give up the old way of life, or find a new one. He became a jumble of sorry fictions, an attitude with nothing behind it but pretense. He retained something that he thought of as his pride, but it had no meaning, and exhibited itself mainly in mounting bitterness toward Mildred. He carped at her constantly, sneered at her loyalty to Mr. Roosevelt, revealed that his mother knew the whole Roosevelt family, and regarded Franklin Delano as a phony and a joke. His gags about the Pie Wagon, once easily patronizing and occasionally funny, took on a touch of malice, and Veda, ever fashionable, topped them with downright insolence. The gay little trio wasn't quite so gay.

And then one night in the den, when Mildred tucked another $20 into his pocket, he omitted his usual mumble about paying it back. Instead, he took out the bill, touched his forelock with it, and said: "Your paid gigolo thanks you."

"I don't think that was very nice."

"It's true, isn't it?"

"Is that the only reason you come here?"

"Not at all. Come what may, swing high, swing low, for better or for worse, you're still the best piece of tail I ever had, or ever could imagine."

He got this off with a nervous, rasping little laugh, and for a few seconds Mildred felt prickly all over, as though the blood were leaving her body. Then her face felt hot, and she became aware of a throbbing silence that had fallen between them. Sheer pride demanded that she say something, and yet for a time she couldn't. Then, in a low, shaking voice, she said: "Monty, suppose you go home."

"What's the matter?"

"I think you know."

"Well, by all that's holy. I *don't* know!"

"I told you to go."

Instead of going, he shook his head, as though she were incredibly obtuse, and launched into a dissertation on the relations between the sexes. The sense of it was that as long as this thing was there, everything was all right; that it was the strongest bond there was, and what he was really doing, if she only had sense enough to know it, was paying her a compliment. What she really objected to was his language, wasn't it? If he had said it flowery, so it sounded poetic, she would have felt differently, wouldn't she?

But every moment or two he gave the same nervous, rasping laugh, and again she was unable to speak. Then, gathering herself with an effort, she rose to one of her rare moments of eloquence. "If you told me that, and intended it as a compliment, it might have been one, I don't know. Almost anything is a compliment, if you mean it. But when you tell me that, and it's the only thing you have to tell me, then it's not a compliment. It's the worst thing I ever had said to me in my life."

"Oh, so you want the I-love-you scene."

"I want you to go."

Hot tears started to her eyes, but she winked them back. He shook his head, got up, then turned to her as though he had to explain something to a child. "We're not talking about things. We're talking about words. I'm not a poet. I don't even want to be a poet. To me, that's just funny. I say something to you my own way, and wham you go moral on me. Well what do I do now? It's a pure question of prudery, and—"

"That's a lie."

Her lungs were filling with breath now, so much that she felt it would suffocate her. Her face screwed up into the squint, and the glittering tears made her eyes look hard, cold, and feline. She sat perfectly still, her legs crossed, and looked at him, where he stood facing her on the other side of the room. After a long pause she went on, in a passionate, trembling voice. "Since you've known me, that's what I've been to you, a piece of tail. You've taken me to mountain shacks and back-street speakeasies, you've never introduced me to your friends—except for a few men you've brought over to dinner sometimes—or your mother, or your sister, or any member of your family. You're ashamed of me, and now that you're in my debt, you had to say what you just said to me, to get even. It's not a surprise to me. I've known it all along. Now you can go."

"None of that is true."

"Every word of it is true."

"So far as my friends go—"

"They mean nothing to me."

"—It hadn't occurred to me you'd care to meet any of them. Most of them are dull, but if meeting them means anything to you, that's easy fixed. So far as my mother goes—"

"She means nothing to me either."

"—So far as my mother goes, I can't do anything about her now, because she's away, and so is my sister. But you may have forgotten that with this restaurant of yours you keep somewhat peculiar hours. To have arranged a meeting would have been idiotically complicated, so I did the best I could. I took your daughter over there, and if you knew anything about social conventions at all, you'd know that I was dealing in my own way with what otherwise would have been a situation. And certainly my mother took all the interest in Veda she could be expected to take—a little more interest than you seemed to be taking, I sometimes thought."

"—I didn't complain on that score."

In her heart, Mildred knew that Monty was being as dishonest about Veda as he was being about the rest of it. Obviously, he liked Veda, and found her an amusing exhibit to drag around, no doubt because she was precisely the kind of snob that he was himself, and that most of his friends were. And also, by doing so much for the child, he could neatly sidestep the necessity of doing anything about the mother. But to argue about it would jeopardize the enchanted life that Veda now led, so Mildred veered off in a new direction. "Monty, why don't you tell the truth? You look down on me because I work."

"Are you crazy?"

"No. You look down on everybody that works, as you practically admitted to me the first night I was with you. All right, I work. It's not at all elegant work, but it's the only work I can do. I cook food and sell it. But one thing you'd better get through your head sooner or later: *You'll* have to go to work—"

"Of course I'm going to work!"

"Ha-ha. When?"

"As soon as I get the damned house sold, and this mess straightened out that we've got ourselves into. Until that's over, work, for me, is out of the question. But as *soon* as it's over—"

"Monty, you just make me laugh. I used to be married to a real-estate company, and there's no use trying to kid me about houses, and how to get rid of them. There's nothing about the place that can't be put in the hands of an agent, and handled like any other. No, it's not that. You'd rather live there, so you can have an address on Orange Grove Avenue, and cook your own eggs in the morning, and drive over to the club in the afternoon, and have your dinner here with Veda, *and take your spending money from me*—than work. That's all, isn't it?"

"Sure."

His face broke into a sunny smile, he came over, roughly pushed her into a little heap, took her in his arms. "I don't know anybody I'd rather take money from than you. Your paid gigolo is damned well satisfied."

She pushed his arms away, trying to repulse him. But she was taken by surprise, and her struggles had no steam in them. Try as she would, she couldn't resist the physical effect he had on her, and when she finally yielded, the next hour was more wanton, more shamefully exciting, than any she remembered.

And yet, for the first time, she felt an undertone of disgust. She didn't forget that not once had the $20 bill been mentioned, not once had he offered to give it back. They parted amicably, he apologizing for the offending remark, she telling him to forget what she had said, as she was upset, and didn't mean it. But both of them meant it, and neither of them forgot.

CHAPTER

11

"Baby, what are you doing about Repeal?"

"You mean Repeal of Prohibition?"

"Yeah, just that."

"Why, I don't see how it affects me."

"It affects you plenty."

Mrs. Gessler, having coffee with Mildred just before closing time, began to talk very rapidly. Repeal, she said, was only a matter of weeks, and it was going to stand the whole restaurant business on its head. "People are just crazy for a drink, a decent drink, a drink with no smoke or ether or formaldehyde in it, a drink they can have out in the open, without having to give the password to some yegg with his face in a slot. And places that can read the handwriting on the wall are going to cash in, and those that can't are going to pass out. You think you've got a nice trade here, don't you? And you think it'll stick by you, because it likes you, and likes your chicken, and wants to help a plucky little woman get along? It will like hell. When they find out you're not going to serve them that drink, they're going to be sore and stay sore. They're going to tag you for a back number and go someplace where they get what they want. You're going to be out of luck."

"You mean I should sell *liquor?*"

"It'll be legal, won't it?"

"I wouldn't even consider such a thing."

"Why not?"

"Do you think I'd run a *saloon?*"

Mrs. Gessler lit a cigarette, began snapping the ashes impatiently into Mildred's Mexican ashtrays. Then she took Mildred to task for prejudice, for stupidity, for not being up with the times. Mildred, annoyed at being told how to run her business, argued back, but for each point she made Mrs. Gessler made two points. She kept reminding Mildred that liquor, when it came back, wasn't going to be the same as it had been in the old days. It was going to be respectable, and it was going to put the restaurant business on its feet. "That's what has ailed eating houses ever since the war. That's why you're lucky to get a lousy 85 cents for your dinner, when if you could sell a drink with it, you could get a buck, and maybe a buck and a quarter. Baby, you're not talking sense, and I'm getting damned annoyed at you."

"But I don't know anything about liquor."

"I *do.*"

Something about Mrs. Gessler's manner suggested that this was what she had been trying to lead up to all the time, for she lit another cigarette, eyed Mildred sharply, and went on: "Now listen: You know and I know and we all know that Ike's in the long- and short-haul trucking business. Just the same, Repeal's going to hit him hard. We'll have to do something, quick, while he reorganizes. That means *I'll* have to do something. So how's this? You put in the booze, and I'll take charge of it for you, for a straight ten per cent, of what I take in, plus tips, if, as, and when there are any, and if, as and when I'm not too proud to pick them up—which ain't likely, baby. It ain't even possible."

"You? A *bartender?*"

"Why not? I'll be a damned good one."

This struck Mildred so funny that she laughed until she heard a girdle seam pop. In spite of work, worry, and everything she could do about it, she was getting the least little bit fat. But Mrs. Gessler didn't laugh. She was in dead earnest, and for the next few days nagged Mildred relentlessly. Mildred still regarded the whole idea as absurd, but on her trips downtown in connection with the pie business, she began to hear things. And then, as state after state fell in line for Repeal, she hardly heard anything else: every proprietor, from Mr. Chris to the owners of the big cafeterias, was in a dither to know what to do, and she began to get frightened. She had to talk to somebody, and on such matters she hadn't much confidence in Bert, and none at all in Monty. On a sudden inspiration she called up Wally. She saw him quite a lot, in connection with their real-estate relations, but their previous relation, by the curious twists of human memory, had by tacit consent been completely erased, so it had never existed. Wally came over one afternoon, listened while Mildred explained her quandary, then shook his head. "Well I don't know what you're backing and filling about. Course you'll sell liquor."

"You mean I'll have to, to hold my trade?"

"I mean there's *dough* in it."

He looked at her with his familiar stare, that was at the same time so vague and so shrewd, and her heart gave a little thump. It was the first time, for some reason, that this aspect of the problem had occurred to her. He went on, a little annoyed at her stupidity: "What the hell? Every drink you sell will be about eighty per cent profit, even at what you have to pay for your liquor. And it'll pull in more people for the dinner trade. If Lucy Gessler wants to take it over, then O.K. If she don't know about booze, I don't know who does. Get going on it, and get going now. It's coming, fast. And be sure you put on your sign, *Cocktails*. That's what they're waiting for. Put a red star in front of it, so they know *you* know it's important."

"Will I need some kind of a license?"

"I'll fix that up for you."

So the next time Mrs. Gessler came in, she found Mildred in

a different frame of mind. She nodded approval of what Wally had said about the sign, then became coldly businesslike about other obligatory preparations. "I'll need a bar, but there's no room for one until you make alterations, so I'll have to get along with a portable. It'll be a perambular thing that I'll wheel from table to table—the same as most other places are going to use, temporarily. It'll have to be specially made and it'll cost you about three hundred bucks. Then I'll need a couple of hundred dollars' worth of liquor. I ought to have more, but it'll be all I can get, in the beginning. Then I want a couple of leather seats, near the door, with a low table between. Between trips to the tables, I'll be running my own little soiree over here, and I'll sell plenty of drinks to people waiting to be seated for dinner. Then I'll want a special bus, assigned to me alone. Your kid Pancho has a pal that'll do, by the name of Josie. He won't be available for general work, because he'll have to wash glasses for me all the time, and wash them the way I want them washed, and bring beer from the icebox when I call for it, and ice whatever wine we sell, and he'll have all he can do, just helping me. Then I'll need a full set of cocktail, highball, and wine glasses—not too many, but we'll have to have the right glasses for the right drinks. Then, let's see. You'll need pads of special bar checks, to run separate from the others. It's the only way we can keep it straight. That's about all I can think of now."

"How much, all in all?"

"About five hundred to start—for the bar, glasses, furniture and checks. The liquor will be over and above the five hundred, but you won't pay till the Monday after delivery, and by that time we ought to have a few dollars coming in."

Mildred gulped, told Mrs. Gessler she would let her know next day. That night she lay awake, and her mind darted first to this scheme, then to that, whereby she could furnish five hundred dollars. She kept a little reserve of two or three hundred dollars, but she dared not dip into it, as sad experience had taught her that emergencies arose constantly that demanded instant cash. It was a long time before her mind darted at last to the only way she could get the money: by robbing the special account for Veda's piano. It now amounted to $567, and the moment she thought of it she tried not think of it, and began once more her frantic questing for schemes. But soon she knew this was what she had to do; knew that Veda couldn't have her piano for Christmas. Then once more rage began to suffocate her—not at Mrs. Gessler, or Repeal, or any of the circumstances that made this new outlay necessary, but at Monty, for the money he had cost her, those endless $10's and $20's which now, if she had them, would see her through. She worked herself into such a state that presently she had to get up, put on a kimono, and make herself a cup of tea, so she could quiet down.

Christmas morning Mildred woke up with one of her rare hangovers. It had indeed been a gay night at the little restaurant, for the bar, opening promptly on December 6, had outdone all that had been expected of it. Not only had it taken in large sums itself, but it had drawn a bigger dinner trade, and a better dinner trade. Mrs. Gessler, in gabardine slacks and the same brickred as the waitresses' uniforms, white mess jacket with brass buttons, and red ribbon around her hair, seemed to catch the diners' fancy, and certainly she was expert enough to please the most fastidious. Tips went up, and when the kitchen celebration finally got going, it was exceedingly festive. Hans, the baker, was supposed to be off at night, but he showed up anyway, and got the party started with a bang by feeling Sigred's leg. Sigrid was a Swedish girl Mildred had hired mainly for her looks, and then found out was one of the best waitresses she had ever seen. Then, just to be impartial, Hans felt Arline's leg, and Emma's, and Audrey's. Emma and Audrey had been taken on the day after the opening, just to forestall the possibility of another jam-up. The ensuing squeals were enjoyed by Pancho and Josie, who sat apart, not quite of things, yet not quite out of them; and by Mrs. Kramer, an assistant cook Mildred was training. They were emphatically not enjoyed by Carl, a seventeen-year-old who drove the little secondhand delivery truck Mildred had bought, and painted cream, with *"Mildred Pierce, Pies"* lettered on it in bold red script. He concentrated on ice cream and cake, and eyed Hans's efforts with stony disapproval, to the great delight of Arline, who kept screaming that he was learning "the facks of life."

Mildred had sat down with them, and put out wine and whiskey, and taken two or three drinks herself. What with the liquor, and the thanks she received for the $10 she had given each of them, she began to feel so friendly that she weakened in her resolve to give Monty nothing whatever for Christmas. First she took his orchids out of the icebox and pinned them on, to a loud chorus of applause. Then she had another drink, went over to the cash box, and smooched four $10 bills. These she put in a little envelope and wrote on it, "Merry Christmas, Monty." Then, hearing from Mrs. Gessler that he had arrived, she went into the dining room, weaving slightly, and elaborately took him outside. Under the trees she slipped the envelope into his pocket and thanked him for the orchids, which she said were the most beautiful she had ever had. Then she invited him to smell them. Laughing a little, obviously delighted at her condition, he reminded her that orchids had no smell. "Smell'm anyway." So he smelled, and reported that the orchids still had no smell, but that she smelled fine. She nodded, satisfied, and kissed him. Then she took him inside, where Bert, Wally, Mrs. Gessler, and Veda were sitting at a table, having a little celebration of their own.

And yet the evening had had an unpleasant finish: Monty and Veda began whispering together, and went into gales of laughter at some joke of their own. Mildred heard the words "varlets' yulabaloo," and concluded, probably correctly, that they were laughing at the party in the kitchen. She launched into a long, boozy harangue on the rights of labor, and how anybody who worked for a living was as good as anybody else. Wally tried to shush her down and Mrs. Gessler tried to shush her down, but it was no use. She went on to the bitter end. Then, somewhat inconsistently, she lurched to her feet, went to the kitchen, and asked how people could enjoy themselves with all that yelling going on. This had the effect of ringing down the curtain, front and rear.

Now, as she got up and dressed, she had a sour recollection of the harangue, and a still sourer recollection of the four $10's that had followed their predecessors down a bottomless rathole. She had given Letty the day off, so she went to the kitchen, made herself coffee, and drank it black. Then, hearing Veda's water running, she knew she had to hurry. She went to her bedroom, got a pile of packages out of the closet, and took them to the living room. Quickly she arranged a neat display around the base of the tree that had already been set up and decorated. Then she took out her own offering and looked at it. It was a wristwatch. She had put off buying it until the last moment, hoping the profits from the bar would permit her to order the piano anyway. But the unforeseen had again intervened. During the first hectic days of Repeal, Mrs. Gessler had a devil's own time finding liquor, and for much of it had to pay cash. So the hope died, and at the last minute, Mildred had dashed downtown and bought this gaud for $75. She listened close and heard its tiny tick, but it didn't sound much like a grand piano. Glumly she wrapped it, wrote a little card, tucked it under the ribbon. Then she set it beside the package from Bert.

She had hardly stood up to survey the general effect when there came a tap on the door, and Veda, in her most syrupy Christmas voice, asked: "May I come in?" Mildred managed a soft smile, and opened the door. Suddenly Veda was smothering her with kisses, wishing a merry Christmas to "you darling, darling Mother!" Then, just as suddenly, the kisses stopped and so did the greetings. Veda was staring at the Pierce upright, and by the look on her face Mildred knew she had been told about the grand, by Bert, by Monty, by the cashier at the bank, by somebody—and had expected to see it there, as a fine surprise, this Christmas morning.

Mildred licked her lips, opened her mouth to make explanations, but at the cold look on Veda's face, she couldn't. Nervously she said something about there being a great many presents, and hadn't Veda better make a list, so she would be sure who sent what? Veda made no reply, but stooped down and began pulling ribbons. When she got to the wristwatch she examined it with casual interest, laid it aside without comment. At this Mildred went back to her bedroom, lay down on the bed, tried to stop trembling. The trembling went on. Presently the bell rang, and she heard Bert's voice. Going to the living room again, she was in time to hear Veda ecstatically thank him for the riding boots he had given her, and call him "you darling, darling Father." A little scene ensued, with Bert saying the boots could be exchanged if they weren't the right fit, and Veda trying them on. They were perfect, said Veda, and she wasn't going to take them off all day. She was even going to *sleep* in them.

But Veda never once looked at Mildred, and the trembling kept on. In a few minutes Mildred asked Bert if he was ready, and he said any time she was. They went to the kitchen for the flowers they were going to put on Ray's grave, but Bert quickly closed the door. Jerking his thumb toward the living room he asked: "What's the matter with her? She sick?"

"It's about the piano. What with the bar and one thing and another I couldn't get it. This Christmas, I mean. But somebody kindly tipped her off."

"Not me."

"I didn't say so."

"What *did* you give her?"

"A wristwatch. It was a nice watch, a little one, the kind they're all wearing, and you'd think she'd at least—"

But the trembling had reached Mildred's mouth by now, and she couldn't finish. Bert put his arm around her, patted her. Then he asked: "Is she coming with us?"

"I don't know."

They went out the back door to get the car out of the garage, and Mildred drove. As they were backing down the drive, Bert told her to hold it. Then, lightly, he tapped the horn. After a few seconds, he tapped it again. There was no response from the house. Mildred eased into the street, and they drove to the cemetery. Mildred threaded her way slowly along the drive, so as not to disturb the hundreds of others who were out there too. When they came to the Pierce plot she stopped and they got out. Taking the flowers, they walked over to the little marker that had been placed there by the Pierces a short time before. It was a plain white stone, with the name, and under it the dates of the brief little life. Bert mumbled: "They wanted to put a quotation on it, 'Suffer the little children,' whatever it is, but I remembered you like things plain."

"I like it just like it is."

"And another thing they wanted to put on it was: 'Erected by her loving grandparents Adrian and Sarah,' but I told them 'Hey, keep your shirt on. You'll get your names in this marble orchard soon enough without trying to beat the gun in any way.' "

This struck Mildred as funny, and she started to titter, but somewhere down the drive a child began to laugh. Then a great lump rose in her throat and Bert quickly walked away. As she stood there she could hear him behind her, walking back and forth. She stood a long time. Then she put the flowers on the grave, paused for one last look, turned, and took his arm. He laced his fingers through hers, squeezed hard.

When Mildred got home, she found Veda exactly where she had left her: in the chair near the Christmas tree, the boots still on, staring malevolently at the Pierce upright. Mildred sat down and opened a package Bert had brought with him when he came, a jar of preserved strawberries from Mrs. Biederhof. For a few moments, except for the crackle of paper, there was silence. Then, in her clearest, most affected drawl, Veda said: "Christ, but I hate this dump."

"Is there anything in particular that you object to?"

"Oh, no, Mother, not at all, not at all—and I do hope you don't begin changing things around, just to please me. No, there's nothing in particular. I just hate every lousy, stinking part of it, and if it were to burn down tomorrow *I* wouldn't shed a furtive tear from the Elixir of Love, by Gaetano Donizetti, seventeen ninety-eight–eighteen forty-eight."

"I see."

Veda picked up a package of the cigarettes Mildred kept on hand for Monty, lit one, and threw the match on the floor. Mildred's face tightened. "You'll put out that cigarette and pick up the match."

"I will like hell."

Mildred got up, took careful aim, and slapped Veda hard, on the cheek. The next thing she knew, she was dizzy from her head to her heels, and it seemed seconds before she realized, from the report that was ringing in her ears, that Veda had slapped her back. Blowing smoke into Mildred's face, Veda went on, in her cool, insolent tone: "Glendale, California, Land where the Orange Tree Blows, from Mignon, by Ambroise Thomas, eighteen eleven–eighteen ninety-six. Forty square miles of nothing whatever. A high-class, positively-restricted development for discriminating people that run filling stations, and furniture factories, and markets, and pie wagons. The garden spot of the world—in the pig's eye. A wormhole, for grubs!"

"Where did you hear that?"

Mildred had sat down, but at these last words she looked up. She was wholly familiar with Veda's vocabulary, and she knew that this phrase was not part of it. At her question, Veda came over, leaned down close. "Why the poor goddam sap—do you think he'd marry *you?*"

"If I were willing, yes."

"Oh! Yee gods and little fishes hear my cynical laughter, from Pagliacci, by Ruggiero Leoncavallo, eighteen fifty-eight–nineteen nineteen. If you were willing—! Pardon me while I regain my shattered composure. Stupid, don't you know what he sees in you?"

"About what you see, I think."

"No—it's your legs."

"He—told you—*that?*"

"Why certainly."

Veda's manner showed that she relished Mildred's consternation. "Of course he told me. We're very good friends, and I hope I have a mature point of view on these matters. Really, he speaks very nicely about your legs. He has a theory about them. He says a gingham apron is the greatest provocation ever invented by woman for the torture of man, and that the very best legs are found in kitchens, not in drawing rooms. 'Never take the mistress if you can get the maid,' is the way he puts it. And another thing, he says a pretty varlet is always agreeably grateful, and not too exacting, with foolish notions about matrimony and other tiresome things. I must say I find his social theories quite fascinating."

Veda went on at some length, snapping her cigarette and when it went out lighting another one and throwing the match on the floor. But for some time Mildred found her taunts nothing but a jumble. She was so stunned at the discovery that this man, whom she had put up with because he brought Veda closer to her, had all the time been sneering at her behind her back, making fun of her most intimate relations with him, setting the child against her, that every part of her seemed to have turned to jelly. Presently, however, words began to have meaning again, and she heard Veda saying: "After all, Mother, even in his darkest days, Monty's shoes are custom made."

"They ought to be. They cost me enough."

Mildred snapped this out bitterly, and for a second wished she hadn't. But the cigarette, suddenly still in midair, told her it was news to Veda, quite horrible news, and without further regret, she rammed home her advantage: "You didn't know that, did you?"

Veda stared incredulously, then decided to play it funny. "You buy his shoes? Yee gods and little—"

"His shoes and his shirts and his drinks and everything else he's had in the last few months, including his polo dues. And you needn't call on your gods and little fishes anymore, or mention any more dates from the operas. If you want to see some dates I have them all written down, with an exact amount beside each one. Miss Pierce, you made a slight mistake. It's not my legs that he likes me for, it's my money. And so long as it's that, we'll see who's the varlet and who's the boss. It may interest you to know that *that's* why he's such a very good friend of yours. He doesn't haul you over to your music lesson because he wants to. In fact, he often complains about it. He does it because he has to. And surprising though it be to you, he'll marry me, or not marry me, or do anything I say, so his proud, gentlemanly belly can have something to eat."

Mildred got up, something haughty in her manner for a moment suggesting Veda. "So you see, what he sees in me *is* about what you see, isn't it? And unfortunately, you're in exactly the position he's in, too. You have to do what I say. The hand that holds the money cracks the whip. And I say there'll be no more money for you, not one cent, until you take back everything you've said, and apologize for it."

Veda's answer was to abandon the grand manner, and become a yelling, devilish adolescent of fourteen. Coldly, Mildred listened to her curses, watched her kick at the Pierce upright with Bert's riding boots. "And that's the piano you're going to practice on, until I get ready, in my own good time, to buy you another."

Veda screamed at the top of her lungs, then leaped at the piano and began playing the Can-Can from Orpheus. Mildred didn't know what it was, but she knew it was wild, obscene music. Picking up her coat, she stalked out of the house and headed up the street toward the restaurant.

So far as Monty was concerned, Mildred knew this was the end, but she didn't do anything about it at once. She received him as usual when he dropped in at the restaurant that night, and the next two or three nights. She even submitted to his embraces, deriving a curious satisfaction from the knowledge that his access to the very best legs was rapidly drawing to a close. Stoppage of the spending money brought Veda to her milk, as no beating had ever done, and when it did, Mildred forgave her quite honestly, in a teary little scene two or three days after Christmas. It was almost automatic with her by now to acquit Veda of wrongdoing, no matter how flagrant the offense. In her mind, the blame was all Monty's, and presently she knew exactly how she would deal with him, and when. It would be at the

New Year's party he had invited her to, a week or so before. "I thought I'd ask Paul and Louise Ewing—polo players, but you might like them. We could meet at my house around ten, have a drink, then go in to the Biltmore, for the noisy part."

This had obviously been an effort to kill two birds with one stone, to give some plausibility to what he had said about her hours, and at the same time introduce her to somebody, quite as though he would have done so all along if only the right kind of evening had presented itself. She had taken it as evidence of a change of heart, and accepted. Indeed, she had more than accepted. She had consulted anxiously with Mrs. Gessler over what she should wear, and gone into Bullock's and picked out an evening gown. Then she had gone into a veritable agony over the question of a coat. She didn't have a fur coat, and the prospect of making her debut in the world of mink with nothing but her battered blue haunted her horribly. But Mrs. Gessler, as usual, stepped into the breach. She knew a lady, it seemed, with a brocade coat. "It's a beautiful thing, baby, ashy rose, all crusted with gold, just what you want with your hair. It's really a Chinese mandarin's coat, but it's been re-cut, and you couldn't put a price on it. There's nothing like it on sale anywhere. It'll be the snappiest thing in the room, even at the Biltmore, and—she's broke. She needs the money. I'll see what I can do."

So for $25, Mildred got the coat, and when the dress arrived, she caught her breath at the total effect. The dress was light blue, and gave something to the rose of the coat, so she was a-shimmer with the delicate colors that her general colorlessness needed. She bought gold stockings and gold shoes, and her panic changed to smug complacency. All this had been before Christmas, and her choice of the New Year's party as the occasion for the break with Monty may possibly have been prompted by a matter-of-fact determination not to let such a costume go to waste, as well as a vivid recollection of the $40 she had contributed to the expense. However, no such motive obtruded on her own virtuous consciousness. It was merely, she told herself, that a resolve had to be made, and New Year's morning was a very good time to make it. As she rehearsed the scene mentally, it became clear in its details, and she knew exactly how she would play it. At the Biltmore, she would be gay, and rattle her rattle, and throw her balloon, and tell the story of Harry Engel and the anchors. Back at Monty's house, she would watch the Ewings take their departure, and then, at his invitation to come in, she would decline, and climb into her car. Then, at his surprised look, she would make a little speech. She would say nothing of Veda, or money, or legs. She would merely remark that all things had to come to an end sometime, and it looked as though he and she had reached that point. It had been very pleasant, she had enjoyed his company, every minute of it, she wished him the very best in the world, and she certainly hoped he would regard her as his friend. But—and at this point she saw herself putting out a graceful hand, and in case he merely stood there looking at it, as stepping on the starter.

The whole thing, perhaps, was a little stuffy, and certainly it was singsongy, as she kept adding to it. But it was her valedictory, and no doubt her privilege to deliver it any way she chose.

December 31, 1933, dawned dark in California, and before the morning was over, quite a little rain was falling. By midafternoon, tall tales interrupted the broadcasts: of washouts in the hills, of whole families evacuated from this village and that village, of roads blocked, of trains held in Arizona pending dispatcher's orders. But in Glendale, except for the wet, and quite a little rubble that washed down on the streets, nothing ominous met the eye, and Mildred viewed the downpour as an annoyance, a damper on business, but nothing to get excited about. Around five o'clock, when it didn't let up, she stopped Mrs. Kramer from sectioning more chickens, on the ground that nobody would be there to eat them, and they could wait until next day. When Arline, Emma, and Audrey successively called up to say they couldn't get there, she thought little of it, and when Sigrid came, she set her to cleaning silver.

Around six, Monty called up to know if she had cold feet. Laughing, she asked: "What from?"

"Well, it's a little wet."

"Do you mean *you're* getting cold feet?"

"No, not at all. Just being the perfect host and giving you one last chance to back out if you want to."

"Why, this little shower is nothing."

"Then I'll be expecting you."

"Around ten."

By seven thirty not one customer had showed up, and Mrs. Gessler abruptly suggested that they close, and begin getting Mildred dressed, if she was still fool enough to go to the damned party. Mildred agreed, and started her preparations to lock up. Then she, Mrs. Gessler, Mrs. Kramer, Pancho, Josie, and Sigrid all burst out laughing at the discovery that there *were* no preparations—no dishes to wash, no bottles to put out, no cash to count. Mildred simply cut the lights and locked the door, and as the others went scuttling off into the night, she and Mrs. Gessler climbed into her car and drove down Pierce Drive. It was a little windswept, a little rough from the stones that had washed down on it, but otherwise as usual. Mildred parked close by the kitchen door and dived inside, then held out her hand to Mrs. Gessler.

She was surprised to find Letty and Veda there. Letty had been afraid to start home, and timidly asked Mildred if she could spend the night. Veda, due long ago at the Hannens' for dinner, a party, and an overnight visit, said Mrs. Hannen had called to say the party had been postponed. At this, Mrs. Gessler looked sharply at Mildred, and Mildred went calmly to her room and began taking off her uniform.

By nine, Mildred was powdered, puffed, perfumed, and patted to that state of semi-transparency that a woman seems to achieve when she is really dressed to go out. Her hair, waved the day before, was fluffed out softly; her dress adjusted to the last fold and flounce; her face fashioned to the fish-eyed look that marks the last stage of such rites. Letty was entranced, and even Veda admitted that "you really look quite nice, Mother." Mildred stood before the full-length mirror for a final critical inspection, but Mrs. Gessler disappeared for a final look at the night. When she came back she camped on the bed, and looked moodily at Mildred. "Well, I hate to say it after taking all that trouble over you, but I wouldn't go to that party, if I were you."

"Why, for heaven's sake?"

"Because it's bad out there. You call that idiot up and tell him you're not coming."

"Can't."

"Oh he'll understand. He'll be relieved."

"His phone's disconnected."

"It would be. Then send him a wire. It won't be delivered till tomorrow, but it'll prove you got manners."

"I'm going."

"Baby, you *can't*."

"I said I'm going."

Irritated, Mrs. Gessler ordered Veda to get the trench coat she wore to school, and her galoshes. Mildred protested, but when Veda appeared with the things, Mrs. Gessler went to work. She pinned Mildred's dress up, so it was a sort of sash around her hips, with a foot of white slip showing. Then she put on the galoshes, over the gold shoes. Then she put on the evening coat, and pulled the trench coat over it. Then she found a kerchief, and bound it tightly around Mildred's head. Mildred, suddenly transformed into something that looked like Topsy, sweetly said good-bye to them all. Then she went to the kitchen door, reached out into the wet, and pulled open the car door. Then she hopped in. Then she started the motor. Then she started the wiper. Then she tucked the robe around her. Then, waving gaily to the three anxious faces at the door, she started the car, and went backing down to the street.

Turning into Colorado Boulevard, she laughed. Snug in her two coats, with the motor humming smoothly and the wiper chattering cheerfully against the glass, she thought it funny that people should get so excited over a little rain.

Heading down into Eagle Rock, she was halted by two men with lanterns. One of them came over, and in a hoarse voice asked: "Pasadena?"

"Yes."

"You can't get through. Not without you detour."

"Well? Which way do I go?"

He took off his hat, swooshed the water out of it, then quickly put it on again and gave intricate directions as to how she was to drive up to the hills, then turn and follow along the higher ground until she came to Colorado Boulevard again. "That is, if you don't hit washouts. But believe me, lady, unless you got to get there tonight, it'll be a whole lot better to turn back."

Mildred, perfectly familiar with the road, took up her journey again. She came to a washout, where part of the hill had slid down on the road, but one track was still open, and she slipped easily by. She came back to Colorado Boulevard at a point not far from the high bridge, so popular with suicides at the time, and went splashing across. At the traffic circle she turned right into Orange Grove Avenue. Except for a few tree limbs that had blown down on it, and a lot of leaves, it was clear. As she rolled over its shining black expanse, she laughed again at the way people got all worked up over nothing.

On the portico of the Beragon mansion a light was lit. She turned in through the pillars and followed the drive up past the big trees, the iron dogs, and the marble urn. She parked at the steps, and had hardly cut the motor when Monty popped out of the door, in a dinner coat, and stared as though he could hardly believe his eyes. Then he yelled something at her, popped in the house again, and emerged, carrying a big doorman's umbrella with one hand and dragging a gigantic tarpaulin with the other. The tarpaulin he hurriedly threw over her hood to keep the rain out of the motor. The umbrella he opened for her, and as she made a nimble jump for the portico, said: "God, I had no idea you'd show up. It didn't even enter my mind."

"You put the light on, and got all dressed up. If you don't look out I'll begin wondering who you *were* expecting."

"All that was before I turned on the radio and heard what it's really like out there. How in the *hell* did you get here anyway? For the last hour it's been nothing but a story of bridges out, roads blocked, whole towns under water, and yet—here you are."

"Don't believe everything you hear."

Inside, Mildred saw the reason for the tarpaulin he had produced so unexpectedly, quite as though he kept such things around in case they were needed. The whole place was under gray, ghostly cloths that covered rugs, furniture, even paintings. She shivered as she looked into the great dark drawing room, and he laughed. "Pretty gloomy, hey? Not quite so bad upstairs." He led the way up the big staircase, snapping on lights and then snapping them off when she had passed; through several big bedrooms, all under cloths as the drawing room was, to a long narrow hall, at the end of which was the tiny apartment where he lived. "This is my humble abode. How do you like it?"

"Why it's—quite nice."

"Really servants' quarters, but I moved into them because I could have a little fire—and they seemed cozier, somehow."

The furnishings had the small, battered, hand-me-down look of servants' quarters, but the fire was friendly. Mildred sat down in front of it and slipped off the galoshes. Then she took off the kerchief and trench coat, and unpinned her dress. His face lit up as she emerged like a butterfly from her very drab cocoon, and he turned her around, examining every detail of her costume. Then he kissed her. For a moment he had the old sunny look, and she had to concentrate hard to remember her grievances. Then he said such grandeur deserved a drink. She was afraid that with a drink she couldn't remember any grievances at all, and asked if they hadn't better wait until the Ewings got there. "The—who did you say?"

"Isn't that their name?"

"Good God, they can't get here."

"Why not?"

"They live on the other side of Huntington Avenue, and it's three feet deep in water, and—how in the *hell* did you get here? Haven't you heard there's a storm going on? I think you were hiding two blocks up the street, and just pretended to drive over from Glendale."

"*I* didn't see any storm."

Following him into the bedroom, to see if she could be of help with the drink, she got a shock. It was a tiny cubicle, with one window and a hummocksy bed, on which were her trench coat and a cocktail service, consisting of a great silver shaker, a big B on its side, and beautiful crystal glasses. But not seven feet away, in the smallest, meanest bathroom she had ever seen, he was chopping away at a piece of ice he had evidently procured earlier in the day. Near him, on a small table, she could see a little two-burner gas fixture, a box of eggs, a package of bacon, and a can of coffee. Wishing she hadn't come, she went back and resumed her seat by the fire.

He served the drinks presently, and she had two. When he reached for the shaker to pour her a third, she stopped him. "If I'm going to drive, I think I've had enough."

"Drive? Where to?"

"Why—isn't the Biltmore where we're going?"

"Mildred—we're not going anywhere."

"Well we certainly are."

"Listen—"

He stepped over and snapped on a small radio. An excited announcer was telling of bridges down between Glendale and Burbank, of a wrecked automobile on the San Fernando Road, of the fear that a whole family had been lost with the car. She tossed her head petulantly. "Well, my goodness, the Biltmore's not in Burbank."

"Wherever it is, and however we go to get to it, we have to cross the Los Angeles River, and by last report it's a raging torrent, with half the bridges out and three feet of water boiling over the rest. We're not going. The New Year's party is here."

He filled her glass and she began to sulk. In spite of the liquor, the main idea of the evening was still clear in her mind, and this turn of events was badly interfering with it. When he put his arm around her, she didn't respond. Amiably, he said she was a very problematical drunk. On two drinks she'd argue with Jesus Christ, on three she'd agree with Judas Iscariot. Now would she kindly tilt over No. 3, so she'd be in a frame of mind to welcome the New Year the way it deserved? When she didn't touch the drink, he asked for her key, so he could put her car in the garage. When she made no move to give it to him, he went downstairs.

Somewhere in the house, water began to drip. She shivered, for the first time really becoming aware of the rain that was cascading down the windows, roaring on the roof. She began to blame him for that too. When he came back, and took a sharp look at her face, he seemed a little bored. "Well, if you still feel like that, I suppose there's nothing to do but go to bed. . . . I pulled that cloth clear over your car, so it'll probably be all right. I have green pajamas and red. Which do you prefer?"

"I'm not going to bed."

"You're not very amusing here."

"I'm going home."

"Then good night. But in case you change your mind, I'll put out the green pajamas, and—"

"I haven't gone yet."

"Of course you haven't. I'm inviting—"

"Why did you tell her that?"

What with the liquor, the rain, and his manner, her grievances had heavy compression behind them now, and she exploded with a snarl that left her without the least recollection of all the stuffy little things she had intended to say. He looked at her in astonishment. "Tell whom what? If you don't mind my asking."

"You know perfectly well what I'm talking about. How could you say such things to that child? And who gave you the right to talk about my legs anyhow?"

"Everybody else does. Why not me?"

"What?"

"Oh come, come, come. Your legs are the passion of your life. They all but get a cheer when you appear with them in that Pie Wagon, and if you don't want them talked about, you ought to wear your skirts longer. But you *do* want them talked about, and looked at, and generally envied, so why this howling fit? And after all, they *are* damned good-looking."

"We're talking about my child."

"Oh for God's sake, what do you mean, child? If she's a child, she's forgotten more about such things than you'll ever know. You ought to keep up with the times. I don't know how it was once—maybe the sweet young things were told by their mothers at the age of seventeen and were greatly surprised, you can't prove it by me. But now—they know all there is to know before they've even been told about Santa Claus. Anyway, she knows. What am I supposed to do? Act like a zany when I drive off with you at night and don't bring you back until the next morning? Do you think she doesn't know where you've been? Hell she even asks me how many times."

"And you tell her?"

"Sure. She greatly admires my capacity—and yours. Yours she simply can't get over. 'Who'd think the poor mope had it in her?'"

As Monty mimicked Veda, Mildred knew this was nothing he had invented, as a sort of counter-offensive. Her rage mounted still higher. She said "I see," then said it over again, three or four times. Then, getting up and going over to him, she asked: "And how about the best legs being found in kitchens, not in the drawing room?"

"What in the hell are you talking about?"

"You know what I'm talking about."

Monty stared, touched his brow, as though in a great effort of recollection. Then, snapping his fingers briskly, he said: "Oh, I knew there was something familiar about that. Yes, I did give a little dissertation along those lines one afternoon. We passed a girl—she had on a uniform of some sort, and an apron— quite a pretty little thing, especially around the ankles. And I got that off—what you've just quoted. Nothing original, I assure you. I had almost forgotten it. . . . How does that concern us?"

He was plausible, circumstantial, casual, but a little flicker around the eyes betrayed him. Mildred didn't answer his question. She came over close, and there was something snakelike about her as she said: "That's a lie. You weren't talking about any girl you saw on the street. You were talking about me."

Monty shrugged and Mildred went back to her chair and sat down. Then she began to talk slowly, but with rising stridency. She said he had deliberately tried to set Veda against her, to hold her up to ridicule, to make the child think of her as an inferior, somebody to be ashamed of. "I see it all now. I always thought it was funny she never invited any of these people over here in Pasadena to see *her* once in a while. Not that I don't give her the opportunity. Not that I don't remind her that you can't accept invitations all the time without giving any in return. Not that I didn't do my part. But no. Because you were filling her up with all this foolishness, she's been ashamed to ask these people over. She actually believes Glendale is not good enough for them. She thinks I'm not good enough. She—"

"Oh for God's sake shut up."

Monty's eyes were black now, and had little hard points of light in them. "In the first place, what invitations did she accept? My mother's, right here in this house. Well, we went all over that once, and we're not going over it again. And to the Hannens'. And so far as I know the only invitation Charlie and Roberta ever got out of you was an invitation to go over and buy their dinner in that Pie Wagon, and they did go over, and—"

"No check was ever presented to them."

"O.K., then you're square. For the rest, who the hell would expect a kid of fourteen to be doing something about every cocktail party I dragged her to? She asked about it, and I said it would be silly. Come on. What else?"

"That may be all right, for older people. But there have been plenty of others she's met, girls her own age—"

"No, there haven't. And right there's where I suggest you get better acquainted with your own daughter. She's a strange child. Girls her own age don't interest her. She likes older women—"

"If they're rich."

"Anyway, she's damned nice to them. And it's unusual as hell. And you can't blame them for liking it. And liking her. But as for her trying to throw some kind of a shindig for them, what are you trying to do, make me laugh?"

In some elusive, quicksilver way that she couldn't get her finger on, Mildred felt the argument slipping away from her, and like Veda, she abandoned logic and began to scream: "You've set her against me! I don't care a bit for your fine talk—*you've set her against me!*"

Monty lit a cigarette, smoked sullenly a few moments without speaking. Then he looked up. "Ah! So this is why you came. Stupid of me not to have thought of it sooner."

"I came because I was invited."

"On a night like this?"

"It's as good a time as any other."

"What a nice little pal *you* turned out to be.... Funny—I had something to say, too."

He looked with a little self-pitying smile into the fire, evidently decided to keep his intentions to himself, then changed his mind. "... *I* was going to say you'd make a fine wife for somebody—if you didn't live in Glendale."

She had been feeling outpointed, but at this all her self-righteousness came back. Leaning forward, she stared at him. "Monty, you can still say that? After what I've said to you? Just to have somebody take care of you, you'd ask me to marry you? Haven't you any more self-respect than that?"

"Ah, but that's what I *was* going to say."

"Monty, don't make it any worse than it is. If I got excited about it, you were going to let it stay said. If I didn't, you were going to pretend that was what you *were* going to say. Gee, Monty, but you're some man, aren't you?"

"Now suppose you listen to what I *am* going to say."

"No, I'm going home."

She got up, but he leaped at her, seized her by both arms, and flung her back in her chair. The little glittering points of light in his eyes were dancing now, and his face was drawn and hard. "Do you know why Veda never invites anybody to that house of yours? Do you know why nobody, except that string-bean that lives next door, ever goes there?"

"Yes—because you set her against me and—"

"Because you *are* a goddam varlet, and you're afraid to have people come there, because you wouldn't know what to do about them—you just haven't got the nerve."

Looking into his contorted face, she suddenly had the same paralyzed, shrunken feeling she had had the morning Miss Turner told her off, and sent her over to the housekeeper's job, because there was nothing else she could do. And she kept shrinking, as Monty went on, pouring a torrent of bitter, passionate invective at her. "It's not her. It's not me. It's you. Doesn't that strike you as funny? That Veda has a hundred friends, here, there, everywhere she goes, and that you haven't any? No, I'm wrong—you have one. That bartender. And that's all. Nobody ever gets invited to your house, nobody—"

"What are you talking about? How can I give parties, or invite people, with a living to make? Why you—"

"Living, my eye! That's the alibi, not the reason. You damned little kitchen scullion, you'd tell *me* who's setting your child against you? *Me?* Listen, Mildred. Nobody but a varlet would give a second's thought to what you've been talking about tonight. Because that's the difference. A lady doesn't care. A varlet does."

He walked around, panting, then turned on her again. "And I like a fool, like a damned idiot, I once thought maybe I'd been mistaken, that you were a lady, and not a varlet. That was when you handed me the $20 bill that night, and I took it. And then I took more. I even gave you credit for something. God knows what it is, some sense of humor that only an aristocrat ever has, and *asked* you for money. And then what? Could you go through with it? The very thing that you yourself started? A lady would have cut her heart out before she let *me* know the money meant anything. But you, before I had even fifty bucks out of you, you had to make a chauffeur out of me, didn't you? To get your money's worth? A lackey, a poodle dog. You had to rub it in. Well no more. I've taken my last dime off you, and God willing, before my sun goes down, I'll pay you back. Why you scum, you—waitress. I guess that's one reason I love Veda. She wouldn't pick up a tip. That's one thing she wouldn't do— and neither would I."

"Except from me."

White with rage, she opened her evening bag, took out a crisp $10 bill, threw it at his feet. He took the fire tongs, picked it up, dropped it on the fire. When the flame flared up he took out a handkerchief and mopped his face.

For a time, nothing was said by either of them, and when their panting had died down, Mildred began to feel ashamed, defeated, and miserable. She had said it all, had goaded him to say it all too, those things that she knew he felt, and that left her crumpled and unable to answer. Yet nothing had been settled: there he was and there she was. As she looked at him, she saw for the first time that he was tired, worn, and haggard, with just a touch of middle age dragging at what she had always thought of as a youthful face. Then a gush of terrible affection for him swept over her, compounded of pity, contempt, and something motherly. She wanted to cry, and suddenly reached over and rubbed his bald spot. For a long time, it had been a little joke between them. He made no move, but he didn't repulse her either, and when she leaned back she felt better. Then again she heard the rain, and for the first time was afraid of it. She drew the coat around her. Then she picked up Manhattan No. 3, drank half of it, set it down again. Without looking at her, he filled her glass. They sat a long time, neither of them looking at the other.

Then abruptly, as though he had solved a very difficult problem, he banged his fist on the arm of his chair, and said: "Damn it, what this needs is the crime of rape!"

He came over, put one arm around her, slipped the other under her legs, and carried her into the bedroom. A little moaning laugh escaped her as he dumped her down on the hummocksy bed. She felt weak and drugged. In a moment, the brocaded coat was off, was sliding to the floor. She thought of her dress, and didn't care: she wanted him to rip it off her, to tear it away in shreds, if he had to, so he got her out of it. But he wasn't ripping it off. He was fumbling with the zipper, and for a moment her fingers were over his, trying to help. Then something stirred inside of her, an unhappy recollection of what she had come for, of what had been piling up between them these last few months. She fought it off, tried to make it sink under the overwhelming blend of liquor, man, and rain. It wouldn't sink. If she had lifted a mountain, it couldn't have been harder than it was to put both palms in Monty's face, push him away, squirm off the bed, and lurch to her feet. She grabbed both coats, ran into the other room. He was after her, trying to drag her back, but she fought him off as she snatched up the galoshes and dashed into the dark hall.

Somehow, she got through the ghostly rooms, down the stairs, and to the front door. It was locked. She twisted the big brass key, and at last was on the portico, in the cold wet air. She pulled on both coats, stepped into the galoshes. Then suddenly the light came on, and he was beside her, reaching for her, trying to pull her back. She dashed out into the rain, yanked the cloth off the car, let it fall in the mud, and jumped in. As she snapped on the lights and started the motor, she could see him under the light, gesticulating at her, expostulating with her. There was nothing of passion in his face now. He was angrily telling her not to be a fool, not to go out in the storm.

She started out. On Orange Grove Avenue more tree limbs were down, and it didn't look so sleek and harmless. She pulled in to the curb, found the kerchief in the trench coat pocket, tied it around her head. Then, cautiously, feeling a throb of fright every time the car bucked in the wind, she went on. As she turned at the traffic circle, she caught the lights of another car, behind.

There were no men with lanterns now, nothing but the black, wild, and terrible night. She got over the bridge without trouble, but when she came to the detour, she was afraid, and waited until the other car caught up a little. Then she went on, noting with relief that the other car turned into the detour too. She had no trouble for a mile or so, and then she came to the washout. To her dismay it had spread: the road was completely blocked. All resolution having deserted her, she stopped and waited, to see what the other car was going to do. It stopped, and she watched. A door slammed, and she strained her eyes to see. Then Monty's face was at the window, not six inches from her own. Water was pouring off an old felt hat, and off the slicker that was buttoned to his ears. Furiously he pointed at the washout. "Look at that! It never occurred to you there'd be something like that, did it? Damn it, the trouble you're putting me to!"

For a moment or two, as he savagely ordered her to lock the car, get out, and come back with him, she had a happy, contented feeling, as though he were her father, she a bad little girl that would be taken care of, anyway. Then once more her fixed resolve rose in her. She shifted into reverse and backed. She backed past his car, came to a corner, headed into it. When she had followed the new road a few feet, she saw it led down into Eagle Rock. It was full of rubble, and she proceeded by inches, rolling and braking, then rolling on again. Then ahead of her she saw that the rubble stopped, that a black shining road lay ahead. She stepped on the gas. It was the check of the car that told her the black shining road was black shining water. When she stepped on the brake the car slid right on. The lights went out. The motor stopped. The car stopped. She was alone in a pool that extended as far as she could see. When she took her foot off the brake she felt it splash into a puddle. She screamed.

The rain was driving against her, and she wound up the window. Outside, she could hear the purling of the torrent against the wheels, and in a moment or two the car began to move. She guided it to the right, and when she felt it catch the curb, pulled up the hand brake. Then she sat there. In a few minutes, her breath had misted the glass so she could see nothing. Then the door beside her was jerked open, and once more Monty was standing there. He had evidently gone back to his car to take off his trousers, for as the slicker floated on the pool she could see he was in his shorts. He braced his right arm against the doorjamb. "All right, now throw your legs over my arm, and put your arm around my neck. Hold on tight, and I think I can get you to the top of the hill."

She lifted her feet to the seat, took off the gold shoes and stockings, put them in the dashboard compartment. Then she put on the galoshes, over her bare feet. Then she wriggled out of both coats and the dress. The dress and the brocaded coat she stuffed over the shoes, closed the compartment and locked it. Then shivering, she got into the trench coat. Then she motioned to Monty to move his hand. When he did, she pulled the door shut and snapped the catch. Then she slipped out the opposite door, locking it. A yelp came out of her as she stepped off the running board and felt the water around her thighs, and the current almost swept her off her feet. But she held on to the door handle and steadied herself. Above her was a high bank, evidently with some sort of sidewalk on top of it. Paying no attention to Monty and his barely audible shouts, she scrambled up, and then slipped, slid, and staggered home through the worst storm in the annals of the Los Angeles weather bureau, or of any weather bureau.

She passed many cars stalled as hers was stalled, some deserted, some full of people. One car, caught between vast lakes of water, was standing near a curb, its top lights on, filled with people in evening clothes, helpless to do anything but sit. She slogged on, up the long hill to Glendale, down block after block of rubble, torrents, seas of water. Her galoshes filled repeatedly, and periodically she stopped, holding first one foot high behind her, then the other, to let the water run out. But she couldn't let the sand and pebbles out, and they cut her feet cruelly. She was in a hysteria of weakness, cold, and pain when she finally reached Pierce Drive, and half ran, half limped, the rest of the way to the house.

Veda and Letty, like two frightened kittens, hadn't slept very well that night, and when lights began to snap on in the house, and a sobbing, mud-spattered, staggering apparition appeared at their door, they screamed in terror. When they realized it was Mildred, they dutifully followed her to her room, but it was seconds before they got readjusted to the point of helping her out of her clothes and getting her into bed. But suddenly Letty recovered from her fright, and was soon running around frantically, getting Mildred what she needed, especially whiskey, coffee, and a hot-water bottle. Veda sat on the bed, chafing Mildred's hands, spooning the scalding coffee into her mouth, pushing the covers close around her. Presently she shook her head. "But Mother, I simply can't understand it. Why didn't you stay with him? After all, it wouldn't have been much of a novelty."

"Never mind. Tomorrow you get your piano."

At Veda's squeal of delight, at the warm arms around her neck, the sticky kisses that started at her eyes and ended away below her throat, Mildred relaxed, found a moment of happiness. As the gray day broke, she fell into a deep sleep.

For some time after that, Mildred was too busy to pay much attention to Veda. Relieved of Monty, she began to have money, above installments on the piano and everything else. In spite of hard times, her business grew better; the bar shook down into a profitable sideline; most important of all, she paid off the last of the $4,000 she had owed for the property, and last of her equipment notes. Now the place was hers, and she took a step she had been considering for some time. The pies put a dreadful strain on her kitchen, so she built an annex, out back of the parking space, to house them as a separate unit. There was some little trouble about it, on account of the zoning regulations. But when she submitted acceptable exterior plans, which made it look like a rather large private garage, and agreed to display no advertising except the neon sign she was already using, the difficulty was smoothed out. When it was finished, she added pastries to her list, clever items suitable for restaurant perambulators, and had little trouble selling them. Hans presently needed an assistant, and then another. She bought a new truck, a really smart one. About the same time she turned in the car, never quite recovered from the battering it took in the storm, and bought a new one, a sleek maroon Buick with white tires that Veda kissed when the dealer delivered it.

But when Ida, who was a regular visitor now, saw the annex, she grew thoughtful, and then one night started a campaign to get Mildred to open a branch in Beverly, with herself as manager. "Mildred, I know what I'm talking about. That town is just crying for a place that will put out a real line of ready desserts. Think of the entertaining they do over there. Them movie people giving parties every night, and the dessert nothing but a headache to them women. And look how easy you can give them what they want—why you're making all that stuff right now. And look at the prices you'll get. And look at the sidelines you got. Look at the fountain trade. Look at the sandwich trade. And I can do it all with four girls, a fountain man, a short-order cook, and a dish washer."

Mildred, not wanting to assume risk when she had a certainty, was in no hurry about it. But she drove over to Beverly and made inquiries, and began to suspect that Ida was right. Then, snooping around one afternoon, she ran into a vacant property that she knew would be right for location. When she found out she could get a lease for an absurdly small rental, she made up her mind. There followed another hectic month of furniture, fixtures, and alterations. She wanted the place done in maple, but Ida obstinately held out for light green walls and soft, upholstered booths where people would find it comfortable to sit. Mildred gave way, but on the day of the opening she almost fainted. Without consulting her, Ida had ordered a lot of preserves, cakes, health breads, and other things she knew nothing about. Ida however said *she* herself knew all about them, at any rate all that was necessary to know. By the end of the week, Mildred was not only convinced, but completely flabbergasted. Ida's report was ecstatic: "Mildred, we're in. In the first place I got a lunch trade that's almost like the Brown Derby. People that don't *want* planked whitefish and special hamburgers. They want those little sandwiches I got, and the fruit salads, and you just ought to hear the comment. And I don't hardly get them cleared out before I got a college trade, wonderful refined kids on their way home from Westwood that want a chocolate soda or a malt before they start playing tennis. And when they go my tea trade starts, and on top of that I got a little dinner trade, people that want to eat light before they catch a preview or something. And then on top of that I got a late trade, people that just want a cup of chocolate and a place to talk. From twelve noon until twelve midnight I got *business*. And the take-out trade from those people, it's enough to take your breath away." The receipts bore her out. Ida was to get $30 a week, plus 2 per cent of the gross. She had hoped, in time, to make $50 a week. That very first Saturday night Mildred wrote her a check for $53.71.

But it wasn't all smooth sailing. Mrs. Gessler, when she heard what Mildred was up to, flew into a rage, and wanted to know why Ida had been singled out to manage the Beverly branch, instead of herself. Mildred tried to explain that it was all Ida's idea, that some people are suited to one thing, some to another, but got nowhere. Mrs. Gessler continued bitter, and Mildred grew worried. She had come to depend on her tall, thin, profane bartender as she depended on nobody else, not only for shrewd business advice but also for some sort of emotional support that her nature demanded. Losing her would be a calamity, and she began to consider what could be done.

At that time there was considerable talk about the rise of Laguna Beach, a resort along the coast, a few miles below Long Beach. Mildred began to wonder if it would be a good place for still another branch, with Mrs. Gessler in charge. She drove down a number of times and looked it over. Except for one place, she found no restaurants that impressed her, and unquestionably the resort was coming up, not only for summer trippers, but for year-round residents as well. Again it was the lease that decided her. She found a large house, with considerable land around it, on a bluff, overlooking the ocean. With an expert eye, she noted what would have to be done to it, noted that the grounds would be expensive to keep up. But when the terms were quoted to her, they were so low that she knew she could make a good profit if she got any business at all. They were so low that for a brief time she was suspicious, but the agent said the explanation was simple enough. It had been a private home, but it couldn't be rented for that, as it was entirely too big for most of the people who came down from the city just to get a coat of tan. Furthermore, the beach in front of it was studded with rocks and was therefore unsuitable to swimming. For all ordinary purposes it was simply a turkey, and if she could use it, it was hers at the rate quoted. Mildred inspected the view, the house, the grounds, and felt a little tingle inside. Abruptly, she paid $25 cash for a ten-day option, and that night held Mrs. Gessler after closing time for a little talk. But she barely got started when Mrs. Gessler broke in: "Oh shut up, will you for God's sake shut up?"

"But—aren't you *interested?*"

"Does a duck like water? Listen, it's halfway between L.A. and San Diego, isn't it? Right on the main line, and Ike still has his trucks. It's the first honest-to-God's chance he's had to get started again, in a legal way, since—well, you know. And it gets him out of this lousy place. Do you want me bawling right on your shoulder?"

"What's the matter with this place?"

"It's not the place, it's him. O.K., I'm working, see, and he has to find something to do with himself, at night. So he finds it. He says it's pool, and he does come home with chalk all over him. I'll say that for him. But he's a liar. It's a frazzle-haired blonde that works in one of those antique furniture factories on Los Feliz. Nothing serious maybe, but he sees her. It's what I've been so jittery about, if you've got to know. And now, if I can just get him out of here, and in business again so he can hold his head up—well, maybe that'll be that. Go on, tell me some more."

So once again Mildred was in a flurry of alterations, purchases of inventory, and arguments about policy. She wanted a duplicate of the Glendale place, which would specialize in chicken, waffles, and pies, and operate a small bar as a sideline. Mrs. Gessler, however, had other ideas. "Do they come all the way to the ocean just to get chicken? Not if I know them. They want a shore dinner—fish, lobster, and crab—and that's what we're giving them. And that's where we make the dough. Don't forget: fish is cheap. But we've got to have a little variety, so we give them steak, right from our own built-in charcoal broiler."

When Mildred protested that she knew nothing about steaks, or fish, or lobster, or crab, and would be helpless to do the marketing, Mrs. Gessler replied she could learn. It wasn't until she sent for Mr. Otis, the federal meat inspector who had been romantic about her in her waitress days, that her alarm eased a little. He came to the Glendale restaurant one night, and confirmed her suspicions that there were about a hundred different ways to lose money on steaks. But when he talked with Mrs. Gessler he was impressed. He told Mildred she was "smart," and probably knew where she was coming out. It depended mainly, he said, on the chef, and to Mildred's surprise he recommended Archie, of Mr. Chris's establishment. Archie, he assured her, had been wasted for years in a second-class place, but "he's still the best steak man in town, bar none. Any bum can cook fish and make money on it, so don't worry about that. But on steaks, you've got to have somebody that knows his stuff. You can't go wrong on Archie."

So Mildred stole Archie off Mr. Chris, and under his dour supervision installed the built-in charcoal broiler. Presently, after signs had been put up along the road, and announcements inserted in the Los Angeles papers, the place opened. It was never the snug little gold mine that Ida's place was, for Mrs. Gessler was careless of expenses, and tended to slight the kitchen in favor of the bar. But her talent at making a sort of club out of whatever she touched drew big business. The ingenuity with which she worked out the arrangements drew Mildred's reluctant admiration. The big living room of the house was converted into a maple-panelled bar, with dim lights. The rooms behind it were joined together in a cluster of small dining rooms, each with a pleasant air of intimacy about it. One of them opened on a veranda that ran around the house, and out here were tables for outdoor drinkers, bathing suiters, and the overflow trade. But the most surprising thing to Mildred was the flower garden. She had never suspected Mrs. Gessler of any such weakness, but within a few weeks the whole brow of the bluff was planted with bushes, and here, it appeared, was where Mrs. Gessler spent her mornings, spading, pruning, and puttering with a Japanese gardener. The expense, what with the water and the gardener, was high, but Mrs. Gessler shrugged it off. "We're running a high-class dump, baby, and we've got to have something. For some reason I don't understand, a guy with an old-fashioned on the table likes to listen to the bumblebees." But when the flowers began to bloom, Mildred paid without protest, because she liked them. At twilight, just before the dinner rush, she would stroll among them, smelling them and feeling proud and happy. On one of these strolls Mrs. Gessler joined her, and then led her a block or two down the main road that ran through the town. Then she stopped and pointed, and across the street Mildred saw the sign:

GESSLER
LONG & SHORT DISTANCE
HAULING
DAY & NIGHT
SERVICE!

Mrs. Gessler looked at it intently. "He's on call all the time, too. All he needed was a chance. Next week he's getting a new truck, streamlined."

"Is everything all right upstairs?"

Mildred had reference to the terms of Mrs. Gessler's employment. She didn't get $30 a week and 2 per cent of the gross, as Ida did. She got $30 and 1 per cent, the rest of her pay being made up of free quarters in the upper part of the house, with light, heat, water, food, laundry, and everything furnished. Mrs. Gessler nodded. "Everything's fine. Ike loves those big rooms, and the sea, and the steaks, and—well, believe it or not he even likes the flowers. 'Service with a gardenia'—he's thinking of having it lettered on the new truck. We're living again, that's all."

Mildred never cooked anything herself now, or put on a uniform. At Glendale, Mrs. Kramer had been promoted to cook, with an assistant named Bella; Mrs. Gessler's place was taken by a man bartender, named Jake; on nights when Mildred was at Beverly or Laguna, Sigrid acted as hostess, and wore the white uniform. Mildred worked from sunup, when her marketing started, until long after dark; she worked so hard she began to feel driven, and relieved herself of every detail she could possibly assign to others. She continued to gain weight. There was still something voluptuous about her figure, but it was distinctly plump. Her face was losing such little color as it had had, and she no longer seemed younger than her years. In fact, she was beginning to look matronly. The car itself, she discovered, took a great deal out of her, and she engaged a driver named Tommy, older brother to Carl, who drove the truck. After some reflection she took him to Bullock's and bought him a uniform, so he could help on the parking lots. When Veda first saw him in this regalia, she didn't kiss him, as she had kissed the car. She gave her mother a long, thoughtful look, full of something almost describable as respect.

And in spite of mounting expenses, the driver, the girl Mildred engaged to keep the books, the money kept rolling in. Mildred paid for the piano, paid off the mortgages Bert had plastered on the house; she renovated, repainted, kept buying new equipment for all her establishments, and still it piled up. In 1936, when Mr. Roosevelt came up for reelection, she was still smarting from the tax she had paid on her 1935 income, and for a few weeks wavered in her loyalty. But then business picked up, and when he said "we planned it that way," she decided she had to take the bitter with the sweet, and voted for him. She began to buy expensive clothes, especially expensive girdles, to make her look thin. She bought Veda a little car, a Packard 120, in dark green, "to go with her hair." On Wally's advice, she incorporated, choosing Ida and Mrs. Gessler as her two directors, in addition to herself. Her big danger, Wally said, was the old woman in Long Beach. "O.K., she's crossing against the lights, Tommy had his brakes on when he hit her, she's not hurt a bit, but when she finds out you've got three restaurants just watch what she does to you. And it works the other way around too. Sooner or later you're going to have those five people that got ptomaine poisoning, from the fish, or say they did. And what those harpies do to you, once they get in court, will be just plain murder. You incorporate, your *personal* property is safe." The old woman in Long Beach, to say nothing of the five harpies on their pots, fretted Mildred terribly, as many things did. She bought fantastic liability insurance, on the car, on the pie factory, on the restaurants. It was horribly expensive, but worth it, to be safe.

Through all the work, however, the endless driving, the worry, the feeling there were not enough hours in the day for all she had to do, one luxury she permitted herself. No matter how the day broke, she was home at three o'clock in the afternoon, for what she called her "rest." It was a rest, to be sure, but that wasn't the main idea. Primarily it was a concert, with herself the sole auditor. When Veda turned sixteen, she persuaded Mildred to let her quit high school, so she could devote her whole time to music. In the morning she did harmony, and what she called "paper work." In the afternoon she practiced. For two hours she practiced exercises, but at three she began to practice pieces, and it was then that Mildred arrived. Tiptoeing in the back way, she would slip into the hall, and for a moment stand looking into the living room, where Veda was seated at the satiny black grand. It was a picture that never failed to thrill her: the beautiful instrument that she had worked for and paid for, the no less beautiful child she had brought into the world; a picture moreover, that she could really call her own. Then, after a soft "I'm home, darling," she would tiptoe to her bedroom, lie down, and listen. She didn't know the names of many of the pieces, but she had her favorites, and Veda usually played one. There was one in particular, something by Chopin, that she liked best of all, "because it reminds me of that song about rainbows." Veda, somewhat ironically, said: "Well

Mother, there's a reason"; but she played it, nevertheless. Mildred was delighted at the way the child was coming along; warm, shy intimacy continued, and Mildred laughed to think she had once supposed that Monty had something to do with it. This, she told herself, was what made everything worthwhile.

One afternoon the concert was interrupted by a phone call. Veda answered, and from the tone of her voice, Mildred knew something was wrong. She came in and sat on the bed, but to Mildred's "What is it darling?" returned no answer at once. Then, after a few moments of gloomy silence, she said: "Hannen's had a hemorrhage."

"Oh my, isn't that awful!"

"He knew it was coming on. He had two or three little ones. This one caught him on the street, while he was walking home from the post office. The ambulance doctor made a mess of it— had him lifted by the shoulders or something—and it's a lot worse than it might have been. Mrs. Hannen's almost in hysterics about it."

"You have to go over there. At once."

"Not today. He's all packed in icebags, and they give him some kind of gas to inhale. It's just hell."

"Is there something I could do? I mean, if there are any special dishes he needs, I can send anything that's wanted, hot, all ready to serve—"

"I can find out."

Veda stared at the Gessler house, now for rent. Then: "God, but I'm going to miss that damned he-bear."

"Well my goodness, he's not *gone* yet."

Mildred said this sharply. She had the true California tradition of optimism in such matters; to her it was almost blasphemous not to hope for the best. But Veda got up heavily and spoke quietly. "Mother, it's bad. I know from the way he's been acting lately that he's known it would be bad, when it came. I can tell from the way she was wailing over that phone that it's bad. . . . And what I'm going to do I don't know."

Special dishes, it turned out, were needed desperately, on the chance that the stricken man could be tempted to eat, and in that way build up his strength. So daily, for a week, a big hamper was delivered by Tommy, full of chicken cooked by Mildred herself, tiny sandwiches prepared by Ida, cracked crab nested in ice by Archie, sherries selected by Mrs. Gessler. Mildred Pierce, Inc., spit on its hands to show what it could do. Then one day Mildred and Veda took the hamper over in person, together with a great bunch of red roses. When they arrived at the house, the morning paper was still on the grass, a market circular was stuffed under the door. They rang, and there was no answer. Veda looked at Mildred, and Tommy carried the things back to the car. That afternoon, a long incoherent telegram arrived for Mildred, dated out of Phoenix, Ariz., and signed by Mrs. Hannen. It told of the wild ride to the sanitarium there, and begged Mildred to have the gas turned off.

Three days later, while Mildred was helping Ida get ready for the Beverly luncheon rush, Veda's car pulled up at the curb. Veda got out, looking half combed and queer. When Mildred unlocked the door for her, she handed over the paper without speaking, went to a booth, and sat down. Mildred stared at the unfamiliar picture of Mr. Hannen, taken before his hair turned white, read the notice of his death with a blank, lost feeling. Then, noting that the funeral was to be held in New York, she went to the phone and ordered flowers. Then she called Western Union, and dictated a long telegram to Mrs. Hannen, full of "heartfelt sympathy from both Veda and myself." Then, still under some dazed compulsion to do something, she stood there, trying to think what. But that seemed to be all. She went over and sat down with Veda. After a while Veda asked one of the girls to bring her coffee. Mildred said: "Would you like to ride to Laguna with me, darling?"

"All right."

For the rest of the day, Veda tagged at Mildred's heels, silent about Mr. Hannen, but afraid, apparently, to be alone. The next day she hung around the house, and when Mildred came home at three, the piano was silent. The day after that, when she still moped, Mildred thought it time to jog her up a bit. Finding her in the den, she said: "Now darling, I know he was a fine man, and that you were very fond of him, but you did all you could do, and after all, these things happen, and—"

"Mother."

Veda spoke quietly, as one would speak to a child. "It isn't that I was fond of him. Not that I didn't love the shaggy brute. To me he'll always be the one and only, and—oh well, never mind. But—he taught me *music,* and—"

"But darling there are other teachers."

"Yes, about seven hundred fakes and advertisers in Los Angeles alone, and I don't know one from another, and besides—"

Veda broke off, having evidently intended to say something, and then changed her mind. Mildred felt something coming, and waited. But Veda evidently decided she wasn't going to say it, and Mildred asked: "Can't you make inquiries?"

"There's one man here, just one, that Hannen had some respect for. His name is Treviso, Carlo Treviso. He's a conductor. He conducts a lot of those operas and things out at the Hollywood Bowl. I don't know if he takes piano pupils or not, but he might know of somebody."

"Do you want me to call him up?"

Veda took so long answering that Mildred became impatient, and wanted to know what it was that Veda was holding back, anyway. "Has it anything to do with money? You know I don't begrudge anything for your instruction, and—"

"Then—call him up."

Mr. Treviso's studio was located in downtown Los Angeles, in a building with several signs beside the door, and as Mildred and Veda walked up to the second floor, a bedlam of noises assailed their ears; tenors vocalizing, pianists running dizzy scales, violinists sawing briskly in double stops. They didn't get in to Mr. Treviso at once. Their knock was answered by a short, fat woman with an Italian accent, who left them in a windowless anteroom and went into the studio. At once there were sounds from within. A baritone would sing a phrase, then stop. Then there would be muffled talk. Then he would sing the same phrase again, and there would be more talk. This went on and on, until Mildred became annoyed. Veda, however, seemed mildly interested. "It's the end of the Pagliacci Prologue, and he can't hit the G on pitch. Well, there's nothing to do about *him*. Treviso might just as well save his time."

"To say nothing of *my* time."

"Mother, this is a wop. So we sit."

Presently the baritone, a stocky, red-faced boy, popped through the door and left sheepishly, and the woman came out and motioned them in. Mildred entered a studio that was rather different from Mr. Hannen's. It was almost as large, but nothing like as austere. The great black piano stood near the windows, and the furniture matched it, in size as well as elegance. Almost covering the walls were hundreds of photographs, all of celebrities so big that even Mildred had heard of some of them, and all inscribed personally to Mr. Treviso. That gentleman himself, clad in a gray suit with black piping on the waistcoat, received them as a ducal counselor might have received a pair of lesser ladies in waiting. A tall, thin Italian of perhaps fifty, with bony face and sombre eyes, he listened while Mildred explained what they had come for, then bowed coldly and waved them to seats. When Veda cut in with what Mildred had neglected to mention, that she had studied with Mr. Hannen, he became slightly less formal, struck a tragic pose and said: "Poor Charl'. Ah, poor, poor Charl'." Then he paid tribute to the Hannen tone, and said it marked him as a great artist, not merely as a pianist. Then, smiling a little, he permitted himself to reminisce. "I first know Charl', was in 1922. We make tour of Italy together, I play Respighi program wit' orchestr', Charl' play Tschaikowsky concerto. Was just after Mussolini come in, and Charl', 'e was afraid somebody make him drink castor oil. Was bad afraid. 'E buy gray spat, black 'at, learn Giovanezaz, change name to Annino, do ever' little t'ing to look like wop. So last concert, was in Turino. After concert, all go to little cafe, 'ave last drink, say good-bye. So concertmaster, 'e make little spich, tell how fine Charl' play Tschaikowsky concerto, say whole orchestr' want make Charl' little gift, express happreciation. 'E give Charl' big mahogany box, look like 'ave gold cup in it, somet'ing pretty nice. Charl', 'e make little spich too, say t'anks boys, sure is big surprise. 'E open box—was roll toilet paper!''

Mr. Treviso's smile had broadened into a grin, and his black eyes sparkled so brightly they almost glared. Mildred, whether because of the anecdote itself, or the recent death of its subject, or the realization that she was in the presence of a point of view completely alien to her, wasn't amused, though she smiled a little, to be polite. But Veda affected to think this was the funniest thing she had ever heard in her life, and egged Mr. Treviso on to more stories. He looked at his watch and said he would now listen to her play.

The Veda who sat down at the piano was a quite different Veda from the one who had so airily entertained Mr. Hannen three years ago. She was genuinely nervous, and it occurred to Mildred that her encouragement to Mr. Treviso's storytelling might have been a stall for time. She thought a moment, then with grim face launched into a piece known to Mildred as the Brahms Rhapsody. Mildred didn't like it much. It went entirely too fast, for her taste, except for a slow part in the middle, that sounded a little like a hymn. However, she sat back comfortably, waiting for the praise that Mr. Treviso would bestow, and that she would tell Ida about, that night.

Mr. Treviso wandered over to the window, and stood looking down at the street. When Veda got to the slow part, he half turned around, as though to say something, then didn't. All during the slow part he stared down at the street. When Veda crashed into the fast part again, he walked over and closed the piano, elaborately giving Veda time to get her hands out of the way. In the bellowing silence that followed, he went to the far corner of the studio and sat down, a ghastly smile on his face, as though he had been prepared for burial by an undertaker who specialized in pleasant expressions.

It was an appreciable interval before it dawned on Mildred

what he had done, and why. Then she looked toward the piano to suggest that Veda play one of her slower pieces. But Veda was no longer there. She was at the door, pulling on her gloves, and before Mildred could say anything, she dived out the door. Mildred jumped up, followed, and in the hall called to her. But Veda was running down the stairs and didn't look up. The next Mildred knew, Tommy was driving them home, and Veda was sitting with writhing face and clenched hands, staring horribly at the floor. Even as Mildred looked, a white line appeared on the back of one of the gloves and it popped.

All the way home Mildred fumed at the way Mr. Treviso had treated them. She said she had never seen anything like that in her life. If he didn't like the way Veda had played the piece, he could have said so like a gentleman, instead of acting like that. And the very idea, having an appointment with two ladies for four o'clock, keeping them waiting until a quarter to five, and then, when they had barely got in the door, telling them a story about *toilet paper*. If that was the only man in Los Angeles that Mr. Hannen had any respect for, she certainly had her opinion of Mr. Hannen's taste. A lot of this expressed Mildred's very real irritation, but some of it was to console Veda, by taking her side after an outrageous episode. Veda said nothing, and when they got home she jumped out of the car and ran in the house. Mildred followed, but when she got to Veda's room, it was locked. She knocked, then knocked again, sharply. Then she commanded Veda to open the door. Nothing happened, and inside there was silence. Letty appeared, and asked in a frightened way what the trouble was. Paying no attention to Letty, Mildred ran out to the kitchen, grabbed a chair, and ran outside. A sudden paralyzing fear had come over her as to what Veda might be doing in there. Putting the chair near the house, she stood on it and raised the screen. Then she stepped into the room. Veda was lying on the bed, staring at the ceiling in the same unseeing way she had stared at the floor of the car. Her hands were still clenching and unclenching, and her features looked thick. Mildred, who had expected at the very least to see an empty iodine bottle lying around somewhere, first felt relieved, then cross. Unlocking the door, she said: "Well my goodness, you don't have to scare everybody to death."

"Mother, if you say my goodness one more time I shall scream, I shall scream!"

Veda spoke in a terrible rasping whisper, then closed her eyes. Stiffening and stretching out her arms as though she were a figure on a crucifix, she began to talk to herself, in a bitter voice, between clenched teeth. "You can kill it—you can kill it right now—you can drive a knife through its heart—so it's dead, dead, *dead*—you can forget you ever tried to play the piano—you can forget there ever was such a thing as a piano—you can—"

"Well my g—. Well for heaven's sake, the piano isn't the only thing on earth. You could—you could *write* music." Pausing, Mildred tried to remember what Bert had said that day, about Irving Berlin, but just then Veda opened her eyes. "You damned, silly-looking cluck, are you trying to drive me *insane?* ... Yes, I could write music. I can write you a motet, or a sonata, or a waltz, or a cornet solo, with variation—anything at all, anything you want. And not one note of it will be worth the match it would take to burn it. You think I'm hot stuff, don't you? You, lying there every day, dreaming about rainbows. Well, I'm not. I'm just a Glendale Wunderkind. I know all there is to know about music, and there's one like me in every Glendale on earth, every one-horse conservatory, every tank-town university, every park band. We can read anything, play anything, arrange anything, and we're just no good. Punks. Like you. God, now I know where I get it from. Isn't that funny? You start out a Wunderkind, then find out you're just a goddam punk."

"Well, if that's the case, it certainly does seem peculiar that he wouldn't have known it. Mr. Hannen, I mean. And told you so. Instead of—"

"Do you think he didn't know it? And didn't tell me? He told me every time he saw me—my tunes stunk, my playing stunk, everything I did stunk—but he liked me. And he knew how I felt about it. Christ, that was something, after living with *you* all my life. So we went on with it, and he thought perhaps Old Man Maturity, as he called him, might help out, later. He will like hell. In this racket you've got it or you haven't, and— *will you wipe that stupid look off your face and stop acting as if it was somebody's fault?*"

"It certainly would seem, after all that work—"

"Can't you understand anything at all? They don't pay off on work, they pay off on talent! *I'm just no good!* I'M NO GOD-DAMN GOOD AND THERE'S NOTHING THAT CAN BE DONE ABOUT IT!"

When a shoe whizzed past her head, Mildred went out, picked up her handbag, and started over to Beverly. She felt no resentment at this tirade. She had got it through her head at last that something catastrophic had happened to Veda, and that it was completely beyond her power to understand. But that wouldn't stop her from trying, in her own way, to think what she could do about it.

13

In a day or so, feeling that Veda was the victim of some sort of injustice, Mildred decided that the Messrs. Hannen and Treviso weren't the only teachers in Los Angeles; that battles aren't won by quitting, but by fighting hard; that Veda should go on with her music, whether the great masters liked it or not. But when she outlined this idea to Veda, the look from the bed cut her off in the middle of a sentence. Then, unable to give up the idea that Veda was "talented," she decided that aesthetic dancing was the thing. There was a celebrated Russian dancer who often dined at Laguna, and this authority was sure that with Veda's looks and good Russian instruction, things might still be straightened out. But at this Veda merely yawned. Then Mildred decided that Veda should enter one of the local schools, possibly Marlborough, and prepare herself for college. But this seemed a bit silly when Veda said: "But Mother, I can't roll a hoop anymore."

Yet Veda continued to mope in her room, until Mildred became thoroughly alarmed, and decided that whatever the future held, for the present something had to be done. So one day she suggested that Veda call up some of her friends and give them a little party. Conquering her loyalty to the house, the conviction that it was good enough for anything Veda might want to do in it, she said: "If you don't want to ask them here, why not Laguna? You can have a whole room to yourself. I can have Lucy fix up a special table, there's an orchestra we can get, and afterwards you can dance or do anything you want."

"No, Mother. Thanks."

Mildred might have persisted in this, if it hadn't been for Letty, who heard some of it. In the kitchen she said to Mildred: "She ain't going to see none of them people. Not them Pasadena people."

"Why not?"

"Don't you *know?* After she's been Mr. Hannen's candy kid? The one that was going to New York and play the pyanner so they'd all be hollering for her? You think she's going to see them people now, and just be Veda? Not her. She's the queen, or she don't play. She ain't giving no party, and you ain't either."

"I've simply got to do something."

"Can't you leave her *alone?*"

Letty, a devoted worshipper of Veda's by now, spoke sharply, and Mildred left the kitchen, lest she lose her temper. Leaving Veda alone was something that hadn't entered her mind, but after she cooled off she thought about it. However, she was incapable of leaving Veda alone. In the first place, she had an honest concern about her. In the second place, she had become so accustomed to domineering over the many lives that depended on her, that patience, wisdom, and tolerance had almost ceased to be a part of her. And in the third place, there was this feeling she had about Veda, that by now permeated every part of her, and colored everything she did. To have Veda play the piece about rainbows, just for her, was delicious. To have her scream at her was painful, but bearable, for at least it was she that was being screamed at. To have her lying there on the bed, staring at the ceiling, and not even thinking about her, was an agony too great to be borne. Even as she was trying to be detached, to weigh Letty's remark fairly, she was deciding that where Veda really belonged was in pictures, and meditating a way whereby a director, one of Ida's customers, could be induced to take an interest. This brilliant scheme, however, was never put to the test. Veda snapped out of it. Appearing at Laguna one night, she blithely ordered a cocktail, downed a $3.50 steak, and mingled sociably with everybody in the place. Casually, before she left, she asked Mildred if she could order some new clothes, explaining she had been embarrassed to go anywhere "in these rags." Mildred, delighted at any sign of reviving interest, overlooked the cocktail and told her to order anything she wanted.

She was a little stunned when the bills began to come in, and they footed up to more than $1,300. And she was disturbed when she saw the clothes. Up to now, Veda had worn the quiet, well-made, somewhat sexless toggery sanctioned by Pasadena, as suitable to girls of her age. Now, in big, expensive hats and smart, striking dresses, with powder, rouge, and lipstick thick on her face, she hardly looked like the same girl. She was, by any standard, extraordinarily good-looking. Her hair, still a soft, coppery red, was cut and waved to flow over her shoulders. Her freckles were all gone, leaving the upper part of her face, which so much resembled Bert's, even handsomer than it had been before: the shadows under her eyes gave her true beauty, and if the light blue of the eyes themselves, as well as the set of the resolute mouth, were a little hard, they were also suggestive of the modern world, of boulevards, theatres, and streamlined cars. She had grown but little these last three years. Though her carriage enhanced her height, she was actually but a shade taller than Mildred. And her figure had filled out, or taken on form, or undergone some elusive change, so the Dairy was no longer the bulging asymmetry it had been in the days when Monty complained about it. It melted pleasantly, even excitingly, into the rest of her. But what shook up Mildred, when this new finery arrived, was the perception that this child was no longer a child. At seventeen she was a woman, and an uncommonly wise one at that. Mildred tried to like the clothes, couldn't. Unable to indict them, she harped on the three-quarter mink coat, the exact model she had picked out for herself, years before, and never yet bought. Querulously, she said such a purchase should never have been made "without consulting her." But when Veda slipped it on, and called her "darling Mother," and kissed her, and begged to be allowed to keep it, she gave in.

Thereafter, she hardly saw Veda. In the morning, when she went out, Veda was still asleep, and at night, when she came in, Veda wasn't home yet, and usually didn't arrive until two or three in the morning. One night, when Veda's car backed and started several times before making the garage, and the footsteps sounded heavy in the hall, Mildred knew that Veda was drunk. But when she went to Veda's door, it was locked, and there was no answer to her knock. Then one afternoon, when she came home for her rest, Veda's car was there, and so was a dreadful girl, named Elaine. Her place of residence, it turned out, was Beverly, her occupation actress, though when Mildred asked what pictures she had acted in, the answer was merely, "character parts." She was tall, pretty, and cheap, and Mildred instinctively disliked her. But as this was the first girl Veda had ever chosen as a friend, she tried to "be nice to her." Then Mildred began to hear things. Ida cornered her one night, and began a long, whispered harangue. "Mildred, it may be none of my business, but it's time you knew what was going on with Veda. She's been in here a dozen times, with that awful girl she goes around with and not only here but at Eddie's across the street, and at other places. And all they're up to is picking up men. And the men they pick up! They're driving all around in that car of Veda's, and sometimes they've got one man with them and sometimes it's five. Five, Mildred. One day there was three inside, sitting all over the girls' laps, and two more outside, one on each running board. And at Eddie's they *drink . . .*"

Mildred felt she had to talk to Veda about this, and one Sunday morning screwed up her courage to start. But Veda elected to be hurt. "After all, Mother, it was you that said I couldn't lie around here all the time. And just because that prissy Ida—oh well, let's not get on that subject. There's nothing to be alarmed at, Mother. I may go into pictures, that's all. And Elaine may be a bum—well there's no use being silly about it. I grant at once that she's nothing but a tramp. But she knows directors. Lots of them. All of them. And you *have* to know directors to get a test."

Mildred tried conscientiously to accept this version, reminded herself that the picture career had been her own idea, too. But she remained profoundly miserable, almost physically sick.

One afternoon, at the Glendale restaurant, Mildred was checking inventory with Mrs. Kramer when Arline came into the kitchen and said a Mrs. Lenhardt was there to see her. Then, lowering her voice, Arline added excitedly: "I think it's the director's wife."

Mildred quickly scrubbed up her hands, dried them, and went out. Then she felt her face get prickly. Arline had said Mrs. Lenhardt, but the woman near the door was the very Mrs. Forrester to whom she had applied, years before, for the job as housekeeper. She had just time to recall that Mrs. Forrester had expected to be married again when the lady turned, then came over beaming, with outstretched glove and alarming graciousness. "Mrs. Pierce? I've been looking forward *so* much to meeting you. I'm Mrs. Lenhardt, Mrs. John Lenhardt, and I'm *sure* we're going to work out our little problem *splendidly.*"

This greeting left Mildred badly crossed up, and as she led Mrs. Lenhardt to a table she speculated wildly as to what it might mean. She had a panicky fear that it had something to do with that visit years before, that Veda would find out she had once actually applied for a servant's job, that the consequences would be horrible. As she faced her visitor, she suddenly made up her mind that whatever this was about, she was going to deny everything; deny that she had ever seen Mrs. Forrester before, or been to her house, or even considered a position as housekeeper. She had no sooner made this decision than she saw Mrs. Forrester eyeing her sharply. "But haven't we met *before,* Mrs. Pierce."

"Possibly in one of my restaurants."

"But I don't *go* to restaurants, Mrs. Pierce."

"I have a branch in Beverly. You may have dropped in for a cup of chocolate sometime, many people do. You probably saw me there. Of course, if I'd seen you I'd remember it."

"No doubt that's it."

As Mrs. Lenhardt continued to stare, Arline appeared and began dusting tables. It seemed to Mildred that Arline's ears looked bigger than usual, so she called her over, and asked Mrs. Lenhardt if she could offer her something. When Mrs. Lenhardt declined, she pointedly told Arline she could let the tables go until later. Mrs. Lenhardt settled into her coat like a hen occupying a nest, and gushed: "I've come to talk about our children, Mrs. Pierce—our *babies,* I'm almost tempted to say, because that's the way I really feel about them."

"Our—?"

"Your little one, Veda—she's such a *lovely* girl, Mrs. Pierce. I don't know *when* I've taken a child to my heart as I have Veda. And . . . my boy."

Mildred, nervous and frightened, stared for a moment and said: "Mrs. Lenhardt, I haven't any idea what you're talking about."

"Oh come, come, Mrs. Pierce."

"I don't know what you mean."

Mildred's tone was sharp, and Mrs. Lenhardt looked at her steadily, her lips smiling, her eyes not believing. Then she broke into a high, shrill laugh. "Of course you don't! How stupid of me, Mrs. Pierce. I should have explained that my boy, *my* baby, is Sam Forrester."

As Mildred still stared, Mrs. Lenhardt saw at last that this might not be pretense. Her manner changing, she leaned forward and asked eagerly: "You mean Veda hasn't told you anything?"

"Not a word."

"Ah!"

Mrs. Forrester was excited now, obviously aware of her advantage in being able to give Mildred her own version of this situation, whatever it was, first. She stripped off her gloves and shot appraising glances at Mildred for some time before proceeding. Then: "Shall I begin at the beginning, Mrs. Pierce?"

"Please."

"They met—well it seems only yesterday, actually it was several weeks ago, at my house. My husband, no doubt you've heard of him—he's a director, and he was considering Veda for a part. And as he so often does with these kids, when we have a little party going on, he asked her over—Veda and her little friend Elaine, another lovely child, Mrs. Pierce. My husband has known her for years, and—"

"Yes, I've met her."

"So it was at my own house, Mrs. Pierce, that Veda and Sam met. And it was *simply* love at first sight. It must have been, because that boy of mine, Mrs. Pierce, is so sincere, so—"

"You mean they're *engaged?*"

"I was coming to that. No, I wouldn't say they were engaged. In fact I *know* that Sammy had no such thing in mind. But Veda has somehow got the idea that—well, I *understand* it, of course. Any girl wants to get married, but Sam had no such thing in mind. I want that made clear."

Mrs. Lenhardt's voice was becoming a little high, a little strident, and she waggled a stiff forefinger at Mildred as she went on. "And I'm *quite* sure you'll agree with me, Mrs. Pierce, that any discussion of marriage between them would be *most* undesirable."

"Why?"

So far as Mildred was concerned, marriage for Veda would have been a major calamity, but at Mrs. Lenhardt's manner she bristled with hot partisanship. Mrs. Lenhardt snapped: "Because they're nothing but children! Veda can't be over nineteen—"

"She's seventeen."

"And my boy is twenty. That's too young. Mrs. Pierce, it's

entirely too young. Furthermore, they move in two different worlds—"

"What different worlds?"

Mildred's eyes blazed, and Mrs. Lenhardt hastily backed off. "That isn't quite what I mean, Mrs. Pierce, of course. Let us say different *communities*. They have different backgrounds, different ideals, different friends. And of course, Sam has always been used to a great deal of money—"

"Do you think Veda hasn't?"

"I'm sure she has everything you can give her—"

"You may find she's been used to just as much as your boy has, and more. I'm not exactly on relief, I can tell you."

"But you didn't let me *finish*, Mrs. Pierce. If Veda's accustomed to wealth and position, so much the *more* reason that this thing should not for a second be considered. I want to make this clear: If Sammy gets married, he'll be *completely* on his own, and it will certainly be hard for two young people, both born with silver spoons in their mouths, to live on what *he* can earn."

Having made this clear, Mrs. Lenhardt tried to calm down, and Mildred tried to calm down. She said this was the first she had heard of it, and she would have to talk to Veda before she could say what she thought. But as Mrs. Lenhardt politely agreed that this was an excellent idea, Mildred began to have a suspicion that the whole truth had not been told. Suddenly and sharply she asked: "Why should Veda feel this way about it, and your boy not?"

"Mrs. Pierce, I'm not a mind reader."

Mrs. Lenhardt spoke angrily, the color appearing in her cheeks. Then she added: "But let me tell you one thing. If you, or that girl, or anybody, employ any more *tricks*, trying to blackmail my boy into—"

"Trying to—*what?*"

Mildred's voice cracked like a whip, and for a few moments Mrs. Lenhardt didn't speak. Apparently she knew she had said too much, and was trying to be discreet. Her effort was unsuccessful. When her nostrils had dilated and closed several times, she exploded: "You may as well understand here and now, Mrs. Pierce, that I shall *prevent* this marriage. I shall prevent it in any way that I can, and by legal means, if necessary." The way she said *"necess'ry"* had a very ominous sound to it.

By now the reality behind this visit was beginning to dawn on Mildred, and she became calm, cold, calculating. Looking up, she saw Arline at her dusting again, her ears bigger than ever. Calling her, she told her to straighten the chairs at the next table, and as she approached turned pleasantly to Mrs. Lenhardt. "I beg your pardon. For a moment I wasn't listening."

Mrs. Lenhardt's voice rose to a scream. "I say if there are any more threats, any more officers at my door, any more of these tricks she's been playing—I shall have her arrested, I shall have her prosecuted for blackmail, I shall not hesitate for one moment, for I've quite reached the limit of my patience!"

Mrs. Lenhardt, after panting a moment, got up and swept out. Mildred looked at Arline. "Did you hear what she said?"

"I wasn't listening, Mrs. Pierce."

"I asked if you heard what she said?"

Arline studied Mildred for a cue. Then: "She said Veda was trying to blackmail her boy into marrying her and if she kept it up she'd have the law on her."

"Remember that, in case I need you."

"Yes'm."

That night Mildred didn't go to Laguna or to Beverly. She stayed home, tramping around, tortured by the fear that Arline had probably told everybody in the restaurant by now, by uncertainty as to what dreadful mess Veda had got herself into, by a sick, nauseating, physical jealousy that she couldn't fight down. At eleven, she went to her room and lay down, pulling a blanket over her but not taking off her clothes. Around one, when Veda's car zipped up the drive, she took no chances on a locked door, but jumped up and met Veda in the kitchen. "Mother! ... My, how you startled me!"

"I'm sorry, darling. But I have to talk to you. Something has happened."

"Well—at least let me take off my hat."

Mildred went to the den, relieved that she had smelled no liquor. In a minute or two Veda came in, sat down, lit a cigarette, yawned. "Personally, I find pictures a bore, don't you? At least Nelson Eddy pictures. Still, I suppose it's not his fault, for it isn't how he sings but what he sings. And I suppose he has nothing to do with how dreadfully long they are."

Miserably, Mildred tried to think how to begin. In a low, timid voice, she said: "A Mrs. Lenhardt was in to see me today. A Mrs. John Lenhardt?"

"Oh, really?"

"She says you're engaged to marry her son, or have some idea you want to marry him, or—something."

"She's quite talkative. What else?"

"She opposes it."

In spite of her effort, Mildred had been unable to get started. Now she blurted out: "Darling, what *was* she talking about? What does it all mean?"

Veda smoked reflectively a few moments, then said, in her clear, suave way: "Well, it would be going too far to say it was my idea that Sam and I get married. After the big rush they gave me, with Pa breaking his neck to get me a screen test and Ma having me over morning, noon and night, and Sonny boy phoning me, and writing me, and wiring me that if I *didn't* marry him he'd end his young life—you might say it was a conspiracy. Certainly I said nothing about it, or even thought about it, until it seemed advisable."

"What do you mean, advisable?"

"Well, Mother, he was certainly very sweet, or seemed so at any rate, and they were most encouraging, and I hadn't exactly been happy since—Hannen died. And Elaine did have a nice little apartment. And I was certainly most indiscreet. And then, after the big whoop-de-do, their whole attitude changed, alas. And here I am, holding the bag. One might almost say I was a bit of a sap."

If there was any pain, any tragic overtone, to this recital, it was not audible to the ordinary ear. It betrayed regret over folly, perhaps a little self-pity, but all of a casual kind. Mildred, however, wasn't interested in such subtleties. She had reached a point where she had to know one stark, basic fact. Sitting beside Veda, clutching her hand, she said: "Darling, I have to ask you something. I have to, I have to. Are you—going to have a baby?"

"Yes, Mother, I'm afraid I am."

For a second the jealousy was so overwhelming that Mildred actually was afraid she would vomit. But then Veda looked at her in a pretty, contrite way, as one who had sinned but is sure of forgiveness, and dropped her head on Mildred's shoulder. At this the sick feeling left, and a tingle went through Mildred. She gathered Veda to her bosom, held her tight, patted her, cried a little. "Why didn't you tell me?"

"I was afraid."

"Of me? Of Mother?"

"No, no! Of the suffering it would bring you. Darling Mother, don't you know I can't bear to see you unhappy?"

Mildred closed her eyes for a moment, to savor this sweet blandishment. Then, remembering, she asked: "What did she mean about officers?"

"You mean police?"

"I guess so. At her door."

"My, that *is* funny."

Veda sat up, lit another cigarette, and laughed in a silvery, ironical way. "From what I've learned of the young man *since* this happened, I'd say that any girl from Central Casting, perhaps all eight thousand of them for that matter, could have sent officers to his door. He has a very inclusive taste. Well, that's really funny, when you stop to think about it, isn't it?"

Hoping for more saccharine remarks, Mildred asked Veda if she'd like to sleep with her, "just for tonight," but Veda said it was something she'd have to face alone, and went to her room. All through the night, Mildred kept waking with the jealousy gnawing at her. In the morning, she went to the Glendale restaurant and called Bert. Dispensing with Tommy, she went down to Mrs. Biederhof's corner and picked him up. Then, starting for the hills, she started to talk. She put in everything that seemed relevant, beginning with Mr. Hannen's hemorrhage, and emphasizing Veda's forebodings about it. When she got to Mr. Treviso, Bert's face darkened, and he exclaimed at the "rottenness" of a dirty wop that would treat a young girl that way. Then, finding the going more difficult, Mildred told about Elaine, the drinking, and Ida's harrowing tales. Then, disconnectedly, hardly able to speak anymore, or to drive, she told about Mrs. Lenhardt. Then, trying to tell about her talk with Veda, she broke down completely, and blurted: "Bert! She's going to have a baby! She's in a family way!"

Bert's grip tightened on her arm. "Hold it! Stop this goddam car. I got to—get someplace where I can move around."

She stopped, and pulled to one side, on Foothill Boulevard. He got out, began tramping up and down beside the car. Then he began to curse. He said goddam it, he was going to kill that son of a bitch if it was the last thing he did on earth. He said he was going to kill him if they hung him for it and his soul rotted in hell. With still more frightful oaths, he went into full particulars as to where he was going to buy the gun, the way he would lay for the boy, what he would say when he had him face to face, and how he would let him have it. Mildred watched the preposterous little figure striding up and down, and a fierce, glowing pride in him began to warm her. Even his curses gave her a queer, morbid satisfaction. But after a while she said: "Get in, Bert."

He climbed in beside her, held his face in his hands, and for a moment she thought he was going to weep. When he didn't, she started the car and said: "I know you'd kill him, Bert. I know you would, and I glory in you for it. I love you for it." She took his hand, and gripped it, and tears came to her eyes, for he had reached her own great pain, somehow, and by his ferocity, eased it. "But—that wouldn't do Veda any good. If he'd dead, that's not getting her anywhere."

"That's right."

"What are we going to do?"

Gagging over her words, Mildred presently broached the subject of an operation. It was something she knew little about, and hated, not only on account of its physical aspect, but because it went counter to every instinct in her wholly feminine nature. Bert cut her off with a gesture. "Mildred, girls die in that operation. They die. And we're not going to let her die. We lost one, and that's enough. By God, I'll say she's not going to have any operation, not to make it easy for a dirty little rat that took advantage of her and now wants to do a run-out."

Bert now turned toward Mildred, his eyes flashing. "He's going to marry her, that's what he's going to do. After he's given her child a name, then he can do his run-out. He *better* do a run-out, and do it fast, before I catch up with him. He can go to hell, for all I give a damn, but before he does, he'll march up beside her and say 'I do.' I'll see to that."

"It's the only thing, Bert."

Mildred drove along, and presently had a hollow feeling they were right back where they started. It was all very well to say the boy had to marry Veda, but how could they make him do it? Suddenly she burst out: "Bert, I'm going to get a lawyer."

"It's just what I've been thinking."

"You and I, we can't do a thing. Precious time is going by, and something has to be done. And the first thing is to get that lawyer."

"O.K. And get him quick."

When Mildred got home, Veda was just getting up. Closing the door, she addressed the tousled girl in the green kimono. "I told your father. We had a talk. He agrees that we need a lawyer. I'm going to call up Wally Burgan."

"Mother, I think that's an excellent idea.... As a matter of fact, I've already called him up."

"You—*what?*"

Veda spoke sleepily, and a little impatiently. "Mother, can't you see that I'm trying to arrange things myself, without putting you to all kinds of trouble about it? I've been trying to spare you. I want to make things easy for you."

Mildred blinked, tried to adjust herself to this astounding revelation.

Wally arrived around three. Mildred brought him to the privacy of the den, then went and sent Letty on an errand that would take her all afternoon. When she got back to the den, Veda was there, in a simple little blue frock that had cost Mildred $75, and Wally was looking at the pictures of Bert attending the banquets. He said things certainly did look familiar, and casually got down to business. He said he had done a little inquiring around, and the situation was about what he figured it was. "The kid comes into dough on his twenty-first birthday, that's the main thing. How much I don't exactly know, but it's well up in six figures. He's got to inherit. There's no way the mother, or the stepfather, or any of them can juggle the books to keep him out of it, and once he dies, whoever is married to him at the time cuts in for her share of the community property. That's what this is all about, and it's all it's all about. That's why they're breaking their necks to head it off. It's got nothing to do with their being too young, or loving each other, or not loving each other, or the different ways they've been brought up, or any of the stuff that mother has been dishing out. It's nothing but the do-re-mi—the old army game."

When Wally stopped Mildred drew a deep breath and spoke slowly, raising her voice a little: "Wally, I'm not interested in whether he inherits, or how much he inherits, or anything of that kind. So long as I'm here, I don't think Veda will be in want. But a situation has been created. It's a terrible situation for Veda, and the only thing that boy can do about it is marry her. If he's a decent boy, he'll do the right thing on his own initiative, regardless of what his family says. If he's not, he'll have to be made. Wally, that woman had a great deal to say that I haven't told Veda, but that I have witnesses to substantiate—about law, and what she'll do, and other things. *I'll go just as far as she will.* If it's the only way, I want that boy arrested—and you can tell him he can be very glad it's only the police he has to face, instead of Bert."

"Arresting him may be a little tough."

"Haven't we got laws?"

"He's skipped."

Wally shot a glance at Veda, who considered a few moments, then said: "I think you'd better tell her."

"You see, Mildred, just happens we already thought of that. Two, three days, maybe a week ago, I took Veda over to the sheriff's office and had her swear out a warrant for Sam. No statutory rape, nothing unpleasant like that. Just a little morals charge, and same afternoon, couple of the boys went over to serve it. He wasn't there. And so far—"

"So that's what she meant by officers!"

Veda stirred uneasily under Mildred's accusing eyes. "Well Mother, if you're talking about what I said last night, I didn't know at that time that any officers had actually *been* there."

Mildred turned on Wally. "It does seem to me that on a thing of this kind, a matter as serious as this, I should have been the first one you would have talked to about it. Why the very idea, of legal steps being taken without my knowing anything whatever about it!"

"Now just hold your horses a minute."

Wally's eyes became very cold, and he got up and marched up and down in front of Mildred before he went on. "One thing you might consider: I've got a little thing called legal ethics to consider. Sure, I'd have been willing to talk to you. We've talked plenty before, haven't we? But when my client makes an express stipulation that I not talk to you, why—"

When Mildred turned, Veda was ready. "Mother, it's about time you got it through your head that after all, I, and not you, am the main figure in this little situation, as you call it. I'm not proud of it. I readily admit it's my own fault, and that I've been very foolish. But when I act on that assumption, when I try to relieve you of responsibility, when I try to save you unhappiness, it does seem to me you could give me credit for some kind of decent motives, instead of going off the handle in this idiotic way.'

"I *never* in all my *life—!*"

"Now, Mother, nobody was asking any help from you, and as Wally has taken my case as a great favor to me, I think the least you can do is let him tell us what to do, as I imagine he knows much more about such things than you do."

As Mildred subsided, a little frightened at Veda's tone, Wally resumed in the casual way he had begun: "Well, so far as his doing anything goes, I'd say the next move was up to them. Way I look at it, we've taken Round 1. When we got out that warrant, that showed we meant business. On a morals charge, all the jury wants to know is the age of the girl—after that it's dead open and shut. When they got him under cover quick, that shows they knew what they're up against. And what they're up against is tough. So long as that warrant is out against him, he dare not come back to the state of California, he can't go back to college, or even use his right name. Course there's a couple of other things we might do, like suing the mother, but then we're in the newspapers, and that's not so good. I'd say leave it like it is. Sooner or later they got to lead to us, and the more we act like we don't care, the prettier we're sitting."

"But Wally!"

Mildred's voice was a despairing wail. "*Wally!* Time is going on! Days are passing, and look at this girl's condition! We can't wait! We—"

"I think we can leave it to Wally."

Veda's cool tone ended the discussion, but all that day and all that night Mildred fretted, and by next morning she had worked herself into a rage. When Tommy reported, at noon, she had him drive her over to Mrs. Lenhardt's, to "have it out with her." But as they whirled up the drive, she saw the house man that had let her in, that morning long ago, talking to the driver of a delivery truck. She knew perfectly well *he* would remember her, and she called shrilly to Tommy to drive on, she had changed her mind. As the car rolled around the loop in front of the house, she leaned far back, so she wouldn't be seen. Then she had Tommy drive her to Ida's, and telephoned Bert.

Leaving Tommy in Beverly, she again picked up Bert at Mrs. Biederhof's corner, and headed up to the hills.

Bert listened, and began shaking his head. "Gee Mildred, I wish you'd told me you had Wally Burgan in mind. I'm telling you, I don't like the guy, and I don't like the way he does business. Telling him to step on the gas is like—well, he's been liquidating Pierce Homes for eight years now, hasn't he? And they're not liquidated yet. He's not trying to get Veda married. He's just running up a bill."

They rode along, each trying to think of something, and suddenly Bert had it. "To hell with him! What we want is to find that boy, isn't it? Isn't that right?"

"That's it! Instead of—"

"What this needs is a private detective."

A hot, savage thrill shot through Mildred. At last she knew they were getting somewhere. Excitedly they talked about it, and then Bert told her to get him to a drugstore, or any place where he could get to a phone book. She stopped in San Fernando, and Bert hopped out before the car stopped rolling. He was back in a minute or two, a slip of paper in his hands. "Here's three, with phone numbers and addresses. I'd say let's go first to this Simons agency. I've heard of it, for one thing, and it's right there in Hollywood, not too far away."

The Simons Detective Agency was located in a small, one-story office on Vine Street, and Mr. Simons turned out to be a friendly little man with bushy black hair. He listened attentively as Bert stated the problem, and refrained from asking embarrassing questions. Then he tilted back in his chair and said he saw no particular difficulty. He got jobs of this sort all the time, and on most of them was able to show results. However, since time seemed to be of the essence, there would be certain expenses, and he would have to ask for an advance. "I'd have to have two fifty before I can start at all. First, to get the young man's picture and other information I'll need, I'll have to put an operative to work, and he'll cost me ten dollars a day. Then I'll have to offer a reward, and—"

"Reward?"

Mildred suddenly had visions of a horrible picture tacked up in post offices. "Oh, don't worry, Mrs. Pierce." Mr. Simons seemed to divine her fear. "This is all strictly confidential, and nobody'll know anything. Just the same, we work through our connections, and they're not in business for their health. I'd say, on this, a $50 reward should be ample. Then there's the printing of our fliers, and the pay of a girl to address a couple thousand envelopes and ..."

Bert suggested that half the advance should be paid now, the other half when the boy was found, but Mr. Simons shook his head. "This is all money I'll have to pay out before I can start at all. Mind, I haven't said anything yet about my services. Of course, other places may do it cheaper, and you're perfectly welcome to go where you please. But, as I always say, the cheaper the slower in this business—and, the riskier."

Mildred wrote the check. On the way home, both of them applauded themselves handsomely for what they had done, and agreed it should be between themselves, with nothing said to Wally or Veda until they had something to "lay on the line," as Bert put it. So for several days Mildred was ducking into phone booths and talking in guarded tones to Mr. Simons. Then one afternoon he told her to come in. She picked up Bert, and together they drove to the little frame office. Mr. Simons was all smiles. "We had a little luck. Of course it wasn't really luck. In this business, you can't be too thorough. We found out that when he left town, the young man was driving one of his step-father's cars, and just because I was about to put that information on the flier, now we've got something. Here's the itemized bill, and if you'll just let me have the check while the girl is typing out the address for you ..."

Mildred wrote a check for $125, mainly for "services." Mr. Simons put a card in her hand, with an address on it. "That's a dude ranch near Winslow, Ariz. The young man is using his right name, and I don't think you'll have any trouble locating him."

Driving back, they stared at one of Mr. Simons's fliers, bearing the weak, handsome face of the boy they had chosen for a son-in-law. Then, nervously, they discussed what was to be done, and came to the conclusion, in Bert's phrase, that they had to "go through with it." When Mildred dropped him off, they agreed that the time had come to get action out of Wally, and rather grimly Mildred drove home. Going to the kitchen, she sent Letty on another protracted errand. Then, when the girl had gone, she hurried into the den and called Wally. Shrilly, she told what she had done, and read him the address furnished by Mr. Simons. He said hey wait a minute, till he got a pencil. Then he made her repeat the address slowly, and then said: "Swell. Say, that's a help. It's a good thing to have, just in case."

"What do you mean, in case?"

"In case they get tough."

"Aren't you calling the sheriff's office?"

"No use going off half-cocked. We've got them right where we want them, and as I said before, our play is to make them come to us. Just let it ride, and—"

"Wally, I want that boy arrested."

"Mildred, why don't you let me—"

Mildred slammed up the receiver and jumped up, her eyes blazing, her hat slightly askew. When she turned to dash out, Veda was at the door. At once she launched into a denunciation of Wally. "That man's not even trying to do anything. I've told him where that boy is. I had a detective find out—and still he does nothing. Well that's the last he'll hear from me! *I'm* going over to the sheriff's office myself!"

Quivering with her high, virtuous resolve, Mildred charged for the door. She collided with Veda, who seemed to have moved to block her path. Then her wrist was caught in a grip like steel, and slowly, mercilessly, she was forced back, until she plunged down on the sofa. "You'll do nothing of the kind."

"Let go of me! What are you pushing me for? What do you mean I'll do nothing of the kind?"

"If you go to the sheriff's office, they'll bring young Mr. Forrester back. And if they bring him back, he'll want to marry me, and that doesn't happen to suit me. It may interest you to know that he's been back. He sneaked into town, twice, and a beautiful time I had of it, getting him to be a nice boy and stay where Mamma put him. He's quite crazy about me. I saw to that. But as for matrimony, I beg to be excused. I'd much rather have the money."

Mildred took off her hat, and stared at the cold, beautiful creature who had sat down opposite her, and who was now yawning as though the whole subject were a bit of a bore. The events of the last few days began ticking themselves off in her mind, particularly the strange relationship that had sprung up, between Veda and Wally. The squint appeared, and her face grew hard. "Now I know what that woman meant by blackmail. You're just trying to shake her down, shake the whole family down, for money. You're *not* pregnant, at all."

"Mother, at this stage it's a matter of opinion, and in my opinion, I am."

Veda's eyes glinted as she spoke, and Mildred wanted to back down, to avoid one of those scenes from which she always emerged beaten, humiliated, and hurt. But something was swelling within her, something that began in the sick jealously of a few nights before, something that felt as though it might presently choke her. Her voice shook as she spoke. "How could you do such a thing? If you had loved the boy, I wouldn't have a word to say. So long as I thought you had loved him, I didn't have a word to say, not one word to blame you. To love is a woman's right, and when you do, I *hope* you give everything you have, brimming over. But just to pretend you loved him to lead him on, to get money out of him—*how* could you do it?"

"Merely following in my mother's footsteps."

"What did you say?"

"Oh, stop being so tiresome. There's the date of your wedding, and there's the date of my birth. Figure it out for yourself. The only difference is that you were a little younger at that time than I am now—a month or two anyway. I suppose it runs in families."

"Why do you think I married your father?"

"I rather imagine he married you. If you mean why you got yourself knocked up, I suppose you did it for the same reason I did—for the money."

"What money?"

"Mother, in another minute I'll be getting annoyed. Of course he has no money now, but at the time he was quite rich, and I'm sure you knew it. When the money was gone you kicked him out. And when you divorced him, and he was so down and out that the Biederhof had to keep him, you quite generously stripped him of the only thing he had left, meaning this lovely, incomparable, palatial hovel that we live in."

"That was his idea, not mine. He wanted to do his share, to contribute something for you and Ray. And it was all covered with mortgages, that he couldn't even have paid the interest on, let alone—"

"At any rate, you took it."

By now, Mildred had sensed that Veda's boredom was pure affectation. Actually she was enjoying the unhappiness she inflicted, and had probably rehearsed her main points in advance. This, ordinarily, would have been enough to make Mildred back down, seek a reconciliation, but this feeling within kept goading her. After trying to keep quiet, she lashed out: "But why? *Why*—will you tell me that? Don't I give you everything that money can buy? Is there one single thing I ever denied you? If there was something you wanted, couldn't you have come to me for it, instead of resorting to—blackmail. Because that woman was right! That's all it is! Blackmail! Blackmail! *Blackmail!*"

In the silence that followed, Mildred felt first frightened, then coldly brave, as the feeling within drove her on. Veda puffed her cigarette, reflected, and asked: "Are you sure you want to know?"

"I dare you to tell me!"

"Well, since you ask, with enough money, I can get away from you, you poor, half-witted mope. From you, and your pie wagon, and your chickens, and your waffles, and your kitchens, and everything that smells of grease. And from this shack, that you blackmailed out of my father with your threats about the Biederhof, and its neat little two-car garage, and its lousy furniture. And from Glendale, and its dollar days, and its furniture factories, and its women that wear uniforms and its men that wear smocks. From every rotten, stinking thing that even reminds me of the place—or you."

"I see."

Mildred got up and put on her hat. "Well it's a good thing I found out what you were up to, when I did. Because I can tell you right now, if you had gone through with this, or even tried to go through with it, you'd have been out of here a little sooner than you expected."

She headed for the door, but Veda was there first. Mildred laughed, and tore up the card Mr. Simons had given her. "Oh you needn't worry that I'll go to the sheriff's office now. It'll be a long time before they find out from me where the boy is hiding, or you do either."

Again she started for the door, but Veda didn't move. Mildred backed off and sat down. If Veda thought she would break, she was mistaken. Mildred sat motionless, her face hard, cold, and implacable. After a long time the silence was shattered by the phone. Veda jumped for it. After four or five brief, cryptic monosyllables, she hung up, turned to Mildred with a malicious smile. "That was Wally. You may be interested to know that they're ready to settle."

"Are you?"

"I'm meeting them at his office."

"Then get out. Now."

"I'll decide that. And I'll decide when."

"You'll get your things out of this house right now or you'll find them in the middle of Pierce Drive when you come back."

Veda screamed curses at Mildred, but presently she got it through her head that this time, for some reason, was different from all other times. She went out, backed her car down to the kitchen door, began carrying out her things, and packing them in the luggage carrier. Mildred sat quite still, and when she heard Veda drive off she was consumed by a fury so cold that it almost seemed as though she felt nothing at all. It didn't occur to her that she was acting less like a mother than like a lover who has unexpectedly discovered an act of faithlessness, and avenged it.

CHAPTER

14

It was at least six months after this that Bert called up to invite her to the broadcast. For her, it had been a dismal six months. She had found out soon enough where Veda was staying. It was in one of the small, swank apartment houses on Franklin Avenue, in Hollywood. Every fibre of her being had wanted to pay a visit there, to take back what she had said, to reestablish things as they had been, or try to. But when this thought entered her mind, or rather shot through her heart like a hot arrow, she set her face as if it had been cast in metal, and not once did she even drive past Veda's door. And yet, even in her loneliness, her relation with Veda was developing, twisting her painfully, like some sort of cancer. She discovered rye, and in the boozy dreams of her daily rest, she pictured Veda as going from bad to worse, as hungering and mending threadbare finery, until she had to come back, penitent and tearful, for forgiveness. This view of the future was somewhat obscured by the circumstance that Mildred didn't know exactly how much Veda had obtained from the Lenhardts, and thus couldn't calculate, with any degree of accuracy, when destitution was likely to strike. But Bert contributed a thought that assisted drama, if not truth. Bert, having tried unsuccessfully to stand on his rights as a father to bluff information out of Wally, and having threatened even to "hold up the settlement" unless full data were furnished, had learned only that his consent was not needed for a settlement; all the Lenhardts wanted was a release from Veda, a signed letter denying promises, intimidation, or pregnancy. But the episode had left him with a lower opinion of Wally's honesty than he had had before, if that were possible, and he hatched the theory that "Wally would have every damned cent of it before the year was out, didn't make a bit of difference what they paid, or what he got, or what she got." On this theory Mildred eagerly seized, and pictured the cheated Veda, not only as cold, hungry, and in rags, but as horribly bruised in spirit, creeping to the strong, silent mother who could cope with Wally or anybody else. When the scene materialized almost daily before her eyes, with a hundred little variations and embellishments, she always experienced the same brief ecstasy as she lifted the weeping Veda into her arms, patted her, inhaled the fragrance of the soft, coppery hair, and bestowed love, understanding, and forgiveness. One slight incongruity she overlooked: Veda in real life, rarely wept.

At Bert's mention of a broadcast it took her a moment or two to collect her wits. "What broadcast?"

"Why, Veda."

"You mean she's playing on the air?"

"Singing, the way I get it."

"Veda? *Singing?*"

"Maybe I better come over."

By the time he got there, she was a-tremble with excitement. She found the radio page of the Times, and there, sure enough, was Veda's picture, with the news that "the popular singer will be heard tonight at 8:30, on the Hank Somerville (Snack-O-Ham) program." Bert had seen the Examiner, but hadn't seen the Times, and together they looked at the picture, and commented on how lovely Veda looked. When Mildred wanted to know how long this had been going on, meaning the singing,

Bert said quickly you couldn't prove it by him, as though to disclaim participation in secrets that had been withheld from Mildred. Then he added that the way he got it, Veda had been on the air quite a lot already, on the little afternoon programs that nobody paid any attention to, and that was how she'd got this chance on a big national hook-up. Mildred got the rye she had been sipping, poured two more drinks, and Bert revealed that his invitation had really been Mrs. Beiderhof's idea. "She figured it meant a lot more to you than it would to her, so that's how I came to call you up."

"It was certainly nice of her."

"She's a real friend."

"You mean we'll go to the *studio?*"

"That's it. It's going out from the NBC studio right here in Hollywood, and we'll be able to see it and hear it."

"Don't we have to have tickets?"

"... I got a couple."

"How?"

"It's taken care of."

"From Veda?"

"Never mind. I got 'em."

At the look on Mildred's face, Bert quickly crossed over, took her hand. "Now what's the use of acting like that? Yes, she called me up, and the tickets are there waiting for me. And she'll call you up, of course she will. But why would she be calling you in the morning, like she did me? She knows you're never home then. And then another thing, she's probably been busy. I hear they run those singers ragged, rehearsing them, the day of a broadcast. O.K., they've got her there, where she can't get to a phone or anything, but that's not her fault. She'll call. Of course she will."

"Oh no. She won't call me."

As Bert didn't know the full details of Veda's departure from home, his optimism was understandable. He evidently regarded the point as of small importance, for he began to talk amiably, sipping his rye. He said it certainly went to show that the kid had stuff in her all right, to get a spot like that with a big jazz band, and nobody giving her any help but herself. He said he knew how Mildred felt, but she was certainly going to regret it afterwards if she let a little thing like this stand in the way of being there at the kid's first big chance. Because it was a big chance all right. The torch singers with these big name bands, they're in the money, and no mistake about it. And sometimes, if they had the right hot licks on their first broadcast, they hit the big time overnight.

Mildred let a wan, pitying smile play over her face. If Veda had got there, she said, it was certainly all right with her. Just the same, it certainly seemed funny, the difference between what Veda might have been, and what she was. "Just a year or two ago, it was a pleasure to listen to her. She played all the classical composers, the very best. Her friends were of the best. They weren't my friends, but they were of the best. Her mind was on higher things. And then, after Mr. Hannen died, I don't know what got into her. She began going around with cheap, awful people. She met that boy. She let Wally Burgan poison her mind against me. And now, Hank Somerville. Well, that's the whole story—from Beethoven to Hank Somerville, in a little over a year. No, I don't want to go to the broadcast. It would make me too sad."

Truth to tell, Mildred had no such critical prejudice against Mr. Somerville, or the torch canon, as her remarks might indicate. If Veda had called her up, she would have been only too glad to regard this as "the first move," and to have gone adoringly to the broadcast. But when Veda called Bert, and didn't call her, she was sick, and her sickness involved a bad case of sour-grapes poisoning: so far as she was concerned, torch was the lowest conceivable form of human endeavor. Also, she hated the idea that Bert might go without her. She insisted that he take Mrs. Biederhof, but he got the point, and miserably mumbled that he guessed he wouldn't go. Then suddenly she asked what advantage there was in going to the studio. He could hear it over the radio. Why not ride with her to Laguna and hear it there? He could have his dinner, a nice big steak if he wanted it, and then later she would have Mrs. Gessler put the radio on the veranda, and he could hear Veda without going to a lot of useless trouble. At the mention of steak, poor Bert perked up, and said he'd often wanted to see her place at Laguna. She said come right along, she'd be starting as soon as Tommy brought the car. He said O.K., and went legging it home to change into clothes suitable to a high-class place.

At Laguna, Mildred was indifferent to the impending event, and had little to say to the girls, the cooks, and the customers who kept telling her about Veda's picture in the paper, and asking her if she wasn't excited that her daughter was on the air. Bert, however, wasn't so reticent. While his steak was on the fire, he held court in the bar, and told all and sundry about Veda, and promised that if hot licks were what it took, the kid had them. When the hour drew near, and Mrs. Gessler plugged in the big radio on the veranda, he had an audience of a dozen around him, and extra chairs had to be brought. Two or three were young girls, there were two married couples, and the rest were men. Mildred had intended to pay no attention to the affair at all, but along toward 8:25, curiosity got the better of her. With Mrs. Gessler she went outside, and there was a lively jumping up to give her a seat. One or two men were left perched on the rail.

The first hint she got that Veda's performance might not be quite the torchy affair that Bert had taken for granted came when Mr. Somerville, early in the program, affected to faint, and had to be revived, somewhat noisily, by members of his band. The broadcast had started in the usual way, with the Krazy Kaydets giving the midshipmen's siren yell and then swinging briskly into Anchors Aweigh. Then Mr. Somerville greeted his audience, and then he introduced Veda. When he asked if Veda Pierce was her real name, and she said it was, he wanted to know if her voice was unduly piercing. At this the kaydets rang a ship's gong, and Veda said no, but her scream was, as he'd find out if he made any more such remarks. The studio audience laughed, and the group on the veranda laughed, especially Bert, who slapped his thigh. A man in a blue coat, sitting on the rail, nodded approvingly. "She put that one across all right."

Then Mr. Somerville asked Veda what she was going to sing. She said the Polonaise from Mignon, and that was when he fainted. While the kaydets were working over him, and the studio audience was laughing, and the ship's gong was clanging, Bert leaned to the man in the blue coat. "What's it about?"

"Big operatic aria. The idea is, it's a little over the kaydets' heads."

"Oh, now I get it."

"Don't worry. They'll knock it over."

Mildred, who found the comedy quite disgusting, paid no attention. Then the kaydets crashed into the introduction. Then Veda started to sing. Then a chill, wholly unexpected, shot up Mildred's backbone. The music was unfamiliar to her, and Veda was singing in some foreign language that she didn't understand. But the voice itself was so warm, rich, and vibrant that she began to fight off the effect it had on her. While she was trying to get readjusted to her surprise, Veda came to a little spray of rippling notes and stopped. The man in the blue coat set his drink on a table and said: "Hey, hey, *hey!*"

After a bar or two by the orchestra, Veda came in again, and another chill shot up Mildred's back. Then, as cold prickly waves kept sweeping over her, she really began to fight her feelings. Some sense of monstrous injustice oppressed her: it seemed unfair that this girl, instead of being chastened by adversity, was up there, in front of the whole world, singing, and without any help from her. Somehow, all the emotional assumptions of the last few months were stood on their head, and Mildred felt mean and petty for reacting as she did, and yet she couldn't help it.

Soon Veda stopped, the music changed slightly, and the man in the blue coat sipped his drink. "O.K. so far. Now for the flying trapeze." When Veda started again, Mildred gripped her chair in sheer panic. It seemed impossible that anybody could dare such dizzy heights of sound, could even attempt such vocal gymnastics, without making some slip, some dreadful error that would land the whole thing in ruin. But Veda made no slip. She went on and on, while the man in the blue coat jumped down from the rail, squatted by the machine, and forgot his drink, forgot everything except what was pouring out into the night. Bert and the others watched him with some sort of fascinated expectancy. At the end, when the last, incredibly high note floated over the finale of the orchestra, he looked up at Mildred. "Jesus Christ, did you hear it? Did you—"

But Mildred didn't wait for him to finish. She got up abruptly and walked down toward Mrs. Gessler's flowers, waving back Bert and Mrs. Gessler, who called after her, and started to follow. Pushing through the bushes, she reached the bluff overlooking the sea, and stood there, lacing her fingers together, screwing her lips into a thin, relentless line. This, she needed nobody to tell her, was no descent from Beethoven to Hank Somerville, no cheap venture into torch. It was the coming true of all she had dreamed for Veda, all she had believed in, worked for, dedicated her life to. The only difference was that the dream that had come true was a thousand times rosier than the dream she had dreamed. And come what might, by whatever means she would have to take, she knew she would have to get Veda back.

This resolve remained hot in her mouth, but back of it, like a fishbone across her throat, was her determination, that Veda, and not herself, would have to make the first move. She tried to put this aside, and drove to Veda's one morning with every intention of stopping, ringing the bell, and going in. But as she approached the little white apartment house, she hurriedly told Tommy to drive on without stopping, and leaned far back in the car to avoid being seen, as she had done that morning at Mrs. Lenhardt's. She felt hot-faced and silly, and the next time she decided to visit Veda she drove the car herself, and went alone. Again she went by without stopping. Then she took to driving past Veda's at night, and peeping, hoping to see her. Once she did see her, and quickly pulled in at the curb. Taking care not to slam the car door, she slipped out of the car and crept to the window. Veda was at the piano, playing. Then suddenly the miracle voice was everywhere, going through glass and masonry as though they were air. Mildred waited, a-tremble, until the song was finished, then ran back to her car and drove off.

But the broadcasts continued, and Mildred's feeling of being left out in the cold increased, until it became intolerable. Veda didn't appear again on the Snack-O-Ham program. To Mildred's astonishment, her regular spot on the air was Wednesdays, at 3:15, as part of the Treviso Hour, offered by star pupils of the same Carlo Treviso who had once closed the piano so summarily over her knuckles. And then, after listening to two of these broadcasts, and drinking in Veda's singing and everything the announcer said about her, Mildred had an idea. By making use of Mr. Treviso, she could compel Veda to call her on the phone, to thank her for favors rendered. After that, pride would be satisfied and almost anything might happen.

So presently she was in the same old anteroom, with the same old vocalizing going on inside, and her temper growing hotter and hotter. But when Mr. Treviso finally received her, she had herself under what she thought was perfect control. As he gave no sign of recognition, she recalled herself to him, and he looked at her sharply, then bowed, but otherwise made no comment. She then made her little speech, which sounded stiff, and no doubt was supposed to sound stiff. "Mr. Treviso, I've come on a matter that I shall have to ask you to keep confidential, and when I tell you the reason, I'm sure you'll be only too glad to do so. My daughter Veda, I believe, is now taking lessons from you. Now for reasons best known to herself, she prefers to have nothing to do with me at the moment, and far be it from me to intrude on her life, or press her for explanations. Just the same, I have a duty toward her, with regard to the expenses of her musical education. It was I, Mr. Treviso, who was responsible for her studying music in a serious way, and even though she elects to live apart from me, I still feel that her music is my responsibility, and in the future, without saying anything to her, without saying one word to her, Mr. Treviso, I'd like you to send your bills to me, and not to her. I hope you don't find my request unreasonable."

Mr. Treviso had seated himself, and listened with his death-mask smile, and for some moments he studied his fingernails attentively. Then he stood up. "Am ver' sorry, Madame, but dees is subject w'ich I cannot discuss wit' you."

"Well I'm very sorry too, Mr. Treviso, but I'm afraid you'll have to discuss it with me. Veda is my daughter, and—"

"Madame, you excuse me, 'ave engagement."

With quick strides, he crossed to the door, and opened it as though Mildred were the queen of Naples. Nothing happened. Mildred sat there, and crossed her still shapely legs in a way that said plainly she had no intention of going until she had finished her business. He frowned, looked at his watch. "Yes, himportant engagement. You excuse me? Please."

He went out, then, and Mildred was left alone. After a few minutes, the little fat woman came in, found a piece of music, sat down at the piano, and began to play it. She played it loud, and then played it again, and again, and each time she played it was louder and still louder. That went on perhaps a half hour, and Mildred still sat there. Then Mr. Treviso came back and motioned the little fat woman out of the room. He strode up and down for a few minutes, frowning hard, then went over and closed the door. Then he sat down near Mildred, and touched her knee with a long, bony forefinger, "Why you want dees girl back? Tell me that?"

"Mr. Treviso, you mistake my motives. I—"

"No mistake, no mistake at all. I tell Veda, well you pretty lucky, kid, somebody else pay a bill now. And she, she got no idea at all, hey? Don't know how to call up, say thanks, sure is swell, how you like to see me again, hey?"

"Well that wasn't my idea, Mr. Treviso, but I'm sure, if Veda did happen to guess who was paying the bill, and called up about it, I could find it in my heart to—"

"Listen, you. I tell you one t'ing. Is make no difference to me who pay. But I say to you: you want to 'ear dees girl sing, you buy a ticket. You pay a buck. You pay two bucks. If a ticket cost eight eighty, O.K. you pay eight eighty, but don't try to 'ear dees girl free. Because maybe cost you more than a whole Metropolitan Grand Opera is wort'."

"This is not a question of money."

"No by God, sure is not. You go to a zoo, hey? See little snake? Is come from India, is all red, yellow, black, ver' pretty little snake. You take 'ome, hey? Make little pet, like puppy dog? No—you got more sense. I tell you, is same wit' dees Veda. You buy ticket, you look at a little snake, but you no take home. No."

"Are you insinuating that my daughter is a snake?"

"No—is a coloratura soprano, is much worse. A little snake, love mamma, do what papa tells, maybe, but a coloratura soprano, love nobody but own goddam self. Is son-bitch-bast', worse than all a snake in a world. Madame, you leave dees girl alone."

As Mildred sat blinking, trying to get adjusted to the wholly unexpected turn the interview had taken, Mr. Treviso took another turn around the room, then apparently became more interested in his subject than he had intended. He sat down now, his eyes shining with that Latin glare that had so upset her on her first visit. Tapping her knee again, he said: "Dees girl, she is coloratura, inside, outside, all over."

"What *is* a coloratura soprano?"

"Madame, is special fancy breed, like blue Persian cat. Come once in a lifetime, sing all a trill, a staccato ha-ha-ha, cadenza, a tough stuff—"

"Oh, now I understand."

"Cost like 'ell. If is *real* coloratura, bring more dough to a grand opera house than big wop tenor. And dees girl, is coloratura, even a bones is coloratura. First, must know all a rich pipple. No rich, no good."

"She always associated with nice people."

"Nice maybe, but must be rich. All coloratura, they got, 'ow you say?—da *gimmies*. Always take, never give. O.K., you spend plenty money on dees girl, what she do for you?"

"She's a mere child. She can't be expected to—"

"So—she do nothing for you. Look."

Mr. Treviso tapped Mildred's knee again, grinned. "She even twiddle la valiere all a coloratura, sit back like a duchess twiddle a la valiere." And he gave a startling imitation of Veda, sitting haughtily erect in her chair, twiddling the ornament of her neck chain.

"She's done that since she was a little girl!"

"Yes—is a funny part."

Warming up now, Mr. Treviso went on: "All a coloratura crazy for rich pipple, all take no give, all act like a duchess, all twiddle a la valiere, all a same, every one. All borrow ten t'ousand bucks, go to Italy, study voice, never pay back a money, t'ink was all friendship. Sing in grand opera, marry a banker, get da money. Got da money, kick out a banker, marry a baron, get da title. 'Ave a sweetie on a side, guy she like to sleep wit'. Den all travel together, all over Europe, grand opera to grand opera, 'otel—a baron, 'e travel in Compartment C, take care of dog. A banker, 'e travel in Compartment B, take care of luggage. A sweetie, 'e travel in Drawing Room A, take care of coloratura—all one big 'appy family. Den come a decoration from King of Belgium—first a command performance, Theatre de la Monnaie, den a decoration. All coloratura 'ave decoration from King of Belgium, rest of life twiddle a la valiere, talk about a decoration."

"Well—Los Angeles is some distance from Belgium—"

"No, no distance. Dees girl, make you no mistake, is big stuff. You know what make a singer? Is first voice, second voice, t'ird voice—yes, all know dees gag. Was Rossini's gag, but maybe even Rossini could be wrong. Must 'ave voice, yes. But is not what make a singer. Must 'ave music, *music* inside. Caruso, 'e could no read one note, but 'e have music in a soul is come out ever' note 'e sing. Must have rhythm, feel a beat of a music before conductor raise a stick. And specially coloratura—wit'out rhythm, wit'out music, all dees ha-ha-ha is vocalize, not'ing more. O.K., dees Veeda. I work on dees girl one week. She sing full chest, sound very bad, sound like a man. I change to head tone, sound good, I t'ink, yes, 'ere is a voice.

'Ere is one voice in a million. Den I talk. I talk music, music, music. I tell where she go to learn a sight-read, where learn 'armonia, where learn piano. She laugh, say maybe I 'ave somet'ing she can read by sight. On piano is a Stabat Mater, is 'ard, is tricky, is Rossini, is come in on a second beat, sing against accompaniment t'row a singer all off. I say O.K., 'ere is little t'ing you can read by sight. So I begin to play Inflammatus, from a Rossini Stabat Mater. Madame, dees girl hit a G on a nose, read a whole Inflammatus by sight, step into a C like was not'ing at all—don't miss one note. I jump up, I say Jesus Christus, where you come from? She laugh like 'ell. Ask is little 'armonia I want done maybe. Den tell about Charl', and I remember her now. Madame, I spend two hours wit' dees girl dees afternoon, and find out she know more music than I know. Den I really look dees girl over. I see dees deep chest, dees big bosom, dees 'igh nose, dees big antrim sinus in front of a face. Den I know what I see. I see what come once in a lifetime only—a great coloratura. I go to work. I give one lesson a day, charge one a week. I bring dees girl along fast, fast. She learn in six mont' what most singer learn in five year, seven year. Fast, fast, fast. I remember Malibran, was artist at fifteen. I remember Melba, was artist at sixteen. Dees girl, was born wit' a music in a soul, can go fast as I take. O.K., you 'ear Snack-O-Ham program?"

"Yes, I did."

"A Polonaise from Mignon, is tough. She sing like Tetrazzini. Oh, no, Madame, is not far from Los Angeles to Belgium for dees girl. Is no good singer. Is great singer. O.K., ask a pipple. Ask a pipple turned in on a Snack-O-Ham."

Mildred, who had listened to this eulogy as one might listen to soul-nourishing organ music, came to herself with a start, and murmured: "She's a wonderful girl."

"No—is a wonderful singer."

As she looked at him, hurt and puzzled, Mr. Treviso stepped nearer, to make his meaning clear. "Da girl is lousy. She is a bitch. Da singer—is not."

This seemed to be all, and Mildred got up. "Well—we're all

entitled to our opinion, but I would like it, if you don't mind, if you'd send your bills hereafter to me—"

"No, Madame."

"Have you any *particular* objection?"

"Yes, Madame. I no enjoy a snake bite. You come in 'ere, you try to make me play little part, part in intrigue to get your daughter back—"

"Mr. Treviso, that is your surmise."

"Is no surmise. For last two weeks, ever since Snack-O-Ham broadcast, dees little bitch 'ave told me a poor dumb mother will try to get 'er back, and a first t'ing she do is come here, offer pay for singing lesson."

"She—!"

"Yes! Dees girl, she live for two t'ing. One is make a mother feel bad, odder is get back wit' all a rich pipple she know one time in Pasadena. I tell you, is snake, is bitch, is coloratura. You want Veda back, you see Veda self. I 'ave not'ing to do wit' dees intrigue. She ask me, I say you not been 'ere at all— any'ow, *I* no see."

Mildred was so shaken up by Mr. Treviso's last revelation, that she wasn't capable of plans, schemes, or intrigues for the rest of that day. She felt as if she had been caught in some shameful act, and drove herself with work so as not to think about it. But, later that night things began to sort themselves out into little piles. She found some consolation in the certitude that at least *Veda* wouldn't know what she had done. And then, presently, she sat up in bed, hot excitement pulsing all through her. At last she knew, from that disclosure of Veda's desire to get back with the rich Pasadena people, how she would get her, how she would make even a coloratura come grovelling, on her knees.

She would get Veda through Monty.

15

Without making any special effort to do so, Mildred had kept track of Monty these last three years, had even had a glimpse of him once or twice, on her way back and forth to Laguna. He was exactly where she had left him: in the ancestral house, trying to sell it. The place, no more saleable, even in its palmiest days, than a white elephant, had a run-down look to it by now. The grass was yellow, from lack of water; across the lawn, in a bleary row, were half a dozen agents' signs; the iron dogs looked rusty; and one of the pillars, out front, had evidently been hit by a truck, for there was a big chip out of it, with raw brick showing through. However, though she knew where to find him, Mildred didn't communicate with Monty at once. She went to the bank, opened her safe-deposit box, and made an accurate list of her bonds. She looked at her balances, both checking and savings. She went to Bullock's, bought a new dress, new hat, new shoes. The dress was simple, but it was dark, and soft. She then called an agent, and without giving her name, got the latest asking price on the Beragon mansion.

All this took two or three days. Just how exact her plan was it would be hard to say. She was wholly feminine, and it seems to be part of the feminine mind that it can tack indefinitely upwind, each tack bearing off at a vague angle, and yet all bearing inexorably on the buoy. Perhaps she herself didn't quite know how many tacks she would have to make to reach the buoy, which was Veda, not Monty. At any rate, she now sent him a telegram, saying she wanted help in picking a house in Pasadena, and would he be good enough to call her around eight that night, "at the Pie Wagon"?

She was a little nervous that evening, but was as casual when Monty called as though there were no buoys in her life whatever. She explained chattily that she simply had to move soon, to live in some place that was more centrally located; that Pasadena would be most convenient, and would he be good enough to ride around with her, and let her get her bearings before she actually got around to picking out a house? He seemed a little puzzled, but said he would do what he could, and how about calling some agents, so they could ride around too, and show what they had? Agents, she said, were exactly what she wanted to avoid. She could see them any time. What she wanted was to get the feel of a town that he knew a great deal better than she did, perhaps peep at a few places, and get some idea where she wanted to live. Monty said he had no car at the moment, and could she pick him up? She said that was exactly what she wanted to do, and how about the next afternoon at three?

She dressed with a great deal of care the next afternoon, and when she surveyed herself in the long mirror, it was with quite a little satisfaction. For the last few months, perhaps as a result of the woe that had weighted her down, she hadn't put on any more weight, and the special girdle certainly held her belly in quite nicely. The new dress had a smart, casual look to it, and was of a becoming length, so that enough of her legs showed, but not too much. The big hat gave her a slightly flirty, Merry Widow look. The shoes flattered her feet, and set off the whole costume with a bit of zip. She tried a silver fox fur, decided it was right, and wore it. In truth, although she didn't look quite as she imagined she did, she looked rather interesting. She looked like a successful woman of business, with the remains of a rather seductive figure, a face of little distinction but considerable authority, a credit to the curious world that had produced her, Southern California.

It didn't suit her plans to have Tommy along, so she stepped into the car herself and was pleased at the expert way she handled it. She went zipping over the bridge to Pasadena, from the traffic circle down Orange Grove Avenue. When she got to the Beragon mansion, Monty was sitting on the steps waiting for her. She went roaring up the drive, stopped in front of him, said "Well!" and held out her hand. He took it, then jumped in beside her. Both were smiling, but a little pang shot through her at the change in him. He wore slacks, but they were cheap and unpressed. His bald spot was bigger; it had grown from the size of a quarter to the size of a big silver dollar. He was thin and lined, and had a brooding, hangdog look that was very different from the jaunty air he had once had. As to how she looked, he made no comment, and indeed indulged in no personal talk of any kind. He said he wanted her to see a place in the Oak Knoll section, quite decent, very reasonable. Would she care to drive over there? She said she'd love to.

By the time they had looked at places in the Oak Knoll section, the Altadena section, and the South Pasadena section, and nothing quite suited her, he seemed a little irritated. From the glib way he quoted prices, she knew he *had* called up the agents, in spite of her telling him not to, and that he would get a little split if she bought. But she paid no attention, and around five headed for Orange Grove Avenue again, to bring him home. Rather curtly, he said good-bye, and got out, and started inside, and then, as a sort of afterthought, stood waiting for her to leave. Pensively, she sat at the wheel, looking at the house, and then she cut the motor, got out, and stood looking at it. Then she let a noisy sigh escape her, and said, "Beautiful, beautiful!"

"It *could* be, with a little money spent on it."

"Yes, that's what I mean. . . . What do they want for it, Monty?"

For the first time that afternoon, Monty really looked at her.

All the places he had taken her to had been quoted around $10,000: evidently it hadn't occurred to him she could possibly be interested in this formidable pile. He stared, then said: "Year before last, seventy-five flat—and it's worth every cent of it. Last year, fifty. This year, thirty, subject to a lien of thirty-one hundred for unpaid taxes—all together around thirty-three thousand dollars."

Mildred's information was that it could be had for twenty-eight and a half, plus the tax lien, and she noted ironically that he was a little better salesman than she had given him credit for. However, all she said was: "Beautiful, beautiful!" Then she went to the door, and peeped in.

It had changed somewhat since her last visit, that night in the rain. All the furniture, all the paintings, all the rugs, all the dust cloths, were gone, and in places the paper hung down in long strips. When she tiptoed inside, her shoes gritted on the floor, and she could hear gritty, hesitant echoes of her steps. Keeping up a sort of self-conscious commentary, he led her through the first floor, then up to the second. Presently they were in his own quarters, the same servants' apartment he had occupied before. The servants' furniture was gone, but in its place were a few oak pieces with leather seats, which she identified at once as having come from the shack at Lake Arrowhead. She sat down, sighed, and said it certainly would feel good to rest for a few minutes. He quickly offered tea, and when she accepted he disappeared into the bedroom. Then he came out and asked: "Or would you like something stronger? I have the heel of a bottle here."

"I'd love something stronger."

"I'm out of ice and seltzer, but—"

"I prefer it straight."

"Since when?"

"Oh, I've changed a lot."

The bottle turned out to be Scotch, which to her taste was quite different from rye. As she gagged over the first sip he laughed and said: "Oh, you haven't changed much. On liquor I'd say you were about the same."

"That's what *you* think."

He checked this lapse into the personal, and resumed his praise of the house. She said: "Well you don't have to sell me. I'm already sold, if *wanting* it is all. And you don't have to sit over there yelling at me, as though I was deaf. There's room over here, isn't there?"

Looking a little foolish, he crossed to the settee she was occupying. She took his little finger, tweaked it. "You haven't even asked me how I am, yet."

"How are you?"

"Fine."

"Then that's that."

"How are you?"

"Fine."

"Then that's that."

She tweaked his little finger again. He drew it away and said: "You know, gentlemen in my circumstances don't have a great deal of romance in their lives. If you keep this up, you might find yourself the victim of some ravening brute, and you wouldn't like that, would you?"

"Oh, being ravened isn't so bad."

He looked away quickly and said: "I think we'll talk about the house."

"One thing bothers me about it."

"What's that?"

"If I should buy it, as I'm half a mind to, where would you be? Would there be a brute ravening around somewhere, or would I have it all to myself?"

"It would be all yours."

"I see."

She reached again for his finger. He pulled it away before she caught it, looking annoyed. Then, rather roughly, he put his arm around her. "Is that what you want?"

"H'm-h'm."

"Then that's that."

But she had barely settled back when he took his arm away.

"I made a slight mistake about the price of this house. To you, it's twenty-nine thousand, five hundred, and eighty. That'll square up a little debt I owe you, of five hundred and twenty dollars, that's been bothering me for quite some time."

"You owe me a debt?"

"If you try, I think you can recall it."

He looked quite wolfish, and she said "Booh!" He laughed, took her in his arms, touched the zipper on the front of her dress. Some little time went by, one half of him, no doubt, telling him to let the zipper alone, the other half telling him it would be ever so pleasant to give it a little pull. Then she felt her dress loosen, as the zipper began to slide. Then she felt herself being carried. Then she felt herself, with suitable roughness, being dumped down on the same iron bed, on the same tobacco-laden blankets, from which she had kicked the beach bag, years before, at Lake Arrowhead.

"Damn it, your legs are still immoral."

"You think they're bowed?"

"Stop waving them around."

"I asked you—"

"No."

Around dark, she grew sentimentally weepy. "Monty, I couldn't live here without you. I couldn't, that's all."

Monty lay still, and smoked a long time. Then, in a queer, shaky voice he said: "I always said you'd make some guy a fine wife if you didn't live in Glendale."

"Are you asking me to marry you?"

"If you move to Pasadena, yes."

"You mean if I buy this house."

"No—it's about three times as much house as you need, and I don't insist on it. But I will not live in Glendale."

"Then all *right!*"

She snuggled up to him, tried to be kittenish, but while he put his arm around her he continued sombre, and he didn't look at her. Presently it occurred to her that he might be hungry, and she asked if he would like to ride to Laguna with her, and have dinner. He thought a moment, then laughed. "You'd better go to Laguna alone, and I'll open myself another can of beans. My clothes, at the moment, aren't quite suitable to dining out. Unless, of course, you want me to put on a dinner coat. That mockery of elegance happens to be all I have left."

"We never had that New Year's party yet."

"Oh didn't we?"

"And we don't *have* to go to Laguna … I love you in a dinner coat, Monty. If you'll put one on, and then drive over with me while I put on *my* mockery of elegance, we can step out. We can celebrate our engagement. That is, if we really are engaged."

"All right, let's do it."

She spanked him on his lean rump, hustled him out of bed, and jumped out after him. She was quite charming in such moments, when she took absurd liberties with him, and for one flash his face lit up, and he kissed her before they started to dress. But he was sombre again when they arrived at her house. She put out whiskey, ice, and seltzer, and he made himself a drink. While she was dressing he wandered restlessly about, and then put his head in her bedroom and asked if he could put a telegram on her phone. "I'd like Mother to know."

"Would you like to talk to her?"

"It's a Philadelphia call."

"Well my goodness, you act as if it was Europe. Certainly call her up. And you can tell her it's all settled about the house, at thirty thousand, *without* any foolish deductions of five hundred and twenty dollars, or whatever it was. If that's what's been worrying her, tell her not to worry anymore."

"I'd certainly love to."

He went to the den, and she went on with her dressing. The blue evening dress was long since outmoded, but she had another one, a black one, that she liked very well, and she had just laid it out when he appeared at the door. "She wants to speak to you."

"Who?"

"Mother."

In spite of success, money, and long experience at dealing with people, a qualm shot through Mildred as she sat down to the phone, in a hastily donned kimono, to talk to this woman she had never met. But when she picked up the receiver and uttered a quavery hello, the cultured voice that spoke to her was friendship itself. "Mrs. Pierce?"

"Yes, Mrs. Beragon."

"Or perhaps you'd like me to call you Mildred?"

"I'd love it, Mrs. Beragon."

"I just wanted to say that Monty has told me about your plan to be married, and I think it splendid. I've never met you, but from all I've heard, from so many, many people I always felt you were the one wife for Monty, and I secretly hoped, as mothers often do, that one day it might come to pass."

"Well that's terribly nice of you, Mrs. Beragon. Did Monty tell you about the house?"

"He did, and I do want you to be happy there, and I'm sure you will. Monty is so attached to it, and he tells me you like it too—and that's a big step toward happiness, isn't it?"

"I would certainly think so. And I do hope that some time you'll pay us a visit there, and, and—"

"I'll be delighted. And how is darling Veda?"

"She's just fine. She's singing, you know."

"My dear, I heard her, and I was astonished—not really of course, because I always felt that Veda had big things in her. But even allowing for all that, she quite bowled me over. You have a very gifted daughter, Mildred."

"I'm certainly glad you think so, Mrs. Beragon."

"You'll remember me to her?"

"I certainly will, Mrs. Beragon."

She hung up flushed, beaming, sure she had done very well, but Monty's face had such an odd look that she asked: "What's the matter?"

"*Where* is Veda?"

"She—took an apartment by herself, a few months ago. It bothered her to have all the neighbors listening while she vocalized."

"That must have been messy."

"It was—terrible."

Within a week, the Beragon mansion looked as though it had been hit by bombs. The main idea of the alterations, which were under the supervision of Monty, was to restore what had been a large but pleasant house to what it had been before it was transformed into a small but hideous mansion. To that end the porticoes were torn off, the iron dogs removed, the palm trees grubbed up, so the original grove of live oaks was left as it had been, without tropical incongruities. What remained, after all this hacking, was so much reduced in size that Mildred suddenly began to feel some sense of identity with it. When the place as it would be began to emerge from the scaffolding, when the yellow paint had been burned off with torches and replaced with a soft white wash, when green shutters were in place, when a small, friendly entrance had taken the place of the former Monticello effect, she began to fall in love with it, and could hardly wait until it was finished. Her delight increased when Monty judged the exterior sufficiently advanced to proceed with the interior, and its furnishings. His mood continued dark, and he made no more allusions to the $520, or Glendale, or anything of a personal kind. But he seemed bent on pleasing Mildred, and it constantly surprised her, the way he was able to translate her ideas into paint, wood, and plaster.

About all she was able to tell him was that she "liked maple," but with this single bone as a clue, he reconstructed her whole taste with surprising expertness. He did away with paper, and had the walls done in delicate kalsomine. The rugs he bought in solid colors, rather light, so the house took on a warm, informal look. For the upholstered furniture he chose bright, inexpensive coverings, enunciating a theory to Mildred: "In whatever pertains to comfort, shoot the works. A room won't look comfortable unless it is comfortable, and comfort costs money. But on whatever pertains to show, to decoration alone, be a little modest. People will really like you better if you aren't so *damned* rich." It was a new idea to Mildred, and appealed to her so much that she went around meditating about it, and thinking how she could apply it to her restaurants.

He asked permission to hang some of the paintings of his ancestors, as well as a few other small pictures that had been stored for him by friends. However, he didn't give undue prominence to these things. In what was no longer a drawing room, but a big living room, he found place for a collection of Mildred Pierce, Inc.: Mildred's first menu, her first announcements, a photograph of the Glendale restaurant, a snapshot of Mildred in the white uniform, other things that she didn't even know he had saved—all enlarged several times, all effectively framed, all hung together, so as to form a little exhibit. At first, she had been self-conscious about them, and was afraid he had hung them there just to please her. But when she said something to this effect, he put down his hammer and wire, looked at her a moment or two, then gave her a compassionate little pat. "Sit down a minute, and take a lesson in interior decorating."

"I love lessons in decorating."

"Do you know the best room I was ever in?"

"No, I don't."

"It's that den of yours, or Bert's rather, over in Glendale. Everything in that room meant something to that guy. Those banquets, those foolish-looking blueprints of houses that will never be built, are a part of him. They do things to you. That's why the room is good. And do you know the worst room I was ever in?"

"Go on, I'm learning."

"It's that living room of yours, right in the same house. Not one thing in it—until the piano came in, but that's recent—ever meant a thing to you, or him, or anybody. It's just a room, I suppose the most horrible thing in the world. . . . A home is not a museum. It doesn't have to be furnished with Picasso paintings, or Sheraton suites, or Oriental rugs, or Chinese pottery. But it does have to be furnished with things that mean something to *you*. If they're just phonies, bought in a hurry to fill up, it'll look like that living room over there, or the way this lawn looked when my father got through showing how much money he had. . . . Let's have this place the way *we* want it. If you don't like the Pie Wagon corner, I do."

"I love it."

"Then it stays."

From then on, Mildred began to feel proud of the house and happy about it, and particularly relished the last hectic week, when hammer, saw, phone bell, and vacuum cleaner mingled their separate songs into one lovely cacophony of preparation. She moved Letty over, with a room of her own, and Tommy, with a room and a private bath. She engaged, at Monty's request, Kurt and Frieda, the couple who had worked for Mrs. Beragon before "es went kaput," as Kurt put it. She drove to Phoenix, with Monty, and got married.

For a week after this quiet courthouse ceremony she was almost frantic. She had addressed Veda's announcement herself, and the papers were full of the nuptials, with pictures of herself and lengthy accounts of her career, and pictures of Monty and just as lengthy accounts of *his* career. But there was no call from Veda, no visit, no telegram, no note. Many people dropped in: friends of Monty's, mostly, who treated her very pleasantly, and didn't seem offended when she had to excuse herself, in the afternoon at any rate, to go to work. Bert called, with all wishes for her happiness, and sincere praise for Monty, whom he described as a "thoroughbred." She was surprised to learn that he was living with Mom and Mr. Pierce. Mrs. Biederhof's husband having struck oil in Texas, and she having joined him there. Mildred had always supposed Mrs. Biederhof a widow, and so apparently had Bert. Yet the call that Mildred hoped for didn't come. Monty, well aware by now that a situation of some sort existed with regard to Veda, rather pointedly didn't notice her mood, or make any inquiries about it.

And then one night at Laguna, Mrs. Gessler appeared around eight in a bright red evening dress, and almost peremptorily told Mildred to close the place, as she herself was invited out. Mildred was annoyed, and her temper didn't improve when Archie took off his regimentals at nine sharp, and left within a minute or two. She was in a gloomy irritable humor going home, and several times called Tommy down for driving too fast. Until she was at the door of her new house, she didn't notice that a great many cars seemed to be parked out front, and even then they made no particular impression on her. Tommy, instead of opening for her, rang the bell twice, then rang it twice again. She was opening her mouth to say something peevish about people who forget their keys, when lights went up all over the first floor, and the door, as though of its own accord, swung slowly open, wide open. Then, from somewhere within, a voice, the only voice in the world to Mildred, began to sing. After a long time Mildred heard a piano, realized Veda was singing the Bridal Chorus from Lohengrin. "Here comes the bride," sang Veda, but "comes" was hardly the word. Mildred floated in, seeing faces, flowers, dinner coats, paper hats, hearing laughter, applause, greetings, as things in a dream. When Veda, still singing, came over, took her in her arms, and kissed her, it was almost more than she could stand, and she stumbled hurriedly out, and let Monty take her upstairs, on the pretext that she must put on a suitable dress for the occasion.

A few years before, Mildred would have been incapable of presiding over such a party: her commonplaceness, her upbringing, her sense of inferiority in the presence of "society people," would have combined to make her acutely miserable, completely incompetent. Tonight, however, she was a completely charming hostess and guest of honor, rolled into one. In the black evening dress, she was everywhere, seeing that people had what they wanted, seeing that Archie, who presided in the kitchen, and Kurt, Frieda, and Letty, assisted by Arline and Sigrid, from the Pie Wagon itself, kept things going smoothly. Most of the guests were Pasadena people, friends of Veda's and Monty's, but her waitress training, plus her years as Mildred Pierce, Inc., stood her in good stead now. She had acquired a memory like a filing cabinet, and had everybody's name as soon as she heard it, causing even Monty to look at her with sincere admiration. But she was pleased that he had asked such few friends as she had: Mrs. Gessler, and Ida, and particularly Bert, who looked unusually handsome in his dinner coat, and helped with the drinks, and turned music for Mr. Treviso when Veda, importuned by everybody, graciously consented to sing.

Mildred wanted to cry when people began to leave, and then discovered that the evening had hardly begun. The best part came when she, and Veda, and Monty sat around in the small library, across from the big living room, and decided that Veda should spend the night, and talked. Then Monty, not at all reverent in the presence of art, said: "Well goddam it, how did you get to be a singer? When *I* discovered you, practically pulled you out of the gutter, you were a pianist, or supposed to be. Then I no sooner turn my back than you turn into some kind of a yodeler."

"Well goddam it, it was an accident."

"Then report."

"I was at the Philharmonic."

"Yes, I've been there."

"Listening to a concert. And they played the Schubert Unfinished. And afterwards I was walking across the park, to my car, and I was humming it. And ahead of me I could see him walking along—"

"Who?"

"Treviso."

"Oh yes, the Neapolitan Stokowski."

"So I had plenty of reason for not walking to meet the honorable signor, because I'd played for him once, and he wasn't at all appreciative. So I slowed down, to let him get ahead. But then he stopped, and turned around, and looked, and then he came over to me, and said: 'Was that you singing?' Well, I have to explain that I wasn't so proud of my singing just about that time. I used to sing Hannen's songs for him, whenever he wrote one, but he used to kid me about it, because I sang full chest, and sounded exactly like a man. He called me the Glendale Baritone. Well, that was Charlie, but I didn't know why I had to take any kidding off Treviso. So I told him it didn't concern him whether I was singing or not, but he grabbed me by the arm, and said it concerned him very much, and me. Then he took a card from his pocket, and a pen, and ran under a light, and wrote his address on it, and handed it to me, and told me to be there the next day at four o'clock, that it was important. So that night I had it out with myself. I knew, when he handed me the card, that he had no recollection he had ever seen me before, so there was no question of kidding. *But*—did I want to unlock that door again or not?"

"What door?"

Monty was puzzled, but Mildred knew which door, even before Veda went on: "Of music. I'd driven a knife through its heart, and locked it up, and thrown the key away, and now here was Treviso, telling me to come down and see him tomorrow, at four o'clock. And do you know why I went?"

Veda was dead serious now, and looking at them both as though to make sure they got things straight. "It was because once he had told me the truth. I had hated him for it, the way he had closed the piano in front of me without saying a word, but it was his way of telling me the truth now. So I went. And for a week he worked on me, to get me to sing like a woman, and then it began to come the right way, and I could hear what he had heard that night out there in the park. And then he began to tell me how important it was that I become a musician. I had the voice, he said, if I could master music. And he gave me the names of this one and that one, who could teach me theory, and sight-reading, and piano, and I don't know what-all."

"Oh yeah?"

"Yeah, and did I get my revenge, for that day when he closed the piano on me. I asked him if there was a little sight-reading he wanted done, and he handed me the Inflammatus from Rossini's Stabat Mater. Well nuts. I went through that like a hot knife through butter, and he began to get excited. Then I asked him if he had a little job of arranging he wanted done, and then I told him about Charlie, and reminded him I'd been in there before. Well, if he'd hit gold in Death Valley he couldn't have acted more like a goof. He went all over me with instruments, little wooden hammers that he used on my knuckles, and caliper things that went over my nose, and gadgets with lights on them that went down my throat. Why he even—"

Veda made curious, prodding motions just above her midriff, while Monty frowned incredulously. "Yes! Believe it or not, he even dug his fingers in the Dairy. Well! I didn't exactly know what to think, or do."

Veda could make a very funny face when she wanted to, and Monty started to laugh. In spite of herself, so did Mildred. Veda went on: "But it turned out he wasn't interested in love. He was interested in meat. He said it enriched the tone."

"The *what?*"

Monty's voice rose to a whoop as he said this, and the next thing they knew, the three of them were howling with laughter, howling at Veda's Dairy as they had howled at Mrs. Biederhof's bosom, that first night, many years before.

When Mildred went to bed her stomach hurt from laughter, her heart ached from happiness. Then she remembered that while Veda had kissed her, that first moment when she had entered the house, she still hadn't kissed Veda. She tiptoed into the room she had hoped Veda would occupy, knelt beside the bed as she had knelt so many times in Glendale, took the lovely creature in her arms and kissed her, hard, on the mouth. She didn't want to go. She wanted to stay, to blow through the holes in Veda's pajamas. And when she got back to her room she couldn't bear it that Monty should be there. She wanted to be alone, to let these little laughs come bubbling out of her, to think about Veda.

Monty agreed to withdraw to the tackroom as he called the place where he stored his saddles, bridles, and furniture from the shack, with complete good humor—with more good humor, perhaps, than a husband should show, at such a request.

CHAPTER
16

Mildred now entered the days of her apotheosis. War was crashing in Europe, but she knew little of it, and cared less. She was drunk with the glory of the Valhalla she had entered: the house among the oaks, where dwelt the girl with the coppery hair, the lovely voice, and the retinue of admirers, teachers, coaches, agents, and thieves who made life so exciting. For the first time, Mildred became acquainted with theatres, opera houses, broadcasting studios, and such places, and learned something of the heartbreak they can hold. There was, for example, the time Veda sang in a local performance of Traviata, given at the Philharmonic under the direction of Mr. Treviso. She had just had the delightful sensation of beholding Veda alone on stage for at least ten minutes, and at the intermission went out into the lobby, to drink in the awestruck comment of the public. To her furious surprise, a voice behind her, a man's voice, with effeminate intonation, began: "So that's La Pierce, radio's gift to the lyric muse. Well, there's no use telling me, you can't raise singers in Glendale. Why, the girl's simply nauseating. She gargles it over her tonsils in that horrible California way, she's off pitch half the time, and as for acting—did you notice her routine, after Alfredo went off? She had no routine. She planted one heel on that dime, locked both hands in front of her, and just stayed there until ..."

While Mildred's temples throbbed with helpless rage, the voice moved off somewhere, and another one began, off to one side: "Well, I hope you all paid close attention to the critique of operatic acting, by one who knows nothing about it—somebody ought to *tell* that fag that the whole test of operatic acting is how few motions they have to make, to put across what they're trying to deliver. John Charles Thomas, can he make them wait till he's ready to shoot it! And Flagstad, how to be an animated Statue of Liberty! And Scotti, I guess he was nauseating. He was the greatest of them all. Do you know how many gestures he made when he sang the Pagliacci Prologue? One, just one. When he came to the F—poor bastard, he could never quite make the A flat—he raised his hand, and turned it over, palm upward. That was all, and he made you *cry.* . . . This kid, if I ever saw one right out of that can, she's it. So she locked her hands in front of her, did she? Listen, when she folded one sweet little paw into the other sweet little paw, and tilted that pan at a forty-five-degree angle, and began to warble about the delicious agony of love—I saw Scotti's little girl. My throat came up in my mouth. Take it from me, this one's in the money, or will be soon. Well, hell, it's what you pay for, isn't it?"

Then Mildred wanted to run after the first man, and stick out her tongue at him, and laugh. Some things, to be sure, she tried not to think about, such as her relations with Monty. Since the night Veda came home, Mildred had been unable to have him near her, or anybody near her. She continued to sleep alone, and he, for a few days, to sleep in the tackroom. Then she assigned a bedroom to him, with bath, dressing room, and phone extension. The only time the subject of their relations was ever discussed between them was when he suggested that he pick out his furniture himself; on that occasion, she had tried to be facetious, and said something about their being "middle-aged." To her great relief, he quickly agreed, and looked away, and started talking about something else. From then on, he was host to the numerous guests, master of the house, escort to Mildred when she went to hear Veda sing—but he was not her husband. She felt better about it when she noted that much of his former gaiety had returned. In a way, she had played him a trick. If, as a result, he was enjoying himself, that was the way she wanted it.

And there were certain disturbing aspects of life with Veda, as for example the row with Mr. Levinson, her agent. Mr. Levinson had signed Veda to a radio contract singing for *Pleasant,* a new brand of mentholated cigarettes that was just coming on the market. For her weekly broadcast Veda received $500, and was "sewed," as Mr. Levinson put it, for a year, meaning that during this period she could do no broadcasting for anybody else. Mildred thought $500 a week a fabulous stipend for so little work, and so apparently did Veda, until Monty came home one day with Mr. Hobey, who was president of Consolidated Foods, and had decided to spend part of his year in Pasadena. They were in high spirits, for they had been in college together: it was Mr. Hobey's mountainous, shapeless form that reminded Mildred that Monty was now in his forties. And Mr. Hobey met Veda. And Mr. Hobey heard Veda sing. And Mr. Hobey experienced a slight lapse of the senses, apparently, for he offered her $2,500 a week, a two-year contract, and a guarantee of mention in 25 percent of Consol's national advertising, if she would only sing for *Sunbake,* a new vitamin bread he was promoting. Veda, now sewed, was unable to accept, and for some days after that her profanity, her studied, cruel insults to Mr. Levinson, her raving at all hours of the day and night, her monomania on this one subject, were a little more than even Mildred could put up with amiably. But while Mildred was trying to think what to do, Mr. Levinson re-revealed an unexpected ability to deal with such situations himself. He bided his time, waited until a Sunday afternoon, when highballs were being served on the lawn out back, and Veda chose to bring up the subject again, in front of Mildred, Monty, Mr. Hobey, and Mr. Treviso. A pasty, judgy little man in his late twenties, he lit a cigar, and listened with half-closed eyes. Then he said: "O.K. ya dirdy li'l rat. Now s'pose ya take it back. Now s'pose ya 'pologize. Now s'pose ya say ya sorry."

"*I?* Apologize? to *you?*"

"I got a offer for ya."

"What offer?"

"Bowl."

"Then, accept. . . . If the terms are suitable." .

Mr. Levinson evidently noted how hard it was for Veda to say anything at all about terms, for the Hollywood Bowl is singer's heaven. He smiled a little, and said: "Not so fast, baby. It's kind of a double offer. They'll take Pierce or they'll take Opie Lucas—they leave it to me. I handle ya both, and Opie, she don't cuss me out. She's nice."

"A contralto's no draw."

"Contralto gets it if you don't 'pologize."

There was silence in the sunlight, while Veda's mouth became thick and wet, and Mr. Treviso smiled at a dancing mote, looking like a very benign cadaver. After a long time, Veda said: "O.K., Levy. I apologize."

Mr. Levinson got up, walked over to Veda, and slapped her hard, on the cheek. Monty and Mr. Hobey jumped up, but Mr. Levinson paid no attention. His soft, pendulous lower lip hanging down, he spoke softly to Veda: "What ya say now?"

Veda's face turned pink, then crimson, then scarlet, and her light blue eyes stared at Mr. Levinson with a fixity characteristic of certain varieties of shark. There was another dreadful pause, and Veda said: "O.K."

"Then O.K. And lemme tell ya someth'n, Pierce. Don't ya start noth'n with Moe Levinson. Maybe ya don't know where ya comin' out." Before sitting down, Mr. Levinson turned to Mr. Hobey. "Opie Lucas, she's free. She's free and she's hot. You want her? For twenty-five hunnerd?"

". . . No."

"I thought not."

Mr. Levinson resumed his seat. Monty and Mr. Hobey resumed their seats, Mr. Treviso poured himself a spoonful of the red wine he had elected, instead of a highball, and shot a charge of seltzer into it.

For the rest of the summer Mildred did nothing, and Veda did nothing, but get ready for this appearance at the Bowl. There were innumerable trips to buy clothes: apparently a coloratura couldn't merely buy a dress, and let it go at that. All sorts of questions had to be considered, such as whether the material took up light, from the spots, or reflected it, whether it gave, or whether it took. Then the question of a hat had to be decided. Veda was determined she must have one, a little evening affair that she could remove after the intermission, "to give some sense of progression, a gain in intimacy." These points were a little beyond Mildred, but she went eagerly to place after place, until a dressmaker in the Sunset Strip, near Beverly Hills, seemed to be indicated, and presently made the dress. It was, Mildred thought, incomparably lovely. It was bottlegreen, with a pale pink top, and a bodice that laced in front. With the little green bonnet it gave a sort of French garden-party effect. But Veda tried it on a dozen times, unable to make up her mind whether it was right. The question, it seemed, was whether it "looked like vaudeville." "I can't come out looking like both Gish sisters," said Veda, and when Mildred replied that neither of the Gish sisters had ever been in vaudeville, so far as she knew, Veda stared in the mirror and said it was all the same thing. In the end, she decided the bodice was "too much," and took it off. In truth, Mildred thought, the dress did look a little fresher, a little simpler, a little more suitable to a girl of twenty, than it had before. Still unsatisfied, Veda decided presently she would carry a parasol. When the parasol arrived, and Veda entered the living room, one night, as she would enter the Bowl, she got a hand. Mildred knew, and they all knew, that this was it.

Then there was the question of the newspapers, and how they should be handled. Here again, it seemed out of the question merely to call up the editors, tell them a local girl was going to appear, and leave the rest to their judgment. Veda did a great deal of telephoning about the "releases," as she called them, and then when the first item about her came out, she went into a rage almost as bad as the one that had been provoked by Mr. Hobey. At the end of an afternoon in which she tried vainly to locate Mr. Levinson, that gentleman arrived in person, and Veda marched around in a perfect lather: "You've got to stop it, Levy, you've got to kill this society girl stuff right now! And the Pasadena stuff! What do they want to do, kill my draw? And get me razzed off the stage when I come on? How many society people are there in this town, anyway? And how many Pasadena people go to concerts? Glendale! And radio! And studied right here in Los Angeles! There's twenty-five thousand seats in that place, Levy, and those boobs have got to feel that I'm their little baby, that I'm one of them, that they've got to come out there and root for me."

Mr. Levinson agreed, and seemed to regard the matter as important. Mildred, despite her worship of Veda, felt indignant that she should now claim Glendale as her own, after all the mean things she had said about it. But the mood passed, and she abandoned herself to the last few days before the concert. She took three boxes, holding four seats each, feeling sure that these would be enough for herself, Monty, and such few people as she would care to invite. But then the Bowl began calling up, saying they had another lovely box available, and she began remembering people she hadn't thought of before. In a day or so, she had asked Mom and Mr. Pierce, her mother and sister, Harry Engel and William, Ida and Mrs. Gessler, and Bert. All accepted except Mrs. Gessler, who rather pointedly declined. Mildred now had six boxes, with more than twenty guests expected, and as many more invited to the supper she was giving, afterwards.

According to Bert, who sat on the edge of her box and unabashedly held her hand, it had been a magnificent job of promotion, and the thing was a sell-out. So it seemed, for people were pouring through all entrances, and Bert pointed to the upper tiers of seats, already filling up, by which, he said, "you could tell." Mildred had come early, so she "wouldn't miss anything," particularly the crowd, and knowing that all these people had come just to hear her child sing. It was almost dark when Monty, who had driven Veda, slipped into the box and shook hands with Bert. Then the orchestra filed into the shell, and for a few minutes there was the sound of tuning. Then the lights went up, and the orchestra came to attention. Mildred looked around, and for the first time felt the vastness of the place, with these thousands of people sitting there waiting, and still other thousands racing up the ramps and along the aisles, to get to their seats. Then there was a crackle of applause, and she looked around in time to see Mr. Treviso, who was to conduct, mounting his little stand, bowing to the audience and to the orchestra. Without turning around, Mr. Treviso raised his hand. The audience stood. Bert and Monty stood, both very erect, both with stern, noble looks on their faces. Bewildered, Mildred stood. The orchestra crashed into *The Star-Spangled Banner,* and the crowd began to sing.

The first number, called *The Firebird,* meant nothing to Mildred. She couldn't make out, after reading her program, whether there was to be a ballet or not, and she wasn't at all certain, after it finished, whether there had been one or not. She concluded, while Mr. Treviso was still acknowledging his applause, that if there had been one she would have noticed it. He went out, the lights went up, and for a long time there was a murmur like the murmur of the ocean, as the later comers ran, beckoned to each other, and followed hurrying ushers, to find their seats. Then the murmur died off a little. The lights went out. A drawstring pulled tight on Mildred's stomach.

The parasol, wide open and framing the bonnet in a luminous pink circle, caught the crowd by surprise, and Veda was in the center of the stage before they recovered. Then they decided they liked it, and the applause broke sharp. For a moment Veda stood there, smiling at them, smiling at the orchestra, smiling at Mr. Treviso. Then expertly, she closed the parasol, planted it on the floor in front of her, and folded both hands over its rather high handle. Mildred, having learned to note such things by now, saw that it gave her a piquant, foreign look, and something to do with her hands. The first number, *Caro Nome*, from Rigoletto, went off well, and Veda was recalled for several bows. The second number, *Una Voce Poco Fa*, from the Barber of Seville, ended the first half of the concert. The lights went up. People spilled into the aisles, smoking, talking, laughing, visiting. Bert was sitting on the box again, saying it was none of his business, but in his opinion that conductor could very well have allowed Veda to sing an encore after all that applause. By God, that was an ovation if he ever heard one. Monty, not much more of an authority in this field than Bert was, but at least a little more of an authority, said it was his impression that no encores were ever sung in the first half of a program. All that, said Monty, in his understanding at least, was reserved for the end. Mildred said she was sure that was the case. Bert said then it was his mistake and that explained it. Because if he knew anything about it, these people were eating it up, and it did look as though Treviso would want to give the kid a break, if he could. All agreed that the people were eating it up.

The New World Symphony had little effect on Mildred, except that three airplanes went over while it was being played, and she became terrified lest one go over while Veda was singing, and ruin everything. But the sky was clear when she appeared again, looking much smaller than she had in the first half, quite girlish, a little pathetic. The parasol was gone, and the bonnet, instead of being on Veda's head, was carried in her hand. A single orchid was pinned to Veda's shoulder, and Mildred fiercely hoped that it was one of the six *she* had sent. The program said merely "Mad Scene from Lucia di Lammermoor," but there seemed to be a little more tension than usual before Mr. Treviso raised his stick, and presently Mildred knew she was present at a tremendous vocal effort. She had never heard one note of this music before, so far as she knew; it must have been rehearsed at the studio, not at home. After the first few bars, when she sensed that Veda was all right, that she would make no slip, that she would get through to the end, Mildred relaxed a little, permitted herself to dote on the de-

mure, pathetic little figure pouring all this elaborate vocal fret-
work out at the stars. There came a tap on her shoulder, and
Mr. Pierce was handing her a pair of opera glasses. Eagerly she
took them, adjusted them, levelled them at Veda. But after a
few moments she put them down. Up close, she could see the
wan, stagey look that Veda turned on the audience, and the
sharp, cold, look that she constantly shot at Mr. Treviso, particularly when there was a break, and she was waiting to come in.
It shattered illusion for Mildred. She preferred to remain at
a distance, to enjoy this child as she seemed, rather than as
she was.

The number was quite long, was in fact the longest number
Mildred had ever heard, but when it was done the sound that
swept over the vast amphitheatre was like thunder. Veda came
out for bow after bow, and presently, after her dozenth or so
reappearance, she came out followed by Mr. Treviso, and without hat or any encumbrance, just a simple, friendly little girl,
hoping to be liked. A gentleman with a flute stepped forward,
carrying a chair, and camped near Veda. When she saw him
she went over and shook his hand. Then Mr. Treviso took the
orchestra briskly through the introduction of *Lo, Hear the Gen-
tle Lark,* and there was a ripple of applause, for this was one
of the things that Veda had made popular on the radio. When
she got through there were cheers, and she began a whole series
of her radio numbers: *Love's Old Sweet Song,* Schubert's *Ave
Maria,* an arrangement of the *Blue Danube Waltz* that permitted her to do vocal gingerbread while the orchestra played the
tune, and a Waldteufel waltz Mr. Treviso had dug up for her,
called *Estudiantina.*

Many of these had been called for, with insistent shouting,
by the audience, and toward the end, the orchestra sat back
and listened while Mr. Treviso accompanied her on the piano
that had been pushed out during the intermission. Now Veda
came out, and said: "Even if it's not a song that's supposed to
be sung on a symphony program, may I sing a song just because
I want to sing it?" As the audience broke into amiable applause, Monty looked at Mildred, and she sensed something

coming. Then Mr. Treviso played a short introduction, and Veda began the song about rainbows that had been Mildred's favorite back in the happy days when she used to come home for her rest, and Veda would play the numbers she liked to hear.

It was all for her.

Veda began it, but when she finished it, or whether she finished it, Mildred never quite knew. Little quivers went through her and they kept going through her the rest of the night, during the supper party, when Veda sat with the white scarf wound around her throat, during the brief half hour, while she undressed Veda, and put the costume away; in the dark, while she lay there alone, trying to sleep, not wanting to sleep.

This was the climax of Mildred's life.

It was also the climax, or would have been if she hadn't got it postponed, of a financial catastrophe that had been piling up on her since the night she so blithely agreed to take the house off Mrs. Beragon's hands for $30,000, and pay the tax lien of $3,100. She had expected, when she made that arrangement, to do the major part of the financing through the Federal Homes Administration, about which she had heard. She received her first jolt when she paid a visit to this authority, and found it made no loans of more than $16,000. She had to have at least $20,000, and wanted $25,000. She received another jolt when she went to her bank. It was willing to lend her whatever she wanted, seemed to regard her as an excellent risk, but refused to lend anything at all until repairs were made to the property, particularly in the way of a new roof.

Up to then, she had known there would be outlays, but thought of them vaguely as "a couple of thousand to put the place in order, and a few thousand to furnish it." After the bank's report, however, she had to consider whether it wouldn't be better to give the place a complete overhaul, so that she would have a property that somebody might conceivably want to buy, instead of a monstrosity. That was when Monty was called into consultation. She didn't tell him about the financial problem, but she was delighted when he hit on the plan of restoring the house to what it had been before Beragon, Sr., put into effect his bizarre ideas for improvement. But while this satisfied the bank, and qualified her for a $25,000 loan, it cost upwards of $5,000, and cleaned out her personal cash. For the furnishings, she had to sell bonds. When she married Monty he had to have a car, or she thought he had. This meant $1,200 more. To get the money, and cover one or two other things that had come up by then, she dipped into the reserves of the corporation. She drew herself a check for $2,500 and marked it "bonus." But she didn't use a check from the big checkbook used by Miss Jaeckel, the lady she employed to keep the books. She used one of the blanks she always carried in her handbag, in case of emergency. She kept saying to herself that she must tell Miss Jaeckel about the check, but she didn't do it. Then, in December of 1939, to take care of Christmas expenses, she gave herself another bonus of $2,500, so that by the first of the year there was a difference of $5,000 between what Miss Jaeckel's books showed and what the bank was actually carrying on deposit.

But these large outlays were only part of her difficulties. The bank, to her surprise, insisted on amortization of her loan as well as regular interest payments, so that to the $125 a month in carrying charges were added $250 in reduction charges, a great deal more than she had anticipated. Then Monty, when he sold her Kurt and Frieda at $150 a month, put her to somewhat heavier expenses in the kitchen than she had expected. Then the endless guests, all of whom seemed to have the thirst of a caravan of camels, ran up the bill for household entertainment to an appalling figure. The result was that she was compelled to increase her salary from the corporation. Until then, she had allowed herself $75 a week from each of the corporation's four component parts: the Pie Wagon, the pie factory, the Beverly restaurant, and the Laguna restaurant, or $300 a week in all. This was so grotesquely in excess of her living expenses that the money piled up on her account, and it was so much less than the corporation's earnings that a nice little corporate reserve piled up too. But when she hiked it to $400, the reserve ceased growing, and in fact Miss Jaeckel, with stern face, several times notified her that it would be necessary to transfer money from *Reserve,* which was carried on a special account, to *Current Cash,* which was carried on another account. These transfers of $500 each Mildred O.K.'d hurriedly, and with averted eyes, feeling miserable, and like a thief.

Reserve, being a sort of sacred cow outside the routine bookkeeping system, didn't often come into Miss Jaeckel's purview, so there was no immediate danger she would learn of Mildred's withdrawals. And yet in March of 1940, when Miss Jaeckel made up the income statements, and took them down to the notary and swore to them, and left them, with the tax checks, for Mildred's signature, Mildred was in a cold sweat. She couldn't now face Miss Jaeckel and tell her what she had done. So she took the statements to an accountant, and swore him to secrecy, and told him what she had done, and asked him to get up another set, which she herself would swear to, and which would conform with the balance at the bank. He seemed upset, and asked her a great many questions, and took a week making up his mind that nothing unlawful had been done, so far. But he kept emphasizing that *"so far,"* and looking at Mildred in an accusing way, and he charged $100 for his services, an absurd sum for what amounted to a little recopying, with slight changes. She paid him, and had him forward the checks, and told Miss Jaeckel she had mailed them herself. Miss Jaeckel looked at her queerly, and went back to her little office in the pie factory without comment.

Then, within a week or two, two things happened, of an elusive, tantalizing sort, and it was hard to say what was cause and what was effect, but the Laguna business took an alarming drop, and didn't recover. The Victor Hugo, one of the oldest and best of the Los Angeles restaurants, opened a place not far from Mrs. Gessler's place, and at once did a thriving trade. And Mrs. Gessler, white-lipped and tense, informed Mildred one night that "that little bitch, that trollop from Los Feliz Boulevard, had moved down here."

"Is Ike seeing her?"

"How do I know who Ike sees? He's out on call half the time, and who knows where he goes, or when he comes back."

"Can't you find out?"

"I've found out, or tried to. No, he's not seeing her, that I know of. Ike's all right, if he gets half a break. But she's *here*. She's working in that pottery place, up the road about three miles, in a smock and—"

After that, it didn't seem to Mildred that Mrs. Gessler quite had her mind on her work. Trade slacked off, and Mildred couldn't think of any way to get it back. She cut prices, and that didn't help. She would have closed the place down, but she was bound by a lease, unless she could get rid of it, and the other three places wouldn't yield enough to pay rent under the lease, and maintain her establishment in Pasadena too. It was almost weekly now that Miss Jaeckel came to her for more cash, and the transfers from *Reserve,* instead of being $500 each, dwindled to $250, to $150, to $100, to $50, and still the spiral was going downwards. Mildred lived a queer, unnatural life. By day she was nervous, worried, hunted, afraid to look Miss Jaeckel in the eye, sure all her employees were whispering about her, suspecting her, accusing her. By night, when she came home to Monty, to Veda, to the inevitable guests, she abandoned herself to quiet, mystical, intense enjoyment. In these hours, she sealed herself off from the crises of the day, permitted herself no anxious thoughts, stared at Veda, drew deep, tremulous breaths.

But there came a day when *Reserve,* on the books, was $5,003.61 and at the bank was $3.61. She had to tell a long story to Miss Jaeckel, to cover her inability to make another transfer. Two days after that she couldn't pay her meat bill. Bills of all kinds, in the restaurant business, are paid on Monday, and failure to pay is a body blow to credit. Mr. Eckstein, of Snyder Bros. & Co., listened to Mildred with expressionless eyes, and agreed to deliver meat until she "straightened this little matter out." But all during the following week, Archie was raging at the inferior quality of the top sirloins, and Mrs. Gessler had to be restrained from calling Mr. Eckstein personally.

By Monday, Snyder Bros. were paid, but Mildred was asking time on other bills, particularly her liquor bill, most of which she owed Bodega, Inc. And then one day Wally Burgan strolled into the Pie Wagon, and it developed that he had been retained by several of her creditors. He suggested a little conference. As most of the trouble seemed to be at Laguna, how would she like to meet them down there the following night? They could have dinner, and then talk things over. The following night was the night Veda was to sing at the Bowl. Mildred shrilly said it was impossible, she had to be at the Bowl; nothing could interfere. Then, said Wally, how about one night next week? How about Monday?

The delay made matters worse, for Monday saw more unpaid bills, and in addition to Mr. Eckstein, Mr. Rossi of the Bodega, and representatives of three wholesale grocers, Mildred had to face Mr. Gurney and several small-fry market men who had previously been flattered if she so much as said good morning. Wally, however, kept everything on a courteous plane. He enjoined silence about the matter in hand while dinner was being served, lest waitresses hear things. He insisted that Mildred give him the check for the creditors' banquet, as he somewhat facetiously called it. He encouraged her to talk, to lay her cards on the table, so something could be arranged. He kept reminding her that nobody wanted to make trouble. It was to the interest of all that she get on her feet again, that she become the A1 customer she had been in the past.

Yet, at the end of two or three hours of questions, of answers, of figures, of explanations, the truth at last was out, and not even Mildred's stammering evasions could change it: All four units of the corporation, even the Laguna restaurant, would be showing a profit if it were not for the merciless milking that Mildred was giving them in order to keep up the establishment in Pasadena. Once this was in the open there was a long, grave pause, and then Wally said: "Mildred, you mind if we ask a few questions about your home finances? Kind of get that a little straightened out?"

"That's nobody's business but mine."

"None of it's anybody's business, so far as that goes. If we just went by what was our business, we'd have gone to court already, asking for receivers, and strictly kept our questions to ourselves. We didn't do that. We wanted to give you a break. But looks like we're entitled to little consideration too, don't it? Looks like we could go into what *we* think is important. Maybe you don't think so. Maybe that's where the trouble is. It's you that's behind the eight ball, not us."

"... What do you want to know?"

"How much does Veda pay in?"

"I don't charge my own child board, I hope."

"She's the big expense though, isn't she?"

"I don't keep books on her."

"This is what I'm getting at: Veda, she's making plenty. She had some dough, that I got for her, and she was smart the way she invested it. She's dragging down $500 a week from Pleasant, and even after she pays all them agents, teachers, and chiselers, she must have quite a lot left over. Well, wouldn't you be justified in deducting an amount to pay for her keep? If you did, that would kind of ease the pressure all around."

Mildred opened her mouth to say she couldn't do any deducting, that she had nothing to do with Veda's income. Then, under Wally's bland manner she noted something familiar, something cold. As her heart skipped a beat, she knew she mustn't fall into any traps, mustn't divulge any of her arrangements with Veda. She must stall, say this was something she hadn't thought of before, insist there were legal angles she would have to look into before she would know how she felt. So mumbling, she kept watching and saw Mr. Rossi look at Mr. Eckstein. Then she knew what this was about. Wally was engineering a little deal. The creditors were to get their money, the corporation was to be placed on a sounder basis, and Veda was to foot the bill. It didn't occur to her that there was an element of justice in this arrangement: that the creditors had furnished her with goods, and were entitled to payment; that Veda earned large sums, and had run a lengthy bill. All she knew was that hyenas were leaping at her chick, and her craftiness, her ability to stall, deserted her. She became excited, said that no child of hers was going to be made the victim of any such gyp, if she had anything to do with it. Then, looking Wally in the eye, she went on: "And what's more, I don't believe you or anybody has any right, even any legal right, to take what belongs to me, or what belongs to my child, to pay the bills of this business. Maybe you've forgotten, Mr. Wally Burgan, that it was you that had me incorporate. It was you that had the papers drawn up and explained the law to me. And your main talking point was that if I incorporated, then my personal property was safe from any and all creditors of the corporation. Maybe you've forgotten that, but I haven't."

"No, I haven't forgotten it."

Wally's chair rasped as he stood to face her, where she was already standing, a few feet back from the big round table. "I haven't forgotten it, and you're quite right, nobody here can take one dime of your money, or your personal property, or Veda's, to satisfy the claims they got, makes no difference how reasonable the claims may be. They can't touch a thing, it's all yours and a yard wide. All they can do is go to court, have you declared a bankrupt, and take over. The court will appoint receivers, and the receivers will run it. You'll be out."

"All right, then I'll be out."

"You'll be out, and Ida'll be in."

"... Who?"

"You didn't know that, did you?"

"That's a lie. She wouldn't—"

"Oh yes she would. Ida, she cried, and said at first she wouldn't even listen to such a thing, she was such a good friend of yours. But she couldn't get to you, all last week, for a little talk. You were too busy with the concert. Maybe that hurt her a little. Anyway, now she'll listen to reason, and we figure she can run this business as good as anybody can run it. Not as good as you, maybe, when you've got your mind on it. But better than a stagestruck dame that would rather go to concerts than work, and rather spend the money on her child than pay her creditors."

At the revelation about Ida, tears had started to Mildred's eyes, and she turned her back while Wally went on, in a cold, flat voice: "Mildred, you might as well get it through your head you got to do these things. You got to cut down on your overhead, so you can live on what you make. You got to raise some money, from Veda, from the Pierce Drive property, from somewhere, so you can square up these bills and start over. And you got to cut out this running around and get down to work. Now, as I said before, there's no hard feelings. We all wish you well. Just the same, we mean to get our money. Now you show us some action by a week from tonight, and you can forget it, what's been said. You don't and maybe we'll have to take a little action ourselves."

It was around eleven when she drove up to the house, but she tapped Tommy on the shoulder and stopped him when she saw the first floor brightly lit, with five or six cars standing outside. She was on the verge of hysteria, and she couldn't face Monty, and eight or ten polo players, and their wives. She told Tommy to call Mr. Beragon aside, and tell him she had been detained on business, and wouldn't be in until quite late. Then she moved forward, took the wheel, and drove out again into Orange Grove Avenue. It was almost automatic with her to turn left at the traffic circle, continue over the bridge, and level off for Glendale and Bert. There was no light at Mom's, but she knew he was home, because the car was in the garage, and he was the only one who drove it now. At her soft tap he opened a window, and told her he would be right out. At the sight of her face, he stood for a moment in his familiar, battered red bathrobe, patted her hand, and said goddam it this was no place to talk. Mom would be hollering, wanting to know what was going on, and Pop would be hollering, trying to tell her, and it just wouldn't work. He asked Mildred to wait until he got his clothes on, and for a few minutes she sat in the car, feeling a little comforted. When he came out, he asked if she'd like him to drive, and she gladly moved over while he pulled away from the curb in the easy, grand style that nobody else quite seemed to have. He said it sure was one swell car, specially the way it held the road. She hooked her arm through his.

"Veda has to kick in."

They had driven to San Fernando, to Van Nuys, to Beverly, to the ocean, and were now in a little all-night cocktail bar in Santa Monica. Mildred, breaking into tears, had told the whole story, or at least the whole story beginning with Veda's return home. The singular connection that Monty had with it, and particularly the unusual circumstances of her marriage, she conveniently left out, or perhaps she had already forgotten them. But as to recent events, she was flagitiously frank, and even told about the two $2,500 checks, as yet undiscovered by Miss Jaeckel. At Bert's whistle there was a half-hour interlude, while he went into all details of this transaction, and she spoke in frightened whispers, yet gained a queer spiritual relief, as though she were speaking through the lattice of a confessional. And there was a long, happy silence after Bert said that so far as he could see, there had been no actual violation of the law. Then solemnly he added: "Not saying it wasn't pretty damn foolish."

"I *know* it was foolish."

"Well then—"

"You don't have to *nag* me."

She lifted his hand and kissed it, and then they were back to the corporation and its general problem. It could only be solved, he had insisted, through Veda. Now, on his second highball, he was even more of that opinion. "She's the one that's costing you money, and she's the one that's making money. She's got to pay her share."

"I never wanted her to know."

"I never wanted her to know, either, but she found out just the same, when I hit the deck. If she'd had a little dough when Pierce Homes began to wobble, and I'd taken it, and Pierce Homes was ours right now, she'd be better off, wouldn't she?"

Mildred pressed Bert's hand, and sipped her rye, then she held his hand tight, and listened to the radio for a minute or two, as it began moaning low. She hadn't realized until then that Bert had been through all this himself, that she wasn't the only one who had suffered. Bert, in a low voice that didn't interfere with the radio, leaned forward and said: "And who the hell put that girl where she is today? Who paid for all the music? *And* that piano. *And* that car? *And* those clothes? And—"

"You did your share."

"Mighty little."

"You did a lot." Intermingling of Pierce Homes, Inc., with Mildred Pierce, Inc., plus a little intermingling of rye and seltzer, had brought Bert nearer to her than he had ever been before, and she was determined that justice must be done him. "You did plenty. Oh we lived very well before the Depression, Bert, as well as any family ever lived in this country, or any other. And a long time. Veda was eleven years when we broke up, and she's only twenty now. I've carried on nine years, but it was eleven for you."

"Eleven years and eight months."

Bert winked, and Mildred quickly clutched his hand to her cheek. "All right, eleven years and eight months, if you've got to bring that up. And I'm *glad* it was only eight months, how do you like that? Any boob can have a child nine months after she gets married. But when it was only eight, that proves I loved you, doesn't it?"

"Me too, Mildred."

Mildred covered his hand with kisses, and for a time they said nothing, and let the radio moan. Then Bert said: "You want me to talk to that girl?"

"I can't ask her for money, Bert."

"Then I'll do it. I'll drop over there this afternoon, and bring it up friendly, and let her know what she's got to do. It's just ridiculous that you should have your back to the wall, and she be living off you, and rolling in dough."

"No, no. I'll mortgage the house. In Glendale."

"And what good will that do you? You raise five grand on

it, you square up for a few weeks, and then you're right back where you started. She's got to kick in, and keep on kicking."

They ran up the beach to Sunset Boulevard and rode homeward in silence. Then unexpectedly Bert pulled over, stopped, and looked at her. "Mildred, you've got to do it yourself."

"... Why?"

"Because you've got to do it tonight."

"I can't, it's late, she'll be asleep—"

"I can't help how late it is, or whether she's asleep, or she's not asleep. You've got to see her. Because you forgot, and I forgot, and we both forgot who we're dealing with. Mildred, you can't trust Wally Burgan, not even till the sun comes up. He's a cheap, chiseling little crook, we know that. He was my pal, and he crossed me, and he was your pal, and he crossed you. But listen, Mildred: He was Veda's pal too. Maybe he's getting ready to cross *her*. Maybe he's getting ready to grab her dough—"

"He can't, not for corporate debts—"

"How do you know?"

"Why, he—"

"That's it, he told you. Wally Burgan told you. You believe everything he says? You believe *anything* he says? Maybe that meeting tonight was just a phony. Maybe he's getting ready to compel you to take over Veda's money, as her guardian, so he can attach it. She's still a minor, remember. Maybe you, I, and Veda will all have papers slapped on us today. Mildred, you're seeing her tonight. And you're getting her out of that house, so no process server can find you. You're meeting me at the Brown Derby in Hollywood for breakfast, and by that time *I'll* be busy. There'll be four of us at that table, and the other one will be a lawyer."

Conspiratorial excitement carried Mildred to Veda's room, where necessity might never have driven her there. It was after three when she came up the drive, and the house was dark, except for the hall light downstairs. She put the car away, walked on the grass to keep from making a noise, and let herself in the front door. Putting the light out, she felt her way upstairs, carefully staying on the carpeting, so her shoes would make no clatter. She tiptoed along the hall to Veda's room and tapped on the door. There was no answer. She tapped again, using the tips of her fingers, to make only the softest sound. Still there was no answer. She turned the knob and went in. Not touching any light switch, she tiptoed to the bed, and bent down to touch Veda, to speak to her, so she wouldn't be startled. Veda wasn't there. Quickly she snapped on the bed light, looked around. Nobody was in the room, and it hadn't been slept in. She went to the dressing room, to the bathroom, spoke softly. She opened a closet. Veda's things were there, even the dress she had put on tonight, before Mildred went to Laguna. Now puzzled and a little alarmed, Mildred went to her own room, on the chance Veda had gone there to wait for her, and fallen asleep, or something. There was no sign of Veda. Mildred went to Monty's room, and rapped. Her tempo was quickening now, and it was no finger rap this time. It was a sharp knuckle rap. There was no answer. She rapped, again, insistently. Monty, when he spoke, sounded sleepy, and quite disagreeable. Mildred said it was she, to let her in, she had to see him. He said what about, and why didn't she go to bed and let him sleep? She rapped again, imperiously this time, and commanded him to let her in. It was about Veda.

When he finally came to the door, half opened it, and found what Mildred wanted, he was still more annoyed. "For God's sake, is she an infant? Suppose she's not there, what do I do then? I went to bed—I don't know what she did. Maybe she went somewhere. Maybe she had a blowout. Maybe she's looking at the moon. It's a free country."

"She didn't go anywhere."

"How do you know?"

"Her dress is there."

"Couldn't she have changed it?"

"Her car is there."

"Couldn't she have gone with somebody else?"

This simple possibility hadn't even occurred to Mildred, and she was about to apologize and go back to her room when she became aware of Monty's arm. He was leaning on it, but it was across the door, in a curious way, as though to bar her from the room. Her hand, which was resting on the door casing, slipped up, flipped the light switch. Veda was looking at her, from the bed.

Monty, his voice an emasculated, androgynous yell, crammed all the bitterness, the futility of his life into a long, hysterical denunciation of Mildred. He said she had used him for her special purposes ever since she had met him. He said she was incapable of honor, and didn't know what it meant to stand by her commitments. He recalled the first $20 she had given him, and how she had later begrudged it. He worked down to their marriage, and correctly accused her of using him as bait to attract the errant Veda. But, he said, what she had forgotten was that he was live bait, and the quarry and the bait had fallen in love, and how did she like that? And what was she going to do about it? But there was considerable talk about money mixed in with the chase, and what it added up to was that he had shown his independence of one woman who had been keeping him, with a pie wagon, by switching over and letting another woman keep him, with a voice.

Mildred, however, barely heard him. She sat in the little upholstered chair, near the door, her hat on the side of her head, her handbag in her lap, her toes absurdly turned in. But while her eyes were on the floor, her mind was on the lovely thing in the bed, and again she was physically sick at what its presence there meant. When Monty had talked some little time, stalking gauntly about in his pajamas, Veda interrupted him with affectionate petulance: "Darling! Does it make any difference what such nitwits do, or whether they pay, or even know what a commitment is? Look what a pest she is to me. I literally can't open my mouth in a theatre, or a radio studio, or anywhere, that she isn't there, bustling down the aisle, embarrassing me before people, all to get *her* share of the glory, if any. But what do I do? I certainly don't go screaming around the way *you're* doing. It would be undignified. And very—" here Veda stifled a sleepy yawn—"*very* bad for my throat. ... Get dressed now, and we'll clear out, and leave her to her pie plates, and by lunch time it'll merely seem funny."

Monty went to his dressing room, and for a time there was silence, except for Mildred's breathing, which was curiously heavy. Veda found cigarettes on the floor, and lit one, and lay there smoking in the way she had acquired lately, sucking the smoke in and letting it out in thick curls, so it entered her mouth but didn't reach her throat. Mildred's breathing became heavier, as though she were an animal, and had run a distance, and was panting. Monty came out, in tweeds, a blue shirt, and tan shoes, his hat in one hand, a grip in the other. Veda nodded, squashed out her cigarette. Then she got up, went to Monty's mirror, and began combing her hair, while little cadenzas absentmindedly cascaded out of her throat, and cold drops cascaded over Mildred's heart. For Veda was stark naked. From the massive, singer's torso, with the Dairy quaking in front, to the slim hips, to the lovely legs, there wasn't so much as a garter to hide a path of skin.

Veda, still humming, headed for the dressing room, and Monty handed her the kimono, from the foot of the bed. It was then that Mildred leaped. But it wasn't at Monty that she leaped, her husband, the man who had been untrue to her. It was at Veda, her daughter, the girl who had done no more than what Mildred had once said was a woman's right. It was a ruthless creature seventeen years younger than herself, with fingers like steel from playing the piano, and legs like rubber from riding, swimming, and all the recreations that Mildred had made possible for her. Yet this athlete crumpled like a jellyfish before a panting, dumpy little thing in a black dress, a hat over one ear, and a string of beads that broke and went bouncing all over the room. Somewhere, as if from a distance, Mildred could hear Monty, yelling at her, and feel him, dragging at her to pull her away. She could feel Veda scratching at her eyes, at her face, and taste blood trickling into her mouth. Nothing stopped her. She clutched for the throat of the naked girl beneath her, and squeezed hard. She wrenched the other hand free of Monty, and clutched with that too, and squeezed with both hands. She could see Veda's face getting red, getting purple. She could see Veda's tongue popping out, her slaty blue eyes losing expression. She squeezed harder.

She was on the floor, beside the bed, her head ringing from heavy blows. Across the room, in the kimono now, huddled in a chair, and holding on to her throat, was Veda. She was gasping, and Monty was talking to her, telling her to relax, to lie down, to take it easy. But Veda got to her feet and staggered out of the room. Mildred, sensing some purpose in this exit, and taking its evil nature for granted, scrambled up and lurched after her. Monty, pleading for an end to "this damned nonsense," followed Mildred. Letty and Frieda, in night dresses, evidently aroused by the commotion, stared in fright at the three of them, as Veda led the way down the big staircase. They made in truth a ghastly procession, and the gray light that filtered in seemed the only conceivable illumination for the hatred that twisted their faces.

Veda turned into the living room, reeled over to the piano, and struck a chord. Then her breath came fast, as though she was going to vomit, but Mildred, a horrible intuition suddenly stabbing at her, knew she was trying to sing. No sound came. She struck the chord again, and still there was no sound. On the third try, a dreadful croak, that was like a man's voice and yet not like a man's voice, came out of her mouth. With a scream she fell on the floor, and lay there, writhing in what appeared to be convulsions. Mildred sat down on the bench, sick with the realization of what she had done. Monty began to weep hysterically, and to shout at Mildred: "Came the dawn! ... Came the dawn—God, what a dawn!"

CHAPTER

17

It was Christmas again on Pierce Drive, a balmy golden California Christmas. Mildred, after the most crushing period of life, was beginning to live again, to hope that the future might hold more than pain, or even worse, shame. It wasn't the mad, spinning collapse of her world that had paralyzed her will, left her with the feeling that she must wear a veil, so she needn't look people in the eye. The loss of Mildred Pierce, Inc., had been hard. It had been doubly hard because she would always know that if Wally Burgan had been a little less brutal, if Mrs. Gessler had been a little more loyal, and not gone off on her four-day drunk, telephoning the news of Ike's blonde at hourly intervals, with reversed charges, from Santa Barbara to San Francisco—she might have weathered the storm. These calls had been one of the features of her stay in Reno, that six-week fever dream in which she constantly listened to Mr. Roosevelt, and couldn't get it through her head that she couldn't vote for him this year, as she would be a resident of Nevada, not of California. And it had been hard, the wilting discovery that she could no longer do business under her own name. That, it turned out, was still owned by the corporation, and she thought bitterly of the many debts she owed to Wally.

But what had left her with a scar on her soul that she thought nothing could ever heal, was a little session, lasting barely an hour, with a stenographer and a pair of attorneys. It seemed that Veda, the day after she left the hospital, reported as usual at the broadcasting studio, for rehearsal with the Pleasant Orchestra. The rough, male voice that came out of the amplifiers wasn't quite what Pleasant had contracted for, and the conductor had called the rehearsal off. Veda, that day and the day after, had insisted that she was willing to go through with her contract. Thereupon Pleasant had gone to court to have the contract annulled, on the ground that Veda was no longer able to fulfill it.

Veda's attorney, brother of Mr. Levinson, her agent, felt it necessary to prove that Veda's vocal condition was due to no fault of her own. Thus it was that Mildred, before she moved out of the Beragon mansion and advertised it for rent, before she went to Reno for the divorce, before she even got the icebags off her head had to give a deposition, telling about her quarrel, and how she had throttled Veda, so she had lost her voice. This was painful enough, even though neither attorney pressed her for an exact account of what the quarrel was about, and let her ascribe it to "a question of discipline." But the next day, when the newspapers decided this was a strange, exciting, and human story, and published it under big headlines, with pictures of Mildred and Veda, and insets of Monty, and hints that Monty might have been back of the "question of discipline," then indeed was the albatross publicly hung on Mildred's neck. She had destroyed the beautiful thing that she loved most in the world, and had another breakdown, and couldn't get up for some days.

Yet when Veda came to Reno, and elaborately forgave her, and there were more pictures, and big stories in the papers, Mildred was weepily grateful. It was a strange, unnatural Veda who settled down with her at the hotel, a wan, smiling wraith who talked in whispers, on account of the condition of her throat, and seemed more like the ghost of Veda than Veda herself. But at night, when she thought about it, it all became clear to Mildred. She had done Veda a wrong, and there was but one way to atone for it. Since she had deprived Veda of her "means of livelihood," she must provide the child a home, must see that she would never know want. Here again was a familiar emotional pattern, with new excuses. But Bert felt about it as she did. She sent him $50, asking if he could come up and see her, and explaining that she couldn't go to see him, as she wasn't permitted to leave the state of Nevada until her divorce was granted. He came up the next weekend, and she took him for a long ride, down toward Tonopah, and they threshed it out. Bert was greatly moved by the details of Veda's arrival, and forgiveness. Goddam it, he said, but that made him feel good. It just went to show that when the kid was seeing the right kind of people, she was true blue inside, just what you'd want her to be. He agreed that the least Mildred could do was provide Veda a home. To her stammering inquiry as to whether he wanted to help her provide it, he gravely said he didn't know anything he'd like better. He was up for two more weekends, and after the divorce there was a quiet courthouse wedding. To Mildred's surprise, Veda wasn't the only guest. Mr. Levinson showed up, saying he happened to be in town on business, and was a sucker for rice.

The days after Thanksgiving had been bleak and empty for Mildred: she couldn't get used to it that the Pie Wagon was no longer hers, that she had nothing to do. And she couldn't get used to it that she was cramped for small money. She had mortgaged the house on Pierce Drive, into which she had now moved, obtaining $5,000. But most of this had been spent in Reno, and the rest of it was rapidly melting. Yet she had resolved they were going to have Christmas, and bought Bert a new suit, and Veda one of the big automatic phonographs, and several albums of records. This bit of recklessness restored her to a touch of her old self, and she was a little gay as Letty announced dinner. Bert had made eggnog, and it felt warm and pleasant, and as the three of them went back to the dining room she suddenly remembered she had bumped into Mr. Chris the day before, at the Tip-Top, and he was furious at the pies that were being delivered to him by Mildred Pierce, Inc. "He couldn't believe it when I told him I have nothing more to do with it, but when I asked him how he'd like to have some of *my* pies, he almost kissed me. 'Hokay, hokay, any time, bring'm in, appliss, limmon, e poomkin!' "

She was so pleased at the way she imitated Mr. Chris's dialect that she started to laugh, and they all started to laugh. Then Bert said if she felt like making pies again, just leave the rest to him. He'd sell them. Veda laughed, pointed at her mouth, whispered that she'd eat them. Mildred wanted to jump up and kiss her, but didn't.

The doorbell rang. Letty went to answer it, returned in a moment with a puzzled look on her face. "The taxi man's there, Mrs. Pierce."

"Taxi? I didn't order any taxi."

"Yes'm, I'll tell him."

Veda stopped Letty with a gesture. "I ordered it."

"*You* ordered it."

"Yes, Mother."

Veda got up from her untouched turkey, and calmly faced Mildred. "I decided some time ago that the place for me is New York, and I'm leaving in a little while from Union Air Terminal, in Burbank. I meant to tell you."

Bewildered, Mildred blinked at Veda's cold, cruel eyes, noted that Veda was now talking in her natural voice. A suspicion flashed into her mind. "Who are you going with?"

"Monty."

"Ah."

All sorts of things now began to flit through Mildred's mind, and piece themselves together: remarks by Mr. Hobey, the *Sunbake* promoter, the big forgiveness scene in Reno, featured by the newspapers, the curious appearance of Mr. Levinson at her wedding. Then, while Veda still stood coldly smiling, Mildred began to talk, her tongue licking her lips with quick, dry motions like the motions of a snake's tongue. "I see it now. . . . You didn't lose any voice, you just thought faster than anybody else, that night. . . . If you could make me say I choked you, then you could break your contract with Pleasant, the company that gave you your first big chance. You used to sing full chest, like a man, and you could do it again, if you had to. So you did, and you made me swear to all that, for a court record, so the newspapers could print it. But then you found out you'd gone a little too far. The newspapers found out about Monty, and that wasn't so good for the radio public. So you came to Reno, and had pictures of yourself taken, with me in your arms. And at my wedding, to your father. And you even invited that Levinson to be there, as though he meant anything to me. Anything to cover up, to hide what had really been going on, the love affair you'd been having with your mother's husband, with your own stepfather."

"Anyway, I'm going."

"And I know perfectly well why you're going. Now the publicity has blown over a little, you're going to sing for Sunbake, for $2,500 a week. All right—but this time, don't come back."

Mildred's voice rose as she said this, and Veda's hand involuntarily went to her throat. Then Veda went to her father, and kissed him. He kissed her, and patted her, but his eyes were averted, and he seemed a little cold. Then she left. When the taxi door slammed, and it had noisily pulled away, Mildred went to the bedroom, lay down, and began to cry. Perhaps she had something to cry about. She was thirty-seven years old, fat, and getting a little shapeless. She had lost everything she had worked for, over long and weary years. The one living thing she had loved had turned on her repeatedly, with tooth and fang, and now had left her without so much as a kiss or a pleasant goodbye. Her only crime, if she had committed one, was that she had loved this girl too well.

Bert came in, with a decisive look in his eye and a bottle of rye in his hand. In masterful fashion he sloshed it once or twice, then sat down on the bed. "Mildred."

"Yes."

"To hell with her."

This remark only served to step up the tempo of Mildred's sobs, which were approaching a wail already. But Bert took hold of her and shook her. "I said to hell with her!"

Through the tears, the woe, Mildred seemed to sense what he meant. What it cost her to swallow back her sobs, look at him, squint, and draw the knife across an umbilical cord, God alone knows. But she did it. Her hand tightened on his until her fingernails dug into his skin, and she said: "O.K., Bert. To hell with her!"

"Good*dam* it, that's what I want to hear! Come on, we got each other, haven't we? Let's get stinko."

"Yes—let's get stinko."

ABOUT THE AUTHOR

JAMES M. CAIN (1892-1977) is recognized today as one of the masters of the hard-boiled school of American novels. Born in Baltimore, the son of the president of Washington College, he began his career as reporter on the Baltimore papers, served in the American Expeditionary Force in World War I and wrote the material for *The Cross of Lorraine*, the newspaper of the 79th Division. He returned to become professor of journalism at St. John's College in Annapolis and then worked for H. L. Mencken on *The American Mercury*. He later wrote editorials for Walter Lippmann on the *New York World* and was for a short period managing editor of *The New Yorker*, before he went to Hollywood as a script writer. His first novel, *The Postman Always Rings Twice*, was published when he was forty-two and at once became a sensation. It was tried for obscenity in Boston, was said by Albert Camus to have inspired his own book, *The Stranger*, and is now a classic. Cain followed it the next year with *Double Indemnity*, leading Ross MacDonald to write years later, "Cain has won unfading laurels with a pair of native American masterpieces, *Postman* and *Double Indemnity*, back to back." Cain published eighteen books in all and was working on his autobiography at the time of his death.

ALSO BY JAMES M. CAIN

DOUBLE INDEMNITY

Tautly narrated and excruciatingly suspenseful, *Double Indemnity* gives us an X-ray view of guilt, of duplicity, and of the kind of obsessive, loveless love that devastates everything it touches. First published in 1935, this novel reaffirmed James M. Cain as a virtuoso of the *roman noir*.

Crime/Fiction

THE POSTMAN ALWAYS RINGS TWICE

First published in 1934 and banned in Boston for its explosive mixture of violence and eroticism, *The Postman Always Rings Twice* established Cain as a major novelist with an unsparing vision of America's bleak underside, and was acknowledged by Albert Camus as the model for *The Stranger*.

Crime/Fiction

THREE BY CAIN

Serenade describes the lethal triangle of a famous opera singer, a young conductor, and a Mexican-Indian prostitute. In *Love's Lovely Counterfeit* a group of gangsters struggles to maintain its stranglehold on a Midwestern city. Set in the mining town of Appalachia, *The Butterfly* is a hair-raising story of incest and mistaken identity.

Crime/Fiction